A Polwenna Bay novel

by

Ruth Saberton

Copyright

All characters, organisations and events in this publication, other than those clearly in the public domain, are fictitious and any resemblance to real persons, living or dead, is purely coincidental.

The opinions expressed in this book are solely the opinions of the author and do not represent the opinions or thoughts of the publisher. The author has represented and warranted full ownership and / or legal right to publish all materials in this book.

Copyright © 2015 Ruth Saberton
Cover illustration copyright © Carrie May
Editor: Jane Griffiths
The moral right of the author has been asserted.

All rights reserved. No part of this publication may be reproduced, stored in a retrieval system or transmitted, in any form or by any means, without the prior permission of the publisher.

Also by Ruth Saberton

Escape for the Summer

Escape for Christmas

Dead Romantic

Hobb's Cottage

Weight Till Christmas

Katy Carter Wants a Hero

Ellie Andrews Has Second Thoughts

Amber Scott is Starting Over

The Wedding Countdown

A Time for Living: Polwenna Bay 2

Winter Wishes: Polwenna Bay 3

Treasure of the Heart: Polwenna Bay 4

Writing as Jessica Fox

The One That Got Away

Eastern Promise

Hard to Get

Unlucky in Love

Always the Bride

Writing as Holly Cavendish

Looking for Fireworks

Writing as Georgie Carter

The Perfect Christmas

Chapter 1

Summer Penhalligan was only five years old when she stood on the stage of the Polwenna Bay Village Hall and sang *Somewhere over the Rainbow*, but even before the final verse was over her mother knew she was destined for fame and fortune, far away from Cornwall and in the bright lights of the West End. Nothing was going to get in the way of Susie Penhalligan's dreams – least of all her daughter.

Summer had spent most of her childhood learning lines, being trundled up and down the country to rehearsals and practising ballet and tap until her feet hurt. While her siblings had spent their time playing on the beach or surfing – or, later on, drinking scrumpy in The Ship – Summer had focused on her acting and tried not to care that she was missing out on what looked like a lot of fun. On the odd occasion when she'd felt like missing a dance class or Saturday rehearsal to spend time with her best friend Morwenna, just the thought of her mother's disappointment had been enough to stop Summer in her tracks. Susie had lived and breathed Summer's acting, thinking nothing of driving her daughter hundreds of miles to auditions or classes in their exhausted Ford Fiesta, and she'd saved every penny from her job cleaning holiday cottages to help pay for it all. Even Summer's father Eddie, a gruff fisherman who spent more time propping up the bar than he ever did at home, would sometimes make it to a show and then boast drunkenly to all and sundry in The Ship that his girl was going to make them proud. Summer had always known that she *had* to succeed. Letting her parents down hadn't been an option.

Fortunately hard work, dedication and talent had been in Summer's favour, and so had her striking looks and slim figure. Like all of the

Penhalligan family, Summer had been blessed with a combination of inky black hair and olive skin – rumoured to be the legacy of a Spanish Armada survivor who'd been washed ashore in Cornwall and had found comfort in the arms of a local girl – and eyes as sea green as the waves that danced beyond the harbour wall.

It had broken Summer's heart to leave her family and friends behind, especially one friend in particular, whom even now she couldn't think about without her chest constricting. Nevertheless, she'd left Cornwall shortly after her sixteenth birthday and set off for London, where (to her mother's immense pride) she'd managed to secure a place at a top drama school. In the twelve years since, Summer had scarcely had time to breathe. She could certainly count on one hand the amount of times she'd been free to return home.

Home. When she'd first arrived in London, just the thought of Cornwall had been enough to make her eyes prickle. Whenever she'd allowed herself to dwell too much on everything she'd left behind, from the higgledy-piggledy rooftops to the ceaseless crash of the waves breaking on the rocks below her bedroom window, Summer had started to panic – and she'd had to think very hard indeed about how many sacrifices her family had made to send her all the way up country to drama school. Each time she'd thought about that one person in particular, the person whose hurt and anger had made Summer feel as though her own heart was being clawed out, she'd had to screw her eyes tightly shut and concentrate on how proud everyone at home was and just how much they'd given up so that she could be here. It would have been selfish and ungrateful to turn tail to Paddington Station and hurl herself onto the first train home.

Sometimes Summer had resorted to pulling one of her precious Topshop earrings out of her earlobe and digging it into her arm, until the bite of metal managed to blunt the homesickness. Then, when her emotions were back under control, she'd always give herself a stern lecture: about how her mother had toiled for her, clearing the mess left behind by the Range Rover-driving holidaymakers who rented the prettiest cottages down by the harbour, and about how her brothers had chosen to go to sea with Eddie and put money into the family pot rather than take their A levels. She couldn't let them all down. Ironically, even her friend Morwenna had once sacrificed the money she'd saved for a new saddle so that she could buy Summer a beautiful collector's edition of Shakespeare's plays.

As it turned out, though, Mo and the rest of the Tremaine family had ended up letting Summer down in just about the worst way possible…

In those early, lonely days, thinking about her best friend had often meant another earring jab. The two girls had grown up together and been closer than sisters. Although Morwenna was as fair skinned as Summer was dark, they'd often liked to imagine that they were twins. Back then it was certainly true that wherever one girl was, the other was never far away. Even more than a decade on, Summer often still found herself thinking that she must tell Morwenna about some incident or other, or feeling her heart lift when she caught sight of a curly red head in a crowd. The subsequent realisation that the friendship was long gone was every bit as painful as if the loss had happened yesterday. Mo and Summer no longer spoke – and they probably never would again.

In desperation, Summer had thrown herself into her studies, and before long the excitement of her new life in the city had been a balm to the homesickness. The longer she stayed away from Polwenna Bay, the less upsetting the memories became. It was easier not to think about home, Summer had soon learned, to shut the door firmly on the longing to be back and to refuse to dwell on it. Besides, it couldn't have been made any clearer that she was no longer wanted.

There were many advantages to having years of acting classes under her belt; not least of these was discovering that if she played the part of a confident and sassy city chick, she could pretty much convince everyone around her and possibly even herself too. Elocution and acting classes had soon smoothed away the warm Cornish drawl from her voice and with practice Summer had managed to erase Polwenna Bay from her heart as well, or at least lock it away in a very small corner that she was determined to seldom visit.

As time slid past in that imperceptible yet alarming way that years do, Summer found that if she did ever miss the calling of the gulls, the tang of salt in the air or the lemon-sharp light of the bay, then she was able to console herself with the knowledge that at least she'd managed to find the fame that her mother had craved for her.

Had she made her family proud? Summer wasn't so sure. Maybe *proud* wasn't quite the right word; somehow Summer doubted that her Shakespeare-loving mother approved of the direction Summer's career path had taken in the end. Her father had been utterly mortified – no more bragging in the pub from him, she imagined – but at least she'd managed to pay off their mortgage and could make sure they were taken care of. Her brothers were less delicate and had readily accepted the down payment on their new trawler, *Penhalligan Girl*, but Polwenna was a small place and people had long memories, so Summer stayed away. Her face was on billboards and magazines the length and breadth of Britain; she belonged to that small and very select group of celebrities known solely by their first names, and she lived a lifestyle that most people could only dream of.

Summer had never intended to disillusion her family by letting them know that the dream was actually more of a nightmare. But now, suddenly, it seemed that she didn't have much of a choice…

After all those years away, it was a shock to find herself returning to Polwenna Bay, the small Cornish fishing town where she'd grown up. Summer hadn't known that this was where she was heading, or even that she was leaving London. Everything had happened in such a hurry. Her head was still spinning at how an entire life could change in a heartbeat. One minute she'd been sitting at the bottom of the stairs with her head in her hands, an entire galaxy of stars whirling in front of her eyes, and the next she'd been scooping up her car keys from the table and running out of the door, down the scrubbed steps and out into the street. Had she even shut the blue front door of their sweet Kensington mews house? Summer didn't have a clue – and as she'd floored it along the A38, she hadn't really cared. She was away from Justin and that was all that mattered.

Now, as she guided the Audi off the main road, Summer became aware that her heart was racing from more than the adrenalin of her flight from London. These sunken lanes, rendered cool green tunnels by gnarled trees interlocking their limbs above, were achingly familiar. Cornwall, the county of saints and sinners, smugglers and wreckers, she thought – and her stomach tangled with delicious excitement. Driving westwards, Summer knew every twist and turn of the road, and the names of the small villages and hamlets were as familiar as her own. Trerulefoot, Narkurs, Nomansland and Hessenford: strange foreign-sounding names half-forgotten but suddenly as fresh in Summer's mind as though she'd seen them only yesterday. These places unfolded before her just like the landscape that peeled away from the narrow lanes into rolling fields of ripening crops and acid-green pastures, dotted with sheep resembling balls of cotton wool. Any minute now the road would bear sharply to the right, skirting an ancient church that slumbered in the sunshine, and then she'd see it: the glimpse of glittering blue sea that meant she was nearly back at Polwenna Bay.

Sure enough the road right-angled, exactly as she knew it would, and Summer found herself braking hard. Lord! She'd been driving way too fast in her haste to put as much distance as possible between herself and the city. Heaven only knew how many speed traps she'd sailed through. She'd probably lost her licence before she'd even hit the M4. At least moving at speed had meant that she'd avoided the paps, though. There were usually a few hanging around the London house in the hope that they might get a shot of Britain's favourite couple. Usually Summer gave them what they wanted, because it was easier that way – she made sure her image was controlled and they got a picture that could actually be used – but today she'd shot out in such a hurry that the one guy who'd been sunning himself on her wall hadn't even had time to grab his camera before she'd raced away. With any luck Justin wouldn't be home until late, as there was often a function on after a match, and by that time the pap would have pushed off for his tea.

The last thing Summer needed was a story breaking off the back of a typical Justin Anderson episode. If the press got wind that she was in Polwenna Bay then she'd be well and truly stuck. The town was tiny; you could sneeze at one end and have Mrs Keverne in the village shop at the other calling out *bless you*! There wouldn't be many places

Summer could hide, and if some people still held grudges – her stomach lurched at the thought – it wouldn't be hard to drop her in it. She guessed she was counting on the fact that, no matter what had gone on in the past, the Cornish looked after their own. The network of caves and tunnels rumoured to honeycomb the hillside beneath the town, not to mention the amount of cafés and gift shops that bore reference to wreckers and smugglers, certainly stood testament to Polwenna Bay's history of remaining tight-lipped. Be it hiding a smuggler from the excise men or keeping quiet about a runaway actress-turned-model, Summer was hoping that all that had changed was the date displayed on the calendar.

And then, all of a sudden, there it was! On the horizon, the sea was nestling between two perky hills that reminded Summer a little uncomfortably of her latest advertising campaign. Although she was twenty-eight now, she still felt the same excitement that this glimpse of the sparkling ocean had always given her. Summer had woken up to the sea every day for the first sixteen years of her life. Like a stroppy partner, the sea was never the same two days or even two minutes running: it was a constant kaleidoscope of blues and turquoises or greens and greys. Sometimes it turned savage, spitting like a cat and hurling handfuls of brine at the windows of Cobble Cottage, causing Susie to pace and fret until Eddie's trawler was safely moored against the harbour wall and the gate was firmly shut. On other mornings Summer had flung open the curtains and gazed across a sea as oily-smooth as petrol, the bay reflected as though in a mirror and admiring itself in the sunshine. The best days of all had been those when the sun had been out, the waves had been glittering and, craning her neck, Summer had been able to see a red hanky fluttering from the top window of Seaspray House across the bay. She knew then that a small wooden boat was already making its way across to collect her…

No, no, no. Summer shook her head as though trying to shake the image out of her mind's eye. Memories like these were staying securely shut away. She'd had them under lock and key since the day the taxi had driven her slowly through the town and away to a new life; to open her personal Pandora's box now would be nothing short of crazy. The girl who had watched the little boat dancing closer, who had sneaked away from the house to snatch a few forbidden hours exploring the coves and creeks, no longer existed. The feel of that mouth on hers, the blue of his eyes the same as the cobalt water, the way he'd held her face between his hands and looked at her as though he'd never be able to tear his gaze away: all these things that had once meant so much were really as insubstantial as the sea frets that blew in over the bay. That time had gone and Summer knew that her past wasn't so much a foreign country as another world altogether.

Yes, that girl had left a long time ago, but as she drove the last mile towards Polwenna Bay, Summer couldn't help wondering whether maybe, just maybe, the boy with the sea-blue eyes might have stayed…

Chapter 2

Jake Tremaine was never quite certain whether he loved or loathed the Polwenna Bay Festival. On the one hand it was good fun to see the village come back to life after the long winter of empty streets and closed shops, but on the other it meant that getting the pickup truck through the narrow roads was even harder than usual. To continue would risk squashing several dancing locals (all wearing emerald face paints and adorned with greenery, for reasons he'd never quite fathomed in all his years of living in the place) or scraping even more paint from the bumper of the truck if he pulled in tightly against one of the cottages to allow the procession to pass. It was easier to abandon the work vehicle in the tourist car park at the top of the town and walk down to the marina. Not that Jake had ever scraped the truck. Having learned to negotiate the narrow streets as a teenager, knowing how many centimetres were spare at either side of the vehicle was almost a sixth sense; he could coax it through the narrowest spots with an ease that had been the undoing of many holidaymakers who'd attempted to copy him. No, the fresh scars on the side of the Ranger were undoubtedly the work of his younger sister, Issie, whose spatial awareness was in inverse proportion to her ability to cause havoc wherever she went.

As he parked the truck in one of the few spaces left on this sunny May Saturday, Jake reflected on the problem that was the youngest Tremaine sibling. Whereas he was the oldest and practically had dents in his shoulders from the weight of worrying about the family business, Issie was the total opposite, whirling in and out of the family like a blonde-dreadlocked and henna-tattooed tornado. Having recently returned from her latest travelling stint, Issie was no doubt somewhere in the town dressed in a costume, downing scrumpy and getting herself into all kinds of trouble that at the age of twenty-two she really should be beyond. Last night's skinny-dipping in the harbour certainly hadn't been her brightest idea, no matter how earnestly she'd tried to explain that the full moon had restorative powers. Their grandmother, Alice, had been mortified. Jake sighed. The thought of the chaos Issie might cause today was yet another stress he could do without. He was only relieved that her twin, Nick, and the Penhalligan brothers were at sea and not around to encourage her, because when that bunch met up anything could happen. Take the time they'd "borrowed" three thousand pounds' worth of nets from the quay to make a tree house, for example. Eddie Penhalligan had been wild. Jake still remembered how Summer; her green eyes wide as she retold the tale, had said that even the walls of their cottage had shaken with his roars of fury.

Jake smiled at the long-ago memory and sent up a silent prayer of gratitude that it was a flat calm day and perfect for fishing. The perpetrators of that crime might be adults now, but they could still cause trouble when they got together and a few beers were added to the mix. He had enough to do today without having to drag Nick out of a fight or prevent his crazy sister from doing midnight parkour along the harbour wall.

He glanced down at his watch and saw with relief that it was only early afternoon. Great. That left him plenty of time to get everything finished. He could do the final checks on his wealthy customers' boats, make a couple of phone calls to the parts people and, if he felt like it, grab a beer before heading up the hill to Seaspray. With any luck most of the visitors would be watching the tug of war on the beach, leaving the pub relatively quiet. Later on he knew that The Ship Inn would be rammed, visitors squashed together like sardines in a press of Seasalt clothing and Cath Kidston bags while getting merry on Pol Brew Ale. There would be hardly any space between the door and the bar, and any locals would be squeezed out into the small yard at the back to congregate by the beer barrels, where they'd smoke rollups and moan about the *emmets*. Jake didn't smoke or have a burning desire to sit in a dank corner by the bins, and he certainly wasn't going to join in any complaints about the influx of holidaymakers. He knew all the arguments about holiday cottages pricing out the locals and changing the village, and he had his fair share of sympathy with them. Nevertheless, the tourists who flocked to the pretty Cornish fishing village also provided a huge chunk of the Tremaines' income. To make sure that the marina and Seaspray stayed in the family, Jake would willingly grit his teeth and put up with the crowds, the influx of Boden and the gleaming four-by-fours that invariably got wedged when their drivers chose to believe the satnav over the evidence of their own eyes.

Jake swung his tool case from the truck and steeled himself to carry it through the busy village and down to the harbour. He didn't usually work on Saturday afternoons. Not in the marina, anyway – although more often than not he was busy mowing the lawns up at Seaspray or fixing something in a holiday cottage. Today, though, his wealthiest customer had just arrived from London and expected his boat to be ready to go.

This particular customer, Ashley Carstairs, was the worst kind of second-homer. He'd arrived in the Bay six months previously and quickly snapped up one of the premier properties, which he was hell-bent on renovating as fast as possible. The Cornish *dreckly* way of doing things drove Ashley round the twist. As an ex-banker with an annual bonus bigger than most people would earn in a lifetime, he was certainly used to flashing the cash and getting exactly what he wanted – and instantly, too. The pace of life in Cornwall was slower than in London anyway, but Ashley's tutting and eye-rolling in the village shop as the locals chatted over the till only served to make everyone go even slower. He liked to complain, too, and had even found fault with The Plump Seagull, the much-praised Michelin-starred restaurant run by Jake's brother Symon. Not only that, but Ashley had committed an unforgivable Polwenna Bay crime when he'd parked his flash car in the private space belonging to Silver Starr, the tasselled, tarot-card-reading owner of the hippy pisky shop Magic Moon. Silver, whose real but far less romantic name was Shirley Potts, had struggled to park her ancient Mini and had ended up leaving it on the harbour slipway, where it was soon marooned by the incoming tide. Ashley had been unrepentant and, to add insult to injury, had done exactly the same a week later. He was lucky, Jake thought wryly, that the only magic thing about Silver was the mushrooms she liked to pick from the cliff tops; it would have been fitting if she'd been able to turn Ashley into a frog. Parking spaces in Polwenna Bay were like gold dust, and using anyone else's even momentarily put you in the bad books for at least two generations.

As well as upsetting the local New Age brigade and insulting Symon's culinary prowess, Ashley had snapped up Mariners, one of the prettiest houses in the village, and was now busy pulling it apart – another thing that hadn't endeared him to the locals. Not that Cashley, as he was known locally, gave a hoot about this. Property developing was his game and Polwenna Bay was the unfortunate spot where he'd decided to play. He might mention childhood holidays in Cornwall but everybody knew there wasn't a sentimental bone in his body: it was all about making money.

Mariners was a beautiful stone property on the west headland. For sixty years it had stood staunchly through the worst of the winter gales, gazing out at the seascape from its huge ground-floor window. Although it was only accessible by a steep footpath, the inconvenient access was more than compensated for, in Jake's opinion, by the breathtaking views across the bay and out to sea. At night the lights of the village floated below like those of a fairy grotto, and the Eddystone Lighthouse winked out of the darkness. By day anyone standing in the window felt as though they could stretch their wings and fly over Polwenna, just like the circling gulls that called endlessly overhead. Ashley, however, wasn't prepared to lug his belongings up to the house. Nor was he willing to use a quad bike and a trailer like everyone else who could only reach their houses by the cliff path. No. Ashley wanted to bulldoze a road in through ancient woodland; he wanted an underground garage for his cars and, just in case he needed it, a helipad too. The house had already been ripped back to the walls but the project was currently halted in its tracks thanks to a fierce campaign orchestrated by a group of villagers, including Jake's fiery sister, Morwenna.

"Why the bloody hell buy a house he can't get to and doesn't like anyway? Why destroy a thousand years of woodland just because he can't be arsed to walk to his front door?" Morwenna had raged, storming back and forth across Seaspray's kitchen. Her muddy yard boots had been kicked off by the back door, and stomping across the slate floor in thick Toggi socks didn't have quite the same impact, but the tossing of her wild red hair and the determined tilt of her chin spoke volumes about her outrage. She looked like an angry Rossetti painting.

"Because he's a cock?" Nick had offered mildly from his seat at the kitchen table where, feet up amid the debris of unpaid bills, newspapers and mugs, he was simultaneously flicking through *Fishing News* and texting his latest conquest. Even in a tatty smock and with his long blond hair caught up in a rubber-banded ponytail, Nick attracted women like the cream teas in the harbour tea shop attracted wasps. With his dancing blue eyes, stubbled jaw and glinting pirate-style earring, Nick certainly rocked the young-Brad-Pitt-meets-fisherman look. Female holidaymakers swooned when they caught sight of him mending nets on the quay or holding court in The Ship, a pint in one hand and the other leaning against a beam. Wherever he went, a trail of broken hearts followed. Not that Nick meant to upset anyone. There was just so little time and so many pretty girls; besides, going to sea made a man realise he had to grab life hard and squeeze out every drop (or so Nick said). He made Jake, who often ended up opening the door to hopeful females and making tea while his gran mopped their tears, feel as ancient as the weathered granite below Seaspray's limewashed walls.

"A cock with money. Crap combination," Mo had spat, charging to the window and glowering across Polwenna Bay towards Mariners, as though by sheer power of will she could make Ashley Carstairs burst into flames. Actually, Jake wouldn't have put this past her. When it came to determination, his sister had more than her fair share. In fact, she'd probably elbowed the rest of them out of the way when God was dishing it out. From running her equestrian business, to riding horses over cross-country jumps that gave Jake vertigo just looking at them, to fighting her latest cause, Morwenna was a force of nature. She was constantly challenging Jake about his continued acceptance of Ashley's flashy fuel-guzzling "penis boat" in the Tremaine marina. She made it very clear that she thought her brother was letting the side down by not giving the village's arch-enemy his marching orders.

Threading through the ice-cream- and pasty-eating crowds on his way to make sure that the very same floating phallic symbol was fuelled and ready for its owner's arrival, Jake reflected wearily that it was all very well for Morwenna to get on her high horse, both literal and metaphorical, but she wasn't the one who woke up at three in the morning with a racing heart as thoughts of the family's precarious finances whirled around and around in her head. Only Jake and his father, Jimmy, knew the true state of the Tremaine family business and the reasons why a family that had once owned so much of the village now teetered on the brink of losing everything. No, thought Jake bleakly as he dodged the local baker in full morris costume and narrowly missed having his eye put out by a stick with bells, Morwenna didn't have a clue – and he was going to do everything within his power to make sure it stayed that way. Better she thought that he was a spineless coward who just wanted the easy money than that she knew the painful truth. Cashley was indeed a cock but he was a cock who paid their business handsomely. For that, Jake was prepared to grit his teeth and face his sister's scorn. If he were to try to hang on to what little the family did have left, then every penny counted.

The main road into the village began as a fairly wide thoroughfare with enough room for two vehicles to pass. Today, visitors flowed along it like a human tide. The road meandered past the village hall and the old Methodist chapel, following the path of the River Wenn as it leapt and splashed on the final stretch of its journey from the moors to the sea. Little bridges across the river gave the locals access to their homes; nasturtiums and aubrietia tumbled from window boxes and lobelia foamed from the dry stone walls. Brightly painted signs announced the possibility of bed and breakfast in dwellings with romantic names like Seaways and Rivercott. Jake's progress was slowed by groups of people stopping abruptly to point out sights that he had taken for granted for years; now, forced to reduce his speed, he found himself looking at the village through their eyes, and in spite of all his worries his heart lifted.

In all his travels around the globe, from working on the sheep station in Australia to a year crewing in the Caribbean, there was nowhere in the world that had matched up to Cornwall. The sharp scoured light, the headspace that being out on the sea gave him, the wide sweep of lemony sand that was the bay, the endless calling of the gulls as they circled overhead... The tug of homesickness he'd felt whenever he'd thought of Polwenna Bay had told Jake that no matter how far he travelled he would always come home. This place held his heart more firmly than any woman ever had – or, rather, more firmly than he would ever allow any woman to do again.

The holidaymakers were pointing excitedly down into the river as a flotilla of yellow plastic ducks bobbed by, chased by the new vicar, a plump apple-cheeked woman in her early thirties. She was brave on two accounts, Jake thought as he watched her huff and puff after them. Taking on Polwenna Bay's charity duck race was no mean feat. Apart from the logistics involved in selling each numbered bathtub duck for one pound, tipping two hundred of them into the river and then making sure they all floated down to be caught in the harbour, the locals tended to get very competitive about the result. The Tremaine children had loved the duck race – it was always a highlight of the festival – and even now Jake felt an echo of the old excitement as he watched the new vicar splash after the jaunty yellow toys.

The plastic flock would, Jake was certain, be a lot easier to deal with than the human kind, even in a river and with a brisk north-easterly wind sending them scooting downstream. He wasn't a churchgoer himself (having given up pleading with God many years ago, he now left such things to his gran), but Jake knew how central the vicar's role was to Polwenna Bay. In true *Vicar of Dibley* style, the older villagers had been stunned to have a young woman sent to shepherd them. Jake also had a nasty suspicion that pretty St Wenn's, set on the hillside and enjoying a stunning view over the lichen-crusted rooftops and out to sea, was on borrowed time before the Church of England decided to cash in its asset, once it twigged that you could count the congregation on one hand and still have fingers left over. Only a few weeks ago he'd been walking through the village and up the little lane near the church when he'd bumped into Cashley coming through the lych-gate. Since Cashley was a devoted follower of Mammon, it seemed unlikely he'd popped in to say a prayer or two. Now, as Jake watched the new vicar, looking like a cherub who'd fallen out of heaven and guzzled a few too many pasties, he felt a twinge of concern. Maybe he'd ask Granny Alice to introduce her to Mo? If anyone was up for fighting for the underdog, it was his sister.

With the duck race now gone, the tourists surged forward. Each side of the street was lined with gift shops, cafés and pasty shops all vying for trade, with their doors flung open to entice the new arrivals. Jake had seen all of these shops far more often than he cared to think about. He knew them all as well as he knew the creaking of the boats in the harbour, or the three hidden rocks that lurked just beyond the bay and only inches below the surface in deadly wait for the unaware (Morwenna had been furious when Jake had shown Cashley where these were); he didn't even need to look to know what was where. Some of the businesses had been here forever – like the toy shop filled with dusty Lego and run by a woman who quite clearly detested children, or the old bakery which sold pasties the size of trawl doors – whereas others were new and changed every other season.

His toolkit was heavy so Jake switched hands, silently cursing the festival for preventing easier parking down at the harbour. He promised himself that once he'd checked Cashley's boat he would reward himself with a well-deserved hour or two in the pub. To hell with it: he might even throw caution to the wind, take the rest of the day off and actually enjoy the celebrations for once. There was going to be a hog roast on the quay, courtesy of Symon's restaurant, and later on their younger brother Zak's band, The Tinners, would be playing in the square. This event was causing quite a stir. The Tinners had a big following in Cornwall, and legions of devoted fans (whom Jake strongly suspected followed the band more for Zak's rock-star looks than the music) had been arriving all day.

As the street narrowed and the houses edged closer and closer together, Jake was in two minds as to whether or not his brother's band playing tonight was good news. Zak was undoubtedly talented and apparently on the brink of great things, but to be honest Zak had always been on the brink of great things. Unfortunately, his deck-chair laid-back attitude and tendency to spend more time with the groupies than at rehearsals were proving to be stumbling blocks on his road to fame and fortune. At any rate, Jake doubted that Jon Bon Jovi was shaking in his leather trousers.

The main street was barely one car wide now and it was thronging with people. The jingle of Morris dancers and the piping of folk music drowned out the seagulls and went some way towards smothering the hopeless revving of a Range Rover wedged at the narrowest point, the large no-entry sign having experienced yet another fail. Turning right instead as he headed past the post office and down towards the marina, Jake stepped aside to let two pretty girls pass. All tousled hair crowned with daisy-chain headbands, and sporting tight white vests and tiny denim cut-offs displaying their endless honey-hued legs to full advantage, they dimpled up at him and batted mascara-heavy eyelashes. Jake smiled. Nice to know that at thirty and dressed in his tatty old Levi's, work boots and a tee-shirt that had seen better days he still had it! No matter what chaos Zak caused tonight, an influx of twenty-something rock chicks with an urge to party could only be a good thing.

Still, Jake was a busy guy these days and at thirty was wise enough to realise that there came a point in every man's life when chasing holidaymakers was no longer exciting but actually quite sad. He'd been virtually single ever since returning to Polwenna Bay several months earlier – in spite of his grandmother's best efforts to match make. Jake knew everyone in the village but, as fond as he was of many of the women, there was nobody who made his nerve ends fizz or with whom he had a connection. Was he being unrealistic to want something more? Jake didn't know; he didn't let himself dwell on the lurking fear that perhaps that connection, that surety of knowing someone better than you knew yourself, was a once-in-a-lifetime fluke. If it existed at all, that was. He'd been convinced in it once, but how wrong could a man be? He shook his head, unable to believe that even all these years on there was still a dull ache when he allowed his thoughts to wander in this direction.

I need to get a grip, Jake thought. Coming back to Polwenna Bay had unsettled him, that was all. Every corner he turned and every dark head he glimpsed transported him back to another lifetime. He'd thought that going travelling would be the key to escaping those feelings, but the tug of home had been his ever-present companion even when diving the gin-clear Caribbean Sea or galloping a horse across the outback. Finally he'd given in to his grandmother's pleas and returned. Just in the nick of time too, as it had turned out. But maybe this hadn't been a good thing? As much as Jake loved Polwenna Bay, there were far too many memories here.

He sighed. This was hardly a train of thought for a sunny May day when the sky was duck-egg blue and the sun was beaming down for once, rather than playing hide-and-seek behind its usual wrapping of pewter clouds. It wasn't as though he had anything to complain about either – not like his brother Danny. Yes, if anyone was entitled to moan then it was Dan. It was bad enough to be injured on a tour of duty and discharged from the job you loved, but it was worse again to have your wife walk out on you just when you needed her most. Danny was devastated and for some reason seemed to think that it was all his fault, as though getting hit by shrapnel in a roadside attack was something he'd planned just to ruin his wife's plans for a bigger house and another few years of basking in her husband's glory. Jake's jaw clenched. On reflection, he'd come to realise that he'd never liked Tara much anyway. She was certainly pretty and (although these were inappropriate things for a brother-in-law to think) she had great tits and a perfect peach of an ass in the designer jeans she wore like a second skin. Yet there was a calculating coldness in her eyes that had always reminded him of the sharks the Penhalligan boys sometimes caught. Jake was sorry to be proved right, though, and every time he caught sight of his brother nursing a whisky at the bar, he wanted to grab the absent Tara by her bony shoulders and shake her until her teeth rattled. I might be tired of the boatyard and the finances, Jake thought, and my father's certainly responsible for my first few grey hairs, but at least I'm not as miserable as Dan.

Like the rest of his family, Jake was at a loss as to how to help his brother. There were only so many times you were prepared to be yelled at when all you wanted to do was make things better. Granny Alice was worried sick, and Jake could see why. Dan's moods were bleaker than Cornish granite and recently it seemed that Bell's whisky flowed through his veins rather than blood. No doubt he was already at the bar running up yet another tab Jake would have to settle or, even worse, out wandering the cliffs until the light faded from the sky and they were all on the brink of calling out a search party. The last time, Danny had been gone for five hours and, although nobody had said a word, they'd all shared the same unspeakable thoughts. Jake didn't think he'd forget in a hurry the tidal wave of relief when Nick and Issie had finally found their brother in the old shelter at the foot of the higher cliff path.

Although the sunshine was bright, Jake shivered. Christ. He needed to put all these worries aside and get into the party spirit. The festival had always been a great time to have some no-strings fun, and judging by the way the two girls were now giggling and casting glances over their shoulders, today could be the perfect time to end the dry spell.

Arriving at the marina and making his way along the floating pontoon to check on *Big Rod*, Cashley's gleaming fast fisher, Jake was already looking forward to the evening ahead. A night off from worrying about the family was exactly what he needed; a night off from worrying about the family *and* spent with a gorgeous naked girl would be even better. All he had to do was get these last checks finished, call his gran and then haul his ass over to The Ship. Watching the new vicar trying to coax toy ducks down the river's mouth and slithering like a plump Bambi on the green slime, Jake supposed that his lot could be worse. An hour's work on the boat, a few beers and then – well, who knew what the evening would hold? It could be a lot of fun.

Providing, of course, none of his siblings got into trouble and needed rescuing.

Chapter 3

Although the Lord moved in mysterious ways, He had nothing on plastic ducks, thought Jules Mathieson despairingly. In theory catching two hundred toys in a net sounded pretty straightforward, but as they bobbed around her wellies they were proving harder to grab than eels coated in butter. It was all right for Moses; God had allowed him to part the Red Sea. And of course, Jesus was a pro when it came to walking on water. But as a humble and fairly new-to-the-job vicar, Jules couldn't possibly expect to accomplish such feats. To be honest she was just grateful that one of the fishermen had managed to find her a net to try to catch the ducks, or else they'd all be half way to France by now and she'd be even less popular than she already seemed to be...

"Come on, Vicar! You're letting them get by! Quickly, then! Catch the first one!"

This disapproving bellow might have come from high above her head, but rather than being the voice of Jules's number one boss it was the rather less dulcet one of Sheila Keverne, organ player and verger. Then again, in Polwenna Bay Sheila Keverne was every bit as omniscient, omnipotent and omnipresent as the Almighty. The self-appointed guardian of all things St Wenn, Sheila hadn't hidden her bitter disappointment with the new incumbent. Barely a day went by without her mentioning the previous vicar in a mournful and rather resentful fashion, as though the Reverend John had died just to spite Sheila. Insult was further added to injury, Shelia's pursed mouth implied, by the Church of England allowing a woman in her early thirties to take his place; both feminism and *The Vicar of Dibley* had clearly passed Sheila by. Jules often thought that from the way Sheila carried on it was amazing anyone could hear her sermons over the rumbling sound of the Reverend spinning in his grave.

"They're getting away! Catch them in the net!"

Glancing up, and sending a swift plea heavenwards for patience, Jules saw a group of her elderly parishioners huddled together on the bridge and peering down with dismay. Pound coins had been spent on their ducks and they wanted value for money. It didn't matter that the river splashing over Jules's wellies was icy cold, that the chunk of trawl net was unwieldy or that none of the assembled adults had offered to give her a hand: the plastic ducks had to be caught and Jules was failing horribly in even this simple duty.

"If one of those ducks is number forty-three then I'll want my money back!" called Janet Pengelley, another scary member of the blue-rinse brigade. Steely-eyed, with a Bible verse for every occasion and parsimonious to Scrooge-like levels, she made the Pharisees look fun-loving. Now, as Jules floundered about in the river, Janet's words prompted much agreement and nodding.

Jules bit back a sigh. God had a purpose in mind, of this she was certain, but sometimes she wished He'd be a little more vocal about what this might be. Improving her patience maybe? Jules was ready to admit that this really wasn't her strong point. She'd been known to dig up seeds to check whether they were germinating, and her cakes invariably flopped because she kept opening the oven door to sneak a peek. So perhaps this was a lesson? It was a blooming hard one though. She'd only been at St Wenn's for six weeks, but already the Lord must be getting tired of hearing her pray for the strength not to throttle certain members of the congregation.

"Come on, children; help me catch the ducks," Jules said to the small group of excited Sunday-schoolers who'd gathered down in the harbour to watch the ducks arrive. Two small boys had been trying to hold the net, but it was too heavy for their little hands and three yellow dots were already bobbing towards the harbour gates. Within minutes they'd be out into the English Channel. Jules's heart sank because she knew that Janet and Sheila would fully expect her to jump into the sea and swim after them.

There was one major problem with this: Jules couldn't swim. In fact she was terrified of the water, which was ironic in the extreme seeing as she was now living so close to the sea she could practically dip her toes in from the rectory. Maybe this was also part of God's plan? That, and weaning her off exploring shopping malls, Greggs the Bakers and bingo – all activities in which she'd excelled, and skills that the parishioners of her last inner-city church had appreciated wholeheartedly.

Was it wrong to wish that God had sent her to Kensington? Jules wondered as she lumbered over the slimy rocks. Goodness, but she was unfit. It was time to knock all the pasties and cream teas on the head and start walking up on the cliffs a little more often. The thought of surviving the chilly and dishearteningly empty church, the gloomy rectory and the disapproval of her verger without treats was very depressing though. Perhaps this was a test and, like Job, she was just going to have to glorify Him regardless.

But without ice cream and chocolate? No disrespect to Job, but this was going to be exceedingly hard.

"Hurry *up*, Vicar!" screeched one of the old biddies from the bridge, jabbing a finger in the direction of the harbour wall. There was a general outcry – the ducks were making a break for freedom and if Jules didn't move quickly enough they'd be in France before you could say *canard*.

Jolted into action, she tried to double her pace. However, her ancient wellies – pink discount-store cheapies and nothing like the leather country boots everyone in Polwenna Bay favoured – had zero grip and she may as well have been walking on glass.

As she slithered across the slippery harbour, Jules noticed that a tall and broad-shouldered man with a halo of golden ringlets was watching her with a bemused expression as he unlocked the marina gates. Jules really did regret all those unhealthy treats now: she wished she'd gone on a diet weeks before and had actually liberated Davina's workout from its DVD case, rather than just reading about all the wonders it could do whilst working her way through a giant bag of Kettle Chips. And why hadn't she put on any make-up this morning or dragged a brush through her hair? Sometimes Jules wanted to give herself a very hard shake. Just because she spent most of her time with the blue-rinse brigade didn't mean that there weren't any younger people to make friends with, although if she was ever lucky enough to get her hands on a gorgeous specimen like this, being *friends* would be the last thing she had in mind…

At this point Jules guessed she should give herself a sharp telling-off for such lustful thoughts, but she couldn't help turning her head for a second look. Good gracious, he lifted that heavy-looking bag as though it was made of feathers, his biceps swelling deliciously under the white cotton of his tee-shirt. He'd have no problems at all lifting a thirteen-stone girl into his arms. God would surely understand, Jules reasoned as she tried to rip her attention back to negotiating the treacherous surface rather than admiring how his blue jeans clung to his muscular legs and moulded a very cute backside. She was just admiring the Lord's glorious creation, that was all! And this man was gorgeous! For a moment Jules wondered if the Angel Gabriel had been sent to scoop her up and rescue her from the pebbles and seaweed. After all, why shouldn't an archangel look like Heath Ledger at his sexy and dishevelled best? Just one more quick peek…

The last thing she saw before her heavy body slammed onto the boulders was the marina gate opening. She had clawed the air desperately before slipping on the rocks, bashing her knees painfully in the process and covering her jeans with green slime. Jules knew that vicars really shouldn't swear, but the word came out regardless.

"Ouch! Bollocks!"

There was a gasp from the bridge and a ripple of laughter from the gathered children. Jules wished she'd managed to keep her mouth shut. Maybe she wasn't cut out for this job after all. Since she'd arrived at Polwenna Bay all she'd seemed to do was get it wrong. Please Lord, Jules prayed, forgive me for saying "bollocks" out loud and, if it's not too much trouble, let the riverbed swallow me up right now.

But unfortunately the riverbed remained stubbornly hard and wet beneath her now damp jeans. The Almighty, it seemed, wanted her to stay in the village and suffer whatever indignities came along next. Jules felt close to tears. She didn't like to question Him but she was really starting to wish she'd taken physics A level rather than RE.

"Bloody hell, are you all right?"

A small hand, its bitten-nailed fingers crammed with silver rings, reached out to her. Squinting up against the sun, Jules made out a slender girl in her early twenties. She had a snub freckly nose and long blonde dreadlocks held back by a daisy-chain headband, of the kind

Jules secretly wanted but knew was better suited to elfin-limbed fairy people than her. Alas, it would have looked ridiculous on a five-foot-seven cropped-haired vicar. There was a pink stud glittering in this blonde girl's nose. All in all, she didn't look like a Sunday-school mother come to wallop an unfit Rev over the head with her Bible. Instead, her wide mouth was curled into a grin and the little boy next to her was laughing too.

"You said 'bollocks'!" he exclaimed with delight. A hunk of hair fell across his face and he pushed it away impatiently. "You said a bad word."

"Yes, sorry about that. It was really wrong of me." Feeling dreadful, Jules took the girl's hand and allowed herself to be hauled to her feet. For such a slim creature the other girl was surprisingly strong and her grasp was like iron.

"Don't worry; my dad says bad words too," the little boy told her kindly. "He says 'bugger' and 'arse' and—"

"Yes, yes, all right, Morgan. We don't need everyone to know your dad's entire repertoire of swearing," said the girl with blonde dreadlocks quickly.

"But he does and they're only words. They're arbitrary. Language is a system of codes, which don't mean anything at all until people give them meaning. Fact."

Jules raised her hand to her head. How hard was that fall? She could have sworn that an eight-year-old had just given her an explanation of semiotics that an Oxford don would have been proud of.

"Yes, yes, yes. Now shut up about that and go and grab those ducks." The girl gave the boy a shove in the direction of the harbour gate. "Go on, quick, before Sheila explodes. And before you ask," she added quickly, intercepting a question before he could even voice it, "that was a metaphor. She won't really explode." Catching Jules's eye, she winked. "Unfortunately."

Morgan seemed relieved to hear this and tore across the harbour. Moments later he was up to his knees at the river's mouth and fishing out ducks.

"Morgan's got Asperger's," the girl explained once he was out of earshot, "and sometimes he struggles with literal and metaphorical concepts."

"Well, I'm very sorry about swearing," said Jules awkwardly.

The girl laughed. "God, don't be. My family's language makes Gordon Ramsay look half-hearted. Besides, running the duck race would make anyone swear; it's a bloody nightmare. I'm Issie Tremaine, by the way, and Morgan's my brother Danny's son. I've no idea where Danny's got to – pissed up somewhere, probably – so I'm on ankle-biter duty."

"Jules Mathieson," said Jules, and waited for the penny to drop. When it didn't, she added, "I'm the new vicar."

Issie's hand flew to her mouth. "Oops! And there's me blaspheming away. Now it's my turn to say 'bollocks'! Sorry, Rev, I had no idea." Her blue eyes crinkled and Jules felt relieved. Issie was amused and she was still giggling, which was a good sign. All too often once people discovered what Jules did for a living they either ran for the hills or changed the way they treated her. It ruined conversations when friends thought they had to censor their every word and treat her as though she was a prim Victorian catapulted into the wrong century. Most avoided her altogether. Although she understood why and prayed very hard not to feel wounded, Jules was hurt when she was left out of nights in the pub or group holidays. Ever since she'd been ordained, her social life had been emptier than Kerry Katona's bank account – and as for her love life, well if the Catholic Church wanted more nuns then she'd be a perfect candidate. Men tended to freak out about her vocation or, even worse, were desperate to prove themselves by getting off with a vicar.

A veteran of many duck races, Issie proved to be a brilliant help, taking pictures of the three winning ducks on her iPhone and organising all the children to collect the strays. Lots of people waved to her or called hello, and Issie seemed to know them all. Then again, she was a Tremaine. Even though Jules had only lived in the village for a few weeks, she had already learned that the Tremaines were one of the oldest and most established families. The small graveyard was full of tombstones that bore their name, and one of the stained-glass windows was a memorial to three Tremaine boys who'd died in the Great War. Of course Issie was a duck-race pro. It was probably in her DNA.

"To be fair though, you don't look much like a vicar," Issie remarked eventually, helping Jules to scoop the rest of the ducks out of the net and then passing them to Morgan, who was concentrating hard on lining them up in numerical order. "You actually look quite normal." Her hand flew to her mouth again. "Oh God! Sorry – what is it with me today? Everything I say sounds like an insult."

Morgan fixed his big blue eyes on Jules. "You are quite a strange vicar, though. Why's your hair such a funny colour?"

"Oops. That makes two of us being unintentionally rude," said his aunt, ruffling his hair fondly and rolling her eyes.

"I didn't know I was being rude," replied Morgan. "I didn't mean to be."

"It's fine," Jules reassured him. Anyway, it wasn't the first time she'd heard this. When most people imagined a vicar she guessed they were picturing an elderly man with grey hair and a beard, wearing floaty robes and presiding over tea parties. A young woman who wore jeans, dyed her hair aubergine (although in fairness to Morgan it *was* a funny colour; Tinky Winky purple would have been a far better description) and who loved rock music didn't always tick the right boxes. But why should a vicar be boring or staid? The stereotype drove Jules mad. Jesus hadn't been either of those things. He'd been far too busy kicking tables over in temples and taking on the establishment to go to tea parties.

Together Issie and Jules placed the carefully counted ducks in bin bags and carried them away from the harbour and up to the lock-up store at the back of the village green. A stage had been set up and already a crowd was starting to gather in order to bag the best spots for the performance later on. The streets crackled with a carnival atmosphere and the smell of roast pork drifted on the breeze. Jules's tummy rumbled.

"Hungry?" grinned Issie, and Jules flushed. Why was she such a glutton? If only she could be one of those skinny people who said things like, "Oh! I forgot to eat lunch!" and who were full after half a lettuce leaf. Jules couldn't imagine ever forgetting lunch; it was her favourite activity after elevenses. And as far as lettuce went, well it was all very tasty when sandwiched under a burger. She glanced at Issie's slim frame and sighed. Envy was a sin, and so was pride, but Jules would have loved nothing more than to experience even for one minute what it was like to be a pretty skinny girl whom all the men stared at. The hunk from the quay had only looked her way because she'd been making a fool of herself. It was the story of her life.

"My brother Symon's doing the hog roast," Issie continued without even waiting for a reply. "Why don't we go and check it out? He'll give us some crackling if we really grovel – and his cider-apple sauce is to die for."

"My mum says meat is murder," piped up Morgan.

"Your mum says a lot of daft things," Issie told him cheerfully. To Jules she added in a stage whisper, "Utter cow, and had a sense of humour bypass at birth. God knows what Danny ever saw in her. Big boobs, I suppose. Men are thick like that. Don't look so worried," she added, when she caught Jules's gaze flicker to the little boy. "Morgan doesn't mind me saying that. He knows it's true and with any luck he might even repeat it."

"I'm not stupid," said Morgan mildly. "Tell her yourself."

"Don't tempt me," said Issie darkly. "So, do you want to come for some grub?"

Jules patted her tummy ruefully. "I don't think I need it. I've put on at least a stone since I moved here."

"So one pork roll won't make any difference," Issie countered.

"You have to exercise to lose weight," added Morgan. He looked at her critically. "My dad was in the army. He knows all about keeping fit. I could ask him to help you if you like."

A hideous vision of having to do star jumps and sit-ups in an army-style boot camp flashed before Jules's eyes. Just the thought was exhausting. No thanks.

"That's a very kind offer," she told him, "but I'm a bit busy right now."

"I didn't mean right now, obviously," said Morgan.

Issie rolled her eyes. "Can we just get to the hog roast? I swear my stomach is going to start digesting itself otherwise!"

Having safely locked away the ducks, they made their way to the quayside. The hog roast was still cooking, so instead Jules treated her companions to pasties. It was the least she could do after all the help they'd given her with the duck race. The three of them sat on the end of quay to eat, and with the warm sunshine on her face, the salty sea breeze lifting her hair and her new friends next to her, Jules didn't think she'd ever tasted anything so good. Maybe things were looking up.

"Are you coming to see the band tonight?" Issie was asking, brushing flakes of pastry from her chin. She tossed the crust into the sea and instantly several squawking gulls dived for it while about a hundred others flew over on the off chance of further spoils. Jules was so over seagulls. Six weeks of being dive-bombed, pooped on and forced to play bin wars whenever she put the rubbish out had seen to that.

"They're really good. My uncle Zak sings," Morgan added. "All the girls fancy him."

"Not nearly as much as Zak fancies himself," said Issie acidly.

Jules laughed at this. "It sounds fun but I hadn't planned on coming out."

"Well, you should. Festival nights are a brilliant laugh. All the pubs are packed and there's music on pretty much everywhere. Why don't you come out with me? I'll introduce you to everyone. You may even meet some fit guys!" Issie looked pleased with this idea.

But Jules wasn't sure. She was lonely after weeks of rattling around the rectory, and a night out with Issie sounded like great fun, but she was the vicar of the parish and Polwenna Bay was a very small place. Sheila and the rest of the blue-rinse brigade would be horrified if they thought their vicar was listening to rock bands and hanging out in pubs. On the other hand, if Jesus were in Polwenna Bay today, where would he be found? Having tea with the WI or talking to fishermen and sinners in the local?

"She might not want to meet men. She could be married or gay," Morgan pointed out when Jules didn't reply.

"Me and my big mouth!" said Issie. She paused. "Are you?"

"Am I what?" Jules teased, pretending to look insulted. "Married? Or gay?"

"Err, either? Not that I care; of course not!"

For a moment Jules toyed with the idea of really making poor Issie squirm. However, this wouldn't be very kind and she was supposed to be setting an example.

"I'm just winding you up. 'Neither' is the answer to your question," she said with a smile. "In fact, the reason I slipped over in the harbour was because I was far too busy looking at a seriously fit guy who was walking to the boats. Did you see him? About six feet and wearing jeans and a white tee-shirt?"

Issie nodded. "Yep. I saw him."

"And wasn't he gorgeous? Couldn't you just gobble him up?" Jules could still picture the man; his image clung to her memory with as much tenacity as the limpets on the rocks. Not that a guy like that would ever look twice at her, but it was still nice to dream. It was all part of glorifying God by appreciating his creation!

"Err, not really. That was my brother, Jake," Issie revealed with a grin. "Honestly, Vicar, those myths about the Cornish being inbred aren't really true, you know."

"Fact," said Morgan.

"Oh!" Now it was Jules's turn to feel embarrassed. "I'm really sorry."

"Don't be sorry. Lots of women fancy Jake; in fact, I'd say all my friends do. It's very predictable," Issie said airily. "It must be that brooding look he's got going on."

Privately Jules thought it had a lot more to do with the ripped body and strong-boned face, but she'd already said way too much about Jake Tremaine for one lifetime. Knowing her luck, Morgan would repeat everything she'd said word for word and her humiliation would be complete. She'd have to spend the rest of her time here hiding in the rectory. Jules supposed Sheila would be pleased, at least.

"Nobody ever gets anywhere with Jake. He's far too busy for love. He's even turned down Ella St Milton. Her family own the hotel, and she's gorgeous – even if she's such a bitch she should be muzzled and fed Chum."

"Fact," nodded Morgan.

"Will you stop saying that?" Issie raised her eyes to heaven. "It's getting bloody annoying. Fact. Anyway, where was I? Jake's not been back long from travelling – he was in the Caribbean for years, the lucky git – but he's certainly making up for lost time bossing us all about now he's home again. It's probably a big brother thing but it's a major pain in the neck. Even Dad and Gran have to do what they're told, and last night Jake had a huge row with Danny about his bar bill."

"My dad drinks too much," Morgan informed Jules. "Fact."

Jules was losing count. "Sorry, I'm confused. How many are there in your family?"

"Too many," said Issie bluntly. "Huge families are a Polwenna thing. Jake says that there's not enough money to go round anymore and that we all need to pull our weight or we'll lose the lot. Well, that's easier said than done, because there are lots of us." She looked at Morgan. "And now there are the ankle-biters too."

"I do not bite ankles," pointed out Morgan coolly. "Fact."

Issie ignored him. She pulled her blonde dreadlocks into a ponytail and secured it with a rubber band, then started to tick her family members off on her fingers as though in danger of losing count herself.

"Jake's the eldest. He runs the marina and the boatyard and has had a total fun bypass. Then there's Danny, who's Rug Rat's father."

"My dad's a soldier," announced Morgan proudly.

Issie smiled at him. "Yes, he is – and a very brave one too. Dan's been discharged because of his injuries," she explained to Jules in a lower voice. "He had a tough time in Afghanistan. I'll tell you about it sometime. Then there's Morwenna. She's cool; you'll like Mo. But don't get on her bad side, for God's sake, or she'll never forget it. Next there's Symon; he's the chef. And then there's Zak, who's got the band. He's cool too. I reckon you'll like Zak. After him there's my twin Nick, who fishes. And finally there's me. Seven of us. Just as well Seaspray's a big house."

"Seven. Wow." Jules was impressed. It made being an only child feel even lonelier. What must it be like to grow up with all those siblings around you? She could already picture the Tremaines, a golden-haired and glamorous bunch, squabbling in their kitchen, having picnics down on the beach or sailing across the bay on a breezy morning. It was all a bit Famous Five meets the Waltons, but surely a lot more fun than being raised on a housing estate in Basingstoke with a workaholic father and a mother so bitter she'd have passed for a lemon if you'd stuck her in a gin and tonic. Even years on, Jules could still feel the relief of going to the local church and finding a happy family there instead.

"Yep, Tremaines breed like rabbits," Issie finished happily. "You'll never be far from one of us here. It's a bit like never being more than two feet from a rat. You've probably already met Granny Alice? She goes to church and she sometimes helps with the flowers – when Adolf Sheila lets her, obviously."

Jules, who was only just managing to keep up with everything, nodded. She had met Alice Tremaine and had liked her immensely. A slender woman in her seventies with long silver hair and a face traced with laughter lines, Alice had been one of the first to welcome her to the village. She'd brought a delicious tray of saffron buns up to the rectory too. Hadn't Alice said something about losing her daughter? Jules racked her memory but she'd been so busy in the early days of her arrival that the details were all a bit hazy.

"Yes we've met. She's lovely."

"So come up to ours sometime. She'd love to see you. I'll introduce you to everyone tonight too. Then at least you'll get to know a few more people besides those old miseries at the church. Joke!" Issie added swiftly, when Jules opened her mouth to protest at this. "I'm sure they're all lovely really, but you're way too young to hang out with people who were in nappies when Queen Victoria was on the throne." She nudged Jules with a bony elbow. "Please come – if you're really good I'll put in a good word with Jake!"

Jules laughed, although the thought of the gorgeous Jake knowing that she'd spotted him made her want to curl up and die. Luckily being a vicar was usually a pretty sure-fire way of keeping herself a little safe from teasing.

"I'll come," she promised. It was only a few drinks, after all – and what a great way to meet those members of her flock who were highly unlikely to set foot in St Wenn's. The pub was the real heart of the village.

Jules finished her pasty and the crust too, although she was learning that this was the part the old tin miners had held while they ate and traditionally discarded afterwards. She was just about to ask Issie what time to meet when her new friend jumped to her feet as though scalded. Abandoning the bench, Issie raced to the railing, shading her eyes against the glare of the sun as she peered across the bay. Her hands were clutching the rail so tightly that her knuckles were glowing chalky white through the skin.

"Are you OK?" Jules asked. "You look like you've seen a ghost."

"Ghosts don't exist," Morgan piped up. "Fact. And neither does God. Fact."

Jules chose to stay quiet. She was too full and too tired to take on Richard Dawkins Junior right now.

With a trembling finger, Issie pointed to the far side of the bay where a dark-haired woman in huge sunglasses was emerging from a shiny sports car. The breeze stirred her thick hair and even from this distance it was clear that the cut of her clothes was expensive. Jules frowned because there was something very familiar about her, although she couldn't quite place it.

"I don't believe it," Issie said slowly, her voice soft and thrumming with anger. "After all this time she's back. She's really back."

"Who?" Jules asked, but Issie didn't answer. Their evening plans, the rubbish from lunch and even Morgan were all forgotten in a heartbeat. Whoever this mystery woman was, Jules thought, she must have done something pretty terrible to upset Issie this much.

"How dare she come back here?" Issie stormed. "Nobody wants her here!"

"What's she done?" Jules asked. "Surely it can't be that bad?"

Issie was scowling. "Yes it can. That's the girl who broke Jake's heart. It was her fault he went away for so long! If he finds out she's here and it makes him leave again it will break Granny Alice's heart. There's no way that's going to happen. I'm going to find her and tell her where to go!"

And with this passing shot she spun on her Croc-ed heel and strode down the quay before disappearing into the crowd. Jules looked at Morgan, who just shrugged.

"Never upset a Tremaine," he advised sagely. "We have long memories. Fact."

Maybe, Jules thought, life in a Cornish fishing village wasn't going to be quite so dull after all.

Chapter 4

Polwenna Bay really was the land that time forgot, Summer thought. As she'd driven through the village the festival had been in full swing and it had felt like only weeks ago that she and Morwenna had been dancing through the streets in the carnival parade. Most of the shops might be the same ones she'd known as a child – there was Patsy's Pasties, owned by her aunty, and nestling beside it was the Merlin Gift Shop with its windows bristling with postcards and which sold everything from fridge magnets to buckets and spades – but in spite of this Summer knew in her heart that everything else had changed.

Magic Moon was a new arrival, as was a very chic-looking boutique filled with designer clothing. Summer wondered what her Aunt Patsy, a dyed-in-the-wool Cornishwoman who only crossed the Tamar when dire emergency prompted, made of all these changes. Patsy Penhalligan was as much a part of Polwenna Bay as the harbour walls and the calling gulls. She knew everything about everyone and made it her business to keep up to date with everything that went on in the village and a fair bit outside it too. It had been Patsy who'd staunchly kept in touch with Summer, religiously sending her five-pound notes for birthdays and Christmases even when Summer, feeling guilty that she and Justin earned in one week more than Patsy had probably seen in several hardworking years, had protested that she really didn't need the money. The cards had kept coming regardless, and even now and then a box of Polwenna pasties – which Summer, usually on a strict no-carbs regime, had been forced to give away. No, her aunt had never given up on her, even though Summer's career must have embarrassed her horribly at the WI and been a source of grief when the whole village seemed to be against her.

It was to Patsy that Summer had turned when the adrenalin spikes from fleeing from the Kensington house had started to ebb and reality had begun to seep in. As soon as she was on the outskirts of London, Summer had pulled the Audi into a supermarket car park, only realising once she'd killed the engine just how much she was shaking. Her cheekbone had been throbbing too, and with trembling hands Summer had pulled down the vanity mirror, gasping in horror when she saw that her skin was already colouring. A few millimetres higher and her eye would have taken the full brunt of the blow.

Thank God for giant Chanel shades, Summer had thought as she'd dug them out of the glove box and pushed them on, and double thank God for Victoria Beckham making it trendy to wear them even when the sun was in. With the glasses on and her heart rate slowing, she'd grabbed some loose change and ventured to a call box. One short phone call to Patsy – no awkward explanations were required by her aunt – and Summer had had somewhere to lie low for a few weeks. The press were bound to scent blood, especially if Justin kicked off in style, but by the time they came looking for her she'd be more than ready for them. Summer had been filled with relief at this thought. She knew that by the time Justin and his people were through with her she'd make the Ebola virus look popular. After all, what sort of heartless bitch leaves Britain's most loved football star only months after his brave and selfless battle with skin cancer?

Cancer, Summer had reflected bitterly as she'd continued on her way, didn't turn nasty abusive men into saints. Far from it. In her experience they just became nasty abusive men who'd had cancer. Justin was clear now. The moles that had been suspect had been removed, but not before he'd been busy milking the story for all it was worth. He was the nation's golden boy and barely a day went by without him featuring in the papers.

If they only knew the truth.

Having parked the car, Summer was now walking along the small pedestrian street that ran through the village, over a little footbridge and onto the harbour. The tang of salty air was so familiar that a lump rose in her throat and she had to swallow it quickly. If she started crying now she'd probably flood the village, but it felt so good to be home. From the gulls circling and screeching above, to the sparkling sea, to the golden horseshoe-shaped beach, the bay was stunningly beautiful. Standing on the bridge and with the afternoon sunshine warming her face, Summer suddenly realised just how much she'd missed the place. Had fame and fortune really been worth making all these sacrifices for? You did what you had to do, she told herself sternly. Besides, what good would come now of starting to think she'd made a huge mistake? But if she hadn't left, and had instead turned her back on all the childhood dreams, then maybe she would never have…

Taking a deep breath and pushing away the memories that were rising, unbidden, to the surface of her mind, Summer turned away from the harbour and walked on until the narrow street began to rise above the glittering water and the shops were replaced by tiny crumpled cottages the colours of sugared almonds. Dry stone walls frilled with nodding valerian and starred with ox-eye daisies hemmed the street; on one side was the safety of the tarmac path and on the other wild grassland tumbled away to the snaggle-toothed rocks below. The climb up was steep, but it was only once she reached the end of the street –

the section where the road gave up any pretence of looking civilised and petered out into the beginnings of the cliff path – that Summer allowed herself to pause.

There was Polwenna Bay, falling away below her and just as she remembered it. In the marina the boats were riding the tide, their rigging jingling in the gentle breeze. Judging by the absence of the sturdy trawlers that usually hugged the harbour wall, the fishermen were out at sea. Funny to think that somewhere beyond the blue line of the endless horizon were her father and her brothers, casting their nets and hauling in their catch. Summer also knew that in the third small ripple-patterned stone cottage that nestled alongside the harbour her mother would be tackling the usual washing mountain, keeping an eye on the vast stew simmering on the range and listening to Radio Cornwall. Summer might have been away from home for a long time, but she knew that some things would never change.

And what about Jake Tremaine? asked a small voice – the same small voice she'd been trying to ignore for what felt like forever. Was he still working for the family business? Did he still love to set out to sea so early that the sky was rippled pink? Did he still laugh easily, head thrown back and sleepy eyes crinkled with merriment? Did he still think of her?

That was another of those thoughts Summer wasn't prepared to contemplate. Anyway, of course he didn't. Jake Tremaine had made his feelings very clear twelve years ago and, if she was honest, Summer didn't think she could forgive him for that. Even though it was a long time ago, she still felt the pain of having to face everything alone. Sometimes she found herself wondering what her life would have been like if things had worked out differently and if Jake had been willing to put aside the hurt she'd caused. Goodness, but they'd been so young, hadn't they? Little more than kids themselves. Did Jake have a wife now and children of his own? Did blond curly-headed little scamps play on the beach and make Miss Powell, the teacher at Polwenna Primary who seemed to have been there forever, tug her grey hair out with despair? Summer's aunt had never mentioned anything, but then again Patsy Penhalligan knew that Jake Tremaine was a no-go zone, right up there with Area 51 and the Official Secrets Act.

Summer gave herself a mental shake. None of this mattered anyway. Jake had let her down when she'd needed him the most. Their time had been and gone.

She was at the end of the road now and Summer couldn't help laughing; this couldn't be more metaphorical. Harbour Watch was the final cottage in a terrace of six, the last dwelling in Polwenna Bay except for Seaspray, the Tremaines' big white house, which seemed to grow from the acres of grounds and whose big windows had kept watch over the village for generations.

Jake's house.

When Patsy had told Summer that Harbour Watch had had a last-minute cancellation, Summer had almost turned the car back to London rather than stay in this particular cottage. Only the thought of Justin and her throbbing cheek had kept her going. Harbour Watch was practically in the Tremaines' garden and Jake would pass it every day on his journey to the marina – if he was still here, of course. He had always wanted to travel. She recalled that they'd spent many hours on the deserted sand at one of the numerous little coves that could only be reached by boat; they'd be curled up together on the old tartan picnic rug, looking up at the blue sky and dreaming of Spain and Australia and the Caribbean. Maybe even now he was living in one of these far-flung places, gazing up at a sun even brighter than the one that shone down right now. In spite of everything that had happened, Summer hoped his dreams had all come true.

The key was under the potted bay tree, just as Patsy had promised. Once Summer was inside and the door was shut securely behind her, with the heavy brass key turned firmly in the lock, she allowed herself to exhale. She hadn't realised just how tense she'd been. Now that she was here, she felt weak and wobbly.

Buoyed up by having reached safety, Summer set about exploring the cottage. Like her childhood home this was an old fisherman's cottage and didn't have space to swing a hamster, so it wouldn't take long. Downstairs consisted of a tiny kitchen with a deep window seat heaped with faded patchwork cushions. There was also a small scrubbed oak table and a stable door that opened straight out to the pathway. Against the whitewashed cottage wall somebody had placed a simple weathered bench and a couple of pots of leggy geraniums, half hidden beneath nets and lobster pots piled up like a game of seafaring Jenga. A black cat was sunning itself on top of this lot, stretched out and contented in the warmth. Maybe it would come inside and keep her company?

Summer laughed out loud at this. She'd only been single for a few hours and already she was turning into a mad cat lady. That hadn't taken long – although, in fairness, she'd been trying to be single for a very long time…

The rest of the kitchen was little more than a hotchpotch of freestanding cupboards and tables, which would have been quaint if not so tatty. Some money was tucked under the bread bin, exactly as her aunty had promised, and Summer pocketed it with relief. Running away without her bank card hadn't been her smartest move. She was also relieved to discover that Patsy had left her a couple of carrier bags full of spare clothes, since packing a suitcase hadn't been high on Summer's list of priorities when she'd fled from the house. As soon as she'd ordered a new bank card she would pay Patsy back and buy her a very big bottle of wine, Summer decided. It was the least she could do for putting her on the spot like this and forcing her to keep Summer's arrival secret from the rest of the family.

A quick check of the fridge and cupboards in the small kitchen revealed that the thoughtful Patsy had provided some supplies and, most importantly, a jar of coffee. Summer filled the kettle and went to explore the rest of the house while it boiled. The house was only three rooms: the kitchen formed the ground floor; a tiny sitting room with a window seat and a small sofa occupied the first floor; and the bedroom and a miniscule shower room were up in the eaves. Sitting on the bed, Summer could hear the feet of the gulls on the roof and their squabbling over who got prime position on the chimney pot, while the sea crashed against the rocks. These were the sounds of her childhood, and she found them comforting.

She'd go and see her mother soon, Summer decided as she returned to the kitchen and made a strong coffee. Then she caught a glimpse of herself in the mirror at the foot of the narrow stairs and winced. On second thoughts, maybe she ought to give it a day or two? The sad-eyed reflection with the swollen cheek and tangled hair looked nothing like the usual groomed and glossy Summer that the celebrity magazines and tabloids loved to feature. Susie Penhalligan would have a fit and demand to know exactly what had been going on. Summer felt like having a fit herself, and now that the adrenalin of her flight was subsiding she felt dangerously close to tears. There was no way she could tell her mother. No way at all. Susie would be jumping in her ancient Ford Fiesta and zooming up the M5 before you could say *protective mother*, and then all hell would break loose. The tabloids would have a field day and Justin would be even more enraged, which would be very bad news indeed. Who knew what he'd do then?

Summer shivered even though the kitchen was warm with pools of golden-syrup sunshine. If she could pinpoint the exact moment things had gone wrong, then she knew when it would be: back at that awards ceremony five years ago. If she could have returned to that time and changed things, she probably wouldn't have dieted and exercised for weeks, or worn a dress that resembled a piece of dental floss and made Elizabeth Hurley's safety-pin one look like a Burka in comparison. And when Justin Anderson had asked if he could join her, she would definitely have said no.

Yes, that was the moment when her life, or rather her new life, had gone so wrong. The parts with Jake had seemed long ago and, if not forgotten exactly, then at least consigned to the dusty corners of her mind that she didn't often visit. She'd moved on from what had happened (she'd had no choice), and the world had just been starting to open up to her. Justin had wandered over, bow tie undone and inky hair sexily dishevelled, and given her a slow smile that had made Summer's stomach tangle. He'd had two champagne glasses hanging loosely in one hand and a bottle of vintage champagne in the other, and his sherry-hued eyes had held her as he'd joined her and poured them each a glass. Summer had drunk far too much of it far too quickly and by the end of the night was giddy, not just from the Krug but mostly from his undivided attention. He was *Justin Anderson*, the hottest and most talented Premier League star since David Beckham, and he was talking to her – and not just *talking*, either, but hanging on to Summer's every word! As one of several models present, successful but hardly in his league, Summer had been stunned and not a little star-struck in the full beam of Justin's charm offensive. No wonder she'd been bowled over by it.

She looked in the mirror again and the doleful reflection shook her head. What a fool. She really should have known better. One thing was for sure: she knew better *now*. All she could hope was that Justin wouldn't do anything stupid like jumping into his precious red Ferrari and tearing down here on the off chance that he'd find her. If she lay low for a week or two, found a way to explain to her family why she was keeping herself to herself, it was highly likely that he'd give up and move on to somebody else.

She certainly hoped so anyway. Her hands fluttered down to her stomach and rested there for a moment. She had to be strong and she had to make this work. No matter how scared she was or how much Justin threatened her, she had to stay away from him. She had to.

It was no longer just about her.

Chapter 5

With a baseball cap crammed onto her head and her big Chanel sunglasses firmly in place, Summer locked the cottage behind her and headed into the village. It was early evening now and snatches of music floated up from the village green, suggesting that the celebrations were in full swing. The scent of roasting meat drifted on the breeze, reminding her that she hadn't eaten. She'd have to do so at some point, but right now her stomach was churning like a washing machine. There was bread in the cottage, and a toaster. She'd have to try to eat something later on.

If only she'd had time to grab her bag. Then she could have sent Patsy a text and asked her for some help. She wished too that she and Morwenna were still friends. Mo would know what to do; the fiery redhead wouldn't let a bully like Justin intimidate her and would be more than capable of taking on the press if they got in her way. Summer, always shy unless on the stage or in front of a camera, had lost count of the times that her best friend had looked after her at school and fought off the bullies. They'd seemed to hate Summer for no reason other than that she was pretty and dating Jake Tremaine, whom everyone agreed was *way* hot. When Ella St Milton, one of the meanest girls at school, had *accidentally* poured her paint water all over Summer's GCSE art project, Morwenna had *accidentally* cut off Ella's swishy blonde ponytail.

"But I tripped," Mo had insisted, echoing Ella's excuse of moments earlier. Unfortunately, Mo's wide blue eyes and innocent expression had fooled nobody. She'd been excluded for a week and Ella had been whisked off to Plymouth for a full head of hair extensions. On the plus side, Mo had spent the week riding her horses – Alice Tremaine was no fan of bullies – and nobody had ever dared pick on Summer Penhalligan again. Well, not unless they wanted to be scalped, Mo had said cheerfully. On the downside, Summer had been pretty certain that both she and Morwenna had made a dangerous enemy for life in the spoilt and spiteful Ella. Hopefully she wouldn't come across the other girl anytime soon. The St Miltons owned a big hotel just outside the Bay and had always been very wealthy. As a child, Summer had been taunted relentlessly by Ella and her cronies for her cheap clothes and her tiny home. Now she was famous, had a closet full of designer bags, shoes and clothes and a beautiful house in Kensington, Summer would have enjoyed a sense of *Schadenfreude* if it hadn't been for the fact that her life was very far from the happy pictures that *Hiya* and *All Right!* liked to peddle. Her fingers stole to her bruised face and she flinched.

Unfortunately, Summer no longer had Morwenna to fight her corner and, whether or not she bumped into Ella, she was going to do her best to make sure she wasn't discovered. It was holiday season in Cornwall, so Polwenna Bay was thronging with *emmets*, the name the Cornish affectionately gave their seasonal visitors. Besides, Summer was a trained actress (even though her skills hadn't been employed lately, or at least not on the stage). How hard could it be to blend into the crowds? Passing the village shop, she caught a glimpse of her reflection in the window and felt reassured that the slim girl in skinny jeans, a baseball cap and a baggy long-sleeve tee-shirt could be anyone. She certainly didn't bear any resemblance to the glossy-haired, lusciously curved and pouting creature known across the UK simply as Summer.

The village shop looked empty and Summer didn't recognise the chewing teen behind the counter so, glancing around nervously, she stepped inside. She needed to grab a copy of *The Dagger*, just to see exactly what it was that had sent Justin wild this morning. Two holidaymakers were chatting by the Duchy Originals area while the bored teenager played with an iPhone. Nobody took the slightest notice of Summer. Brilliant. Feeling reassured, she scanned the selection of redtops, but there was nothing. Only by flicking through the last remaining copy of *The Dagger* did she finally come across a small picture of her leaning in closely to speak to Max Roberts. So that was what had set Justin off. For him this was actually something she could almost understand; more often than not it was something as trivial as Summer making tea when he wanted coffee, or wearing shoes he didn't like, which made him flip. Max, with whom Summer had recently filmed an episode of the comedy quiz show *Celebrity Squash*, was one of the hottest young actors of the moment and also as gay as a Cath Kidston tea towel. If Justin had actually taken the time to ask, rather than sending Summer flying across their bespoke kitchen and smack into the central island, she'd have been able to tell him so.

"Do you want to buy that paper or not?" asked an impatient voice.

Looking up, Summer saw that a man was staring at her petulantly, a frown creasing the place between his eyes. His face was all sharp planes and perfect bone structure beneath hair that curled to his chin in waves the exact same colour as the chocolate dusting on cappuccino. Mocha-dark stubble sprinkled his jaw and his full mouth was pressed into a very unamused line. If he hadn't been so bad tempered he would have been exceedingly good-looking.

"Well?" he demanded, clearly itching to snatch the paper from her. "Yes or no? The tide won't wait for you to make your mind up. Some of us have got boats to get to."

Oh great. This was a member of the species peculiar to Cornwall in the tourist season: the know-it-all *emmet* with more money than manners. Summer had met enough of these in her time to know one when she saw one, and this guy – dressed from head to foot in Musto, wearing Maui Jim shades perched atop a trendy haircut, and rocking the latest LV man bag – definitely ticked all the boxes.

"Well? I don't have all day," demanded Mr Musto, checking a Rolex the size of the village hall clock. Then his eyes narrowed. "Hey, have we met before?"

Only in my bad dreams, thought Summer darkly. Hastily, and before he could make the connection – unlikely, she knew, but still a risk not worth taking – she thrust the paper at him.

"Here, it's all yours," she told him over her shoulder. "Enjoy the boating!"

Without waiting for a reply she dashed out of the shop. For an awful moment she half expected him to come charging after her shouting that he knew who she was. For once, though, luck was on Summer's side. Musto Man was far too busy elbowing locals out of the way in his haste to catch the tide to pay any more attention to a scruffy girl. Still, Summer knew this was a warning and that she had to do something drastic if she was to stay incognito. Hiding in plain sight, was how Patsy had put it. Then, like an answer to prayer, Summer saw it: the solution to her problems. Or to one of them, at the very least.

Kursa's Kozi Kutz. All big hairdryers and faded 1980s shots of Princess Diana pageboy cuts and curly perms. But who cared? It may not have been Nicky Clarke but she had never been so in need of a salon. This was also a new addition to the village, and Summer was quietly hopeful that the mysterious Kursa wouldn't know who she was. Maybe she could even have a go at doing an American accent. After all, her Blanche DuBois had once won all the critics over. She gave the door a push and dived in.

Over the course of her career Summer had spent a lot of time at the hairdresser's. If she'd ever naïvely thought that being an actress was all about learning screeds of Shakespeare and channelling the muse, then she'd been in for a bit of a disappointment. It was true that she'd spent ages memorising her lines for various plays, but she'd also endured equal amounts of time in the stylist's chair being dyed and blow-dried or styled for shoots. Lately she and Justin had frequented the same salon once favoured by Kate Middleton, and Summer owed her glossy dark mane to their magic rather than any real effort on her own part. Justin spent just as much time in the stylist's chair as she did, knowing full well that every style he wore was going to be copied the length and breadth of the UK. Summer felt confident that she was something of an expert when it came to hairdressers; she didn't think there was anything about a trip to one that could surprise her.

She was wrong.

For a start, was she actually in a salon or had she walked into her Nan's front room by mistake? The walls were smothered with orange and green flowery wallpaper and the floor was carpeted in a lurid swirly shagpile. A carpet like that could only be some sort of 1970s masterpiece, unless the stress had really got to Summer and she was having a violent hallucination. A tiny sink lurked in the corner of the room, its taps jauntily sporting a plastic shower attachment of a kind that Summer hadn't seen since childhood. Two overstuffed red-velour armchairs complete with frothing antimacassars flanked a stone fireplace. Huge dryers loomed over them like diplodocuses, while in another corner there was a tea trolley piled high with a jumble of curlers, perm papers and medieval-looking curling tongs. At least, Summer hoped they were curling tongs.

This *was* a hairdresser's? There wasn't a customer in sight. Summer was contemplating bolting back to the cottage and taking her chances with being spotted, when a figure stepped out of the wallpaper. She was wearing a flowery housecoat and big pink slippers, camouflaging her perfectly with the dahlias and roses in the pattern. Even her hair was tango orange; it was as though one of the plants was walking towards Summer, Triffid-like. Summer couldn't help it. She shrieked.

"Sorry, my love – didn't mean to make you jump," said the Triffid.

"I think I've made a mistake," Summer said quickly, reversing towards the door. "I thought this was a hairdresser's."

"Not a mistake at all, my love! Welcome to Kursa's Kozi Kutz! I'm Kursa. Why don't you take a seat and tell me what you'd like me to do?"

A plump hand rested on her shoulder and guided Summer across the shagpile. Before she could open her mouth to protest, Summer was plopped down into a marshmallow of an armchair that faced a mirror balanced precariously on the mantelpiece. She considered making a dash for freedom, but then she caught sight of her reflection. The baseball cap had slipped and her long hair was falling down loose from underneath it; those trademark dark curls would give her away in an instant. Summer only prayed that Kursa didn't recognise her. That would be a disaster. Checking out the tottering piles of magazines and clocking that *Woman's Weekly* and *The People's Friend* featured heavily, she figured she was pretty safe. *Heat* or *Closer* would have been a bit more of a worry.

Summer took a deep breath and whipped off the hat. "Would you be able to cut my hair? A dry cut would do."

Kursa nodded, already reaching for her scissors. "A couple of inches?"

"No. Not exactly." Summer swallowed. Her hand moved to her stomach. Why on earth was she hesitating? There were far more important things to think about than hair. "I was thinking a bit more."

"No problems. To the shoulder?"

"No. All of it."

The scissors hovered and Kursa's eyes widened.

"All of it? Are you serious, my love? It's beautiful hair. It must have taken ages to grow."

"All of it," Summer said firmly.

"Well if you're sure," said Kursa, sounding doubtful. Her gaze flickered to Summer's cheek and she frowned. "Man trouble?"

"You could say that."

Their eyes met in the mirror. "I came here five years ago from Penzance," Kursa told Summer softly. "My Ted was a bit handy with his fists. Best day of my life when he dropped dead. Better than winning the lottery. I always loved Polwenna, so I sold up and bought this place. Then I went to college and trained as a hairdresser. At my age, would you believe! It was always my dream."

Summer had enjoyed the grieving widow fantasy a few times herself and then felt dreadful afterwards. Lately, though, her dream would be to have a good night's rest without trying not to breathe too loudly, fidget, talk in her sleep or do whatever else might annoy Justin.

"Nothing helps get you over a man like a change of hair," Kursa said when Summer didn't reply. "Like therapy, it is. New hair, new start, new man."

"New man? No thanks." Summer shook her head. "I'm through with men. Believe me, if there was a convent nearby I'd be seriously considering joining up."

"There are still some good ones out there. My son Richard, he's one of the good guys. A doctor too. He's just started to practise here; I can hardly believe it!"

"Mmm," said Summer politely. She was starting to feel twitchy and was hoping that Kursa got a move on in the next decade. What if one of her Polwenna Bay regulars came in? Imagine if it was Sheila Keverne or "Key Hole" Kathy Polmartin? The redtops had nothing on the way those two pillars of the community could spread gossip. She may as well just phone *The Sun*'s news desk herself and be done with it.

"Listen to me going on!" Sensing that her customer wasn't in a chatty frame of mind, Kursa leaned forward and turned the mirror around so that Summer couldn't see her handiwork. "Just leave it with me. If it's a change you want then it's a change you shall have. You're going to be in for a big surprise!"

Summer didn't much like surprises. Justin was full of them, and few of them were pleasant. For instance, there was the surprise she'd got when Justin had… Well, never mind him now. The point was that usually she liked to know exactly what was going on, especially when it came to her appearance. It was how she made her living, after all. But something strange was happening as Kursa cut her hair: with every snip of the scissors it was though the tension was falling away with her curls. Very soon the floor was covered in a mound of the dark locks. Summer couldn't recall ever having short hair, but she was willing to give it a try. After all, hair grew back.

And bruises faded.

Summer was still musing on this when Kursa rubbed some wax on her hands, ran it through what was left of Summer's hair and stepped back to regard her critically through narrowed eyes.

"Proper job," she said, a smile spreading across her face. "Good to know I've still got it."

Turning the mirror around slowly, in the style of Gok Wan about to do a grand reveal, she waited for Summer's reaction. She wasn't disappointed.

Summer gasped.

The reflection in the glass looked nothing like her. Yes, of course the big green eyes and blooming bruises were hers, as was the small freckled nose and too-large pouty mouth, but where on earth had those cheekbones come from? Her hair curled around her face in ringlets like those of an Austen heroine and although she didn't think it had ever been this short she absolutely loved it. She looked so much younger! And just think of the hours she was going to save washing and styling it. No more diffusers or straighteners or curling wands. It was a whole new world of freedom for her follicles – and hopefully nobody would recognise her like this. It felt like a huge leap forward. Could it be possible that things really were going to be OK?

Summer was still smiling five minutes later when she let herself out of the salon. Armed with a tub of gel and a stack of ancient *Woman's Weekly* magazines, she was looking forward to settling into a bath and then devouring a pile of toast before snuggling down for the night. Maybe tomorrow she'd go and see her mum and tell her what had happened. She'd call her agent too and see if she could sort out some financial arrangements; she was getting low on cash, having paid for the haircut with Aunty Patsy's money. She could have a bank card delivered to her parents' place. She'd also need to see a doctor, and sooner rather than later. Maybe Kursa's son would have an appointment.

As she headed back through the village and towards the harbour, Summer marvelled at the change a haircut could make. It was as though the new style had moved her into a different space. Walking back along the street to the waterfront she found that she was looking at the views rather than fixing her eyes on the floor and scuttling along, hoping that nobody noticed her. She didn't see Musto Man again, thank goodness, and nobody gave her a second glance. Maybe things were going to be all right. Perhaps Summer without Justin was invisible.

She could only hope.

Chapter 6

Morwenna Tremaine was not having a good day. It had got off to a bad start when her top event horse, Mr Dandy, had lamed himself carting around the paddock – meaning she'd had to pull out of a major competition and forfeit several hundred pounds worth of entrance fees, which she could ill afford to lose. Then one of her full liveries had handed in their notice, which meant even less money in the pot, and then just to add insult to injury her ancient Discovery had decided it was time to give up the ghost. So when she'd finally got around to opening her mail and discovered that Ashley sodding Carstairs had pulled yet another stunt, it had been the last straw. Mo had screwed up the letter from the Polwenna Action Group and hurled it across the kitchen, wishing with all her heart that it were made of voodoo paper and that somewhere bloody Ashley was clutching his guts and howling. No such luck. Cashley was made of Teflon; nothing ever seemed to stick to him.

Uttering several choice words that she knew Granny Alice certainly wouldn't approve of, Mo tugged on her wellies, pulled her wild red hair onto the top of her head and lassoed it with a scrunchie, then grabbed the last tenner out of the biscuit barrel. The biscuit barrel was supposed to be the place where she kept her emergency funds but, sod it, thought Mo as she stomped out of her static caravan and slammed the door so hard that the flimsy structure wobbled, this was an emergency and she needed a drink. If Cashley managed to grease the right palms on the council and sneak under the planning radar just when most members of

PAG were collapsing under the burden of the holiday trade and simply too exhausted to fight, then their cause was lost.

"Over my dead body," Mo said to the beady-eyed seagull sitting on the caravan's roof. "And his too, if needs be."

The seagull didn't reply. Then again, it didn't need to because unlike Cashley it was born and raised in Polwenna Bay and was therefore Cornish through and through. It was bound to be in agreement with Morwenna Tremaine. Most people tended to be.

It was second nature for Mo to check the yard as she crossed it and, as always, she felt a thrill of pride that all this was hers – even if she was hanging onto it by a wing and a prayer. It might be the case that she lived in a caravan that was such a nineteen-eighties time warp that she half expected to bump into Boy George whenever she went to the kitchenette. It might also be true that when she wasn't in jodhpurs her clothes were an eclectic collection of charity-shop finds and her gran's cast-offs. Nevertheless, her horses lived the lives of pampered A-listers in the American barn and pranced around the paddocks in their fly sheets like supermodels sampling bridal attire. Even if Mo's fingernails were broken from yard chores and her hair hadn't seen a proper cut since Take That were first in the charts, the horses all had perfect hooves – thanks to Tommy Lovell, the sexiest farrier in England (albeit a gay one, sadly for Mo, so there was no chance of paying him in kind) – and their manes were pulled and glossy. Of course, this was as it should be. Mo would have gone without every creature comfort in order to make sure that the horses had exactly what they needed.

Crossing the yard, Morwenna reflected that if things carried on like this then she'd probably have to rethink her career as a three-day eventer. She might have talent, and there was no doubt that she was brave, but eventing was an expensive sport and without a sponsor she was struggling to make her way. No wonder most people on the circuit were either royals or loaded. The entrance fees alone were crippling, never mind the fuel to reach the events and all the costly care that went into bringing on a string of top-level competition horses. Mr Dandy was as highly strung as any Premier League footballer and shared that profession's propensity for exaggerating the slightest injury for maximum dramatic impact. Mo sighed. She dreaded to think how much she owed Lucas Madding, the local equine vet. Probably enough to buy him another Range Rover. Lucas had been kind enough to let her put today's callout fee on the slate, but she'd have to find the money to pay him eventually. Her mortgage was also due next week and she knew that the bank wouldn't be half as understanding. In fact, the last time she'd coaxed the Discovery over the Tamar to Plymouth to grovel to her bank manager, he'd been very unsympathetic.

"There are more important things in life than horses," he'd said disapprovingly to Mo, peering over his bifocals in the manner of Dumbledore giving Harry Potter a dressing down.

There were? Mo couldn't think what. She'd spent most of her life living and breathing horses. Eventually, the bank manager had agreed to extend her overdraft and review the situation in six months, a reprieve that still made Mo feel giddy with relief but which also terrified her. Unless something miraculous happened in the next few months, like Princess Anne popping by and deciding to adopt her, Mo couldn't see a way that she could keep her eventing dream afloat. She couldn't ask her father for a cash injection; Jake was always making it very clear on their father's behalf that the church mice in St Wenn's had more in the pot than the Tremaines these days. Besides, Mo had her pride. Polwenna

Equestrian was *her* baby. She'd find a way to make it pay and keep her horses, even if it meant putting aside her Olympic ambitions and turning to pony trekking for the holidaymakers. Or, even worse, selling her top horse on for good money and starting all over again.

There was a lump the size of a Jolly Ball in her throat at this thought. Morwenna adored Mr Dandy far more than she'd ever loved any man. Of course I do, Mo thought with a grimace as the ghosts of boyfriends past danced through her memory in a mental *most rubbish* ID parade. Not that Mo had much time for dating anyway – it was pretty hard to fit a love life in between all the mucking out, exercising and competing – but the few men who had come and gone from her life had all been pretty useless. Some had been jealous of the horses, one had been terrified (the sight of him quaking when she'd handed him a lead rope had pretty much killed any romance stone dead), and others had just been too much of a pushover. Mo supposed that she was quite bossy; it was the legacy of having to keep all those siblings in line for her formative years. She just couldn't help ordering her boyfriends around. Maybe it was a test and she wanted to see who actually had the balls to stand up to her. This was what her brother Danny thought – and since Danny had spent hours in psychotherapy recently, Mo guessed he knew what he was talking about.

"You want an alpha male," Danny had concluded only yesterday evening as they'd sat in The Ship. He'd smirked at her over the rim of his whisky glass. "Admit it, Mo: you just want a Christian Grey to take control."

"I do not!" Mo had scoffed. "I'm not into perverts, thanks!"

Her brother had raised a quizzical eyebrow, which Mo could see because she was sitting on his good side. "So you say. One woman's pervert is another woman's sex god. I think you protest too much, sis. Mr Grey would have a field day with all that bondage gear of yours."

Mo had laughed. "That's my tack, you moron! And those whips are for schooling horses, not S and M!"

"That's your story," had teased Danny, who'd been at that lovely stage between being just drunk enough to forget his misery and not quite drunk enough to be obnoxious. "But you don't fool me, Morwenna Tremaine. Like all women you want a hero to sweep you off your feet and carry you into the sunset in his manly arms." He'd then glanced down at his own body and Mo's heart had plummeted into her wellies, because she'd known exactly what her brother was thinking. Oh great. Now he'd reached the tipping point at least several drinks earlier than usual. Sure enough, the storm clouds had swiftly come rolling in and the side of his mouth that she could see had shrunk into a tight line.

"Christ. If that's what women want then that's me screwed. No wonder Tara left."

"Tara left because she's a shallow bitch with less depth than a rock pool," Mo had said quickly, but it had already been too late. Her brother was plummeting over the cliff edge of his despair and was signalling with his good arm to the barmaid for another shot. Mo hadn't stuck around to witness the rest of the evening; she hadn't needed to because she'd seen Danny drunk and belligerent far too many times since he'd been discharged from the army. It wasn't pretty; it invariably ended in him getting thrown out of the pub, and she was very afraid that things were only going to get worse. If it hadn't been for his hero status in the village and the fact that everyone loved Granny Alice far too much to rock the boat (for now, at least), Mo was pretty sure that her volatile brother would have been banned from everywhere that sold alcohol.

She leaned against the gate and sighed. Mo had no idea what the answer was for Danny, but she could have cheerfully murdered her ex-sister-in-law for making things a million times worse for him. Sure, Tara had married a strong vital man with a glowing army career, and she certainly hadn't bargained for what had happened to Dan. But he was still her husband. To walk away when he needed her most was unforgivable in Mo's mind, even if Dan was bloody hard to live with at the minute. Anyway, wasn't the whole point of marriage about things being for better or for worse? In sickness or in health?

All this thinking was making Mo's head ache. Watching the horses chomping contentedly at the grass, their tails whisking the flies away, she decided that she was never, ever going to put herself in the dangerous position of being so in love with someone that he became her world. God, no way. Look where that got you. Dan was a wreck, her father missed her mother every day and even Jake had never quite returned to his old carefree self since that bitch, Summer, had ditched him without a second thought. And that was years ago.

No, Mo decided as Mr Dandy ambled up and nudged her hopefully for a treat, if this was what love did for you then she'd stick to the horses, thanks all the same. Besides, how could she respect anyone who wasn't her equal or her sparring partner? She gave her horse a scratch and offered him the last Polo from her gilet pocket. In her eyes there was simply no comparison to Mr Dandy, who was always pleased to see her, kept all her secrets and gave her a great ride every single day!

Satisfied that all her horses were secure for the evening, and sending up a swift prayer of thanks to the gods of good weather and all-night turnout, Mo secured the yard gate and set off for the village. It was a glorious evening but as she stomped down the lane even the sight of the sun slipping behind the hill to bathe the village in honeyed light and gilt-edge the waves didn't improve her state of mind. What she needed was a night off from all the thoughts that were zooming around her head like wasps on speed. An hour listening to Zak's band play, a plate of Symon's hog roast and then a pint of scrumpy in the pub would cheer her up. And if she bumped into Cashley en route and was able to give him a piece of her mind, then so much the better.

There were two ways down to Polwenna Bay from Mo's clifftop yard. The simplest route was to follow the narrow lane that wound its way down the hillside and passed through the westerly side of the village beside the British Legion and the Merry Mackerel Café, before passing the church, skipping over a humpbacked bridge and finally opening up into a street filled with restaurants and gift shops – plus the latest jewel in Polwenna Bay's crown, Symon's Michelin-starred restaurant, The Plump Seagull. Today, Mo wasn't in the mood for simple or straightforward. She also had a vested interest in taking the second route into the village, a muddier and splashier path that split off from the lane just before the jumbled lichen-splattered village rooftops came back into view. This was a scenic and more leisurely path through several acres of ancient woodland. The locals called this area Fernside; in the heat of the summer it was a cool oasis of green shade and in the winter it was the best place in the world to gather kindling for the wood burner or to collect bags full of spiky holly splashed with blood-red berries, to make Christmas garlands.

Mo, who was generally always dressed in boots and jeans, had been taking the Fernside route into the village for as long as she'd had horses up at the top of the hill, and there wasn't an inch of the woodland that she didn't know. Mo always felt that when she slipped into the dappled pools of shade it was as though she'd stepped away from the noise and demands of the real world and travelled backwards to a quieter time. Although the sounds of the village still floated through the valley and the rooks in their treetop perches chattered endlessly like noisy schoolchildren, being in the woods felt like being in another dimension altogether. Whatever the season, Mo loved the peace and quiet of Fernside. In the springtime the floor was an inland sea of bluebells. In the summer wild garlic lent a Parisian scent to the pathways as her boots brushed against the flowers. When autumn came, the leaves turned to russet and scarlet and gold confetti, drifting down silently to carpet the earth. By winter the trees shivered beneath their ivy cloaks and knitted their branches overhead to keep out the rain. Mo had played here as a child, making camps with her siblings, and as an adult it was a place where she liked to come and just be still for a while to escape the pressures of the yard and the knotty business of Tremaine family life. There was something about catching glimpses of Polwenna through the tangled trees, small as a model village from this height, which calmed her down and put everything into perspective.

    Today Mo was walking through Fernside for a very different reason. Rather than feeling soothed, every step she took wound her up so much that she was in danger of chiming like the village hall clock. She splashed through the puddles, kicked branches out of the way and, for once, neglected to admire the village peeping shyly at her through the greenery. Instead of seeing the path and the breathtaking views, all Mo could picture was the pristine tarmac road that Ashley bloody Carstairs wanted to bulldoze through the woods. Mariners, at present his white elephant of a property, couldn't be accessed by road through the village, which was a tragic blow to a man who probably loved his sports car more than his mum (if indeed Cashley had a mum; Mo was convinced that he was actually Satan come to earth as a property developer). But the house was situated right at the end of Fernside, and it hadn't taken Cashley long to figure out that if he flung enough money at the council somebody would agree to sell the woods to him. Today's letter from PAG had carried the devastating news that the woods were indeed going to be sold at auction very soon.

It was a coincidence too far, Mo thought bitterly as she kicked a piece of bark. Of course this was another of the dark doings of Cashley – and unless she came up with a brilliant idea and pretty bloody quickly too, Fernside would be his personal driveway before you could say *tosser*. There had to be a way she could raise the money to beat him to it.

Unable to face walking to the end of the woods and seeing the sad shell of Mariners, Mo turned left when the path fell a little, and took the stepped lane that dropped behind St Wenn's and popped out behind the chip shop. The houses were a cluster of slate roofs and listing chimney pots, speckled with moss and seagull droppings, and the closer she got to the village the louder the music became as The Tinners played their first set on the green.

Maybe Zak would get a big recording deal and lend her the money to buy the woods, Mo thought hopefully. Everyone said he was talented, so if that failed maybe she could persuade him to go on *The X Factor* instead and have a bash at One Direction style world domination? Winning the lottery was another possibility, although since she didn't play it this plan had its flaws. Then there was always the chance of marrying a rich man.

Mo glanced down at her broken nails, calloused hands and tatty clothes. Unless there was a millionaire with a penchant for scruffy girls who smelled of horses and had wild hair, she was on a hiding to nothing. Besides, there was a distinct lack of millionaires in Polwenna Bay; they preferred the smarter Cornish resorts like Fowey and Rock, where they could pose in their boats and pretend that they knew the royals. Unfortunately for Mo the only millionaire in the village was Cashley.

There was nothing else for it: she would have to start buying lottery tickets.

The village green was packed like a sardine tin, with bodies of holidaymakers and locals alike pressed together. Beers in hand and swaying to the catchy harmonies, people had gathered to listen to The Tinners. Mo joined the throng for a couple of songs – and managed to wave at Zak, who grinned and gave her a thumbs-up. Then she went to find her brother Nick over at the hog roast. Clutching their food and dripping apple sauce everywhere, they wandered through the street that led past the shops and along the fish-market area, where the Penhalligan brothers in their dayglow-yellow overalls were landing the day's catch. Continuing past them, they climbed the narrow flight of stone steps leading into the pub.

"Shouldn't you be giving them a hand?" Mo asked her little brother as they stumbled into the candle-lit fug of The Ship. She hated to play the bossy big sister but sometimes Nick brought this side out in her.

Nick shook his shaggy blond head. He was still dressed in his smock and boots and smelled of diesel and sea spray, but the glitter in his blue eyes and the easy smile playing at the corners of his wide mouth suggested that he'd been taking part in the celebrations for some time while his colleagues sorted and weighed the catch.

"Time off for good behaviour. I'm taking the boat again at midnight with Davey Tuckey so that the boys can party tonight," he explained, not quite able to look at his sister – which was typical of Nick when he was being economical with the truth. He waved across the crowded bar to the pretty brunette busy emptying the glass-washer and threw her a smile that could thaw ice caps.

"Hey! Kelly! Pint of Doom Bar for me and a scrumpy for Mo!"

It was a given that women always melted where her brothers were concerned, and Mo pulled a face while the smitten Kelly flicked her hair about and fluttered her lashes so hard that the newspapers piled on the end of the bar were in danger of being blown away. Mo guessed that this did have one advantage – being tall, chiselled and handsome, the Tremaine brothers were pretty hard to miss and in a crowded pub this meant that they tended to be served very quickly. Mo knew she would have been queuing for ages and, being only five feet two, wasn't so easy to spot in a crowd. While Nick paid she hopped onto a bar stool and glanced about the place.

Oh bollocks, there was Danny hunched over the far end of the bar, nursing a whisky as though he were Gollum protecting the precious Ring. Judging from his unfocused expression, he'd been here for some time. There was no sign of Jake yet – Mo guessed he was still at the marina – but Issie was sitting cross-legged in one of the window seats, talking to a plump woman with spiky purple hair who was laughing and gesticulating wildly about something. She was familiar but Mo couldn't quite place her. Pink wellies? She frowned. No local would wear pink wellies. Maybe she was a second-homer?

There were certainly lots of these folk in evidence today, crowding the bar and munching their way through crusty baguettes and plates of mussels. Most of the locals had decamped to the far end of the bar, practically under the stairs with the musty coats and old umbrellas, while the holidaymakers claimed the comfy seats with the best views. This was how it was in the summer, and the residents of Polwenna Bay were more or less resigned to having to step back and make themselves scarce for a few months. After all, these folk paid top dollar to rent the holiday cottages and kept the tills of many village businesses ringing. The Tremaines had two cottages and the marina and, unless things perked up soon, Mo's pony-trekking venture would also rely on the tourists. At this thought she took her drink from Nick, clinked the glasses, and then took a deep swig. Maybe Danny had a point.

Nick downed his pint and held the glass out to Kelly for a refill.

"Stressful day," he explained when Mo raised her eyebrows. "Caught the trawl and came fast. Thought we'd have to cut it off for one bloody awful moment. Can you imagine? Eddie would have gone mental."

Having grown up in a fishing village, Mo spoke fluent trawlerman and knew that *coming fast* was less E L James and more to do with getting your net stuck on a wreck. Since trawl nets were worth thousands and the catch in them just as much on a good day, Mo could well imagine what Eddie Penhalligan's reaction would be to such a mishap. The Penhalligans were a volatile bunch with their mythical Spanish roots and hot Latino tempers, and Big Eddie was famous for exploding. When he'd first seen a picture of Summer posing for *FHM*, all grapefruit cleavage, flowing black gypsy curls and pouting red lips, his roar of fury could be heard in Plymouth. If Mo hadn't hated her former best friend, she would have felt very sorry for her indeed.

Still, even the sheer relief of escaping a verbal tongue-lashing from his boss didn't excuse Nick from getting drunk when he had to take the trawler to sea again at midnight. Alcohol and deep-sea fishing were a deadly combination.

"Should you be having another one if you're saving tide and going at midnight?" Mo asked gently. She glanced at the novelty pasty clock on the wall. It was only half five but, even so, if Nick kept on like this there was no chance he'd be sober enough to skipper *Penhalligan Girl* at midnight.

"Chillax, sis," said Nick airily. "It's nothing I can't handle, OK? Anyway, this is weak beer and I won't have more than four or five anyway. I know what I'm doing."

If Mo drank five pints of beer she would be unconscious until the middle of the next week. Nick though, like most of the fishermen in the village, drank hard and often. Mo worried about him but, as he often reminded her, he was twenty-two and more than capable of making his own decisions. She was wondering whether to persuade him that this particular decision wasn't a sensible one when the pub door burst open and none other than Ashley Carstairs bowled in as though he owned the place.

Well, he didn't own it, thought Mo. Not yet anyway! Just the sight of his smug face, stupid wavy hair and ridiculously expensive clothes was enough to set Mo's teeth on edge. Already seething after her walk through the woods and fired up by half a cider on an empty stomach, she shot Ashley a look that in a fair and just universe should have laid him out at her feet in a crumpled heap of Musto clothing. Unfortunately, Mo lived in the unfair and unjust universe and, as though sensing her vibes, Ashley caught her eye and made a beeline for her.

"Just bloody great," Mo muttered, glancing around for an escape route and, short of leaping the bar and ducking down behind it, not finding one. What on earth did he want now? The last time they'd met had been at an open meeting of the town council where, on the behalf of PAG, she'd opposed his latest plans for a helipad – and been successful, too. There was to be no helipad at Mariners, no matter how many promises he made about improvements to the environment. Cashley's expression when he'd looked across at Mo had been on a par with the one Henry VIII might have worn when sending wives to the Tower. Dark moody guys who got off on the whole broody Heathcliff thing had never done it for Morwenna – she'd gone right off Heathcliff when he hung Isabella's dog – and in spite of herself she shivered. Knowing that somebody hated your guts was not a comfortable feeling.

Well, you hate his guts too, Mo reminded herself sternly as Ashley made his way towards her, cutting through the crowded pub like Moses parting the Red Sea and then looming over her at the bar. It was at times like this that Mo really wished she were six feet tall like her brothers. Being small and looking harmless was such a pain at times.

"You, Red, are costing me far too much money," Ashley Carstairs remarked, staring down at her with his dark eyes. Mo resisted the instinct to shrink away and instead glared up at him. With his hawk-like features and intense gaze, he reminded her of a bird of prey – and there was no way she was letting him swoop in for the kill.

"That's right; it's all about money with you lot, isn't it?" she said, ignoring the annoying name he'd just called her. She wasn't going to acknowledge that Ashley Carstairs had given her a nickname, unless that nickname was *Nemesis*.

"*You lot?*" Ashley sounded amused. "What's that supposed to mean? We incomers? Us *emmets*? People who haven't lived here for ten generations and bred with their kin?" Without missing a beat, he leaned across Mo, brushing up against her and making her hiss like a cat. Ignoring this, he smiled at Kelly and handed her two fifties. "Pint of Carlsberg, angel, and one for yourself and all the other..." he glanced at Mo and winked "...*real locals* in the house. They might all hate me but they never turn down a free drink – just like they'll never turn down a good price for their cottages or their scruffy bits of woodland."

"Oh thanks, Mr Carstairs!" Dimpling at him, Kelly – whom Mo had always suspected was dimmer than The Ship's lighting – trotted off to fetch the drinks while Mo seethed, her hands curling into fists and scoring half moons into her palms.

"Or maybe," Ashley was continuing thoughtfully, "you mean people who choose to invest their money in this town and who want to improve it? Drag it out of the nineteen-seventies and give it the kind of makeover that doesn't seem to have done Rock any harm? The kind of people who keep marinas going, for instance, and who spend the same filthy money you despise in very expensive, and quite frankly overrated, local restaurants? Those people?"

Mo pretended to be fascinated by her drink. She was *not* going to rise to this pathetic baiting, even though she longed to bop him on the nose.

"I meant people who have no sense of heritage, community and history," she replied calmly. "People who have no taste whatsoever and want to ruin ancient woodland just because they're too bloody lazy to walk or don't want to get their stupid penis cars wet."

Ashley raised an eyebrow. "Do we really need to bring my penis into this, sweetheart? Much as I'm flattered that you're thinking about it, I don't really feel it's appropriate. We're virtually strangers. Or is this one of those local customs?"

To her horror, Mo felt a hot tidal wave of a blush start to spread up her neck and sweep towards her cheeks. It was one of the downsides of having flaming red hair. As if she was thinking about Ashley's… Ashley's…

He was grinning at her and Mo blushed even harder.

Well anyway, *that*.

"God, you're pathetic," she said coldly, or rather as coldly as a woman with a face hotter than the nuclear core of Sellafield could. "A total cock."

Ashley shrugged. "Still thinking of my cock, Red? Call me what you like but I'm a cock with lots of money. And whether you like it or not, I will be getting my own way over all of this, because that's what I do. I develop property. Clue's in the job description, sweetheart, and you're starting to get on my nerves with your constant interfering. Just admit defeat. Mariners is going to be rebuilt and I will have my driveway put in through that tatty scrubland you seem so fond of."

"I'll chain myself to the trees," Mo threatened. "You'd have to run me over first."

He regarded her thoughtfully. "I see. Would you be naked?"

She stared at him, wrong-footed. "What?"

Ashley took a long, slow gulp of his drink and studied her over the rim of his pint glass. There was a look in his eyes that made Mo feel very odd indeed and not quite like herself. The hairs on her forearms rippled.

"You heard me. There'd have to be something worth stopping the diggers for, wouldn't there? Otherwise I'd be more than happy to run you over. Would you paint yourself green? It's popular here, I think? Maybe stick a few leaves over your nipples and make a skirt out of twigs? That ridiculous hippy, Silver Starr, was wearing something similar earlier. I bet she'd be pleased to help too. Maybe you could even make a little camp in the trees? Have some tepees and see if that Swampy guy wants to come out of retirement and lend a hand?"

Mo's blood was starting to bubble. "It's all just a joke to you, isn't it?"

"Sweetheart, I'm deadly serious about wanting to see you naked," drawled Ashley, his dark eyes raking over Mo from the top of her tangled head to the bottom of her muddy boots, making her annoying blush grow even hotter. "In fact, I'd go as far as to say that might be the only thing that could save those woods of yours. What do you say? Do we have a deal?"

At that precise second Mo didn't think she'd ever hated anyone quite as much as she hated Ashley Carstairs. He was laughing at her, gloating that his bottomless wallet was going to buy him whatever he wanted. Mo's sense of right and wrong was thumping its fists on the table and throwing an enormous tantrum.

"I'm serious," said Ashley softly. He was still staring at her, the hawk watching its prey. "Generally I like to have dinner with women before I see them naked. So, will you?"

The pub was still noisy but there was a weird buzzing in Mo's ears. The bar stool seemed to be swaying beneath her backside like the deck of Nick's boat.

"Will I what?" she whispered.

"Have dinner with me." Cashley leaned one arm on the low beam of the pub and bent over Mo. Then, voice lowered, he added, "The taking your clothes off bit won't be obligatory, but you'll probably find you want to anyway. Women tend to. Especially once you've seen my penis… car."

He'd been winding her up all along! What a bastard! Enraged, and alarmed at herself because for a brief moment there she'd almost believed he was serious – not that she'd have ever eaten dinner with Cashley, no way, she would rather eat hoof clippings first – Mo leapt off her bar stool and hurled the remains of her cider straight into his horrible, haughty mocking face. Abruptly the pub went silent as heads swivelled to catch this latest Morwenna Tremaine explosion.

"You're pathetic," she hissed to the dripping Ashley. "Utterly pathetic, and all the money in the world can't change that! Take the piss if you like but there's no way you're getting your grubby hands on Fernside woods. No way at all."

"Be very careful, Red," said Ashley. Challenge dripped from his voice just like the cider dripping from his face. "That sounds like a dare to me and I never turn down a dare. And, be warned, I never lose a fight."

Mo raised her chin. Her heart was rattling up and down against her ribcage and her pulse was racing, but it was a good and familiar feeling: the same surge of determination and adrenalin she felt when she rode Mr Dandy at huge fixed fences that, if misjudged by a split second, would mean the end for them both. Ashley wasn't the Badminton water complex, she reminded herself sharply. He was just a knob. She could take him on and win. Of course she could.

"And neither do I," she promised him.

They eyeballed each other, bristling. In the dim light of the pub, shadows played across her adversary's face and made him appear even more determined. His mouth was set in a cruel line and his eyes were harder than the granite rocks outside.

Then Ashley threw back his head and laughed.

"In that case, Red," he said softly, a mocking grin twisting his mouth upwards, "you're on. Let the battle begin."

Chapter 7

Summer knew that she probably should quit while she was ahead, be grateful she'd managed to go this long without being recognised and head straight back to the safety of Harbour Watch. Yes, this was what she *should* do, but her dramatic new haircut was lulling Summer into a false sense of security and, as though her feet had a mind of their own, she headed towards the harbour rather than climbing back up the cliff path to her little cottage.

It was early evening now and the sun was slipping into the sea, spilling liquid gold across the waves. The crowds were starting to thin out as the visitors meandered back to the car park or wandered into the restaurants for supper. Music was thudding from the direction of the green, where the majority of the younger villagers would be listening to the band and getting stuck in to the cider. With her sunglasses still firmly in place and the baseball cap shoved down on her dark ringlets, Summer figured she'd be pretty safe down by the quay. She'd just have a look at the boats and see if her brothers were home yet, Summer decided as she crossed the little bridge that spanned the River Wenn. Then she'd go back to the cottage and lie low while she tried to work out what on earth to do next.

By now Justin would have realised that she'd gone. Just imagining his reaction was enough to make Summer shiver, even though the evening sun was still warm. He'd stride through the house, kicking doors open and yelling for her, before smashing something or maybe – a possibility that was even more troubling – remaining icy calm and waiting, white-lipped, for her to return. Summer had seen this enough times to know that she actually preferred Justin to just lose his temper. That way it was over with. The cold and silent treatment was the worst because she never knew quite when it would end. The eventual eruption of rage would be even more shocking due to its sheer unexpectedness. Whatever his reaction, Summer knew he'd be furious. Justin was High Maintenance with a capital H and a capital M, and he expected his fiancée to be waiting for him, not the other way around. Summer had lost count of the amount of times her heart had gone into free fall when she'd pulled up in her Audi only to see Justin's car already in situ. Even now and despite being over two hundred miles away from him, her pulse began to race.

I'm being ridiculous, Summer told herself sharply. Justin was a bully, albeit a handsome and charming one, and there was nothing he could do to her now. Nobody knew she was here – and even if he did come flying down the motorway to Cornwall, her family didn't have a clue she was staying in the village, so they couldn't give her hiding place away. Only Patsy knew she was here, and Justin would be no match for her aunty if he tried to throw his weight around. Just the thought of the dressing down he'd get if he so much as put a foot over the shop threshold made Summer smile in spite of her fluttering heartbeat. Patsy wasn't impressed by footballers; they were all a bunch of pussies in her opinion. No, she only cared about rugby and her beloved team, the Cornish Pirates. It was time she took a leaf out of her aunt's book and stood up for herself, Summer decided.

This was easier said than done after years of gradually being worn down, but it was something to work on. She'd met Justin at a bad time; she'd been vulnerable and naïve and, even seven years on, desperately looking for someone who might take away the pain of what had happened with Jake. Nobody until Justin had even come close.

She exhaled wearily. She'd got Jake wrong too, hadn't she? She'd truly believed he was one of the good guys, had thought that he loved her just as deeply as she'd loved him. But it had turned out that when the chips were down and she'd really needed him he was no different to any of the other lads just looking for a laugh on a Saturday night.

Do I really have such awful instincts? Summer wondered sadly, walking along to the end of the quay and turning to gaze back at the village. Or had she wanted something to be true and good so badly that she'd closed her eyes to the reality? Justin had been wonderful at first and she'd been thrilled to be with him. Together they were Summer and Justin, the coolest celebrity couple around. Their faces had sold everything from supermarket party food to high-end watches, and she'd been happy to let Justin make the decisions and plan their life together. That was what a loving fiancé did, after all.

Retracing her steps along the quay, Summer sighed. She wasn't quite sure when it was that she'd realised that Justin was controlling her, what jobs she took, what she wore, whom she could spend time with. She was just another of his possessions, like the flash cars, the houses and the Rolex – something he could show off to people and then put away again. He wasn't interested in her as a person. In fact Summer had soon realised that Justin wasn't interested in her at all, unless she was dressed up and hanging off his arm. He didn't care what she thought about things or what she wanted to do; all he'd really been concerned with was adding Summer to his collection of *things everybody else wanted*. He'd never frightened her back then though; that had only started when Summer had dared to voice her doubts about their future.

Summer was so deep in thought that she hadn't noticed a slender girl burst out of the pub and fly down the steps in a blur of flaming red hair and green gilet. It was only when this figure blocked her way that Summer was ripped out of her uncomfortable memories with a jolt.

She froze in shock when she realised who was standing in front of her – Morwenna. Her heart lurched, first with an instinctive happiness before dread rushed in. Mo looked almost exactly as she had the last time they'd spoken, wild red hair tumbling about her shoulders in a fiery halo, blue eyes gas-flame bright with anger and her small hands clenched into fists as she fought to keep a lid on her emotions.

Those same eyes narrowed when Mo saw Summer. The cropped hair and big shades didn't fool her for an instant. Of course they didn't. The two girls had once been closer than sisters and although they no longer spoke their history ran through them just like the river than ran through the village.

"Just bloody great." Mo raised her eyes up to heaven. "Somebody up there must really have it in for me today. It's true what they say: the holiday season really does bring the dregs down to the village." She swept a scornful gaze over Summer and wrinkled her freckled nose. "Winter can't come soon enough for me."

Summer hardly noticed these harsh words; she was far too busy drinking in the sight of her old friend. In an instant the years peeled away and memories were tumbling through her mind. Giggling together over teen magazines, raft races in the icy sea, coughing over their first crafty cigarettes in the bus shelter at the top of the village…

"Mo! I can't believe it! You haven't changed at all!"

Mo's top lip curled. "You have."

Ouch. That blow certainly hit home. "Patsy said you own the yard at the top of the village now? And that you're eventing?"

Summer ploughed on bravely even though the disdain in her old friend's expression felt like a sucker punch to the guts. "That's so brilliant. All your dreams have come true!"

Summer was talking too fast and she knew that it probably sounded like nonsense, but she couldn't help herself. There was so much she wanted to say to Morwenna that she didn't know where to begin. Perhaps they'd be able to talk everything through, she thought with a little leap of hope, and they could put everything that had happened behind them and be friends again?

Mo crushed these hopes in a heartbeat.

"Been spying on us all, have you? My life has nothing to do with you, nothing! You made it abundantly clear what you thought when you left us all behind without even looking back. And now you've got the nerve to stand here and chat away like nothing ever happened?" Mo's voice was getting louder. Several tourists turned and stared. Even the seagulls seemed to pause mid squawk. "Have you any idea what damage you did to our family? How dare you stand there and patronise me with all your talk about how well I've done!"

They were several feet apart but, even so, Summer stepped back. Her heart was racing.

"I'm sorry, Mo. That wasn't what I meant at all. I really don't want to rake up the past."

"Really?" Mo snorted. "Just come back to gloat then?" She glanced around in an exaggerated fashion. "So come on then, where's the entourage? The loaded career-enhancing footballer fiancé? It's funny, Summer, I never had you down as a WAG but I guess that Justin

Anderson is far more your type than the decent, honest guy you turned your back on without a second glance. He's got money and fame, after all – and that was what meant more to you, wasn't it?"

"That's not fair, Mo. It wasn't like that at all. Please, can't we leave all this in the past?"

"You'd like that, wouldn't you?" Mo shot back. "For everyone to pretend that it really didn't matter at all now that everything is great for you?"

Summer's vision blurred. If only she could go back in time and put things right. If only she could tell Mo the truth about Justin and have her friend sort him out like she'd sorted out Ella St Milton all those years ago.

"It isn't great for me," she whispered.

"You got exactly what you wanted," Mo said icily. "The fame, the money, the rich guy. I hope it was all worth it. You might think it was years ago but I'll never forget what you did to Jake. As far as I'm concerned you're dead to me. The Summer I knew died a long time ago."

Summer felt like she'd been slapped. She wasn't proud of how she'd behaved back then but Jake had let her down too, and when she'd needed him most. He'd abandoned *her*, not the other way around. Her eyes filled with tears. Thank goodness she was wearing the sunglasses.

"Mo, I—"

"No, don't." Morwenna held up her hand as though warding off something unpleasant. "I don't want to hear any more. You've got exactly what you wanted and that's your world now. Not me, not Jake and not Polwenna Bay."

Summer wanted nothing more than to turn on her heel and run, but unfortunately there was only the quay behind her and then a sheer drop into the sea. She wasn't going to give Mo the satisfaction of drowning herself, even if it was a tempting option at this exact moment, especially as – horror to top all horrors – Jake was headed in their direction, diverted from his route into the pub by his sister's raised voice.

Summer's legs felt like soggy wool. Almost twelve years might have passed since she'd last seen Jake Tremaine, but they felt like seconds. He was still the most handsome man she had ever seen – and he *was* a man now too, not the boy he had been. The Jake before her now was broad shouldered and muscular, and there were lines fanning from those bright blue eyes. Getting older had only made Jake Tremaine even more attractive. Summer could hardly breathe.

"What the hell is with you today, Mo?" Jake was demanding. Impatiently, he pushed his thick blond curls out of his face so that he could glower at his sister. "I've just heard about your stand-up row with Ashley and now you're yelling at visitors?" He glanced over at Summer and, knowing Jake as she did, she guessed he was on the brink of offering an apology for his sister's outburst. His eyes widened when he realised who was on the receiving end of Mo's temper.

"You cut your hair," he said slowly.

Summer's hand rose and touched her bare neck, which was almost as much of a shock as seeing Jake again after so long.

"Her hair?" Mo rounded on her brother scornfully. "Is that all you can say when she waltzes back here as though nothing ever happened? Who gives a toss about her bloody hair? She's not welcome, that's all that matters!" Turning back to Summer, she added furiously, "Why don't you just crawl back to wherever you came from? Nobody wants you here!"

Her old friend's antipathy was more than Summer could bear.

"I'm so sorry I've upset you," she said, quickly pushing her sunglasses up her nose and hoping that her bruises didn't show. "I didn't mean to. And I won't get in your way, I promise."

Jake's face was brown from hours on the water but beneath the tan he was pale. A muscle ticked in his cheek; a sign of stress that Summer recognised of old. Then he breathed out slowly.

"Mo, you don't own the Bay – luckily for quite a few people today. You can't dictate who's allowed here."

"More's the pity," hissed Morwenna. Her top lip had curled into a sneer and her blue eyes were bright with scorn. "I'd kick out *certain* people so fast their tiny brains would be spinning. You stick around if you want to, Jake, but I can't bear the sight of her, even if I hardly recognise her with her clothes on."

And with that Mo was gone.

"I'm so sorry about that," Jake said regretfully, watching his sister stalk through the crowds. "You know how Mo can be. She has a savage temper."

Summer gulped. She certainly did, but being the focus of her old friend's wrath felt as if somebody had ripped out her soul and kicked it hard.

"She's fiercely loyal and she's protective," Jake went on. His voice still had that West Country richness, as warm and as thick as clotted cream, and just hearing it made her memories race back in a riptide. Summer's own accent had been smoothed away by elocution classes a long time ago; she missed it. "You know Mo: she doesn't forget anything in a hurry."

"I'm sorry." Summer's voice was shaking. "I never wanted to upset anyone."

He shrugged those strong shoulders. "Nobody's upset. Mo's just had a big showdown with somebody and you happened to be in the line of fire. It's nothing personal."

Summer knew this wasn't true. It was totally personal.

"You've every right to visit Polwenna if you want to. Of course you have. Mo knows it," Jake continued. "I really hope you enjoy your stay."

Summer stared at him. If Jake had been surprised to see her he had hidden it well now and appeared indifferent. His distant politeness was worse than rage.

"Jake," she said softly. "Can we talk?"

He shook his head. "I don't think there's any point in that, do you? We said everything that needed to be said all those years ago. There's no point revisiting the past. We've all moved on." He glanced down at her left hand where Justin's enormous diamond heart ring, the one that all the magazines had gone crazy over, sat like a brand on her engagement finger – and a small smile played on his lips. Lips she'd once known so well. Summer could still remember how they'd felt as they'd brushed her throat and traced a trail of fire to her breasts. She shivered in spite of the sun.

"We're different people now," Jake finished coolly. "It's all water under the bridge."

He was standing so close that Summer could have reached out and touched his hand. She really wanted to. Lord. No wonder she'd stayed away from this place. She'd only been here a few hours and already the years were rolling away and she was sixteen again – and her heart knew that Jake was wrong. They weren't different. They were just older.

"I'm sorry if my coming here makes things difficult," she said. "I never meant to upset anyone. I know we ended on a bad note—"

Jake gave her a hard stare, then laughed. "A bad note? I guess you could put it like that." He shook his head and exhaled slowly again. "Look, Summer, this is all screwed up and bloody weird quite frankly. What can I say? I know you had your reasons for what you did and they were right for you, weren't they? You've got the career you always wanted and you've got the whole celebrity thing going on too. A quiet life here would never have been enough. You did the right thing and I'm glad for you, I really am."

"But there are things that I need to—"

Summer didn't get to finish because Jake cut across her. "What happened between us was over a long time ago. My life's moved on and so has yours." His eyes were hard now. "Let's just draw a line under it, shall we? I'm sure you had your reasons for what you did and I've no desire or interest to dredge it up again. Now, if you'll excuse me I'm supposed to be in the pub."

Then he was striding back towards The Ship, leaping the steps two at a time, and leaving Summer watching. Every cell in her body was screaming at her to run after him, grab his arm and demand that he explain to her why he had let *her* down just when she'd needed him the most. Yes, she had walked away but when she'd tried to come back, pouring her heart out in the longest and most tearstained letter she'd ever written in her life, Jake hadn't wanted to know. He'd completely ignored her. A pregnancy scare did that to a young guy, she guessed, although she would never have thought this of Jake. He'd always been so honourable, a gentleman in the truest sense of the word.

As it had turned out, she'd never really known him at all…

Defeated, she turned back towards her cottage. Although her head was thudding and her face throbbing from its earlier encounter with the kitchen island, Summer couldn't help wondering why neither of these things hurt nearly as much as the expression of disinterest on Jake's handsome face.

Hate wasn't the opposite of love after all, she reflected sadly. No, hate would imply that there was still some emotion left, albeit a sad shadow of the powerful passion that had gone before. Meeting Jake today had shown her only too clearly that the emotional counter to love wasn't hatred at all: it was total and utter indifference.

Her heart heavy, Summer swallowed back the words she wished she could have said and headed back to her empty cottage.

Chapter 8

Jake was still shaking when he handed Kelly the money for his pint. Seeing Summer had been the last thing he'd expected. One minute he was all fired up to yank his hot-headed sister back from the brink of yet another potential disaster, and the next he was face to face with the woman he'd spent years trying to forget.

Well, that was a bloody waste of time, he thought bitterly as he tipped his head back and necked his drink until the cold lager was way below the ridge of the glass. The minute those big green eyes behind the shades had met his, Jake had been whizzed straight back in time as though in a particularly trippy episode of *Doctor Who*. The sunglasses hadn't fooled him for a second. Summer might have been thinner and had her thick ebony ringlets cropped into a dark halo, but Jake would have known her anywhere. Thank God he'd managed to hold it together long enough so that she didn't notice just how shocked he'd been to see her.

And, even worse, how much desire for her still flamed through him.

Horrified by this realisation, Jake downed his pint and held the glass out for a refill. Thank goodness it was dark enough in The Ship that nobody could see the heat flooding his face, and so noisy with the chatting drinkers and live music that the crashing of his heart was muffled. As Kelly poured him another pint, Jake took a deep breath and attempted to regain his composure. His reaction was ridiculous. Summer had been a teenage fling; they'd been little more than kids. It hadn't meant anything – or at least, it hadn't meant anything real. They were both adults now, he reminded himself as he passed a crumpled fiver over the bar and curled his hand around the cool glass. The kids they'd once been were long gone, just like the feelings they'd once had. It was just the surprise of seeing her again that was making him feel like this, that was all. No man expected to turn a corner and walk straight into his past. No wonder he needed a drink.

Past or present, the fact remained that Summer Penhalligan was one of the most beautiful women he'd ever laid eyes on. With her silky dark hair, slim body blessed with lush curves, and lips like peony buds, she was every bit as stunning in real life as the magazines and billboards she graced so regularly portrayed. Jake hadn't intentionally followed Summer's career, but it was pretty hard not to when it seemed that she was everywhere. Even on his travels, her image had been in all the media – and it had been worse when he'd returned home. Her high-profile engagement to Justin Anderson had caused a ripple of excitement throughout Polwenna Bay and Jake had caught people looking at him sympathetically on more than one occasion.

It was bad enough to be dumped by your childhood sweetheart, Jake reflected wryly, but worse again when she went on to become a household name lusted after by guys the length and breadth of the UK. Add to this her Premiership footballer fiancé and more column inches than Nelson, and his humiliation was complete. Australia hadn't been far enough…

This was not helping. There was no question about it: even though he hadn't seen her for years, Jake had struggled to put Summer out of his mind. If he didn't get a firm hold on himself fast then he'd be well on his way to slipping back into being the boy he'd once been, which was bloody ridiculous. There'd been a hell of a lot of water under the bridge since then – and plenty of women, too. After spending most of his teenage years with Summer, Jake hadn't seen any reason to hold back once she'd gone. Living in a tourist hotspot and working with boats had meant that there was no shortage of bikini-clad girls wanting to hang out with him and enjoy a holiday romance. He'd be busy at the marina, often bare-chested and in shorts and deck shoes, and eventually a girl would catch his eye and smile. If she took his fancy then Jake would smile back, strike up a conversation and maybe offer to take her out on his boat. Some wine, a sunset, a secluded cove and that was pretty much it: the failsafe way to enjoy some fun without all the complications that inevitably came with a relationship. A two-week turnover of willing partners had suited Jake just fine; he'd quickly realised that being able to take his pick of pretty holidaymakers was a major perk of his job. Before the season was over, Jake had reinvented himself as a player and, like the majority of young guys who lived at the Bay, had made the most of every sunny second.

Over the years women had come and gone – some faster than others, but even so short-term flings had remained pretty much the pattern of Jake's life. Fast-forward to the ripe old age of thirty and the novelty of this had definitely worn off. Maybe he was getting old, or maybe Mo's caustic comment about him fast becoming the Cornish version of *Shirley Valentine*'s Costas had hit home harder than his sister had realised, but Jake no longer felt the need to prove that he was as much a player as the Penhalligan brothers or Teddy St Milton from the hotel. He'd calmed down a lot recently, give or take a few adventures on his travels and the odd drunken dalliance with Ella St Milton.

Talking of Ella St Milton, there she was at the far end of the bar, chatting to Cashley and tossing her blonde hair about in that rather obvious way that women had when trying desperately to catch another man's attention. Sensing Jake looking in her direction, Ella laughed even more loudly. Jake winced. She was undoubtedly attractive, and her worked-out body certainly knew exactly what it was doing when it twined itself around his like a python, but there was something about Ella that always set him on edge, rather like nails being scraped down a chalkboard. Ella's gaze slid from Ashley to Jake, and her pink tongue flickered over her sharp white teeth. Jake looked away quickly. Jesus, the last thing he needed right now was Ella on a mission to jump his bones. Apart from the fact that she was harder to banish than Japanese knotweed, the finances of the Tremaines' marina business were precariously balanced – and there was no way Jake wanted to risk upsetting the wealthy newcomer Cashley, who seemed to think he was in with a chance with Ella. From what Jake could gather, Mo had already done a good job at riling their biggest customer.

Stressing about the business worked wonders for taking his mind off most things, that was for sure. Maybe it would do the same for thoughts of his ex? Jake turned his attention back to his drink, and this time over half the pint disappeared. But it was pointless: neither booze nor stress made much difference to how he was feeling right now. Something in his chest still clenched tight whenever he thought of Summer Penhalligan.

Oh well. At least he'd had good taste when he was eighteen. Glancing across the pub, Jake saw Danny slumped in his usual position at the far end of the bar, practically under the stairs and with his chin resting in his hand. Things could always be worse, Jake thought. *I could have picked Tara Woods rather than Summer.* It was one thing to have to face the ex who'd smashed your heart and all but flushed the pieces down the loo, and another again to have to fight that person to see the child you adored. Danny was proof indeed that Jake had nothing to worry about by comparison. Wounded pride was tough enough to deal with, but a wounded body and mind were something else entirely. Taking the remains of his pint with him, Jake turned his back on Ella and began to wind his way through the press of drinkers, towards his brother.

"Hey, Jake!" The call from across the room caught his attention; Issie was waving at him, her silver rings and nose stud glittering in the fairy lights.

Jake waved back, hugely relieved that his little sister was sitting in the window seat rather than out causing chaos somewhere. One sister on a mission to create havoc was enough for any man; two would no doubt have driven him back up the cliff path to Seaspray and into hiding. The men who ended up with the Tremaine girls would deserve medals and would probably need full body armour if they were to stand an earthly chance of surviving any arguments, Jake concluded. He was now miming a drinking action at his sister, who shook her head and pointed at her full glass.

"Come and meet Jules Mathieson," she hollered over the hubbub, gesturing to the plump woman sitting next to her on a low stool, over which an ample jeans-covered backside spilled like dough rising above the lip of a baking tin. "She's new!"

The Ship was always dimly lit but, even so, there was no mistaking the person with the round face and unfortunate purple hair whom Jake had last seen sprawled on the muddy harbour floor. Was his wild-child little sister really perched next to Polwenna Bay's new vicar, or was the lager here stronger than he'd realised? Seeing Ella making a beeline for him with the single-minded determination of *The Terminator* when spotting Sarah Connor, Jake decided that he needed all the divine intervention he could get. Before Ella could elbow her way through a crowd of Boden-clad visitors and wind herself around him like a chest bandage, Jake was pulling out the stool next to the new vicar and hoping that he was safe for the next ten minutes.

"Salmonella after you again?" Issie's merry face, as freckly as a Mini Egg, beamed at him from across the table. "Don't worry, bro, you're safe with us. And Jules has got God on her side, so she can always throw some holy water at her or something."

Jules rolled her eyes at this and Jake shot Issie a warning look.

"Just kidding," said Issie quickly. "I love Ella really. I'm sure she's a great person deep down." Catching Jules's eye she added, "Like really, really deep down. About Australia deep."

Ignoring his sister, Jake held his hand out to the vicar and smiled at her.

"I'm Jake, Issie's brother, but don't hold that against me. We're not all as tactless as she is – although if you saw my other sister in action just now you're probably thinking we're all mad and wondering what on earth you've done coming here."

As she shook his hand, Jules's face was almost the same colour as her hair. She could hardly look him in the eye, and Jake was touched.

"I was wondering exactly that when I was trying to chase two hundred plastic ducks and fell flat on my backside," she told him with a giggle, looking up shyly from beneath lashes that were surprisingly long and thick. Jake was willing to bet they weren't extensions or spidery fakes like those Ella favoured. Jules was refreshingly make-up free and dressed down in an oversized hoody and baggy jeans. All very *Vicar of Dibley*. Still, maybe that was a rule of lady vicars? Jake supposed that if they looked and dressed like Victoria's Secret Angels it would be rather distracting for the congregation, although he imagined that numbers would certainly improve.

"Falling into the mud during the duck race is a Polwenna Bay rite of passage. You're definitely one of us now," Jake told her warmly, and was rewarded by Jules turning an even deeper pink. Goodness, but that was some blush. She was very sweet but, not wanting St Wenn's new incumbent to spontaneously combust, he figured he'd better give her a moment to recover.

"That's exactly what *I* said," Issie agreed. "Sheila the Squealer's being a pain in the bum as usual, Jake, but even she'll give Jules a break now."

The vicar looked pleased at this idea. "Dear me! I'd have rolled around in the harbour weeks ago if I'd known that was all it took to win her over."

Issie chinked her wine glass against Jules's pint of Pol Brew. Their new vicar was a real-ale drinker, Jake noted with approval. She'd fit in just fine.

"You'll get there. The kids love you and Morgan thinks you're 'all right', which is praise indeed from him. Fact! Welcome to the village!"

"Welcome to Polwenna Bay," Jake echoed, bumping his glass against Jules's.

Jules beamed at them both. She had a smile that lit her entire face and sent dimples burrowing into her cheeks.

"Thanks. I'm really looking forward to getting to know you all," she said.

Once they'd toasted her and the conversation had turned to Issie pointing out the various locals in the pub and delivering a very funny who's who of the villagers, Jake reflected that Jules Mathieson could be exactly what St Wenn's needed if it was to build the congregation and escape falling into the property-developing clutches of people like Cashley. She was young, sociable and happy to get her hands dirty (literally), and hopefully would be a very good influence on his wayward sister too. No wonder their grandmother had already been impressed with her. Maybe the Reverend Jules could even lob a prayer or two the boatyard's way? God knew they needed all the help they could get. Even better, perhaps she could exorcise the ghost of Summer.

Summer. Just the thought of her was enough to make Jake reach for his drink. Seeing her again had resurrected all sorts of feelings he'd thought were as long buried as the ancient remains beneath the lichen-crusted headstones in St Wenn's churchyard. The sound of her voice. Her lush curves. Her skin like the local honey served in all the tearooms. Her beautiful smile…

Jake downed his pint; time for a third and, with any luck, oblivion in the bottom of a pint glass. If Summer didn't go back to London soon he was in danger of ending up like poor bloody Danny.

"Granny Alice is really excited you're here," Issie was telling Jules warmly. "Isn't she, Jake?"

Jake, glad to be dragged away from any more uncomfortable thoughts of Summer, nodded. He was just about to suggest that Jules came up to Seaspray for a family supper one evening when the crash of a bar stool slamming onto the floor – followed by the smashing of glass – brought any hopes of conversation to an abrupt halt.

"You won't take my son away from me! Do you hear me? There's no way I'm letting that happen!" thundered a furious voice, which instantly froze all other chatter. The blues musician in the corner stopped mid chord.

"You don't have any say in it." This determined reply was from a slender dark-haired woman who had her back to everyone in the room. Her voice was trembling but held a determined note as she focused her attention on the tall blond man at the far end of the bar. "Let's be honest, Dan. You're hardly the perfect example of a father who's fit to have custody of a child, are you?"

There was another loud thud as a hand was slammed onto the bar. Several more glasses toppled to the ground and glass sprinkled everywhere like deadly snow. There was a collective gasp of mingled horror and voyeuristic delight from the onlookers.

"He's *my* son!"

"And right now you're a self-pitying, drunken mess!" The woman's scorn was palpable. "Just look at yourself. No court in the land would leave a child with you. You're hardly fit to look after yourself. Deal with it, Danny. Morgan's coming to live in Plymouth with me when I move, and there's nothing you can do about it!"

The woman turned and shoved her way through the crowd and out of the door. She slammed it behind her so hard that the windows rattled.

"What are you all looking at? Well?" roared the figure at the end of the bar. He glowered across the room and everybody tried to pretend that they'd been preoccupied all along with their drinks or deep in their conversations, which now rippled back into full flow. The atmosphere crackled like static.

"I'll have another Scotch," barked the man, thrusting a note at the cowering barmaid. "Go on! Don't just stand there! I need a bloody drink. Now."

Issie drained of colour as she stared at the shattered glasses and the enraged figure that was waving his money across the bar.

"Dan's flipped again! He's getting worse. Jake, you'd better go and talk to him."

"That's your brother? Morgan's dad? The soldier?" The vicar glanced from Jake and Issie to the tall man at the bar who was still demanding another drink. Her big brown eyes were warm with compassion.

Issie nodded. "And that was his cow of an estranged wife coming in to make a scene as usual. Typical bloody Tara. She loves to do everything in public, which is the last thing Danny needs. I bet Afghanistan seemed peaceful after living with her. Go and talk to him, Jakey. He'll listen to you."

Jake wasn't so sure about this. The last time he'd tried to reason with Danny in a mood like this he'd ended up with a fractured cheekbone. Dan had been devastated once he'd sobered up, and for a couple of days had managed to stay away from the pub. A trained soldier who was bitterly frustrated by his injuries, Dan was already volatile – and when he drank, anything could light the touch paper. Jake was torn. He loved his brother and didn't want to upset him but the last thing the family, or even Danny, needed was another ugly scene. He raked a hand through his shaggy blond curls, a gesture that he was sure he repeated far more now that he was back home than he ever had while travelling. Sharks, poisonous outback creatures and drunken Caribbean locals armed with machetes had been nothing in comparison to dealing with his own family.

"I said *I want a drink*, for Christ's sake!" Danny Tremaine yelled. The damaged side of his face was already livid red, but the side untouched by the bomb blast was fast catching up.

Kelly flung a helpless look in Jake's direction. She clearly didn't want to serve Danny but everyone in the village was treating him with kid gloves. He was a hero, after all, and it was obvious just how much he was suffering – but anyone else who dared to behave like this would have been barred long ago.

Jake was on his feet in seconds. It didn't matter how much he cared for Dan or how much he knew his brother was going through; this behaviour had to stop. Nick, cross-eyed with drink and swaying, joined Danny.

Great, thought Jake in despair. Another drunken brother was just what he *didn't* need.

"Come on, Dan. I think you've had enough, mate." Nick placed his hand on Danny's shoulder, only to have it shaken off when his brother rounded on him.

"I haven't had nearly enough! I said I want another drink!" Danny's fist thumped down on the bar and he glared angrily around the pub. "What are you all looking at, eh?"

"You're making a scene." Jake said softly, crossing the bar to his brother's side. "Come on, mate, time to go."

Danny shook his head. The fairy lights on the beams above the bar turned his short hair to a golden halo as though he was some fallen angel. When he spoke his voice was low and laced with danger.

"I'm not going anywhere. I want another drink. Just one bloody drink. Is that too much to ask? Or are you going to try and stop me?" He started to square up to Jake and his one good hand clenched into a fist. Jake eyed him warily. Even with one arm Danny was quick and strong. Could he manage to grab his brother and wrestle him outside? Would Nick be steady enough on his feet to help?

"Well?" Danny's voice rose again. "Are you going to try and stop me?"

Jake was going to attempt it, but quite how he didn't know. He saw Jules slide from her seat, reach into her pocket and pull out her dog collar, which she tucked around the neck of her hoody. She caught his eye and smiled reassuringly, touching the collar with her forefinger.

"Trust me," she mouthed.

Jake trusted Jules but he certainly didn't trust his volatile sibling. Jules ignored his horrified expression, though, and placed herself in between the two brothers. The look of surprise on Danny's face would have been comical if the situation hadn't been so tense. He probably thought he was so drunk that he was hallucinating vicars.

"I don't know what's been happening with your wife," Jules said gently and while Danny was too taken aback to shout, "but please don't take it out on your family or the people in here. It isn't their fault."

Danny's fist was still clenched. Slowly and deliberately he turned his head towards her until Jules could see the full extent of his injuries. Jake always thought it was like looking at two halves of two different men, which some cruel joke had spliced together. The side closest to them was a leaner version of Jake: a high cheekbone and one denim-blue eye starred with dark lashes, a strong jaw sprinkled with golden stubble, a striking profile and a full sensual mouth. But the other side? That was like gazing at a vandalised masterpiece.

Seeing this for the first time was as shocking as it would be to see somebody take a sledgehammer to a Michelangelo sculpture, but Jules remained composed. The cruelly burned flesh, the lid of the eye pulled tightly closed, the downward pluck of what remained of his mouth...

Jake thought that Danny Tremaine had every right to rail against a world and a God that could let this happen.

"This is what's happening with my wife," Danny growled, thrusting his damaged face even closer to the vicar's. "And can you bloody well blame her?"

Jules didn't flinch. "No, not at all. It must have been a huge shock for her."

Danny stared at her, taken aback. "What did you say?"

"I said that your wife must be shocked. What's happened to you is awful because yes, your injuries are shocking when you first see them," Jules told him bluntly. "Nobody can even begin to imagine what it feels like, but it isn't just you who's been affected, is it? Everyone who loves you is hurting."

Danny snorted rudely. "And Jesus wants me for a sunbeam, right? Come on, Rev, don't hold back. Aren't you going to tell me that my wife should love me whatever I look like? Then you can remind me that at least I'm a war hero even if I am hideous?" He laughed, a harsh mockery of a sound. "Come on, aren't you thinking that she ought to just close her eyes when she's with me and put up with it? That's what everyone thinks around here."

The vicar shrugged. "I'm not here to judge your wife, Danny. I don't know her any more than I know you, but I do know that it's your yelling and your breaking glasses that are upsetting everyone in here, not the way you look. It's the way you're behaving that's ugly, not your face." She lowered her voice but held his gaze without fear. "Fact. As your son Morgan would say."

It was as though at just the mention of Morgan something changed in Danny. The anger in him seemed to vanish and his shoulders slumped. Suddenly the raging figure of only moments ago was gone and in its place was a broken man. A tear, as bright and as lonely as the glass strewn on the floor, slipped down his cheek.

"She wants to take Morgan away," he said hoarsely. "I don't think I can deal with it if she does. It's bad enough that Tara's gone; it'll be unbearable without Morgan. What's the point? What am I without them?"

There was a lump in Jake's throat. He could bloody well throttle Tara Tremaine.

"Come on, let me walk home with you. You don't want to be in here anymore," Jules suggested quietly, and Danny nodded.

Jake wasn't sure but it felt to him as though everyone in the place released a breath. His own hands were trembling. To come this close to another fist fight with Danny had unnerved him. His brother was out of control.

"Shit. Did I do that?" Danny said, glancing around the bar and seeming to notice for the first time the smashed glasses and staring customers. He passed a hand over his eye, as though he wanted to wipe away the evidence of what had just occurred. Catching the cowering barmaid's eye he opened his wallet, pulled out a wad of notes and placed them onto the bar, just out of reach of the spilled drink and shattered glass. "Kelly, I'm really sorry. I hope this covers it."

He seemed to shrink into himself as he pushed through the evening drinkers and, stooping through the low doorway, staggered out into the dusk. Jake stared after him in despair. He didn't think he'd ever felt more helpless. How the hell could he help Dan? What on earth could he do to make things better for his younger brother? Not being able to think of a plan was driving him to distraction because Jake was a practical guy; he liked to fix things and make them right again, which was easy to do with boats and engines but a million times more complicated with humans.

What if Danny couldn't be mended? This thought was so agonising that Jake pushed it away as quickly as he could.

"I'll walk him home," he said to Jules. "You've done more than enough just by calming him down."

"I haven't done anything that isn't all in a day's work for a vicar." Looking embarrassed, Jules brushed off Jake's thanks. "He's going to need a bit of time out to clear his head after what's happened here, that's for sure, and I might be able to help. And this," she lifted her fingertips to the dog collar and smiled, "is usually really good at making people feel able to talk, comforted even."

"No offence, but Danny doesn't believe in God," said Nick sharply. "How could he after what's happened to him?"

Jules, who must be used to hearing this kind of thing, nodded. "Don't worry. I'm not about to give the guy a sermon. It's just that sometimes people find it easier to talk to somebody like me. I guess because I'm not family; I'm neutral, a bit like Switzerland?"

Jake wasn't convinced. Much as he was impressed with the way the new vicar had managed to defuse the situation – there was definitely more to her than met the eye – a drunken Danny was not something he would ever allow a woman to handle, vicar or not.

"I appreciate everything you've done but he's not your responsibility," he said firmly. "Enjoy your evening here with Issie. Hopefully the Tremaine family fireworks are over now."

"Chillax, Jake. I'll go with the vicar," Nick offered. He drained his glass and gave his brother a sheepish grin. "I think I ought to knock it on the head anyway, seeing as I'm off to sea later."

There was no arguing with this. Having a stern word with Nick about mixing deep-sea trawling and heavy drinking had been on Jake's (very long) to-do list. Once Jules and Nick had managed to assure him that if there were any problems at all they'd call him, Jake returned to the bar. A headache was starting to beat behind his eyes. Jesus. What a day. He supposed Danny had at least managed to take his mind off Summer, although now that the latest family drama was over thoughts of her were rushing back just like the tide tore back into the harbour. Maybe another drink was what he needed.

"Hey, you." The distinctive scent of Chanel perfume and a soft hand on his forearm announced the arrival of Ella St Milton. She placed a pint of Pol Brew in front of him and hopped onto a bar stool next to him. "Looks like you could do with a drink."

Ella was all wide-eyed concern, sympathy and tight tee-shirt. Her blonde hair was straightened into a sheet of gold and her red lips glistened in the soft lighting. As she leaned forward to reach for her glass of wine her breast brushed against his arm. She smiled slowly when he looked up in surprise, a pink triangle of tongue moistening her lips.

Jake smiled back. The message couldn't have been any clearer and suddenly he was more inclined to listen to it than he'd been for a very long time.

"A drink sounds great," he agreed, picking up the pint glass.

Summer who?

Chapter 9

"Sausages or bacon? Or do you want both?" Alice Tremaine looked up from the Aga and gave Jake an expectant smile. The enormous frying pan on the hotplate was hissing like the waves breaking against the rocks below the house and the whole of Seaspray was filled with the mouth-watering aroma of full English. Normally Jake would have been first in line for one of his grandmother's fry-ups, but this morning the thought alone was enough to make him want to run to the stable door, stick his head out over the bottom half and gulp fresh air.

"Jake?" Alice's spatula hovered over the pan. "Hurry up, love. The eggs will go cold."

At the mere mention of fried eggs, Jake swallowed back a wave of nausea. Christ, just how much had he drunk yesterday evening?

"Nothing for me, thanks," he said weakly, opening the fridge and helping himself to most of the orange juice straight from the carton. A big hit of vitamin C was what he needed, and then some coffee to jump-start his system. Surely after that he would feel slightly more human?

"Jake's hung-over, Grand Gran. Fact," observed Morgan from his seat at the head of the kitchen table. Chewing thoughtfully on a hunk of fried bread, he added kindly, "Don't worry, Jake. You'll feel better soon. My dad looks like that a lot."

Alice shot Jake one of her you-are-such-a-bad-example looks.

"Eat up, Morgan," she said firmly. "We've got to get to church and thank Reverend Jules for helping your dad out yesterday when he was feeling poorly."

Morgan looked confused. "Dad wasn't poorly, Grand Gran. He was drunk. Fact."

"Total fact," nodded Issie. "Well, it *is*!" she insisted when Alice glared at her. "Morgan isn't stupid, Granny: he's got an IQ of 159."

"I'm highly gifted. Fact," said Morgan.

Alice brandished her spatula at Issie. "I don't care what his IQ is! He's still a child – and from some of the behaviour I've seen here lately, so still are all of you. Thank goodness for Reverend Mathieson. I'll be thanking her personally after the service. I don't know how she did it but somehow she managed to calm everything down while all of you were out enjoying yourselves at the festival without a care in the world."

"That's not fair," Issie said. "Jake wanted to take Danny home but Jules insisted and then Nick said he'd go with her too."

Alice's hands were on her hips. Even though she was dressed in the novelty bra-and-stockings print apron that Zak had bought her for Christmas, she managed to assert her authority and quell any further protests with one look. Having raised her grandchildren she was very good at this and, regardless of their age now, they all knew that Granny Alice's *look* was not to be messed with.

"We're Tremaines and we stick together," Alice told them. "That's the way this family's always been and that's the way it stays. We look out for one another." She turned her attention back to the breakfast that was now spitting furiously, and dolloped a huge pile of sausages and bacon onto a plate, which was then deposited with a cross thump onto the kitchen table. "Now eat up."

"I really can't," said Jake regretfully; his grandmother's fry-ups were the stuff of Polwenna Bay legend. He pulled out a chair and reached for the cafetière instead. It was time for a caffeine injection.

"I don't care who eats this, but this isn't going to waste," Alice said sternly. "And no feeding it to Cracker, either," she added to Mo, who was on the brink of taking a sausage for their Jack Russell.

"I'll have some, Granny. It smells wonderful!" Zak waltzed into the kitchen, dropped a kiss onto his grandmother's cheek and plonked himself down at the table. "Load me up! I'm ravenous!"

Zak really was proof that there was no justice in the world, Jake thought with grudging admiration. How his brother managed to be clear-eyed and chirpy when Jake knew for a fact that Zak had been drinking vodka shots and partying into the daylight hours with a bevy of doting girls was a mystery. The sunshine beaming through the big bay window turned Zak's hair to pure gold, and in his white tee-shirt and leather trousers he looked like some kind of rock-music angel come down to earth. Even his stubble didn't look scruffy like Jake's; instead, it glinted like gold dust. Butter wouldn't melt in his mouth as far as Alice was concerned and so, distracted now from the previous conversation, she fussed around Zak, pouring tea and dishing him up a mound of food.

"You don't eat enough, love. You need to come home more often," she told him.

"I really should," Zak agreed, tucking in with gusto. Jake guessed that all the singing, partying and no-strings sex had helped Zak work up quite an appetite. His brother certainly never seemed to put on an ounce of weight. The tallest and most slender of the brothers, Zak was born to swagger about on the stage, showing off flashes of his taut navel and lean hips to crowds of adoring girls. It was a hard life.

Zak was, Jake reflected fondly as he listened to his brother entertain them with stories of his latest tour exploits, one of those magical people who could fall into an open sewer and yet come up smelling of Paco Rabanne. He'd always been this way. Teachers had loved him and had always turned a blind eye when he was naughty; women adored him; and the whole family made allowances for his lack of phone calls and visits because that was *just Zak*. In other words, Zak had buckets of charm and was so much fun that you'd forgive him pretty much anything he did. Like the girl who, Jake was fairly certain, was hiding out in Zak's bedroom right now. She'd be waiting for Alice to leave for church before making her own escape, without even a cup of tea or a slice of toast to see her on her way. Zak wasn't much of a gentleman when it came to his demanding stomach, and he wasn't going to miss out on one of his grandmother's Sunday-morning fry-ups just because he'd scored. Besides, the hungry and neglected rock chick was bound to forgive him because that was *just Zak*, wasn't it?

"The Tinners were so good yesterday," Issie was saying. "Weren't they, Jake?"

But Jake couldn't concentrate enough to comment: as Zak forked black pudding into his mouth and mopped up egg yolk with thick hunks of crusty homemade bread, his own stomach was see-sawing and he felt every one of his thirty years. Still, he was willing to bet that after the antics of the night before Danny was going to feel even worse than he did. Hopefully Danny would sleep it off. Then, when he was sober – or what passed for Dan's version of sober these days – Jake fully intended to have a serious talk with his brother. Alice was right: the Tremaines did stick together and, difficult as Danny was lately, Jake knew he had to try to help him, flying fists or not. After all, Dan couldn't carry on like this. Tara was a piece of work, but even she had a point about the fitness of Morgan staying with a father who was hitting the bottle hard. Jake understood why Danny was angry – and it was clear to him that his brother was also suffering from post-traumatic stress. Nevertheless, causing a scene in the local hadn't done him any favours. In fact, Jake strongly suspected that Tara had provoked Dan publicly so that she had witnesses who could testify to his volatility. It was just the kind of devious plan she'd come up with.

He groaned, and not just because of his throbbing temples. Dealing with the situation wasn't going to be easy, especially if Danny continued to drink so heavily. Jake had wanted to speak to him last night, but by the time he'd finally let himself into Seaspray, there'd been no sign of his brother. The old house had been completely still and Danny's bedroom door had been firmly shut. So far it had yet to reopen.

"Where's Nicky?" Zak was asking through a mouthful of food.

"He's gone to sea with Davey Tuckey while the Penhalligan boys have the morning off," Alice told him. She untied her apron, hung it on the hook by the ancient dresser and frowned. "They went at midnight, saving tide I suppose. I wish he wouldn't do that if he's been out to The Ship."

Jake wished the same. He'd meant to have a word with Nick too, hadn't he? He sighed. Sometimes the responsibility of it all was like a leaden weight on the top of his head. Apart from looking out for his younger siblings' welfare, there was all the stress of trying to find ways to shore up the failing family business – not to mention a father who insisted on doing an ostrich impression and keeping up appearances by flexing the company plastic. Jake's temples began to thud like the bass of one of Zak's songs. And if he even dared to start to thinking about Ella and Summer...

Jake closed his eyes in despair. Maybe he should just take a leaf out of Danny's book and go back to bed. As Alice clattered pans and plates into the dishwasher, his head pounded with each crash of china and chink of cutlery.

"Heavy night?" Mo grinned at him from her perch by the Aga. With her stripy-socked feet up on the laundry basket, she was chomping away on a doorstep of a bacon sandwich while flicking through the equine section of yesterday's *Western Morning News*.

"*Very* heavy by the look of him," Issie laughed. Once Morgan had been dispatched to wash and smarten himself up for church, she added with a wink, "Evil Ella was doing her best to get poor Jake pissed so that she could have her wicked way. When I left the pub they were looking very cosy. I hope you resisted, bro? I couldn't bear her as a sister-in-law. She'd make Tara look like Mary Poppins."

"Ella St Milton?" Alice's wise brown eyes were troubled at the mention of this. "Be careful, Jakey my love. She's one determined young woman. I seem to remember that her grandmother was exactly the same. Poor Jonny St Milton never stood a chance. She was going to marry him whether he liked it or not."

"Ella's well hot. I would," winked Zak. He reached across the table and helped himself to the leftovers on Issie's plate. "She's worth a fortune too, mate. What's stopping you?"

"Err, the fact that she's rancid?" suggested Mo, joining them at the table and helping herself to coffee. Her curled lip spoke volumes.

"Didn't seem to stop Jake last night," teased Issie. "He wasn't exactly fighting her off."

"My goodness, you *were* drunk, weren't you?" Mo said scathingly. "God, we should get this family a group admittance to Al Anon. We're a disgrace to the village."

Jake lifted his head just enough to look at Mo. The sunshine was hurting his eyes. "Just for the record, nothing happened with Ella. Not that it's any of your business."

And this was the absolute truth: nothing had happened, although it hadn't been for want of trying to engineer the situation on Ella's part. Drinks, flirty looks from beneath those thick false lashes, and hundreds of feather-light touches on his shoulder, arm and leg; she'd gone into full attack mode. After last orders they'd walked through the quiet streets together, and when Ella had asked him to come back to the hotel for the night, Jake had certainly been tempted. After all, Zak was right – she was sexy. With her hard gym-honed body and perfect salon grooming, there was no doubt that Ella St Milton was a very attractive proposition. Yet somehow the memories of lush curves and wide-spaced green eyes in a heart-shaped face kept superimposing themselves over Ella's features, and he'd stepped away involuntarily when she'd moved in to kiss him. Getting home to check on Danny had been Jake's excuse, but deep down he knew that as much as he loved his brother it hadn't been Dan that had held him back. Ella hadn't been pleased and they'd parted rather coolly. Lying alone in his bed at Seaspray and listening to the muffled giggles and groans coming from Zak's room, Jake had started to regret turning Ella down. Now, though, in the bright morning light and surrounded by his teasing siblings, he was relieved. The last thing he needed right now were any further complications.

"I can't believe you still hate Ella St Milton," Zak was saying to Mo. "It was years ago that you two fell out. Get over it. You're worse than the Count of Monte Cristo!"

"You know our Mo can hold a grudge for England," sighed Alice. She pulled out a chair and sat next to Morwenna, a gentle squeeze of her granddaughter's shoulder taking any sting out of her words.

"It's not a grudge. I'm just a good judge of character. I was right about Cashley Carstairs too, wasn't I? The tosser's only trying to buy the woods." Mo set her coffee mug down with a thud. "Well, over my dead body! If he wants a fight then he's got one."

"Anger management for you, young lady, after flying off the handle at him yesterday," teased Zak – and predictably Mo flared up like a Roman candle.

"I didn't fly off the handle! I just told him that there's no way that he's going to buy those woods. Somebody has to care about what goes on here while others – no names mentioned, Zak Tremaine – want to waste their time chasing total slappers and pretending to be something out of Bon Jovi or Led Zeppelin!"

Zak's wide blue eyes were the picture of innocence and he placed his hand over his chest. "Ouch, Morwenna. That hurts."

Mo snorted rudely. "Truth tends to, Pound Shop Robert Plant!"

"That's enough!" Alice said. "Zachary, don't tease your sister." She turned to Mo. "But sweetheart, he has a point. You really do need to calm down a little."

Jake didn't think his sore head could cope with much more squabbling. Every time they were back together the Tremaine family rolled the years away and all the old childhood grievances and allegiances surfaced. If Symon, Danny and Nick were present too then there was usually a full-scale fallout guaranteed within ten minutes. It was all pretty harmless stuff and more from force of habit than any real upset, though; when the chips were down they would all fight tooth and nail to defend one another.

"Granny Alice is right, Mo. You do need to watch that temper. You tore a strip off Summer too," he reminded her. "That red hair of yours is getting to be a liability."

Morwenna looked mutinous. "Thanks for the gratitude. I was sticking up for you."

"That's really kind," said Jake, tongue firmly in his cheek. "But I'm big enough to fight my own battles, thanks. Besides, it was all years ago. There's no point dragging it all up now."

Alice's ears were out on elastic. "Did you say Summer? As in Summer Penhalligan? Eddie and Susie's girl?"

Jake could have ripped his tongue out. Great. Now his grandmother had this snippet of information he'd never get a minute's peace. He was about to reply but Issie was staring at him accusingly.

"I knew it was her I saw yesterday, but she'd vanished by the time I got to the car park and I thought I must have been mistaken! How come you never told me?"

Jake shrugged. "There was nothing to tell. She's probably just back for a quick visit and will be gone again in a day or two." God, he certainly hoped so. Something was telling him that it wasn't just a hangover that was making his insides feel so weird this morning.

But Alice was frowning. "That's funny. Susie didn't mention Summer was visiting. In fact she's been getting worried because they haven't heard from her for so long."

Zak leaned across the table, raising his eyebrows at Jake. "Aha! Now I understand why you didn't rock the casbah with Ella last night. Summer's here?" He whistled appreciatively. "Did you see that last advertising campaign she did? That woman is a goddess!"

Unfortunately Jake had seen it. He'd not intended to, but it was pretty hard to ignore six-feet high billboards depicting a gorgeous woman dressed only in wisps of lace and satin. He guessed this was the whole point, given that she'd been promoting a new underwear range, but he'd rather it wasn't his ex who was plastered across most of the UK.

"Err, hello? But have you all gone mad?" interrupted Mo incredulously. "This is the woman who dumped Jake from a vast height, remember? The same one who used to be my best friend and who turned her back on all of us the minute something better came along?"

"That was a long time ago, wasn't it, Jake?" said Alice gently. She smiled at him, and as the sunlight danced across her lined face Jake was struck by how old and tired she looked. Granny Alice was in her seventies and had spent what should have been her quiet retirement looking after her son's motherless brood and running herself ragged. The last thing she needed now that they were supposedly adults was for all of them to start behaving like teenagers again.

Even if his heart was feeling dangerously close to how it had at eighteen…

"Absolutely. It's all water under the bridge," he agreed. "Honestly, Mo, you don't need to look so furious. We were just kids and it wasn't anything serious. I'm well and truly over Summer Penhalligan."

"Morwenna, my love," Alice said softly and with a frown creasing her forehead, "I really do think you should let bygones be bygones. Summer was very young and she made the choices that she thought were the right ones at the time. We may not have liked them but we have to respect them." She gave her grandchildren a stern look. "Surely you're all old enough now to see that?"

Jake exhaled slowly. "Absolutely we are, and nobody is to give Summer Penhalligan a hard time on my account. Is that clear? Absolutely nobody."

Zak opened his mouth, probably to make a quip about how he'd love nothing more than to give Summer a *hard* time, but the determined set of his brother's chin was enough to make him shut up quickly. Meanwhile, easy-going Issie just nodded.

Mo shrugged. "Fine. Whatever you think best, Jake." She pushed her chair away from the table and scooped up her paper. Pausing with her hand on the door handle she shook her head in resignation.

"I'll leave her alone with pleasure," she said, deliberately and scornfully, "but just ask yourself, Jake: why is it you still care what anyone says to her?"

Chapter 10

One hour, two Nurofen and six miles later, Jake was starting to feel slightly more human. Running always helped to clear his mind, mostly because while he was focusing on his breathing and his pace he couldn't think of anything else at all; at the risk of sounding like that dippy hippy Silver Starr, he saw his regular runs as a kind of meditation. It was rare that pounding the fields, roads and cliffs failed to lift his spirits.

Today Jake had taken his usual route that led out through the village, turned left at the car park (he really must liberate the work truck later on, or what little money the boatyard had made so far this season would be gobbled up by parking fees) and wound up a slow and deceptively steep hill to the top of Polwenna Bay. Once at the summit, and with his lungs burning, Jake always ran alongside the main road, criss-crossing from side to side in order to keep on the narrow track masquerading as a grass verge. Then he'd bear right towards the old abbey and pick up the footpath that led through the fields of wheat and maize to the cliff path. The cliff path was always Jake's favourite part of the run, for although it was desperately steep in some places and inexplicably muddy in others, the view never failed to take away what was left of his breath or to compensate for the ache in his muscles.

On this sunny May Sunday, the sea was sparkling and only a few wisps of cloud drifted lazily above Jake's head. He passed a couple of dog walkers and some serious hiker types equipped with maps in plastic neck bags as well as gaiters and walking poles, but apart from these folk the cliff paths were relatively deserted. Jake liked it like this, when it was just the thrashing waves and his heartbeat keeping him company.

Polwenna Bay was just around the next headland and, judging by the amount of small tripping boats trailing white snakes of wake, the village was already bustling with the first influx of visitors. Knowing that the lower path was likely to be choked up with ambling families blocking the way to take pictures or just admire the view, Jake opted instead for the punishingly steep track that led to the highest path. Full of pasties and cream teas, the day trippers were generally unlikely to embark on an almost vertical track that went nowhere except up and then back down. Only locals in pursuit of a little peace and quiet tended to bother with the upper route, and as he climbed upwards the overgrown grasses and wild flowers that hadn't been beaten back by a constant flow of walkers brushed Jake's legs. Several times he had to leap clumps of gorse that ambushed him in the middle of the little-used path – but as soon as he was at the summit and running along a flat grassy expanse for a mile, it was worth every minute. The blue of the sea and the sky seemed to mingle, sheep bounded away as he approached, and suddenly the path twisted and dropped away with dizzying sharpness to reveal Polwenna Bay huddled below in its narrow valley. Jake began to slow his pace; the cliff path ended abruptly in just a hundred metres or so, tumbling away in a series of sharp steps that zigzagged downhill to Seaspray.

Just before the steps, and set back into a little scooped-out area, nestled a weathered bench surrounded by nodding valerian and pink campion. This was where Jake usually stopped to stretch out and cool down. The lichen-speckled wood was powdery with age, and the dedication plaque bore homage to a couple now long forgotten but who'd once loved the view and wanted a seat placed there in their memory. It probably sounded daft, but Jake often felt that by pausing there even for a few minutes and looking down on the village that hadn't changed in centuries, he was, in his small way, respecting them.

He was already looking forward to snatching a few quiet moments there, to calm his ragged breathing and to start collecting together the thoughts he'd been avoiding since Mo had lobbed her earlier verbal grenade at him. But this morning, as he approached the bench, Jake realised that for once it was occupied.

And then he realised by whom.

***

Summer was exhausted. Not just tired; she was absolutely shattered. This was a grinding, deep-to-her bones weariness that no amount of sleeping or just sitting quietly could banish. Maybe it was an early pregnancy symptom, a bit like the metallic taste in her mouth and the waves of nausea? If it was, though, it wasn't one that she'd experienced before when—

No. She wasn't going to think about that. The memories and the feelings from those long-gone days were safely locked up, had been for years, and the mental key had long since been thrown away. It was far better that way.

Summer closed her eyes and turned her face up towards the sun. The calling of the gulls and the distant roar of the waves were a part of the soothing music of being up here, as much an element of the place as the warm wood beneath her legs and the scent of wild garlic tickling her nose. Summer had always thought that there was a special peace about being up on the top path, and in the past this bench had been the place she'd always sought out when she needed space to think.

This morning she'd woken up with a start, her heart crashing against her ribs, and her sheets wet with sweat. For a moment Summer hadn't known where she was, only that the room was inky black and that there was an empty space beside her where Justin should be. Where was he? Was there somewhere she was supposed to be? Had she forgotten something important and been left behind as punishment for some minor misdemeanour? There were so many little things that could easily send him spiralling into one of his lightning-fast rages or, even worse, herald the start of weeks of silences so cold they made the Ice Age look tropical. Alarmed, Summer had dredged through her memories, just in case she'd smiled at somebody the wrong way or not paid Justin enough attention or, crime of crimes, been stupid enough to wear something that resulted in her getting even more attention than him. That was the ultimate betrayal in Justin's eyes. But, try as she might, Summer hadn't been able to think of anything she might have done wrong.

It was only when her heart rate had slowed enough for her to hear the squawk of seagulls that Summer had remembered exactly where she was. The sense of relief had been overwhelming and she'd lain under the duvet feeling weak and wobbly, until the sun's fingers had streaked the sky pink and blushed the small attic bedroom. Then she'd had a shower in the tiny cupboard-like en suite, before dressing in jeans and a light sweater and going downstairs to make a strong coffee and another plate of dry toast.

After breakfast, Summer had felt slightly better. Her hands were less shaky and the nausea was passing. It was a beautiful morning, the world all new and shiny as though it had just been made, and she could hardly wait to venture outside and get some fresh air. She'd decided to avoid the village, though. Yesterday's confrontation with Mo had been deeply upsetting and bumping into Jake worse again. Every time she allowed herself to think about the indifferent expression in his eyes when he'd looked at her, Summer felt the same sharp stab of loss. Even though everything had happened a long time ago, she could feel herself regressing to the unhappy and confused girl she'd once been. Well, that wasn't going to happen today, Summer had told herself as she'd slipped her feet into her Uggs. She was twenty-eight now and had some real and very serious issues to deal with. The past was going to stay where it belonged – twelve years and another lifetime away. Still, knowing it was Sunday and traditionally the day when Alice Tremaine cooked up a massive breakfast for her family and their friends, Summer had decided not to tempt fate by walking through the village, where she was bound to bump into Mo. Instead she'd taken the cliff path out of the village and plumped for the higher route, where she was unlikely to meet anyone.

Summer wasn't sure how long she'd been sitting on the bench. The warmth of the sun had made her drowsy and her eyes had closed. Listening to the droning of bees and the rhythm of the waves slowed the racing of her pulse and made her hopeful that maybe everything would work out just fine. Justin would be pleased to see the back of her and he'd break their engagement off without a fuss. He'd even let her bring the baby up on her own without being difficult.

Yeah right, Summer thought with a mental headshake, and maybe Santa Claus was real too? The climb up was worth every step if it really made her believe that.

"Summer? Are you all right?"

The voice interrupted her thoughts and for a moment, with her eyes still shut, she thought she must have been dreaming – unless this bench was Polwenna Bay's very own time vortex, whisking her back to the early noughties. How wonderful would it be to find herself sixteen again and with her whole life lying before her like freshly fallen snow, instead of the ugly slushy mess she'd made of it?

A hand was touching her shoulder. "Summer? Are you OK? Are you hurt?"

Was it possible to summon somebody just by thinking about them? Surely not? Summer knew she should keep her eyes closed: if she opened them and looked him in the face and saw again that look of indifference, she didn't think she could bear it. As it was, just hearing the concern in this familiar voice hit her right in the solar plexus. Seeing his scorn would be far more painful than her throbbing eye.

Reluctantly, Summer opened her heavy lids. Sure enough Jake Tremaine was crouched down beside her. One look into those eyes, blue with flecks of navy just like the Cornish sea beyond, was all it took to make the past disappear. He was still so ridiculously handsome that she could hardly breathe. She'd only seen him briefly on the quay, where the light had been fading and shadows had been pooling over them, but now in the sunlight she could see that he was just as beautiful as she remembered.

It wasn't that Jake was film-star perfect. No, from what she remembered it was Danny who'd had the monopoly on the male-model looks in the family. She noticed as well that Jake's nose still had the bump in it from when he'd broken it wakeboarding. Even now the memory of all that blood was enough to make her feel queasy! He was unshaven, too, and his curly corn-coloured hair was a little too long. But somehow, with Jake, all these things came together perfectly. His strongly boned face, the broad shoulders, the well-muscled arms and legs, and the way that he always inspired absolute confidence – all of these traits made Summer tremble way more than Justin's fists ever could.

Jake was scanning her face and frowning. "How on earth did you do that to your eye?"

Summer's hand rose to her bruise. In her haste to get outside and stretch her legs she'd forgotten to put her shades on. Big mistake.

"I'm fine," she told him quickly. "It's nothing."

"That doesn't look like nothing to me, Sums. Have you seen a doctor?"

The use of the old nickname made her inhale sharply. His hand was gently moving hers aside, his fingers skimming over the swollen flesh as his eyes narrowed. Shivers that were nothing to do with pain rippled across her body. Oh Lord. One touch from Jake had always been all it took. Summer didn't know whether to be horrified or reassured that even as a teenager her taste in men had been spot on. She knew it had been downhill ever since.

"It's nothing, honestly," she insisted, snapping her head away from his hand. She missed her long hair now. It would have saved a lot of curious looks and awkward questions if she'd been able to hide the bruising beneath it.

"As I said, it doesn't look like nothing to me." Concern furrowed Jake's brow. "Your eye's closing up and I bet it hurts like hell. I should know. I've been punched enough times; it comes with having four brothers."

"I've not been punched. I tripped and walloped my head," Summer said swiftly, knowing she'd better scotch any such rumours right away. Justin's lawyers would make mincemeat of her if they thought she'd been badmouthing him. It didn't matter if what she said was the truth;

in their circles Summer knew that it was always the partner with the most cash and the best lawyer who came out of a relationship whiter than the laundry in a Daz commercial.

Jake was clearly not buying this for a second. "Right. If you say so."

Summer squared her shoulders. "I do say so. I'm fine."

He raised an eyebrow, those compelling eyes holding her in a searching look. Summer looked away first.

"Evidently," he remarked drily. "Still, being fine always was your forte, wasn't it? Forgive me for just being concerned. I was going to say that my friend Richard's one of the GPs here. I know it's Sunday, but I'm sure he'd be happy to look at that for you, if you like? He's a good guy. I think you'd like him."

Of course. A doctor called Richard: Kursa's son, most likely. Sometimes Summer forgot what a small world Polwenna Bay was. It was like living in an episode of *Doc Martin*.

"I'll be OK," she insisted.

There was silence. Then Jake shrugged. "Whatever you say then. It's up to you. Catch you around maybe."

He stepped away and began to head back to the cliff path. He was in running gear, Summer realised, and he was in good shape too. Better, if anything, than when he was eighteen. With his broad shoulders, strong legs and lean hips, Jake was definitely a man now – and a very attractive one. It should be a relief that he'd moved away from her, but Summer couldn't help feeling a stab of regret. They'd once been so close and now they were further apart than strangers.

"Thank you," she called after him, before she could stop herself. "You didn't have to stop and see if I was all right. Especially after yesterday."

Jake turned around slowly. "I wouldn't walk past any woman who looked as though she was in trouble," he told her. "And as for yesterday, forget it. Mo still has a fiery temper but she's calmed down now."

Summer nodded. She was glad to hear it. "I know it was a shock for you both to see me again. Don't worry. I won't stick around for long enough to make life difficult."

Jake's gaze drifted to the bruising on her face and for a moment he looked as though he was about to say something, before thinking better of it.

"Like I said before, stay as long as you need to. It makes no odds to me. Besides, I think you'll find that Mo will be far too busy waging war on the local property developer to worry about you. She's probably boiling oil and cranking up the siege engine as we speak. Christ, I'm almost sorry for Ashley Carstairs."

She laughed. "He should definitely watch out. Mo on a mission is a force of nature. The memory of Ella St Milton without her ponytail will stay with me forever!"

Jake grimaced. "God, I'd forgotten that. Her mum went mad." He paused, and then deadpanned, "Mo hasn't been near you with the scissors too, has she?"

They looked at each other for a second before they both convulsed with mirth. That was one of the things she'd loved about being with Jake, Summer recalled: they'd laughed and laughed until the tears had rolled down their cheeks and their sides had ached. She'd never laughed like that with Justin, or much at all if the truth were told.

"Your friend Richard's mum did this," Summer explained once she'd got her breath back. "I needed a… a change of look."

Jake's eyebrows shot into his thick blond curls. "You must have been desperate! They say Cornwall Council cuts the hedges straighter than Kursa Penwarren cuts hair."

Summer ran a hand through her shorn locks. "She did me a huge favour. I won't hear a word against her."

"Fair enough. It suits you, actually. It makes your eyes look enormous, like a beautiful manga character."

Summer stared at him, taken aback, and Jake coloured.

"Listen to me! I spend far too much time with my nephew. A manga character? I need to get out more."

"I quite like the idea of being a manga cartoon girl," Summer said quickly, touched by his red face. She'd forgotten how easily Jake could be teased. "I could do ninja moves and fight villains." Yes, that would come in very handy when dealing with Justin, she thought privately. "Cowabunga, loser!"

"Cowabunga's *Teenage Mutant Ninja Turtles*," said Jake pityingly. "Typical girl. Just be a Pink Power Ranger or something."

"Pink?" Summer gasped in mock outrage. "Still a sexist Polwenna man then?"

"Oh aye, proper job, maid!" nodded Jake in a thick West Country accent, and they smiled at each other. The tensions of earlier had vanished. Maybe they could still be friends, Summer thought hopefully. After all, they were both adults now. It might be nice.

He held out his hand to her.

"Now, my lover, would 'ee loike a proper Cornish pasty?"

Impulsively, Summer placed her palm in his and allowed Jake to pull her to her feet. Her hand seemed to recall his exactly; it was just as big and as strong as she remembered. Alarmed by the tingling sensation in her fingers, she pulled her hand away as quickly as she could, but not before the flicker of surprise on Jake's face told her that he had felt it too.

Oh dear. This could be complicated…

"Seriously, my offer stands with or without the silly accent," Jake was saying quickly, but not quite quickly enough to cover his shocked expression. "I was hung-over to hell this morning and I couldn't face anything, but I'm starving now. There's a new tearoom down by the museum if you fancy a coffee? I guess you actress types aren't allowed to eat much, but if you are tempted they do an amazing steak and stilton pasty."

Summer looked outraged. "What? Better than Patsy's Pasties?"

"Of course not! Heaven forbid that such a thing could even be imagined, but they are a very close second. And," dropping his voice, Jake leaned forward and whispered in her ear, so close that she could feel his breath flute against her skin and smell the tang of hot male sweat, "rumour has it that the tearoom don't put less filling in just because it's the holiday season!"

She widened her eyes. "As if Patsy would do that! I'm offended on behalf of the entire Penhalligan clan!"

They convulsed into laughter again. Having spent a season working together in the kitchen of the pasty shop, Summer and Jake were under no illusions as to what tricks of the trade were employed to ensure maximum profits.

When their mirth faded away, Jake turned to stare down at her for a moment.

"Will you come for a coffee?" he asked softly. "As friends?"

And Summer, in spite of everything, found that she couldn't say no.

***

Jake wasn't usually a violent man, so when he was suddenly hit by a huge surge of murderous rage, it took him totally unawares. Somebody had assaulted Summer – this was as obvious as the huge bruise on her otherwise flawless face – and he wanted to kill whoever it was. She was absolutely tiny, thinner now and frailer than she'd been as a teenager, and doubtless no match for the coward who'd done this to her. Still, she'd made it more than clear that the subject wasn't up for discussion, so he'd forced himself to swallow back his rising fury. His muscles were tense with anger but for now there was nothing he could do except respect her wishes and step right away from the topic. He knew that Summer was nothing to do with him anymore and that he had no right to feel this rage or to want to protect her, but it was as instinctive to him as breathing.

Right then and there, as they strolled down the hill back into the village, Jake knew he would do anything to stop Summer ever being hurt again. He wanted to track down whoever had done this to her and make sure once and for all that they never, ever managed to do it again. By the time he was finished with the culprit, they'd be lucky to eat through a straw for the rest of their life.

Christ. The strength of his fury terrified Jake. Did feeling like this make him as bad as the bastard who'd done this to her in the first place? That was a thought he'd rather not address, and he pushed it away quickly.

Summer, oblivious to the wild runaway train of thought gathering speed in Jake's mind, was chatting away easily. She seemed happy to talk about the people they both knew in common, and somehow Jake managed to calm down enough to fill her in a little on new arrivals and changes. Lending her his sunglasses also helped: with the violent purple and red bruise hidden from view, he was able to simmer down a little. Once they were seated at one of the tables overlooking the harbour and enjoying pasties the size of their heads, Jake was feeling more like his usual self.

"My career as a model will be over very fast if I stay here too long." Summer looked at her pasty with an alarmed expression.

"You look great," Jake told her. "A bit too thin, if anything, so nothing to worry about on the pasty front. Go on, get stuck in."

To his great surprise Summer did get stuck in. The pasty was wolfed down in almost record time and Jake, who was used to girls like Ella who picked at the odd lettuce leaf while drooling at the mere sight of his steak and chips, was impressed. Putting her knife and fork down with a clatter, Summer placed her hands on her stomach and groaned.

"Oh God, that was wonderful," she said. There was a flake of pastry on her full top lip and he was suddenly struck with the compulsion to lean across the table and kiss it away. He swallowed and pretended to be fascinated by the frothy surface of his coffee. When he was eventually able to look up again, Summer was dabbing her mouth with a napkin and the moment had fortunately passed. Jake couldn't decide if he was relieved or disappointed.

They sipped their lattes in companionable silence while watching the living picture of the harbour shift and kaleidoscope in front of them. The trawlers were all out and the tide had followed, leaving a pale sickle of lemon-coloured beach behind. Seagulls bobbed in the shallows, and on the quay a tall man stood gazing out to sea, his dark jacket lifting in the breeze. Even from here, he had a brooding look about him.

Danny was up then, Jake thought. That was another difficult conversation he was going to have to negotiate. Along with getting his father to face up to the fact that the family finances were about to implode, and trying to stop Mo from flattening Cashley with her four-by-four. When had life become so complex?

He glanced at Summer, who had closed her eyes and raised her face to the sun. With her delicate stem-like neck and tendrils of hair curling against her cheeks like petals, she reminded him of a rare orchid. Hanging out with Summer had always been easy, Jake recalled, and being with her had never been complicated, which had only made what happened later on even harder to accept. He sighed in resignation. As his gran had said, it was a long time ago and they were both different people now. Summer had a whole life in London that he knew nothing about; she was friends with A-list celebrities, for heaven's sake. It was time to let the past go. Life was simpler that way.

But leading a simple life free of complications was far easier said than done when you lived in a small Cornish fishing village. Just as Jake had collected and was about to pay for two more coffees, none other than Ella St Milton came sauntering over to the counter. She looked as though she'd stepped straight out of a salon rather than been up until the small hours winding herself around him like a sexy octopus and downing vodkas with him. No wonder the girl needed coffee. If she'd felt half as bad as he had earlier on, then it was a marvel that she was even walking, let alone bright-eyed and full of beans.

Here was a thought, though: had Ella actually been drinking? Jake racked his brains and couldn't remember whether or not he'd seen Ella with any alcohol last night, after that first glass of wine. She'd certainly been buying a lot of drinks, but whether or not she'd been indulging too was anyone's guess.

Jake was hoping that Ella wouldn't spot him, but when it came to the hotelier it was as though he had some kind of homing beacon. When she caught sight of him, Ella's gaze brightened momentarily; then it flickered to the oblivious Summer, who was still sitting at the table some way away, and her grey eyes narrowed.

"You've got company, I see?" she remarked pointedly as she joined Jake at the counter.

"Not really." Jake fixed his attention on tipping sugar into his latte. Two for the shock of seeing Summer, he decided, and one more to give him the strength to handle whatever abuse Ella was about to hurl at him. Jake knew enough about women to know when he was about to be given a hard time.

"So, you're too busy to spend time with me but not with her?" Ella's voice was light but there was a note of hurt beneath the words, and Jake felt bad for that. Last night when he'd sent her home alone he'd claimed that he had lots to do at the marina in the morning. Ella hadn't bought it then, of course, and she certainly wasn't buying it now. She was glaring in Summer's direction. "What the hell is she doing back here anyway? That *is* Summer over there, isn't it?"

"Yes, it's Summer, and I haven't a clue why's she back. I just ran into her on the cliffs. Literally." Jake indicated his sports gear. "As you can see, I'm hardly dressed for a secret assignation with my glamour-model ex. We're catching up, that's all. It's been a long time."

"Obviously not long enough to get over her. Since when did you take sugar?"

Was there nothing Ella didn't notice? Her eye for detail made her quite scary, Jake thought. Women. Why were they always so competitive?

"I've had an eight-mile run and I need some calories," he said mildly, stirring his coffee and refusing to rise to her bait. Ella loved drama and he wasn't going to give her the scene she wanted. To be honest he didn't care enough about her to waste the energy. "As for your other facetious comment, plenty long enough for that – not that it's any of your business, Ella. Now, how about you stop making a scene and come and join us over there?"

"No thanks; I'm in a hurry," Ella said coolly. "Unlike you, I really am busy. In fact, I don't even think I'll stick around for a takeaway latte. Three's a crowd anyway."

"Ella, you're being ridiculous. It's a coffee with an old friend. We're catching up."

Not that it's any of your concern who I drink coffee with, he added silently. Had he led Ella on? Maybe, but he'd never let her think there was any potential of anything serious. Nevertheless, here she was getting all possessive. He was reminded all of a sudden of Granny Alice's comment about Ella being a determined young woman.

"Well, I'll leave you two to your *catching up*, shall I?" said Ella pointedly. "Oh, don't forget to ask her how Justin Anderson is, will you? Didn't he have cancer not so long ago? I'd have thought his loving fiancée would be spending every minute with him rather than hanging out with her exes. I wonder if he minds? Or even knows? Maybe somebody should tell him?"

Ella turned on her heel and stalked away before Jake could even draw breath to reply, although not before he caught the glint of malice in her eyes and saw her lips shrivel into a tight red slash.

She was being ridiculous, of course, and she probably didn't mean a word of her childish threats – but suddenly, and in spite of the warm sunshine on his skin, Jake felt cold.

Ella St Milton was a dangerous lover and he suspected that she could be an even more dangerous enemy.

Chapter 11

Sundays were always a busy day for a vicar and today was proving no exception for Jules Mathieson, whose Sabbath had started early with a prayer meeting for the lay readers. To her surprise, their emergence from the meeting had distracted a man who was already sitting in a pew, seemingly deep in thought. Jules had tried to reassure him that he was more than welcome to stay, but he'd shot off pretty hastily, clearly not keen on being disturbed. He'd seemed very familiar and it was only halfway through her sermon that Jules had finally twigged that he was the man Mo Tremaine had been arguing with the previous night. No wonder he'd looked so pensive. From the way Mo had flown at him, Jules could hardly blame the guy if he felt he needed to take sanctuary!

By the time the morning service was over, the hymn books were collected up and the last of the congregation was meandering back through the churchyard to the village, Jules was ready to collapse. In spite of only having had a couple of pints and a relatively early night once Danny Tremaine had been safely delivered home, she'd woken up with a pounding head and a mouth drier than the inside of the church font.

Maybe this was the Lord's way of telling her to drink less and not to hang out in pubs, Jules pondered as she gulped the leftover communion wine and then wiped the chalice with a soft cloth. That would make life a bit difficult, though, when the Church of England insisted on using good and wholesome fermented grape juice for the Eucharist; alas, a dwindling congregation meant she had to finish off a third of a bottle of full-bodied claret whenever there was a communion service. I really must pour less next time, Jules thought guiltily. She was in danger of ending up like poor Danny otherwise. Not a comfortable thought.

Hmm. Danny Tremaine. He was without doubt a man on the edge, broken in both heart and body. How did you even dare to presume to try helping a man like him? A man who'd seen horrors most people were lucky enough to not even be able to imagine. Jules couldn't blame him for turning to alcohol. It was one way of coping, after all.

As she moved into the vestry to remove her cassock, Jules's thoughts turned back to the journey up to Seaspray the night before. She and Nick had put their arms around Danny and dragged him, dangling between them, through the streets and up to the house. Danny was still a strong man, over six feet of army-honed muscle, and by the time they'd reached the cliff path Jules had been puffing like a tank engine. If Danny had wanted to talk, rather than been practically unconscious, she would have been no use whatsoever: there had been no breath left in her to speak. *Lord, please help me to resist all the delicious food here and get fit,* Jules prayed to the cheerful stained-glass Jesus above her desk. Surrounded by children and wearing a particularly sunny halo, this version of the Lord always made Jules feel as though he was beaming down at her, ready to hop out of the casement and wander into the village for a chat and a pasty. Goodness, she really wished He would. Fiery fisher folk and social misfits were, after all, His speciality – and Jules was sure that Jesus would have known exactly how to help Danny Tremaine. Why on earth was she wasting His time whining about her weight when there were people here with real problems? Danny couldn't help it that a roadside bomb had caught him unawares, but she knew full well that every packet of Wotsits and bar of Dairy Milk went straight to her hips. Jules felt ashamed.

Please show me what I can do to help Danny, she prayed. *Let me have the right words. Give me a sign.*

A sharp knock at the vestry door made her jump. Seconds later Alice Tremaine's kind face peeked nervously around the door.

Wow. That was quick, Jules thought. Not that she ever doubted her boss, but even so!

"I'm really sorry to disturb you, Jules love," Alice said apologetically, "but I just wanted to catch you while Morgan was out of earshot."

Jules grinned. "I should imagine that's easier said than done. It strikes me that not much gets past that young man. Fact!"

"Fact, indeed, and not always a good thing," Alice Tremaine agreed wryly. Stepping into the small room, she shut the door behind her and then exhaled wearily. "I just wanted to thank you for what you did last night, Vicar. And don't try and fob me off by telling me it was nothing, either!"

Jules smiled. "I wouldn't dream of fobbing you off, Alice, but it really wasn't a major deal. The walk did me good."

Alice shook her head. "Just about everyone in the village is talking about Danny's outburst, and I'm old enough to know that they're probably leaving out the worst of it for my benefit. I'm really grateful to you for stepping in and helping to calm him down. Dan can be volatile at the moment, so that was a brave thing to do."

"I'm not sure about brave," said Jules. She perched on the corner of her desk and picked up her stole, running her hands over the embroidery as though seeking inspiration in the stitches. It was a beautiful design on the top, but underneath it was a confused and knotted mass of thread and oversewing. Maybe Danny was just the other way around? "He's been through a lot," she continued gently. "I think it's understandable he's upset."

"Well, I'm more sorry than I can say that you had to see him like that, my dear," Alice told her apologetically. The older woman's wise eyes were shadowed with a deep sadness. "He wasn't always this way, you know. It's what happened in Afghanistan; it's changed him almost beyond recognition – well, that and Tara not being able to handle it. I think losing her was even worse than losing his arm. Dan adores Tara. By all accounts, while he was in the field hospital it was only thinking of her and Morgan that kept him going. He nearly didn't make it, but he's a Tremaine and a fighter." Her voice shook. "At least, he *was*. Lately I'm really afraid that he's started to give up."

Jules didn't say anything but instead reached forward and laid her hand over Alice's. It felt as light as a bird beneath her touch, the skin papery and the bones fragile. She'd come to realise that words often just got in the way. More often than not, people came to her just to talk through their own thoughts and eventually wound their own way to some kind of absolution. She sometimes thought the Catholics were onto something with confession.

Alice gave Jules a sad smile. Sunshine danced through the stained-glass window, throwing paint-box colours onto the worn stone floor and revealing the dust motes that fell silently through the air. Jules realised that she was holding her breath; she sensed that a story was about to unfold.

"Dan was always such an easy-going boy. He was probably the least trouble out of all the children when he was growing up." Now Alice's gaze was decades away, back in the past where scabby-kneed little boys shinned up trees and rowed their dinghies in the harbour, a world away from the nightmare land of roadside bombs and snipers. "Of course, it wasn't easy for any of them when Penny died," she continued softly. "Jimmy – that's my son – just went to pieces, and he was no use to anyone. The children must have felt as though they'd lost both their parents. The twins were only two, and Zak and Symon weren't that much older. I guess Jake and Danny and Mo were probably hit the hardest because they understood more of what was happening, but I'm afraid that it was exactly *because* they were older I expected them to cope as best they could." Alice had closed her eyes. "I thought I was handling it all by coping alone, but looking back I wonder if it just made a horrible mess even worse. They're all struggling as adults, aren't they? What if it was because I didn't have more time for them when they were children? At the risk of sounding like an episode of *Jeremy Kyle*, maybe I should have sought some help for them?"

Jules thought of Jake in all his sexy snake-hipped, golden-curled, blue-eyed glory and, in spite of the sunshine, goosebumps dusted her arms. He'd not been aware of it, but in the pub last night he'd been a magnet for the gaze of every woman. She'd found it hard enough to string a coherent sentence together from behind the safety of her vicar's status; he really was one of the most striking men she'd ever seen, the type you looked at once and then had to look at again just to check he was real. He hardly seemed like a man who was struggling, except maybe to fight off the rapacious blonde who'd been staring at him across the bar as though he was a Big Mac meal she was about to gobble up. And as for Morwenna – well, she was clearly more than capable of standing up for herself, if Musto Man had to hide out in St Wenn's. Danny was different. He had an air of vulnerability about him that had escaped the rest of the brood.

"I know what you're thinking, but they've had to deal with their loss in their own ways," Alice explained, spotting the doubt on Jules's face. "Mo's been horse mad ever since I can remember. Honestly, if it doesn't have hooves and a mane then she's not interested. When it comes to people, she really isn't bothered. She doesn't let anyone come close. I worry about her because it isn't right, is it? She should have her own family by now."

"You can't live people's lives for them," Jules pointed out gently. "There's plenty of time for Morwenna to find someone."

Alice looked doubtful. "To be honest I can't imagine who'd be able to handle Mo. She's stubborn and fiery, and although I love her she's not easy to live with. And as for Jake, he's never been the same since—"

"You were saying about Jake?" Jules prompted when Alice paused.

"Ah, Jake. Well, he seemed fine for a long time. He worked hard at school, had begun to take over the business and even had a steady girlfriend. I really thought that life was working out for him; they seemed so happy together. But then she broke it off and he couldn't handle it at all. Eventually he went travelling. Like Mo, he's never managed to find anyone either. We hardly saw him for the next ten years. He was in Australia, the States, the Caribbean – anywhere but here. He's only back now because Jimmy's not been well. At least Danny was happy. He had the career he'd always dreamed of and the perfect family. I don't know why it all had to go wrong for him. Hadn't he suffered enough? Has our family done something wrong? Are we being punished?" Her eyes filled with tears and wordlessly Jules passed her the box of Kleenex that lived on her desk, as essential to her role as a vicar as the dog collar and pulpit.

"I can't explain why these things have happened to you." Jules searched her heart for the right words. "Sometimes we can't see the reasons why until we're looking back and then there's some sense to it – and maybe even then it's still inexplicable. Maybe we'll never know the reasons. Or perhaps there simply aren't any? But I do know one thing, Alice, and that is that God doesn't punish us. We do that to ourselves. He loves us."

Alice dabbed her eyes and gave Jules a watery smile. "I know that really, my dear, of course I do. And why not us? All families have their problems, don't they?"

"Absolutely. You should meet mine!" Jules said with feeling. Her father made Richard Dawkins look religious and would probably never get over his only child becoming a vicar. Jules sometimes felt he'd have been less disappointed if she'd turned to crime or joined the Moonies. She often suspected he still lived in hope that she was just going through a phase.

"I just wonder sometimes if they can't settle down now because of what happened all those years ago?" Alice's mouth trembled. "Was there something I should have done?"

"From everything I can see you've done a great job of raising them all," Jules told her warmly. "I don't know any of your grandchildren that well, but the ones I have met seem pretty well adjusted and they all absolutely adore you. I know Danny has issues but those are completely understandable. I really wouldn't worry about Jake and Mo either. Maybe they aren't ready to settle down yet?"

Alice blew her nose. "Ignore me. I'm just being silly. But, Jules, if you'd met Danny before his injuries you'd understand why I think this way. He was the most easy-going young man you could ever meet. We never had a minute's worry about Danny. He loved sport, worked hard at school and went to Sandhurst just as he'd always planned. Then he married Tara, Morgan came along and he was given a promotion. He was on his way to the top all right. Everything was always perfect with our Danny."

Jules was starting to understand a little. Good-looking, well loved and talented, Danny Tremaine had lived an enchanted life until very recently. His landscape had shifted beyond all recognition. No wonder he was savage with rage, grief and fear.

"Alice, his life changed in a heartbeat. He's not the same person that he was, physically or psychologically, and that must be so hard for you to deal with and even harder for him." Jules frowned as a thought occurred to her. "Has he had any help?"

"Like counselling, you mean?"

"That would seem to be a good start."

"He's had countless sessions but he refuses to go to anymore," Alice said wearily. "I've tried to convince him that counselling would help, but he says that talking won't grow his arm back or heal his face. It's pointless trying to reason with him and I can hardly force him. I'm not condoning Tara, and I'm sure there were already issues between them before he was hurt, but he's impossible to live with and the drinking's only getting worse. Nothing I say seems to make any difference. I worry so much because it isn't good for Morgan either. Between you and me, his school have expressed concerns about Morgan seeming very unsettled lately. They want to refer him to someone. We daren't tell Danny."

Jules's heart went out to the older woman. She noticed how thin Alice looked and that her eyes were smudged with purple shadows.

Danny's behaviour was taking its toll on others as well as the man himself; that was for certain.

"There you are Grand Gran!" The vestry door flew open and Morgan hurtled through, the picture of indignation. Shoving a huge watch under Alice's nose, he added, "I've been looking for you everywhere and now it's twelve thirty-two – and we're always home by twelve forty-five on Sundays. Always."

"Hello, Morgan," said Jules.

Morgan ignored her. He was too busy hopping from foot to foot in agitation.

"Come *on* Grand Gran! We've only got thirteen minutes to get back. You're going to have to walk really fast!"

"Dear me, I have been rabbiting on, haven't I?" Alice placed a calming hand on his shoulder. "Morgan, you mustn't just barge in and interrupt people when they're having a conversation, by the way. It's best to knock first. Anyway, say hello to the vicar."

"Yes, yes, hello!" Morgan tugged his great-grandmother's jacket impatiently. He was oblivious to Jules and anything else but his need to be home by the specified time. "*Now* can we go? There's only eleven minutes and thirty-six seconds left now."

"It's fine. Really," Jules said quickly, catching Alice's worried expression. The poor lady certainly had her hands full. "You guys get going. I'll catch up with you later in the week."

After the church door had shut with a firm click, Jules remained leaning against her desk for a long while, lost in thought. There was so much more to being a vicar than the public perception of wafting around in daft robes and doing the odd wedding or funeral. People were so complex; helping to ease their needs and their pain was the biggest part of her job. Jules knew that Jesus would have understood this, but unfortunately Sheila Keverne didn't. Her verger had already made several cutting comments about Jules being seen helping Danny Tremaine home from the pub – and then she'd gone on to pick fault with her sermon too. Maybe I'll do Luke 10:25 next week, Jules thought with a surge of determination. A reminder of the Good Samaritan parable was exactly what Sheila needed, although the bossy old boot probably would have found fault with him too!

Next Sunday's homily decided upon, Jules quickly swapped her cleric's shirt and trousers for jeans and a tee-shirt, and then locked the vestry. St Wenn's would remain open until sunset; it was a pretty church with a breathtaking view of the village, and tourists loved to visit it. Locals also liked to pop in and find a little peace away from the bustle of the streets and busy shops, and Jules was pleased that her little church afforded them a quiet moment or two. There were no real valuables to steal and the climb up was so steep and inaccessible to cars that any thieves would need a good rest after reaching the place anyway. It was also highly unlikely that anyone could make it past Sheila's cottage without being spotted. That woman ought to work for MI5.

It was another glorious May day and the sunshine was pouring down onto Polwenna Bay as though a giant had tipped maple syrup over the clusters of cottages. Jules walked slowly through the small churchyard, raising her face to the warmth and watching the gulls doing aeronautics in the cloudless sky before dive-bombing the tourists. Only yesterday she'd had an ice cream snatched by an opportunistic orange-beaked thief, which had actually made her laugh. Talk about an answer to all her *please make me thinner* prayers!

Jules was just about to let herself out via the little kissing gate that opened onto the winding path into the village, when she spotted a solitary figure seated on the bench overlooking the sea. Although he had his back to her she knew it was Danny Tremaine: there was no mistaking those broad shoulders or that shorn blond hair. Before she had time to think it through, Jules found herself doing a swift about-turn and joining him.

"Oh, it's you," Danny said. He could hardly look her in the eye, even from his good side. A brown paper bag, which was doing a very poor job of concealing a bottle of Jack Daniel's, was nestled by his feet; he made a half-hearted attempt to kick it under the bench when he saw Jules glance down.

"I suppose I ought to thank you for getting me home last night," he added resentfully. "You'll be going to heaven for sure, you will."

The taint of alcohol-laden breath fought with the scent of newly mown grass and salty air. The alcohol won and it took all of Jules's restraint not to shrink away. Resisting the urge to flee, she just shrugged instead and ignored his jibe.

"I was already booked in long before we met. Don't thank me if you don't want to. I wasn't looking for gratitude."

"So what do you want? Some money for the church spire? Me to say a few Hail Marys?"

"Just in case you haven't noticed, we don't have a spire, and if you want Hail Marys then you should pop over to Father William at the abbey." Antagonism was coming from him in waves every bit as rough and as white-tipped as those that came rolling into the bay on stormy days. Jules chose to ignore it. "Actually, what I'd really like is for you to promise never to cause a scene like that again. Smashing glasses and terrifying the poor barmaid? It's hardly kind behaviour, is it?"

He laughed rudely. "Kelly? Terrified? Don't make me laugh. She's as thick as two short planks."

"She might be 'thick', as you so nicely put it, but she wasn't the one making an exhibition of herself in front of the whole village, was she? And no matter what you think of her intelligence she's surely got the right to be safe at work without being accosted by you?" Jules wasn't feeling very patient suddenly. The whiff of the whiskey was making her stomach churn. "Anyway, I didn't do it for you; I did it to help your family out and to stop you causing even more of a scene. "

Danny snorted. "My family? What on earth has my getting drunk got to do with them? We're all grown-ups, Vicar."

Jules thought of Alice, so strained and fragile, and of Morgan who was trying to cling on and cope by whatever means possible, and she felt her temper start to bubble up. Danny might have been horribly injured – she had no way of even starting to understand how he must feel – but he still had a family who loved him. In her ministry Jules had come across endless people who yearned for that, and to see him scorn it made her angry. She really must add patience to her long list of things to ask God to help her with. She took a slow breath to calm herself down.

"The last time I saw him, Morgan wasn't an adult. If you don't give a toss about yourself then try to think about him."

He turned, jolted. The scars seemed even more livid in the daylight but Jules didn't shrink from looking at him. Somehow the physical wounds shocked her far less than those she couldn't see.

"Morgan? What's he got to do with anything? He wasn't there – and if that bitch has her way, he won't be around for much longer either."

"If you carry on like this then it's probably just as well she takes him away." Jules wasn't able to contain herself – her worst flaw as a pastor, she often thought, but her greatest strength too when her instincts were right. Today they were telling her that Danny Tremaine had been handled with kid gloves for far too long and it wasn't doing him any favours. "He's a bright enough boy: of course he's noticed what goes on. One of the first things he told me was that you use lots of rude words when you have a drink. And before you think I was discussing you, I wasn't. I'd not even heard of you. I slipped in the harbour during the duck race and said 'bollocks'. Morgan heard me apologising, so in his own way he was trying to make me feel better." Jules grinned. "It worked, actually. Apparently your collection of obscenities is way bigger than mine!"

Danny stared at her. "Morgan said that about me? That I drink and swear?"

"Yep. He's as sharp as a razor. There's not much that will get past him. Of course he knows what goes on – and I'd bet you anything that he overhears a lot more than people realise, too. He'll know all about last night. Your gran tells me that the school's worried about him too." There was no point holding back now; she'd started, so Jules supposed she ought to finish. "Come on, Danny. Whatever else that bomb might have done to you, it didn't stop Morgan needing you. He looks up to you, and you know as well as anyone that change and uncertainty are difficult for him. He needs his dad, not some drunk wallowing in self-pity. You can turn this around, before it's too late."

Even Danny's scars turned pale. Leaning forward he pushed his ruined face practically into hers and, thrusting his shoulder towards her, waved his empty sleeve. His closed eye seemed to be glowering and it took all of Jules's self-control to remain still.

"Do you see this? Do you? It's fucking monstrous. *I'm* monstrous. No wonder Tara doesn't want me! Would you?"

Jules gulped. He might be injured but Danny Tremaine was still a big man and trained to kill. Right now he looked ready to throttle her with his good hand. Being a good few stones overweight and horribly unfit, Jules didn't fancy her chances of taking him on.

"Well?" thundered Danny. "Wouldn't you be wallowing in self-pity too if you looked like this? If you were just a pathetic wreck of what you once were?"

Her heart was thudding in her ears but somehow Jules managed to sound calm.

"Yes," she said softly. "I would. I'd be angry and bitter and frightened and resentful, and I'd wonder what kind of God would let this happen. I'd shout and I'd rage and I'd cry. Danny, I'm not saying that I'd be any different or any better. In fact, I'd probably not cope nearly as well as you have. But this isn't about me, is it? It's about you."

Jules rose to her feet. This was it. She had to speak before her courage wimped out on her.

"You've got a family who loves you and an amazing son. Maybe even a wife too, if you can work things through rather than flying into a rage. Danny, you still have a life to live, with people who care about you."

"Yeah, *I* do, but some of my mates didn't come out of it alive. Can you imagine how that makes me feel?"

Jules couldn't. "No, of course not. I can't ever imagine what you've been through. I wouldn't presume to pretend I can. But do you honestly think your comrades would have wanted you to drink yourself to death, rather than living?"

Danny said nothing. His mouth was a grim slash.

"Anything else you'd like to add?"

"Yes, actually. You're a hero, Danny Tremaine. I think so, your family thinks so and Morgan certainly thinks so. It's time to start acting like one. Have faith in yourself. There's nothing a man like you can't do."

And with her heart crashing in her chest Jules walked away from him, across the churchyard and through the little gate. With every step she took Jules could feel Danny's gaze boring into her back. He was absolutely livid – and as she'd already seen, an angry Danny was not good to be around.

Whatever had she done?

Chapter 12

Riding a horse when she was in a filthy temper was, as Mo knew from bitter and bruised experience, never a good idea. Horses are herd animals and finely tuned to the slightest tremor. So when Mo tacked up her youngster, Splash, and took him onto the cliffs for a blast, she already had millions of years of evolution working against her, never mind the confrontation with Cashley being on constant replay. The tension in her body transferred itself through her seat and anger fizzed through her reins; by the time she'd reached the first field, Splash was already spinning around like Kylie and snatching at the bit.

"Will you stand still!" snapped Mo, leaning forward out of the saddle and attempting to unfasten the gate. It was an impossible task. Every time she was within millimetres of success, her horse danced away or yanked so hard on the reins that she was almost pulled out of the saddle. With every tug and snatch, Mo grew hotter and crosser.

"For God's sake, Splashy! You've done this a thousand times," she said, exasperated. "Stand bloody still!"

But Splash, convinced even more now by the tone of his rider's voice that there really was a horse-eating monster lurking in the hedge, only upped the ante, his hooves striking sparks from the tarmac and egg-white foam flying from his bit. What Mo should have done, and what her logical voice was telling her to do, was dismount and open the gate that way. Alternatively, and more sensibly, she should just turn around and head back to the manège for an hour of schooling. Unfortunately Mo was still seething from the scene in The Ship and what she needed more than anything was a sprint so fast it ripped away all thought and tore tears from her eyes. Only when she was on the back of half a ton of galloping beast would she feel in control again. There was nothing that soothed Mo's soul like the drumming of hooves and the surging power of a horse, so she'd been determined to take Splash out for a run, even though over twenty years of experience told her this was probably not her best idea.

Finally, and after many frustrated attempts, Mo managed to hook the catch with her whip handle. The gate swung open into ten acres of pasture and Splash exploded through it in a series of bucks that would have had Buffalo Bill's rodeo show frantic to sign him on the spot. Already out of balance from wrestling with the gate, Mo didn't stand a chance of sitting these. She sailed through the air and landed with a heavy thud on the sun-baked earth, her breath punched out of her. With Splash's hooves dancing above her face, there was nothing Mo could do except hope that in his excitement he didn't catch her with a flying metal-tipped foot. That really would be the crappola icing on what was fast turning out to be a crappy day.

Sitting up slowly and with the green grass and blue sky doing a stomach-churning loop the loop, Mo watched her young eventer having a Desert Orchid moment as he raced up the field. Oh God, the long grass was being used for hay and concealed notoriously uneven ground. Mo prayed that Splash didn't slip or put a foot down a rabbit hole. She always cantered up the set-aside at the furthest edge before opening the next gate and then going at full pelt across the next two fields, but Splash didn't think like that. He just saw freedom. As her horse crested the hill, Mo staggered to her feet and hoped that Farmer Pete wasn't out working and that the top gate was closed. The last thing she needed was Splash heading for Fowey and trampling innocent cliff walkers…

Testing her limbs gingerly for damage, Mo decided that she was fine apart from a sore backside and even sorer pride. What a rookie mistake to make. She never, ever did things like this. Mo was a professional – she'd ridden round Badminton, for heaven's sake – and she knew better than to take stupid risks when she wasn't in a fit state of mind to be in the saddle. She was beyond furious with herself.

It was all Ashley Carstairs' fault, Mo decided bitterly as she dragged her aching body up the steep field leading to the cliff path. If he hadn't been so bloody smug and so arrogantly convinced that the future of Fernside was a done deal, she would never have risen to his taunting and put herself in such a foul mood. Summer Penhalligan hadn't helped either, of course, swanning about the place as though the past decade and Jake's broken heart had just been a minor blip. But really the majority of the blame lay with Cashley. Just thinking about how his eyes had swept her body as though she was a horse he was appraising, and recalling his sarcastic invitation to dinner, were enough to make her implode with anger. There was no way he would get his hands on the woods, no way at all. If Mo had to chain herself to a tree or hurl herself in front of a JCB, then she would. Well, either that or sneak into the boatyard when Jake wasn't looking and drill a few holes in the bottom of that ridiculous floating phallic symbol of his. *Big Rod* indeed. What an arse.

Absorbed in a very satisfying daydream where Ashley Carstairs was lost at sea in a mysterious boating tragedy and PAG managed to raise the funds to buy Fernside (perhaps Donald Trump or Richard Branson would come by Polwenna Bay?), Morwenna hardly noticed the throbbing in her right shoulder or that she was limping. Somehow she dragged herself to the top of the field where, mercifully, the gate was firmly shut and Splash, his reins broken and stirrups dangling, was snatching big greedy mouthfuls of grass. The horse whickered in recognition and then carried on guzzling grass while Mo ran a practised hand over his legs, heaving a sigh of relief that there didn't seem to be any damage. Headbutting her in greeting and covering her tee-shirt in acid-green slobber, Splash was up for the next stage of their adventure – but by now Mo had calmed down sufficiently to quit while she was ahead.

"Come on, you," she said, patting his glossy neck and gathering up what was left of the reins. "Let's just go back home, shall we?"

Limping down the field – Splash might not be lame but she certainly was – Mo concluded that she'd have to lunge her youngsters for the next day or two and ask a couple of keen pony-clubbers to help exercise the full liveries. As she was thinking this, she caught sight of a shiny white Range Rover parked up in her yard, and her heart plummeted into her welly boots. There was no mistaking a car that new and clean, or the private plate that read *3LLA*.

Ella St Milton, immaculate in cream jodhpurs and pristine Dubarry boots, was leaning on the yard gate and watching Mo. Although Ella's eyes were shielded by enormous Chanel shades, Mo just knew that the other woman was laughing at her. She must have seen the whole bucking-bronco show. Just bloody great, thought Mo wearily. Fate really must have it in for her today. Why couldn't Salmonella see her looking super smart in her dressage outfit and riding a nearly perfect test, or maybe flying through the heart-stopping water complex at Badminton? Why did it have to be a novice-style dumping and a tee-shirt covered in green slime that Ella would be able to sneer about?

There was no love lost between the two women; there never had been since Mo's Vidal Sassoon moment at school. Why Ella St Milton had turned up now was something of a mystery, as was her equestrian attire. As far as Mo knew, Ella hadn't ridden for donkey's years – and when she had, she hadn't been very good. All the expensive ponies and smart gear in the world couldn't disguise a wobbly seat and hands like cast iron.

"Well, that was an interesting display," Ella remarked when Mo reached the yard. "I thought three-day eventing was your thing, not stunt riding."

Ignoring her, Mo opened the gate and led Splash into his stable, where she proceeded to remove his tack. Unperturbed by this, Ella followed her and leaned over the half-door to watch.

"He's got more bondage gear than Christian Grey," she said idly as Mo slipped the martingale and breastplate over Splash's head. The bridle with its Dutch gag bit followed, and Ella's Botoxed brow attempted to frown. "Is that kit really necessary? It looks a bit cruel, if you don't mind me saying so. My trainer says that gadgets are overrated. He likes Parelli."

Oh great. Ella wanted to talk and, even worse, it sounded as though she was back into horses. Could this day get any worse?

"If your trainer wants to wrestle a sixteen-three Holsteiner around a cross-country course in just a head collar, then he can be my guest," Mo snapped. "Until then, I'll stick to what I know works, thanks."

Ella held up beautifully manicured hands that clearly hadn't been anywhere near a horse lately. "Touchy! Sorry I even mentioned it. I do worry that I love the animals too much sometimes. The trouble is that I've got a very soft heart."

Mo snorted rudely. At school Ella St Milton and her mean-girl posse had made Vladimir Putin look sentimental. She couldn't imagine that much had changed in the years since.

"I have!" Ella insisted. "Look, Mo, I know we haven't always been the best of friends—"

"Friends? Hardly. You did your best to make my life hell at school, remember?" Mo reminded her. "And you weren't exactly nice to Summer either, were you?"

"I think we both know that you managed to hold you own with a pair of scissors. Besides," Ella shot her a sharp glance from narrowed eyes, "you're not so worried about Summer these days, are you? She's hardly bothered with you since she left the village, and most of her clothes, behind. From what I can recall of it she wasn't very nice to Jake either, was she? Didn't he go to Australia because of her?"

Mo said nothing. What could she say? It was true. Summer had left Jake behind without so much as a backwards glance.

There was a silence in the stable, broken only by the occasional stamping hoof and steady munching as Mr Dandy tore into his hay net.

"It's time to move on from the past," Ella said. She reached in and stroked Splash's nose rather tentatively, her own nose wrinkling when she noticed the dirt on her fingers. "Look, I'll be honest, Morwenna: I'm not your greatest fan and I know you don't like me. But we do have something in common."

They did? Mo couldn't think what that might be. Chalk and cheese had more to talk about as far as she could see.

"I mean Jake," Ella continued, brushing her soiled hands on her breeches. "We both really care about him. I know that you Tremaines are a tightly knit bunch and protective as hell of each other – and I admire that, I really do. You wouldn't want Jake to be hurt again, would you?"

"What are you trying to say?"

"That I've seen him with Summer, and from the way it looked she's desperate to get her claws back into him again."

"That's rubbish! Jake wouldn't have anything to do with her again!" Even before the words had left her lips a little knot of unease was tightening deep in Mo's stomach. Jake had stuck up for Summer yesterday and her tender-hearted brother was just the kind of person who could be worked on. He wasn't a single-minded and ruthless type like Ashley Carstairs, for example. Mo couldn't imagine anyone crossing Cashley and being given a second chance. This thought made her shiver.

Ella shrugged. "So why was he buying her pasties and coffee in the harbour café earlier on?"

Morwenna stared at her. "You are kidding me?"

"No. It was like going back in time – only now Summer has a Premier League fiancé in tow, hasn't she? I doubt Justin Anderson will be thrilled."

Mo felt a cold queasy horror, of the kind she usually associated with opening bank statements or approaching big fences. If Summer broke Jake's heart again Australia wouldn't be far enough away for him.

"Listen, I'm not going to lie to you," said Ella, who during all their school years had done exactly that. "I like your brother, *really* like him, and I know he likes me too. Several times we've—"

"Too much information," said Mo quickly. She knew that women loved her brothers, but some things were far better left to the imagination. Ella had been after Jake for years, it was pretty much a family joke, and Jake shouldn't have encouraged her. The woman made hunt terriers look like they let go easily.

Ella laughed and tossed her silky blonde hair – like a mare in season, Mo couldn't help thinking. "Yes, well anyway, things were going really well until she arrived. I know you're no fan of mine, Mo, but surely you can see that being with me is a far better option for Jake? I live in Polwenna Bay, for a start, and I love the place. My life is here and my future too. I've got money that I want to invest in the place, and a local business – an ailing boatyard, for example – could be perfect."

Mo was impressed in spite of herself. "Are you related to Machiavelli by any chance?"

Ella's lip curled. "Machiavelli? Mere amateur." She stepped away from the loose box and glanced around the yard. Mo followed her gaze, wincing at the moss-filled gutters, weed-choked cobbles and flaking paintwork. Carl Hester's pad this was not.

"It must cost a fortune to run this place," Ella continued thoughtfully. "It can't be easy having to pay those entry fees and risk your neck breaking and schooling horses just to earn enough money to keep it ticking over."

"I manage," said Mo shortly. It was almost true, if robbing Peter to pay Paul could be called "managing". The problem was that both Peter and Paul were now skint too and had nothing left for her to rob. Losing her latest livery had meant a massive hole in Polwenna Equestrian's budget. Mo knew she was only weeks away from disaster, and she hated the fact that other people might know this too.

Ella picked a layer of paint from the stable door and raised a beautifully waxed eyebrow. "Really?"

Her temper simmering, Mo let herself out of the stable into the yard. Slinging her saddle onto the rack and draping the bridle across it, she spun round to face the other woman.

"I've not got the time to play games with you, Ella. We're not at school anymore. Why are you here?"

"To talk about livery? What else?"

"Livery? You've seriously got a horse? All that stuff about Parelli wasn't just made up?"

Ella placed her hand on her heart. "I'm offended, Mo. I've always loved horses."

This was blatantly untrue. When she'd fallen off at the local gymkhana Ella had swiftly lost interest in all things equine. Her pony, a gorgeous grey that Mo had secretly coveted, had vanished shortly afterwards and Ella had moved on to boys. As far as Mo knew, that hadn't changed.

"In actual fact I'm buying a horse. You might know it? He's evented and I'm told he has great potential."

Ella was buying an eventer? This was like hearing that Russell Brand had joined the Tory Party. Mo was stunned into silence.

"The horse is called The Bandmaster," Ella continued. "I've bought him from Alex Ennery. You've heard of him, I guess?"

Mo nodded. She'd heard of both the horse and the ex-Olympian who'd bred him. The Bandmaster was tipped for big things and must have cost Ella an absolute fortune. How hard had Mo walloped her head when she fell off just now? None of this made any sense. Ella didn't even ride.

"I'm not going to spare any expense making sure he goes to the top. I want the best yard and the best rider to compete him for me.

Polwenna Bay Hotel's Bandmaster is going to be fantastic publicity for our brand, and as a sponsor I'm going to make sure everything is done to get him in the ribbons. Maybe even to the next Olympics. Who knows? Whoever has my horse on livery and to ride will be pretty much getting a blank chequebook and a ticket to the big time." She looked Mo straight in the eye. "I think we both know where this conversation is going, don't we?"

There was a devil sitting on Mo's shoulder now. Ella was offering her everything she wanted. A lifeline for the yard, financial backing and a top-class horse that Mo knew had exactly what it took to put her right up there with Mary King and Zara Phillips. The Bandmaster jumped like he had springs on his hooves. Temptation whispered in Mo's ear.

"Why would you want to put him here? You don't like me, I'm not at Advanced Level this year and Alex Ennery's yard is only sixty miles away. That's less miles to travel too, if you want to compete. It doesn't make sense to move the horse to Cornwall."

Ella raised her eyes to heaven. "You haven't changed a bit, have you? It's still horses, horses, horses with you, isn't it?"

To be honest, Mo wasn't sure what else really counted in life apart from horses. She'd never felt any differently. Yes, of course there had been the odd boyfriend along the way – a hot farrier or vet could prove a great distraction for an hour or two – but the horses took up most of her spare time and all of her energy. Men didn't tend to like it if they weren't at the centre of her world, and Mo had yet to meet a man who wasn't either a pushover or as dedicated to his career as she was to hers. Therefore she was single and perfectly happy to be so. Mo was determined to get to the top of her sport; from what she could see from eventing friends whose careers had stalled when boyfriends and babies came along, anything serious would only get in the way.

She folded her arms and eyeballed Ella. "I don't understand your sudden interest in this. It doesn't make any sense."

"Let me spell it out then." Ella smiled, but it wasn't a warm smile; rather, it was the sort of smile a crocodile might give before gobbling up its prey. "We can call it a business transaction if that helps? I like Jake, very much, and I know that he likes me too but he's shy."

Shy? This didn't sound like Jake to Mo. Not interested was more like it.

"It doesn't help either that you don't like me," Ella continued. "Jake thinks the world of you and for some bizarre reason your opinion really counts with him. If you were to put in a good word for me it would make all the difference."

Mo goggled at her. "You'd spend a fortune on an eventer and give me the ride just to get in Jake's good books?"

Ella waved a hand as though hundreds of thousands of pounds were nothing. Then again, the woman had handbags that cost more than Mo's saddles, so it was probably all relative. "The horse is great publicity for the St Miltons and it can be written off through the business. Besides, Mummy's mad keen to be in the hospitality tent with Princess Anne and Zara."

Mo opened her mouth to tell Ella that the Princess Royal was far more likely to be found walking the course and cursing the tricky striding her ex had come up with than quaffing champagne in a smart tent, and that Zara would be actually riding – but then she shut it quickly. Who was she to shatter a dream?

"You'll also do a far better job than me at making sure Summer Penhalligan gets nowhere near Jake," Ella continued. "It's money for old rope, Mo, and you know it. So I don't know what you're waiting for. Jake and I would be great together; I've always known it. He just needs a little more encouragement."

Was she mad? wondered Mo. This was like a scene from a Jackie Collins novel.

"You must really want to be with my brother," she said.

"I don't take no for an answer and, believe me, I always get what I want," Ella agreed. Her words were edged with steel and Mo was almost tempted to bolt back into the stable and hide behind Splash. Ella was terrifying in her single-mindedness.

Ella held her hand out. "So, Morwenna Tremaine, do we have a deal?"

Mo hesitated. She thought about Summer and what her former friend had done to Jake, how she'd lied and walked away. Then Jake had left for years and they'd only just got him back. It would break Granny Alice's heart if he left again. Even Evil Ella had to be a better option than watching her brother getting tangled up with his ex. For once, horses didn't even come into Mo's thinking. Her career, The Bandmaster, saving the stables – none of this mattered nearly as much as making sure that Summer Penhalligan never hurt Jake again.

She took Ella's hand and shook it.

"We certainly do," Mo said.

Chapter 13

Summer waited a while before venturing into the village again. This was for two reasons: the first was that she really didn't want to bump into Morwenna and the second was that her spectacular black eye needed to subside before she could face her parents.

Summer knew that she could win an Oscar for her performance of *I Tripped Up and Hit My Face, Silly Old Me* but it wouldn't convince her parents for a second. While she waited for the bruise to fade from angry crimson to purple through to yellow, Summer kept herself busy reading the collection of dog-eared Mills and Boon novels that had been collecting dust on the shelf in the sitting room, and eating her way through the food parcels that her aunty had delivered. She was doing a lot of sleeping too, snuggling down beneath the heavy feather duvet in her crow's nest of a bedroom and waking three or even four hours later, dazed and sometimes disorientated, with her heart thudding as she struggled to remember where she was. It was only when she heard the gulls squabble or the chugging of diesel engines down in the harbour that her pulse slowed and she knew that she was safe.

Or rather, she'd think as her hand rested on her stomach, they were both safe.

Seeing the second line appear on the pregnancy test had been the push that Summer had needed. Instead of the excitement that should have swept through her, she'd felt her blood turn to ice water and her knees had buckled. The last time this had happened she'd been too young to know what to do; she'd been alone and totally let down by the one person she'd truly thought would have been there for her. She'd had no choices and when she'd made the appointment at the clinic, almost too blinded by tears to feed her coins into the payphone and dial the number, Summer really hadn't seen any other way out. This time it was different. She was older, she had money and there was a choice, albeit not an easy one.

The choice had been clear: stay to risk being hurt and bring an innocent being into her messy, dying relationship with Justin, or get out as soon as she could. The latter option was going to be tough. Summer knew Justin inside out and she was well aware that to him she was just another of his belongings. She was slightly more trouble than his Rolex and not nearly as much fun as his Ferrari, but she was his all the same – and Justin Anderson did not like letting go of anything he considered his. At some point he would come looking for her, of that there was no doubt. Summer could only hope that when he did she would be strong enough to stand up to him.

Thank God he didn't know about the baby. There was no chance she'd ever get away if Justin thought for a second that she was pregnant. Summer stared up at the ceiling and tried to focus on the black and white beams rather than the ugly scene that was playing out in the movie theatre of her memory. The beams blurred and danced as she blinked tears away. Summer didn't like to think too much about the worst thing that had happened – there was a very ugly word for it – but at least one good thing was coming from it. Besides, she couldn't help blaming herself sometimes too. Justin had said she drove him to do these things. Summer knew she should have had the guts to walk away a long time ago.

Now, in the safety of the little cottage, Summer tossed her latest saccharine romance across the room in disgust. Hearts and flowers had nothing to do with love. In her experience it more often meant betrayals and bruises. She was through with lying in bed and waiting for Patsy to drop off some more food. It was time to take action. If she sat in the passenger seat of her life for any longer Summer was afraid she'd forget how to drive.

It was early morning and the sky was rosy above the lichen-splattered rooftops. Seagulls were still snoozing on the chimney pots and the streets that teemed with visitors in the daytime were empty now save the odd dog walker. The paper shop was open but Summer didn't dare venture inside just in case a story had broken. So far she was fairly confident that her new haircut was doing a good job of disguising her, but the people who'd known her all her life – like that nosey old trout Sheila Keverne, for instance – wouldn't be fooled for a minute. Jake had spotted her in a heartbeat, but then again she'd have known him anywhere too. He was etched on her soul.

Etched on your soul? Summer scoffed at herself as she crossed over the narrow bridge and headed down towards the harbour. She needed a Mills and Boon detox if she was starting to think like one! Jake was no more than a childhood romance, and if her first love had grown up to make Brad Pitt look plain then surely that was better than him being fat and bald? She'd at least had good taste when she was in her teens. Jake wasn't her soulmate or her one who'd got away: he was just a guy she'd dated once and one who'd let her down pretty badly too, as it had turned out. It was being back home in Polwenna Bay that was making her nostalgic, that was all. Too many pink books with bare-chested brooding heroes and swooning heaving-bosomed maidens on the cover had turned her brain to mush – or maybe the pregnancy hormones were kicking in.

Still, Summer had half expected to see Jake again after their relaxed lunch in the Harbour View Café. It had been so easy spending time with him, the years peeling away like onion layers, and she'd been sure that he'd knock on the door for a chat or a cup of tea. After all, her cottage was practically in Seaspray's garden and he had to walk right past every time he went into the village or to the marina. Now she could only guess that he'd been being polite at the café and that he'd actually been horrified to see her again.

Well, either that or Mo had tied him to a chair and wasn't prepared to let him out until Summer was safely back in the big bad city. Summer couldn't help smiling at this thought. Knowing Mo of old, she could imagine her fiery friend doing exactly that. Summer was still sad that things between them were so broken, especially when Mo didn't know the full story, but she knew she couldn't dwell on the past any longer. Polwenna Bay was full of shadows, and in every doorway she saw a phantom of the girl she used to be. Although the years rolled by, the village never really changed. Sometimes this was comforting, but as a teenager Summer had found it frustrating in the extreme. She and Jake had dreamed of escaping and seeing the world – which they'd both done, of course, just not together as they'd planned. She sighed. There was no point raking over all that again. Mo and Jake had both made their feelings clear and she too had more important matters to think about. It was time to move on.

Nevertheless, Summer couldn't help pausing on the quayside. Shading her eyes with her hand, she scanned the marina just in case a familiar blond-haired figure was already there. It might only be eight-twenty in the morning but Jake liked to start work early.

Had liked, she reminded herself sharply. That was when he was eighteen. She had no idea what he liked to do now. These days he could lie in bed until noon for all she knew. Unbidden, an image of Jake, naked and tanned against white sheets and grinning up at her wickedly, flickered through Summer's memory. She pushed it away firmly and ignored the swift increase of her pulse. Hormones, she told herself; it was hormones making her think like this, that was all.

It was time to see her family, Summer decided, and endure their inevitable interrogation. It would have been fine if she'd only had to face her mother, but unusually *Penhalligan Girl* was still moored up, which meant that her father and the boys would be at home too. With the tide out the trawler was ungainly, fat bellied and balancing precariously on the wooden leg used to steady it. All the other fishing boats were out at sea and, ever a fisherman's daughter, Summer ran through a list of reasons why the boat might be in: hydraulic problems, belly out of the trawl, over quota for the month? She guessed she'd find out soon, once her father had got over his usual embarrassed gruffness sufficiently to talk.

Making her way to the small cottage built into the stone wall, Summer reflected that it couldn't have been easy for her father to have a Page Three pin-up for a daughter. She might call it feminism, a choice, a means to use her assets, but to Eddie Penhalligan it was his little girl that the lads were leering at, and all the money in the world wouldn't take that shame away. These were double standards, of course: Summer knew that her father's berth was stuffed with copies of *Playboy* and pictures of Katie Price back in her Jordan heyday, but the girls in those pictures were nothing to do with him. Not that Summer had ever reached the heady heights of *Playboy*, but she did have her own lingerie line and her calendar was always a bestseller.

"So much for bloody Shakespeare," Eddie had thundered on her first visit home, slamming a yellowed copy of *The Sun* onto the kitchen table. Even the blue and white stripy china on the dresser had leapt in fear. "I suppose they've written your vital statistics in blank bloody verse too, have they?"

"It's a tasteful picture," Summer had pleaded. It was too: you really couldn't see anything at all. Her arm was placed very strategically and the lighting had cast shadows in just the right places. She had thought she looked nice. "It's arty."

"Arty?" Eddie's face had been the same bright red as his fishing boat and a vein had protruded on his forehead. "Arty? It's porn, that's what it is, my girl! Porn!"

"You're being ridiculous. It's not porn; it's fashion." Summer had stood up to him for once. "Besides, the money was good."

"Well that's all right then." Eddie's eyes had been bulging so much at this point that Summer had feared he was about to have a stroke. "There's a picture of my daughter with her tits out that earned her good money! Jesus Christ!"

Summer hadn't bothered to come home very often since then. Interestingly, when she'd presented her father with a cheque to pay off *Penhalligan Girl* he hadn't objected quite so much. Nevertheless, things hadn't improved significantly in the years that followed. Summer had rarely been home and if Susie and Eddie came to London – which was even rarer, given that Eddie had a pathological terror of leaving Cornwall and an even greater fear of the big city – she paid for them to stay at Claridge's and met on neutral territory. Her father's initial reaction had always stayed with her. Summer had a horrible feeling that his respect for her was long gone and never to return, regardless of her property portfolio and impressive bank balance. He'd probably blame her for Justin's behaviour; perhaps he'd say that her early modelling shots were enough to drive any man into a jealous rage.

In her darkest moments Summer feared he was right. Was it her fault that Justin was insecure? Was she to blame for his rages? The logical part of Summer told her that this was nonsense and that the only person culpable here was Justin. Yet there was a small part of her, a part that was maybe still a teenager and in awe of her big and vocal father, that could never forget Eddie's furious words and that wondered…

Susie Penhalligan didn't seem surprised in the least to find her daughter on the doorstep, but simply pulled Summer inside and folded her into a big hug.

"Patsy told you I was here, then," Summer said, hugging her mum back and breathing in the familiar scent of washing powder and Anais Anais. Her eyes filled and there was a lump the size of a pasty in her throat. She was home again and it felt so familiar and safe. Summer couldn't remember how long it was since she'd felt safe.

"Of course she did. Patsy can't keep a secret to save her life; you know that."

Summer's face was still buried in her mother's shoulder.

"I'm sorry I didn't come sooner. I just had some… some stuff I needed to sort out first."

She gulped back a sob, not wanting to alarm Susie by crying. The Penhalligan family weren't criers. They tended to knuckle down and get on with things rather than *scritching*, as Eddie so sensitively put it. A lot of Summer's childhood had been spent pretending that skinned knees didn't hurt or that she wasn't upset when Ella was mean to her. When she'd made friends with the Tremaines, a family who didn't wear their hearts only on their sleeves but just about everywhere else too, it had been a revelation. Her stoic approach had been equally alien to them, and Jake had often complained that he never really knew how she felt. Summer guessed that she was good at keeping her real feelings under wraps, which was handy when she was in role but didn't always make communication easy in a relationship. Meeting Justin, who never enquired how she felt or what she thought, had been something of a relief until Summer had realised that he didn't ask because he simply wasn't interested. Just as his Rolex or his car didn't have a say, neither did the woman on his arm. By the time Summer had figured this out, it was far too late to complain. Instead she'd just acted the part of the perfect model girlfriend and hidden the bruises under expertly applied make-up. It had actually become a point of honour towards the end that nothing Justin said or did could make her cry. A bit like Obi-Wan Kenobi with Luke Skywalker, Summer's father had trained her well. She didn't show a flicker of emotion.

This wasn't always an advantage though. No wonder Mo's parting words all those years ago had been that she was *a cold bitch*. The words cut deeply, even all this time later. Mo had no idea that a calm face could in fact hide a heart that was fragmenting into a thousand bleeding pieces.

Susie Penhalligan knew her daughter well and wasn't the type of mother to make a scene.

"I knew you'd come home when you were ready," she said, dropping a kiss onto Summer's head. Stepping back, she frowned. "Sweetheart, you're so thin!"

Summer shrugged the concern away. Besides, she wouldn't be thin in seven months' time. "I've been busy. Work is hectic and you know I have to watch every mouthful. The camera puts on at least ten pounds."

"Hmm." Susie's brows were still drawn together and her mouth was set in a tight line as she looked at her daughter. "What happened to your face? Patsy said you had a shiner and for once she wasn't exaggerating."

"I just tripped and fell," Summer told her. This wasn't strictly a lie. "It was so silly. I headbutted the kitchen island." When it came to fibbing it always made sense just to include a little smudge of the truth. That way she wouldn't tie herself in knots. Anyway, her mother didn't need to know that Justin had played a major role in helping Summer on her way to making close contact with the finest Italian marble a bespoke kitchen could be made of. Susie might be small but she was five feet two of determined Cornish woman, and likely to take the next train to London and give Justin a piece of her mind. That was the last thing Summer needed right now. Justin was going to have to be handled with kid gloves, otherwise he'd descend on her with his savage attorneys – and she knew from experience that they could twist anything to look like a fact. Panic rose at the thought of what he might do and her hand moved instinctively to her stomach.

Fortunately Susie didn't notice this gesture. She was far too busy making disbelieving sounds and then pushing back Summer's hood, gasping when she saw her daughter's cropped head.

"Oh my God, your beautiful hair! What were you thinking?"

That I needed to hide, thought Summer. Aloud she said, "It's a change, Mum. It should get me noticed."

"It'll get you noticed, all right," Susie tutted. "Love, your hair was beautiful. It's your trademark! I can't believe you've cut it off. That might really affect your career!"

It was on the tip of Summer's tongue to shoot back that her career would have been affected far more if Justin had managed to batter her within an inch of her life, but she shut her mouth hastily. She didn't dare make comments like this. She recalled a time when he'd got into a fight with a younger team member, over something so trivial he couldn't even recall what it was when he'd calmed down. On that occasion Justin had managed to have his people frighten the other guy so much that the incident was never mentioned again. The broken nose and split lip were put down to a fall during training; the tabloids remained in blissful ignorance and football's golden boy continued to bask in the nation's love and adoration. He was a star player and worth a fortune. Sponsorship deals, advertising and the prestige of the team rested on his well-muscled shoulders. Summer knew that nothing would be allowed to jeopardise his reputation, especially an ex-glamour-model girlfriend who'd made her name by posing in her underwear. Nobody would believe her if she dared to tell the truth about football's most charming man. Justin would make sure she was totally destroyed.

No. She'd have to find another way to extricate herself. The problem was, she wasn't sure how long she had left to figure out what this would be.

While Susie continued to chastise her daughter for the radical haircut, Summer stepped from the heat of the porch, past pegs laden with yellow oilskins and mildewed raincoats, and down into the cool of the basement kitchen. The worn, cold flagstones underfoot, the ancient Aga slumbering in the corner, the chipped old sink and the rail hung with stripy tea towels were so familiar that for a moment she could have believed that the past twelve years had just been a weird dream. At any minute her brothers would come hurtling in to raid the fridge, their trainered feet stomping past the low window before they barged through the front door and down the stairs. Then they'd sit at the old pine table and moan about homework while Susie dished up huge portions of stew and tested Summer on the lines for her latest audition piece. Mo would be there too, calming down after the latest row with one of her siblings. Later on, once work at the marina was over for the day, Jake would join them for supper.

It alarmed Summer just how much she longed for this slip back in time to be real. Imagine if she could go back and start over. Would she make the same choices? Somehow, she didn't think so.

Summer sat down at the table in her old place nearest the window, where the red-checked curtains brushed against her as they lifted in the breeze. Meanwhile, Susie switched off the radio and filled the kettle. The kitchen was rich with the scent of bacon, the table still laden with plates and mugs and strewn with crumbs – all evidence of a hearty breakfast for hungry fishermen.

"Where is everyone?" Summer asked. Since the boat was in, she'd expected – dreaded, even – seeing her father today. If not at sea or holding court in the pub and ranting about the evils of the Common Fisheries Policy, Eddie Penhalligan was usually to be found sitting at the kitchen table flicking through a copy of *Fishing News* and bossing his wife about. Summer often thought her mother was either a saint or a total glutton for punishment. As Eddie was a creature of habit, it was most unusual for him not to be there. Her brothers were never very far away either. She frowned. "Why isn't the boat out with the rest of the fleet? It's flat calm out there."

The life of a fisherman's family was a hard one. When it came to income it was always a case of feast or famine. Every day that the weather was fair was a chance to go out to sea and hopefully haul a good catch of flickering silver treasure that would pay the mortgage and put food on the table for another few weeks. Unless there was a problem with the boat, it was unheard of for *Penhalligan Girl* to miss a day at sea.

Susie didn't say anything for a moment. Instead she busied herself placing the kettle on the hotplate and scooping dirty crockery from the table.

"Mum?" Summer leaned across and caught her mother's wrist. "What's wrong? Why isn't Dad at sea?"

There was a pause. Even the kitchen clock seemed to wait before embarking on its next tick. Then Susie sighed, let the plates clatter back onto the table and slid her slight frame onto the seat beside her daughter. Summer realised that she was holding her breath.

"Dad's not been out to sea for a while," her mother told her. She reached out and took one of Summer's hands in hers. It was as cold as the waves breaking below Cobble Cottage, and Summer's heart lurched.

"Is there something wrong with Dad?"

Susie couldn't look her daughter in the eye. "I didn't want to tell you over the phone – and, anyway, Dad was adamant that you didn't come home for any other reason than because you wanted to – but, yes, he's not been well. He's had a few problems with his heart."

Summer stared at her. It was news that Eddie actually had one.

"He had chest pains out at sea a couple of months ago. They had to come back in," Susie continued. Now that she looked more closely, Summer could see the hollows under her mother's eyes and the new lines that traced their way across her brow. "You know your father, Summer; he doesn't make a fuss, so we knew it must be bad. The boys radioed for help and Dr Kussell came down to the quay, took one look at Dad and called an ambulance."

Summer's eyes widened. "An ambulance? Dad went to hospital?" And they hadn't told her?

Her mother nodded. "It was a heart attack. Not the worst kind, thank goodness, but something called an NSTEMI. Dr Penwarren, that's our new GP, says it's like a warning heart attack. Apparently it's done a fair bit of damage already, so unless he takes it easy and makes some changes then the prognosis isn't great. Dad was hooked up to all sorts of machines for a couple of days while they ran tests on him. He was going mad. I thought we'd have to lash him to the hospital bed."

Summer could imagine. Her father hated being cooped up, never mind being told what to do. He would have made a bear with a sore head look good-tempered.

"I wish you'd told me," she said.

Her mother gave her a look. They rarely talked anyway and as far as her father was concerned she was hardly a part of the family. If she'd turned up at his bedside Eddie probably would have combusted with rage and had a full-on heart attack.

"He's going to have surgery at some point: angioplasty, I think they said it was called?" The kettle started to whistle and Susie rose to tend to it. As she put teabags into the flowery teapot that had lived in the Penhalligan kitchen for as long as Summer could remember and then sloshed hot water inside, Susie told Summer about the preventative measures Eddie Penhalligan was supposed to take while he waited for his name to reach the top of the operating list. No drinking, no smoking, no fatty food, some moderate exercise and absolutely no stress.

"As you can imagine, none of this has gone down well with your father," Susie concluded. She placed a mug of strong tea in front of Summer and then leaned against the Aga, curling her hands around her own mug. "I try to cook low-fat food but then Patsy tells me he's in the shop ordering sausage rolls. He's refused to stop smoking and is convinced that drinking halves means cutting down. Added to that, not being allowed to go to sea is making him even more tetchy than normal. I've tried to encourage him to go for walks on the cliffs and I bought us joint membership of the National Trust too, but he says he might as well be dead if this is all he's got to look forward to."

Summer nodded sympathetically. Drinking in The Ship and going to sea was her father's life. Personally, she thought Eddie Penhalligan was a selfish, sexist pig, but he was still her father and she hated to think of the big seafaring giant of a man that she knew reduced to pottering around tea shops and garden centres. She suspected that would finish him off far more thoroughly than any heart attack.

"Anyway, the boys take the boat now with Nick Tremaine, which is a good compromise. Your dad decides what grounds they should visit and helps them land, even though that's probably too physical." Susie took a sip of tea and tried to smile, but Summer wasn't fooled.

"So why's the boat in today?"

"The boys went out last night. Zak Tremaine's band was playing in the Merry Mackerel, and they didn't get in until really late. They were supposed to head out at dawn but Bobby was passed out and Joe was still half-cut. Even Nick was so hung-over he couldn't see straight. Your father went mad. There was no way he was letting them take the boat in that state, even if it meant losing a day at sea." She shook her head wearily. "You know how it is, sweetheart. Fishermen work hard and drink hard, but I sometimes worry that these boys take it too far. They're young and they think they're immortal. Jerry was the same."

Jerry had been Susie's brother, who'd gone missing with his boat when he was barely twenty years old. The wreckage had eventually washed up on the beach but there had been no sign of Jerry and in the end he'd been declared lost at sea. Even now, over forty years on, Summer's grandmother insisted on leaving the porch light burning just in case he came home. Summer shivered just thinking about the tragedy.

Susie finished her tea and placed her mug on the table with a thud.

"Anyway, enough of such miserable talk. The boys are mending the nets now and Dad's with them. He shouted so much this morning that I really thought he was going to have another heart attack, but at least he made his feelings clear. I could throttle the boys, though. They know that stress is the last thing he needs right now." She smiled at Summer. "Still, never mind the menfolk. What about you, sweetheart? I know this isn't just a social visit. Are you going to tell me the real reason why you're back in Polwenna Bay?"

Summer had played a doctor in the TV show *A&E* for two seasons, long enough to glean sufficient knowledge to understand that her father had a serious medical condition. Her mother was right: Eddie Penhalligan most certainly didn't need any more stress and anxiety.

"I'm tired and I just needed a rest," was all she said. "It felt like a good time to come home for a visit."

Summer knew there was absolutely no way she could let her parents know the truth about Justin now, or tell them about the baby. Her father's health issues, her mother's bitten nails and the pile of red bills wedged beneath the fruit bowl suggested that they had enough problems already. She couldn't add to them.

It looked as though she was well and truly on her own.

Chapter 14

A few hours earlier, while most of Polwenna Bay apart from fishermen and runaway celebrities was fast asleep, Jules Mathieson was being roused from her cosy bed by frantic hammering on the rectory's front door.

"I'm coming! I'm coming!" Jules called, kicking off the covers. Her heart thudding in time with the knocking on the door, she snatched up her dressing gown and shoved her feet into her slippers. Being a vicar entailed being prepared for any eventuality; parishioners had a habit of turning up in the small hours, their problems often far too pressing to wait until the daylight. Jules had realised long ago that sleeping naked (Hah! Not much point in that!) or in a cute nightie wasn't a good idea, hence this morning's fleecy and particularly unsexy pyjamas and the novelty pig slippers right by her bed.

Rubbing the sleep from her eyes, Jules stumbled down the stairs yawning and trying not to look in the hallway mirror. She knew that her hair would be standing on end, her eyes would be panda-ed with yesterday's mascara and her bright red dressing gown would make her look like a walking Edam cheese. Why bother to confirm it? Besides, Sheila Keverne, or whichever busybody it was today who'd decided to get the new vicar out of bed at dawn, wouldn't care what she looked like.

"Just a minute," Jules promised as she fumbled with the lock and the chain. Unlike most of the Polwenna residents, who'd never locked their houses in their lives, Jules had experienced city life and old suspicions died hard. Polwenna Bay didn't appear as though it harboured axe murderers or burglars, but you could never be too sure. Besides, if the legends were to be believed, most of her flock were descended from wreckers and smugglers.

The bolt slipped back, the chain clattered against the glass and finally the door swung open. For a moment Jules thought she was still asleep, and she had to rub her eyes again just to make sure. This certainly wasn't Sheila Keverne who was standing on her doorstep at five-thirty in the morning and looking as though being there was the most natural thing in the world.

"Morning, Vicar," said Danny Tremaine cheerfully. "Have you got a moment?"

Jules's mouth fell open. Not only was Danny outside her house at a ridiculously early hour, but he also was freshly shaven and smelling of soap and something lemony rather than drink – and the uninjured part of his face was smiling at her. A black beanie hat perched jauntily on his golden head and his lean body was dressed in trendy sports gear. Morgan, clutching a sophisticated digital camera, was standing beside him and snapping away merrily. Jules felt a bit like Julia Roberts's character in *Notting Hill* being faced by the press pack – except that Jules was much fatter and far more horrified than a gorgeous Hollywood A-lister.

"What on earth are you doing here?"

"And a good morning to you too, Vicar!" replied Danny. His good eye was the same bright blue as the sea that churned endlessly in the distance behind his right shoulder, and his generous mouth was curling upwards into a grin. "Fancy a walk on the cliffs? Morgan and I thought we'd come and show you the beauty of God's glorious creation on this lovely morning."

"God doesn't exist." Morgan was too busy fiddling with his camera to look up. "Fact."

"Not fact, mate. That's just your belief," said Danny. "There's no evidence either way – isn't that right, Vicar? Which is where faith comes in; we have to have faith sometimes, don't we? Even if it doesn't come easy," he added calmly, ruffling his son's hair but still looking at Jules. "Somebody told me that, and quite recently too, I think. Having faith, believing in something, is important. Wouldn't you agree, Vicar?"

Morgan ducked his head away and continued to twiddle with the camera. He was completely absorbed, Jules noticed, and would no doubt be able to give Mario Testino a run for his money in no time at all.

"My dad says you can help him," said Morgan. He looked up. "Can you?"

Jules stared back at Danny, whose gaze was unflinching. Hearing her words lobbed back at her from a man whose dreadful injuries were even more marked in the clean early light, and when he wasn't drunk, made her stomach knot with shame. Who on earth did she think she was to even dare comment, never mind pass judgement on him? When things were tough she couldn't even cope with walking past the biscuit tin without reaching for a cookie, and there was nothing wrong with her. Seeing him now – the livid scars, the closed-up eye, the empty sleeve –humbled her. No wonder Danny had needed the pub. Talk about the sin of pride.

She hung her head. "I'm sorry, Danny. I shouldn't have said those things to you. I didn't have any right."

"Bollocks," said Danny firmly. "You had every right. I've been behaving like an arse and don't deny it; I know it's true. Everyone's usually far too scared to say anything, either in case they push me even closer to the brink or because they're awed by the whole war-hero crap and don't know what to say. How do you dare tell off a man who gave his arm and half his face for his country?"

"It's not crap, Dad: you are a hero," said Morgan, without looking up from his camera. "But you drink far too much alcohol. Fact."

Danny grimaced. "I'm working on it son, OK?"

"OK," said Morgan. "Now can I take some photos?"

"Sure," nodded Danny. To Jules he added softly, "Even my son wants me to get my shit together. I can't argue with that, can I?"

"I guess not," Jules agreed. Then, watching Morgan wander away to start snapping at the view from the churchyard, she asked, "What's with the camera?"

"I think it's Symon's – but Morgan seems to have taken to it, so I guess Sy can kiss that baby goodbye for a good few months. Photography looks set to be Morgan's new obsession, which I must say is something of a relief." Danny grinned at her and it was like the sun had slipped out from behind a cloud. Jules was taken aback by how his face transformed. "Until recently he was into learning all about linguistics. Apart from swearing, at which I am a sodding expert, I'm hopeless at that."

"Yes, your swearing the other night was some of the best I've ever heard," she deadpanned.

"See? I do have other talents apart from the army. There's hope for me yet," laughed Danny. He had a nice laugh, Jules thought. It was rich and warm and rippling, the mirth equivalent of a Cadbury's Flake. She'd like to hear that laugh again. Apart from being much nicer than the swearing and shouting, it was contagious; she found that she wanted to join in.

He stepped forward and laid his hand on her arm. "Seriously though, Vicar, what you said? About living my life? I can't stop thinking about that."

Jules felt her cheeks start to heat up. "Danny, I'm sorry. What do I know about what you've been through?"

"You watch the news, you're intelligent, you have an opinion and you don't know me." Danny's words cut through her protests like a hot knife through rope. "Yes, I'm fucking pissed off with Tara, my face is a mess and my career's over, but you're right: *I'm* still here. I can see my son grow up and I can spend time with my family. Unlike some of my men, who only got to come home in Union Jack draped coffins; I'm still alive, aren't I? Shit, who'd have thought it? I'm actually the lucky one. But why me and not them? How's that fair or just?"

"Danny, I don't know. Maybe that's something only God can understand?"

His lips twitched. "Yeah, right. Maybe we'll leave that discussion for another day. All I know is that everything in my world is upside down."

Jules didn't say anything. She didn't need to because she was sure that Danny was figuring it all out just fine on his own. The sun chose to peek over the top of the valley at this point, slicing the sky with the pink and gold of a new day.

Her heart rose. A new start?

"If there was ever a sign," breathed Danny. "Look, Vicar—"

"Please, call me Jules," she interrupted. "'Vicar' makes me feel like I'm about a hundred years old."

"OK. Jules it is then." He paused for a moment, searching for the right words, before pressing on. "Look, on Sunday night I didn't drink a drop and I didn't sleep much either. I never do these days. It was bloody awful and I'm not going to pretend otherwise, but somehow I made it through the night without my mate Jack Daniel's. Then I started thinking that if I could do it for one night I could do it again, and again. So I did." His face was flushed with the sense of achievement. "I didn't have a drink, Jules! I haven't had one for several days now, and I'll do my best not to have another – although I'm not expecting it to be easy. Of course I'm a mess. I was in a fucking warzone and I saw my friends blown to pieces, for Christ's sake. Sorry for blaspheming, Vic – I mean Jules. But I've lost my wife, I've lost an arm and I don't even look like the man Tara married. I'm in pain from the injuries and I don't sleep because I have nightmares. Drinking's been my way of taking the edge off some of it, but I know I can't go on like this."

Jules was feeling totally out of her depth. What did she know about post-traumatic stress or the experiences of people who'd seen active service?

"I'll make an appointment to see a counsellor again," Danny continued. "I'll listen to what they say and I'll follow the advice of my doctor too. I'll take my medicines, do my exercises and I'll play ball. Jules, I promise that I'll do everything I can to pull it together. I'll do it for Morgan and for my friends. OK?"

"OK," Jules echoed, feeling stunned. This seemed like a pretty dramatic turnaround to her, as well as the most extreme answer to prayer she could have imagined.

"I don't think I need shrinks and I don't think I need drugs either, but then again I wasn't doing so well on my own, so this time I'll do what the experts say I'm supposed to," Danny was telling her. There was a light in his eye now, akin to the light that shone in the eyes of Jules's evangelical colleagues. His hand tightened on her arm. "What I know that I do need, though, is someone to help me take my mind off it all – and that's where you come in."

She did? It took all sorts, but somehow Jules didn't have Danny Tremaine pegged as the type who'd want to sign up for an Alpha Course or join the brass-cleaning rota.

"Me? How exactly can I help?"

"I need to be focused on anything but the pub and booze," Danny explained. He wasn't laughing now. Instead a determined expression had settled across his face. He had the same high cheekbones as Issie and Jake, Jules noticed, and the same dimples too. Even with his injuries, Danny Tremaine was still a striking guy. If only he could see that.

"If I go anywhere near The Ship I'll be staring at the bottom of a glass before you can say 'pisshead'," Danny confessed with a rueful shrug. "Pathetic I know, but that's the truth – and I figure admitting it's half the battle, right? What I need is a distraction, something else to focus on, which is where you come in. You and I could really help each other out here." His hand rose to grab her shoulder in excitement. "Jules! You're the one! You're perfect!"

Eh? What on earth did he mean by this? Jules glanced down at her fleecy dressing gown and novelty pig slippers, and her blush deepened. Perfect? Hardly!

Hang on a minute. Was he suggesting that he and she…

Implying that they…

Did he think they could…

Jules's imagination was in overdrive now. Images that no vicar should ever conjure up whizzed through her mind's eye as though her reading matter of choice had zoomed from the Bible to *Fifty Shades* in a millisecond.

He couldn't mean *that*?

Surely not?

Luckily, before she had the chance to say anything at all and make an idiot of herself in the process, Danny was launching into a speech. He was revealing an idea that he'd obviously put a lot of time and thought into.

"Now, Morgan tells me that you want to lose weight? I want to keep busy, so how about you and I team up and help each other out? I know a lot about fitness and I need to exercise more too, to get my strength back into my leg and keep myself out of the pub. We could meet every day and walk on the cliffs for an hour or use the steps by the church as a workout. We could even swim if it was warm enough!"

He looked so eager that Jules didn't have the heart to point out that she was about as athletic as an arthritic slug and probably the worst choice ever for a fitness buddy. Besides, she hated getting up early. Morning Prayer was bad enough. The Lord had not blessed her with the gift of joyous early rising.

"I only mentioned my weight to Issie and in passing," she protested. "I'm amazed Morgan remembered it."

Danny laughed. "That would be enough for Morgan. He never forgets anything. The boy's got an amazing memory. So, come on, what do you think? Am I or am I not a bloody genius?"

Jules was trying to think of an excuse. "I can't run."

He pointed to his leg. "What makes you think I can? Anyway, who mentioned running? It's going to be a glorious morning. Grab your costume; let's swim in the rock pool!"

Jules crossed her arms mutinously. "No way. Anyhow, I can't swim."

"So I'll teach you. Next excuse?"

"I'm busy?"

"Jules, it's quarter to six in the morning. You wouldn't even be up usually. Next?"

She shook her head. "Do you know what? I think I preferred you when you were drunk and swearing."

"Tough. Those days are behind me, or at least they will be if you'll help." Danny lowered his voice. "Seriously, Jules, I mean it. I really want to change but I'm not sure if I can do it alone. I'm fucking scared, if you want the truth. I know it's too late for Tara and me, but I want to be the father Morgan deserves. You've seen him; he's not like other kids and he needs me. You were spot on. I have been given a second chance, but I'm shit-scared I'm going to blow it on my own. My family is too close; they suffocate me. But you understand. You get it. Jules, I can't explain it but I have a really strong feeling that you and I can help each other. Please, I need you on my side."

It was on the tip of Jules's tongue to refuse point blank. After all, she hated exercise, hardly knew Danny Tremaine (and what she did know wasn't exactly encouraging) and she had a sermon to write as well as a parish council meeting to plan. The thought of going back upstairs and burrowing beneath her duvet to catch another hour's sleep was also a very tempting one. Yes, this was exactly what Jules wanted to do, so why wasn't she telling him thanks but no thanks?

Because, whispered a small voice deep down inside of her, you've been praying really hard to lose weight. And didn't you pray for Danny Tremaine too?

"Well?" said Danny. "What do you say?"

Jules was trembling. This was all a coincidence too far. One thing she knew for certain was that when it came to her boss up there, there were no coincidences – just answers to prayer. What if God, who had a very good sense of humour, had decided to answer both her prayers at once?

Standing on her doorstep in her fleecy pyjamas, silly slippers and bright red dressing gown, Jules knew exactly what her answer had to be and it made her groan.

"I'm probably going to regret this," she said slowly, "but OK then. Let's see if we can help each other."

"Brilliant!" Danny beamed at her and in that instant Jules saw a glimpse of the energetic and vital man he'd been before his injuries. "That's bloody fantastic. You won't regret it, I promise. Well, go on then! Get changed! What are you waiting for?"

Morgan, camera in hand, came racing over when he heard his father's excitement. "Is she coming, Dad?"

Danny smiled at him. "She certainly is, my boy!"

"You want to start right now?" Jules had hoped to at least have twenty-four hours to get her head around this new arrangement – maybe even pop into Plymouth and buy some new sports gear. But it seemed that the Tremaines, a bit like the time and tide, waited for no one. Not even vicars.

Morgan raised his eyes, the same blue as his father's, to the sky and then gave her an impatient look.

"Of course right now! Come *on*! You're wasting time. The light is just right. I'll take some pictures of you. We can do before and after!"

"No time like the present," added Danny.

Jules felt as though she was having a very odd trip. The last time she'd seen Danny, hadn't she been incredibly rude to him and overstepped her mark as a pastor too? She'd expected him to come back half-cut and give her a mouthful of abuse, not show up at the crack of dawn wanting to be friends and to propose they work together to solve their respective problems. Seriously, she thought as she hauled herself back up the stairs to change into her leggings and trainers, life as an inner-city vicar had been a breeze in comparison to being at Polwenna Bay. This Cornish parish was a whole new challenge.

She really hoped she was up to the job.

Chapter 15

"You're a bloody idiot," Jake said to Nick as he fought the urge to grab his younger brother and give him a hard shake. In fact if Nick hadn't been so hung-over that he was likely to vomit everywhere, and if Jake hadn't spent hours yesterday cleaning the marina office, this was exactly what he would have done.

"Don't shout," Nick groaned, massaging his temples and sinking onto a chair. "My head is killing me."

Jake shot his brother a pointed look. "Maybe you should hope your head makes a good job of it before Eddie Penhalligan comes back for another of his special staff briefings?"

Nick turned even greener at this thought. "Christ, I thought he was going to have another heart attack, he was shouting so loudly."

"Do you blame him? Jesus, Nick. What sort of idiot takes a trawler out when they're half pissed?"

Jake's own head was starting to pound. What a start to the day, arriving on the quayside and finding his brother in the middle of another Penhalligan family fracas. Big Eddie was famous for his hot temper and flying fists, and his roars of fury could be heard halfway to Seaspray. Even though it had been early in the morning, a small crowd had already gathered and at the windows of the holiday cottages nervous faces had been peering out to see what all the noise was about. By the time Jake had neared the scene, Big Eddie had been holding Nick by the scruff of his neck while Eddie's boys Joe and Bobby did their best to pull their father away.

Jake leant against the desk and exhaled wearily. Big Eddie's face had been dangerously red. His eyes had bulged like squid and a vein had throbbed in his temple as he'd yelled at his ashen-faced crew. Nick, who was the acting skipper while Eddie was off sick, had taken the brunt of his wrath; at one point Jake had really thought his brother was about to be throttled. No matter how hard Susie had pleaded with her husband to calm down and think of his heart, Eddie had only grown louder and more incensed. In the end, Jake hadn't had much choice but to wade in and rescue his brother. Eddie hadn't appreciated this interference in the slightest, and his swift right hook had caught Jake smack on the jaw. Still, once Nick was extricated and Jake had learned why Eddie was so angry, he hadn't blamed the older man one bit.

He crossed the office and, opening up the small fridge, withdrew a freezer block from the ice compartment and held it against his face. Just great. Now it looked like he'd been brawling. Alice would have a fit.

"Any water in there?" asked Nick. Rigger boots up on the desk now and leaning right back in his chair with his eyes closed, he was the picture of insouciance, seemingly oblivious to the chaos he'd caused and the potential there had been for tragedy. Jake couldn't help himself; pulling out a bottle of Evian and unscrewing the lid, he tipped the contents right over his brother's head.

"What the—" Shocked by the icy drenching, Nick leapt to his feet, spluttering and shaking droplets from his hair. He rounded on Jake, furiously. "What the fuck did you do that for?"

"To sober you up." Lobbing the bottle into the bin, Jake crossed his arms and glared at his brother. "What the hell are you playing at, going to sea drunk? Have you got a death wish?"

Nick, busy mopping his face on the sleeve of his smock, grimaced.

"Chillax, Jake. I wasn't drunk, just a touch hung-over. I'd have been fine to take the boat, especially after some tea and a bacon sarnie. Eddie totally overreacted."

Jake inhaled and counted to ten. "Eddie did not overreact. You're the skipper, Nick. You need to be one hundred per cent alert when you're out at sea. Christ, you know that as well as anyone. One mistake is all it takes. You've got Eddie's sons and his livelihood out there. How could you even think of leaving the harbour in this state?"

"I'm not in a state," Nick insisted, although his sallow face and bloodshot eyes told a very different story. "We had a bit of a heavy night, that was all."

"On a week night?"

Nick looked at his brother as though Jake was a century old, which was exactly how he was starting to feel right now with his throbbing face. Given that he'd had several sleepless nights lately too, the reason for which he hardly dared admit, he could probably add another decade to that.

"Duh. It's the festival," Nick said, as though explaining something simple to an idiot. "Of course we were out. The Tinners were playing and the beer was two pounds a pint in The Ship." He released his ponytail from its rubber band, then shook his head like a dog before flipping his hair back again as if imitating a L'Oréal advert. Even with a savage hangover and after a soaking he looked like a male model.

"If you think I'm in a state then you should see the Penhalligan brothers. They're hanging. Joe even had Guinness for breakfast," added Nick, as though this made everything all right.

Hearing about Joe's liquid breakfast didn't make Jake feel any better. "But *you're* the skipper, Nick. Their safety is your responsibility. Going on the piss in the middle of the working week is just irresponsible. There's going to be a tragedy if you don't grow up; you can't take risks when you're at sea. I wouldn't blame Eddie if he sacked the lot of you."

Nick looked resentful and a little bit ashamed. Jake knew that deep down his brother realised he was in the wrong but, being stubborn and hot-headed, Nick hated to admit it. He took after Mo in that respect.

"I wasn't thinking," he muttered.

"No, you were too drunk to think at all," agreed Jake. He glanced at his diver's watch and saw that it was still early. Outside the office the sun was just waking up and a gentle swell was lifting the boats and clinking the halyards. "If I know Eddie he'll be on *Penhalligan Girl* and cracking the whip. You need to get your ass over there and grovel like you've never grovelled before if you want to still have a job."

Nick sighed and nodded, wincing with the movement of his head.

Once his brother had gone, whipping on a pair of Oakley's the moment he stepped into the sunshine as if he were Dracula braving the daylight, Jake collapsed at his desk and placed his head in his hands. What a week.

His eyes felt gritty from lack of sleep and his body jittery from far too much caffeine. At least, he hoped it was from the caffeine rather than from knowing that Summer Penhalligan was staying only several hundred yards away from him. Ever since their pasty-fuelled truce at the Harbour View Café Jake had gone out of his way to make sure that he avoided the cliff path and headed out to work early in order not to bump into her. It wasn't that he didn't want to see Summer – far from it. Whenever he thought of her, something in Jake's chest clenched tightly and he felt the ground beneath his boots turn to quicksand. For every second that he'd spent with her on the day of their chance meeting on the cliff top, he'd drunk her in like a man who hadn't seen water for a month. He was appalled by just how easy, how right, it had felt to be with her again and by the way that his body still knew hers so well. The scent of her skin was like warm summer grass; the curve of her cheek cried out to be touched by his hand. And then there was the swell of her breast... Jake put the brakes on sharply here as he felt a rush of blood migrate south. Time to derail this particular train of thought. She was absolutely gorgeous, though. If anything, the passing years and the short hair made her even more so, and he'd had to dredge up every drop of self-control he'd possessed not to pull her into his arms and tell her she had to stay with him, that he was never letting her out of his sight again. Jake knew just how she would feel against him, her full breasts soft against his chest, her hips moulding perfectly to his own as the heat flared between them, those rock-pool green eyes staring up at him…

Jake groaned. This was ridiculous. Summer wasn't the same girl who'd walked away from him twelve years ago, however much his senses and his heart might try to tell him otherwise. She was a celebrity and the fiancée of Justin Anderson. She didn't belong in his world any more than he belonged in hers.

Yet the bruise on her face hinted that A-list paradise might not be all that it seemed. Jake brimmed with rage to think that anyone might have hurt her. He'd done his best not to make a big issue of it because Summer had made it very clear that she didn't want to talk. Jake knew when to push and when to step away, and Summer had definitely been giving him *back off* signals. Somebody in her life wasn't listening to her and, however concerned he was, Jake was determined not to join them. Besides, if she trusted him she'd have told the truth. Jake's feelings for

Summer were more knotted and intricate than any nets that Nick could rig, and even more complicated to mend.

She'd be gone soon, he reminded himself; there was no point trying to be friends or to put the past to rest. Summer no longer belonged at Polwenna Bay. With any luck he would be able to avoid her. There was certainly a lot of work to do at the marina, more than enough to distract him from thoughts of her soft skin and how it would feel naked against his.

Enough was enough! Furious with himself for even seeing this road, never mind going down it, Jake abandoned the office for the cool morning air and the calling gulls. It was far too easy for his mind to wander while he was doing bookwork; what was required was some physical activity – well, either that or a cold shower. The next best thing was a hosepipe and some washing down of boats so that they would be sparkling and spotless when their owners arrived. Several buckets of boat-wash and a good couple of hours of hard scrubbing were exactly what he needed.

If anyone was ever under the illusion that working with boats was a glamorous occupation, Jake was sure that spending just ten minutes with him would have shattered that dream. His job most definitely didn't consist of zooming about all day in a sexy speedboat and being surrounded by girls clad in skimpy bikinis, as people liked to imagine. Having spent an hour trying to balance the books but failing miserably, he then got filthy crawling around the bilge in a customer's boat, cut his hand trying to free a seized winch and finally stripped down to his board shorts in order to scrub several boats ready for their owners' arrival at the weekend. By the time he was finishing off Cashley's – hosing the boat-wash from the deck and casting a careful eye over the gleaming fibreglass just in case, God forbid, there might be any marks – Jake was soaking from both water and perspiration. His long hair had twisted into corkscrew curls and even his deck shoes were sodden. Glamorous it was not, and so far not one Victoria's Secret Angel type had wiggled over in her swimsuit and asked if she could pose with him on the pontoon. Such was life!

As the unusually warm May sun shone down, Jake tried to ignore his aching muscles and told himself that at least he'd be getting a tan out of the morning's exertions. The sea beyond the harbour wall was sparkling like jewellery and the village basked sleepily in the golden sunshine. He really shouldn't complain, Jake reminded himself as he collected up his buckets and brushes. After all, how many people had a view like this from their office?

"That looks like hot work!"

Jake looked up, shielding his eyes from the glare of the sunshine, to see Ella St Milton standing on the pontoon. With the light turning her blonde hair to pure gold, her blue mirrored Rayban aviators giving her an alien look and her long brown legs topped by denim cut-offs so short he could almost see her knickers, she looked as though she'd stepped off the set of *Barbarella*. Ella didn't seem to be dressed for boating, especially since she was wearing spiky-heeled sandals. They'd wreck the deck.

"Ella! Hi!" Jake was surprised to see Ella at the marina and even more surprised to see her smiling. After those sharp comments about Summer and the look she'd given him that could have curdled milk, he'd been expecting at best the cold shoulder and at worst some kind of revenge that wouldn't be out of place in a Shakespearean tragedy.

"Did you want *Polwenna Princess* ready for today?" Jake wasn't sure if this was a social visit or a business one. He glanced at his watch and did a quick mental calculation. "If you give me forty minutes I can have her fuelled up, clean and ready to go."

Ella laughed and pushed her sunglasses on top of her head. "Don't look so serious. I haven't come to see the boat. I've come to see you." Her eyes flickered over his wet and gleaming torso and her pupils darkened. "I'm glad I did too. You're Polwenna's own version of the Dreamboys, working half naked like that. You'll give the lady *emmets* heart attacks."

Jake glanced down at his drenched board shorts and sodden Sebagos. "More like a drowned rat, I think, but thanks for the compliment all the same."

He leapt from the boat and onto the pontoon, trying not to notice how the swaying motion made Ella's full breasts jiggle. In fairness, it was hard not to notice: she had the twins racked up and displayed to full effect in a tight white vest, over the edge of which they rose like two scoops of vanilla ice cream. Jake looked away quickly and pretended to be preoccupied with rinsing out his sponges and stowing the buckets away, while Ella chatted easily about the hotel. She made no mention of Summer, which was odd given that when they'd last met Ella had been more or less threatening to call the paps. Jake found himself starting to wonder whether she was a bit unbalanced. There was certainly something of the mad, bad and dangerous to know about her.

"I'm sure this will be the best tourist season for several years," she was concluding. "The hotel is booked solid right the way through to September."

"I really hope you're right," Jake said with feeling. The Tremaines were dependent on the holidaymakers for their income stream, and two consecutive gloomy summers had definitely taken their toll.

Ella's face wore a sympathetic expression and she laid a perfectly manicured hand on his arm.

"Are things still tough with the business?"

"No, no; it's all looking fine," fibbed Jake. The last thing he wanted was for the St Miltons to smell blood. The way they circled an ailing business made Jaws look like a vegan. Unbeknownst to the rest of Jake's family, his father had already propped up the business by borrowing far too much money from Andrew St Milton. So, as well as feeling sick whenever he looked at the rapidly compounding interest, Jake was in constant terror that the loan would be called in. The business simply had no means of repaying it; the only solution would be to sell the family home.

Note to self, thought Jake. Don't upset Andrew's precious only daughter. He'd have to tread very carefully.

"Good," said Ella. She checked her glittery Omega watch. "Look, it's nearly lunchtime. Fancy grabbing a bite to eat?"

The way her small pink tongue whisked over her lips as she spoke suggested that it wasn't just lunch she fancied eating. In spite of everything, Jake was tempted, if only for a split second. Ella was sexy, in a lean and rapacious way. She had great boobs, was dynamite in bed, liked to push the boundaries in a really exciting way and, as the icing on the cake, was loaded too. Most men would leap at the chance of some no-strings fun with a woman like her.

The trouble was that Jake wasn't most men. Besides, he suspected that no-strings fun wasn't what Ella was looking for. Maybe it never had been and she was just playing the long game? This thought made him very uneasy. Ella was attractive and clever, but there was a steely determination in her eyes and she had the oddest knack of always accidentally turning up wherever he happened to be.

Maybe it wasn't quite as accidental as he thought?

Morwenna, unexpectedly, had suddenly become Ella's biggest advocate. When his sister had suggested over supper that Jake should invite Ella up to Seaspray for a dinner party, he hadn't been sure what had alarmed him most: Mo's offer to cook, when she was someone who could burn water, or her sudden championing of the girl she'd spent most of her life loathing. For as long as Jake could remember, his sister and Ella's relationship had been so hostile it had made the Montagues and the Capulets look chummy.

When Jake had managed to retrieve his jaw from the kitchen table and Alice had collapsed into a chair with the shock, he'd asked his sister what on earth was going on. Mo had merely fobbed him off with a line about everyone deserving a second chance and Ella being "all right, really". She hadn't been able to look him in the eye as she'd said this, though.

The whole thing was fishier than *Penhalligan Girl*.

There was also the issue of Summer. Jake knew it was ridiculous but he just couldn't get her out of his head: the way she laughed, the scent of her skin, the way her eyes were a thousand different shades of green…

"We could just pop over to the café and grab a prawn roll?" Ella was suggesting, her fingers on his arm tightening a little and derailing this rather unnerving train of thought. "I haven't got time for a proper lunch and, anyway, I'm watching my figure."

Ella was so slim she made Victoria Beckham look hefty. She couldn't have fished more for a compliment if she'd borrowed a trawler.

"Your figure's fantastic," Jake said dutifully, and was rewarded with a blush. Immediately he knew that this was dangerous territory and that he ought to step right back. He didn't want to toy with Ella's feelings. That wouldn't be fair, but on the other hand neither did he want to risk upsetting her father. Jake knew that he needed to watch his step. "A prawn roll sounds great," he said.

Although it was only just approaching noon, the harbour tearoom was already bustling. All the outside tables were already taken, so Jake and Ella carried their prawn rolls and mugs of tea down onto the slipway where an old wooden bench was settled against the bulging whitewashed wall of a fisherman's cottage. The sun warmed their faces and as they ate they watched two swans glide over hopefully. Ella, who was just picking out and eating the lettuce, threw most of her bread to them and shrieked when a squadron of beady-eyed seagulls dive-bombed her.

"You should know better than that," admonished Jake. His sandwich was delicious, the prawns fat and pink and practically doing breast stroke in the Marie Rose sauce. There was no way he was wasting a mouthful on the bird life!

Ella nodded. "I know, but it's better they eat the carbs than I do. Bread is the devil according to my trainer."

Personally Jake thought Ella's trainer sounded like a knob. Bread was bloody great so far as he was concerned – especially the loaves that his gran baked. He thought of them now, all warm and yeasty from the oven, sliced open and smothered with curls of sunshine-yellow Cornish butter. He glanced at Ella. She was too thin, in his opinion.

"Jake, you know it's the Polwenna Bay Hotel ball soon?" Ella was saying nonchalantly.

He nodded. Everybody knew about that. Each June the St Miltons threw a huge charity fundraising ball at their five-star hotel, opening up the beautiful clifftop gardens to the public, dedicating their Michelin-starred kitchen staff to putting on the most exquisite food, and letting champagne flow faster than the River Wenn. Although tickets cost a hundred pounds, they never failed to sell: this was the must-go-to event of the year and a highlight of Cornwall's social calendar. The hotel's helipad was usually in full use as the county's rich and famous flew in for the night, while the locals had great fun trying to sneak in and snatch pictures of the celebrities on their smartphones. Last year a member of One Direction had been rumoured to be coming, and the lane to the hotel had swarmed with excited tweenagers and their even more excited mothers. Maybe Summer and Justin would attend this year, Jake thought. He was immediately horrified by the knife thrust of jealousy that accompanied this idea. Would Ella be prepared to swallow her dislike of Summer in order to gain the A-list glitter that she would bring to the party? He imagined so. She was a businesswoman and wouldn't let emotion get in the way of good press coverage.

Ella's cheeks were pink and she cleared her throat nervously. "I have a few tickets spare and I was wondering whether you and Mo would like them? I'd love you to be there – as my guests, of course."

"Mo at a ball?" An image of his sister clomping through the hotel's ornate lobby and leaving a wake of mud and straw made him grin. "You *are* kidding?"

"I'm serious. Mo could network with all kinds of people on an occasion like that. The guest list is incredible. There are celebrities, politicians and a couple of oligarchs too, so Daddy says." She slid him a sideways glance. "I've been up to Mo's yard and I can see that things aren't good. She might even meet somebody who'd sponsor her."

Jake knew that Mo was running the yard on fresh air and prayers. It seemed to be the family way. Her talent was going down the drains with the Jeyes Fluid she regularly sluiced across the cobbles. The chance to meet a wealthy sponsor was not to be sniffed at, that was for certain.

"Timmy Eldridge, the music producer, is coming too. He's flying in from his chateau in France," Ella continued. She was into her stride now, growing more confident with each word because she knew she held the winning hand. "Everything he touches turns to gold and I know he's looking for the next big thing." She paused and then said casually, "I was looking for a band to play down on the terrace. Would Zak be interested?"

"What do you think? He'd probably sell Granny Alice for a chance like that."

"I thought he'd be pleased. You just never know where these things can lead. I'll book The Tinners then, if you'll give me your brother's mobile number." Ella was into businesswoman mode now, in control and loving it. It was sexy in a way, Jake supposed; it just wasn't the right way for him.

Ella reached into her Mulberry bag and pulled out her iPhone. Her fingers hovered over the touchpad.

"There's one more thing," she said slowly.

Jake wondered what Ella was going to come up with next. How about *Annie Leibovitz is coming; maybe she could have a chat with Morgan about photography?* or *Jesus is on the guest list; he'll probably work a miracle and heal Danny if I ask him?*

He brushed the crumbs from his shorts, exciting a flotilla of ducks into a crescendo of quacking and sending the seagulls wild, then turned to face her. Her eyes met his and the determination in them was incredible.

"Which is?"

"It's something I want you to do for me."

"And what's that?" Jake stretched his arms above his head. The sun had dried his shorts out now and his shoulders were dusted with cinnamon-coloured freckles. He'd pop home and fetch a new tee-shirt before Cashley turned up with his latest dolly, wanting to show off by bossing his boat wallah around. "Check *Polwenna Princess*'s engines? Swab the decks?"

Ella exhaled slowly. "No, nothing like that. Jake, we're both adults and I think we both know where we stand with each other. We're both single and we have a good time together, don't we? I'm not asking a lot in return for giving Mo and Zak a hand, but the deal is this: if I do, I'd like you to come to the ball as my partner."

"You're asking me to go to the ball with you?" Jake was taken aback. "Ella, I'm really flattered but I don't think it's exactly my scene. You don't want the boatyard grease monkey as your date."

"I think we both know you're a bit more than a 'grease monkey'," said Ella, with a shrug. "But it's up to you. I don't need to beg for dates and I won't ask twice. I just think that we could have fun." She leaned forward and traced her forefinger up his thigh. "A lot of fun."

Her message couldn't have been clearer. Ella was sexy and clever, and Jake didn't doubt for a minute that she could be fun too. He was also aware that an alliance between the Tremaines and the St Miltons would be unstoppable. There was only one problem. The woman he was sitting with wasn't the woman he wanted.

Ella wasn't Summer.

"It's just a masked ball, Jake," said Ella when he didn't instantly leap at the idea. "It's a bit of fun. But hey, up to you. None of you have to come if you'd rather not. Or," she paused, "if there's someone else you'd rather be with?"

"The last time we spoke you weren't exactly in my fan club," Jake reminded her. "What's changed?"

"I know I overreacted then and I'm sorry," Ella said. She actually sounded as though she meant it. "It sounds stupid but I was jealous. I thought you two were seeing each other again, but then I bumped into Susie and she told me that Summer is head over heels in love with Justin. Of course she is! They're Summer and Justin, aren't they? Made for each other. Summer wouldn't cheat on the man she loves."

Jake stared across the harbour. A slight figure in a baggy black hoody was standing at the end of the quay, her arms wrapped tightly around her slender frame. Then she turned on her heel and began to walk back towards the village, her gaze fixed ahead and her thoughts miles away. He didn't even need to see her face to know that it was Summer, but she was completely oblivious to him. Christ, he needed to get her out of his system and fast. He was behaving like a teenager.

Besides, Susie had told Ella that Summer was still crazy about Justin. Thank God he'd not made a fool of himself by saying something to her. Just the mere thought of how close he'd been to total humiliation made him sweat.

Ripping his eyes away from Summer, Jake turned back to Ella. Slim, spiky, sexy, keen Ella. What the hell was he waiting for?

"It sounds like a lot of fun," he said slowly, ignoring the racing of his heart and the desire to leap up and tear after the woman on the far side of the water. He reached down and covered Ella's cool and manicured hand with his own work-roughened one. There was only one way to get over a woman, wasn't there? Now was the time to put the old theory into practice…

"Count me in," he told her.

Chapter 16

Summer was enjoying spending time back at home, chatting with her mother and slowly recovering from the events of the previous few days. Susie was wise enough not to ask any difficult questions and, for the first time in ages, Summer felt able to relax. So far she'd managed to avoid her father on any of her visits to Cobble Cottage, which had certainly made life easier. With every day that passed she was feeling a little more confident. Since the weekend was looming, and this was guaranteed to put Eddie in a good mood because it meant even more time in the pub, she decided that maybe she'd pop back and catch him tomorrow. He had to be faced at some point – just not right now, when there were other priorities to deal with first.

"You don't have to go. Why don't you stay and have some lunch?" Susie insisted when Summer made leaving noises. Already she'd saturated her daughter with tea and filled her up with saffron buns but, worried that Summer was too thin, she was desperate to feed her even more. "I've made some minestrone soup and there's some lovely Cornish brie in the fridge. It's no bother."

"That sounds lovely, Mum, but I've got a few things to do this afternoon." Summer glanced up at the kitchen clock. "Actually, can I use the landline? I need to make a few calls and my mobile's in London."

Phones hadn't been top of Summer's list of must-haves when she'd fled from the house. However, now she needed to call her agent and tell her to cancel the next couple of weeks' jobs, and then pop into the bank to see if she could withdraw some funds. It wasn't going to be easy without a debit card, but surely the bank manager would recognise her even with this haircut? If not, Susie had dug out Summer's birth certificate – although she was obviously puzzled as to why her daughter was in Polwenna Bay without her wallet and her phone. She was clearly desperate to ask about Summer's bruises, but her tentative enquiries hadn't been successful and she'd given up for the time being. Still, Summer suspected that Susie was just biding her time before trying again. Summer would need to summon all her acting skills to convince her mother that everything was fine.

While Susie busied herself setting the table for lunch, Summer went into the hall and perched on the bottom of the stairs with the old telephone wire pulled out as far as possible from the wall socket. This was a real throwback to her teenage years; she must have spent hours sitting here in the chilly gloom and gossiping with Mo until Eddie yelled at her to get off the bloody phone or walk up to Seaspray!

Talk about coming full circle.

Taking a deep breath to steady herself before dipping a toe back into the real world, Summer dialled her agent, Hattie. While the call was being transferred, she prepared for a tongue-lashing.

"Summer? Thank God! Where the hell have you been?" Hattie Lane sounded frantic. Summer could picture her perfectly, the phone tucked between her ear and her shoulder, her razor-sharp bob swinging as she scooted her wheelie chair back and forth in agitation. "Justin must have called the office fifty times! What the hell are you playing at? I've been worried sick."

Hattie and Summer had known each other for over ten years. Summer had been one of the Lane Agency's first clients. The day that Hattie had signed her up, in the small cramped office above a Chinese takeaway in East Ham, had been the day that Summer's career had really taken off – even though it hadn't been quite in the direction she'd originally intended. As Summer's fame and profile had grown, so had the agency's. Today Hattie managed an impressive portfolio of some of the UK's most famous faces, while her partner ran the New York office. The poky room that smelt of dim sum and hoisin sauce was just a distant memory; these days the Lane Agency was homed in a suite of plush offices just off Piccadilly, with floor-to-ceiling windows affording a breathtaking view of the lights and busy city beyond. The Times Square office was even more glamorous. Still, the main thing was that both women knew exactly from where the other had started. Over the course of Summer's career numerous agents had approached Summer, all of them desperate to tempt her away with lucrative offers – but she'd stayed loyal to Hattie. There was something of the Jerry Maguire about her that Summer respected.

Hattie also knew far too many of Summer's secrets.

"You missed the shoot we had booked for Monday," Hattie was saying over the top of Summer's apologies. "Have you any idea how bloody difficult that was for me? I had to seriously kiss ass and promise them an exclusive with you and Justin for the October issue. And before you say it, I don't give a fuck that Justin doesn't like doing shoots for women's mags. You owe me, Summer Penhalligan, so just make it happen. If anyone asks, you've had seriously bad flu, OK? That's the excuse I've given, although they probably all think you've gone abroad for a boob job."

Although she knew that Hattie had more chance of flying to Mars than of getting her and Justin to take part in a couples photo shoot, Summer found herself agreeing. There was no point upsetting Hattie just yet; until she managed to sort herself out a bit, she'd need the other woman on side to assist her financially.

"The shoot was a great one, just beauty work for that new brand, Glitter. It was an exclusive too," Hattie sighed. "We'd have syndicated the images. I have kids to put through private school you know. Don't make a habit of ducking out on me."

Summer made the right regretful noises while thinking privately that with her black eye and bruises the magazine would have had a very different kind of exclusive. There was no way she could say this out loud though, not with Susie's ears out on elastic. Besides, ever since the phone-tapping scandal she was paranoid about whoever else might overhear. She wouldn't put it past Justin to have had Hattie's phone bugged; he was that paranoid.

"Hattie, I'm so sorry," Summer said again, once her agent had run out of steam. "I just had to get away and fast. That's why I'm calling you. I left without my bag or my phone and I really wasn't thinking."

"Without your bag?" Hattie's brain was working so rapidly that Summer could hear the cogs whirring. "Jesus wept, Summer. Justin again, I take it?"

Summer didn't say anything.

"Can't speak, eh?" said Hattie when Summer remained silent. "I get it. I've got teenagers, remember? Parent over shoulder?"

"Something like that," Summer agreed.

"Well I can talk, so you just listen to me. He's a bastard, Summer, even if he is famous and loaded. Sod the magazines and sod the rest of it. If you're somewhere safe then stay put, OK? Don't come back until we've worked something out. Just tell me what you need and I'll sort it."

"Thanks, Hats." Summer closed her eyes. It felt good to have somebody fighting her corner.

"Don't thank me; what are friends for? Besides, you know me, babe – always an eye for business. We could spin this story our way and make a killing if you like? Justin won't know what's hit him. Oh! Unfortunate turn of phrase, but you know what I mean."

"No! Don't do that. Please! You don't know what he's like." Summer's heart lurched. Justin would bury Hattie too: he'd warned her enough times what he would do if she ever crossed him. Summer believed him and she wasn't going to risk upsetting him any more than she had to. "Let me handle this my way, OK?"

Hattie sighed. "I don't like this at all but it's your call, babe. So, I take it you're in Cornwall with your folks and you don't have any access to your money. Do you want me to pop over to your house, grab your bag and FedEx the cards over?"

"No, don't do that. He'll probably have stopped them anyway as they're in joint names. Could you possibly pay some money into an old account of mine if I give you the details? I'm going to head over to Liskeard in a minute and I could withdraw it then."

"Sure. I've just had a cheque come in from *Hiya* – remember that shoot you did before the Beckhams' charity gala? That's a nice big sum and should keep you going for a while. Hang on, let me grab a pen." Summer could hear Hattie rummaging through the detritus on her desk, which was always topped with papers, cuttings and empty takeaway cartons. Some habits died hard, even when you were a big success and had an office in the West End. "OK, babe, shoot."

Once Hattie had the bank details so that she could make an instant online transfer, Summer finished the call, promising she'd be in touch very soon. Although Hattie didn't say so, it was obvious that she was worried at the way the situation had escalated. Summer was worried too, and she was going to do something about it this time – although she wasn't sure what. One thing was a certainty though: she wasn't going back to Justin.

With this thought still at the forefront of her mind, Summer pulled on her black hoody, kissed Susie goodbye and walked along the quay until she was standing right at the furthest end. The sea was rougher today and although the sun was still shining, a line of dark cloud bruised the horizon, a threat of bad weather to come. Maybe it was a metaphor, thought Summer. Just as her life felt calm right now, as soon as Justin knew that she was breaking things off there was going to be one hell of a storm.

The big diamond on her left hand caught the light and glittered. It was a huge heart-shaped stone, two and a half carats set in a band of white gold, and had been the subject of much admiration from the celebrity magazines. Justin had flown Summer to New York on a private jet and then swept through Tiffany's as though he owned the place, making Summer cringe at his blatant showing off. If she was honest, she'd started to have her doubts right there and then. Justin had been oblivious to her embarrassment; twenty minutes and goodness knew how many thousands of dollars later, the enormous ring had taken pride of place on her engagement finger.

And it was a beautiful ring. The stuff of fairy tales, only this fairy-tale had soon switched genre and become a horror story. Justin might have paid cash for it but Summer had paid a much higher price.

Slowly and deliberately she eased the ring off her finger. For a moment she held it in her right hand, letting the light play over it and watching the rainbows dance across the quay, before raising her arm and hurling it high into the sky. The ring arced through the air for a moment before plummeting into the sea, vanishing as the waves closed over it.

It was probably the most expensive symbolic gesture she'd ever made, Summer thought as she turned on her heel and retraced her steps, but it felt great. She hoped that in years to come a child crabbing in the harbour might find it, or maybe on a winter's day a woollen-hatted visitor with a metal detector would strike lucky. She wiggled her hand and smiled; not only did her fingers feel lighter, but her heart did too.

The drive to Liskeard was only eleven miles, but it was eleven miles of twisty-turny lanes that wound their way through the interlocked hills and narrow valleys. Summer could have taken the main roads, but she'd always loved the quieter back lanes with their cool green depths and grassy central ridges. There were landmarks too that she'd loved from childhood, like the forgotten postbox set in the crumbling wall of a long-deserted cottage and hidden by a tangled fringe of ivy, or the huge wrought-iron gates that guarded the sweeping drive of a mysterious manor house. Seeing these again was like unlocking a treasure chest of memories.

She and Jake had driven these lanes a thousand times in his ancient Jeep, her hand resting easily on his jeaned thigh, sensing those strong muscles tighten beneath her fingertips as he worked the clutch. At other times she'd be busy passing him cola bottles and jelly rings from a giant packet of Haribo, laughing until her sides hurt as he messed about with them and poked his tongue out at her. Sometimes Jake would pull the car into a shady gateway where they'd watch the setting sun slide into the sea, so orange and so bright that they almost expected to hear it sizzle when it reached the water. Then he'd draw Summer into his arms and kiss her until she felt dizzy with the kind of longing and happiness that only teenagers can feel.

As she drove those same lanes now, a wave of nostalgia swept over Summer and she wished that she could be that happy carefree girl again, even if it was only for few minutes. Her Audi might be smooth and the height of luxury with its cream leather seats and surround-sound Bose stereo, but right now Summer would have swapped it in a heartbeat for that tired old Jeep with its faint smell of mildew and the leaky sunroof. No car rides since had ever been as thrilling or as much fun as those she'd shared with Jake. Now that the ridiculous diamond ring was gone and she was away from London, Summer could freely admit that Justin and the Ferrari hadn't even come close.

Talking of leaky sunroofs, the clouds that had threatened on the horizon half an hour before had now rolled inland and the sunshine had turned to a sickly lemon hue. The sky had become the same angry purple as Justin's face when he was in a rage; fat splats of rain began landing on the windscreen. Moments later there was a downpour, followed by an enormous clap of thunder as the wipers swiped over the windscreen like crazy. It was at this point that Summer's car decided to cough and splutter and finally peter out to a stop.

"What?" Taken aback, Summer stamped on the gas, but to no avail. A closer inspection of the dashboard revealed that the empty fuel light was blinking at her angrily. Lost in her daydreams earlier, this had barely registered. Lord, she must have been driving on fumes: she hadn't filled up since London. Letting the car roll gently to the side of the lane where there was a gateway, Summer yanked up the handbrake and then thumped her head on the steering wheel in despair. Just great. She was miles from anywhere and on a back road that few people used, so the chances of flagging down the AA were slim. If she was lucky a farmer might chug past in an hour or two – but he'd be on his way to milk the cows and hardly inclined to drive five miles out of his way just because she'd run out of petrol.

It might make more sense to wait in the car, but Summer was desperate to get to the bank before it shut. The way the sky looked, this weather wasn't about to pass anytime soon, so there was no point attempting to sit it out. Without a phone she couldn't call for help either. There was nothing for it but to walk towards the next hamlet and hope that somebody would take pity on her and give her a can of fuel. For the first time since she'd arrived in Cornwall, Summer found herself wishing that she'd be recognised. Fame was a great oiler of wheels. Whether she'd get as far resembling a drowned rat as she would looking like her polished celebrity alter ego was anyone's guess.

She pushed the car door open and stepped out into the deluge. The force of it stung her cheeks and within seconds she was drenched. The Cornish rain was being driven in icy sheets that Summer could see racing in from the coast and ripping across the countryside. The early wheat rippled like an inland sea, and once she was away from the cover of the trees there was no shelter at all. Gritting her teeth and wishing she'd worn boots rather than sandals, Summer trudged forwards with her head bent against the weather.

Just as she'd suspected, the lanes were empty and the farmhouse on the hill was a lot further away in reality than it had appeared from the comfort of the Audi. Summer was wet through to her knickers now, but there was nothing to be gained from turning back at this stage. She was so far down the road that she may as well just carry on. The bank had better let her access her account after all this effort.

Summer continued along the lane. Her legs and arms were dusted with goosebumps and she shivered. May was a fickle month, as warm as blood one moment and then arctic cold the next, and Summer remembered her father saying that hypothermia could take hold in seconds. He'd been talking about falling into the cold waters of the Channel, but Summer was rather worried that the principle was the same. She was just about to climb over a stile and make a shortcut through a field of cows when headlights scattered diamonds through the puddles. A truck had come up behind her; she turned and saw the figure of a broad-shouldered man silhouetted behind the wheel. As it drew alongside her, the vehicle slowed.

All alone in a wet and isolated lane, out of shouting distance and without a mobile phone, Summer suddenly felt very vulnerable. Maybe she should just keep walking. You heard some awful things about women who accepted lifts with strangers…

She heard the whirr of an electric window winding down as the driver stared out at her, and adrenalin flooded her nervous system.

"Summer? What on earth are you doing out here? You're soaked! Get in, for heaven's sake!"

Summer gasped. Her heart was really thumping hard now because the driver of the truck was none other than Jake Tremaine.

Chapter 17

Jake couldn't quite believe what he was seeing. For a moment he thought his eyes were playing tricks on him, but a quick blink and swipe of the wipers soon confirmed that he wasn't imagining things: the slender and sodden figure at the side of the lane really was Summer. Of course it was; he would have recognised her anywhere. After winding down the window and calling out to her, Jake leaned across the cab of the Ranger, sweeping the newspapers and sweet wrappers from the passenger seat and opening the door.

"Hurry up, Sums," he urged. "You're soaked."

Summer didn't need asking again and moments later she was sitting beside him and dripping all over the faux leather seats. Her short hair was plastered to her head and her green eyes seemed bigger than ever in her pale face, while her teeth chattered so much he could hear them.

Jake removed his navy blue sweater and tossed it to her. "Pop that on."

"I'll get it wet," Summer protested. Her teeth worried her full bottom lip in the way that he remembered so well and Jake was suddenly unable to think of anything else but taking it between his own teeth and biting gently before straying down to the soft skin of her throat…

This wasn't a time to have thoughts like that. In fact there was no time that warranted them. Summer was his ex and he'd just agreed to take things a stage further with Ella. Annoyed with himself, Jake turned away to fiddle with the car heater. Moments later the cab was blasted with hot air and Summer, now swathed in his sweater, was shivering slightly less than before. Jake wished now that he'd splashed out on the top-spec model with heated seats rather than watching the pennies and plumping for this no-frills workhorse. Summer still looked half frozen.

"How long have you been out in this?" he asked.

Summer shrugged. "Not long. Fifteen minutes maybe? It was fine when I set out."

Jake laughed. "That's Cornish weather for you. I watched this lot roll in across the bay just before I left. It's heavy but it should pass in another hour or so."

She mopped her face with his sleeve. It was far too long and flopped over her hand. Seeing her huddled in clothes that were too big made Jake feel protective of her. He wanted to wrap her up, sweep her into his arms and carry her away somewhere safe where he could look after her. His groin tightened and Jake gave himself a mental shake. How was it that, even looking like a drowned rat, Summer Penhalligan moved him in a way that no other woman ever could? Ella, for all her workouts, facials and expensive clothes, didn't come close to Summer's natural beauty.

"Where were you going anyway?" Jake asked. His voice sounded hoarse. Summer literally took his breath away. It was ridiculous. Even the scent of her damp skin was driving him wild in a way that Ella's bucket loads of Chanel never would.

"The bank." Summer's wet clothes were starting to steam in the heat. Condensation blurred the windows and Jake had the nebulous sensation that, enclosed in the cab, they were in their own world. She wiped her face with the end of the sleeve again and smiled. "It's a bit of a long story but I set off from London in rather a hurry and left my purse behind. A friend of mine was going to transfer some money to my old account and I was on my way to withdraw it when I ran out of petrol. I feel pretty stupid."

It was a few days since Jake had seen Summer, and the bruise on her face was starting to fade from livid purple to brown and yellow smudges. He had a strong suspicion why Summer might have fled without her money and it made him sick to the stomach. There was no point asking her though. Jake had sisters and he knew that women could be stubborn when they chose to be. If Summer wanted to confide in him then she would. Until then he would just do all he could to help.

"That Audi in the hedge is yours, then?"

She nodded. "I feel so stupid for letting it run this low. I'll buy some more fuel when I've got my money. Hey! What are you doing?"

Jake was reversing the truck. "We're going back to the village. You need to get dry and warmed up."

"No way." Summer's voice was determined. "I need to draw that money out. Anyway, aren't you going into town?"

"I was only popping to the farm store to get some engine oil. That can wait until tomorrow."

She crossed her arms and gave him a determined look. "Well I can't, Jake. I really need to get some money out. Besides, I can't leave the car here. If you take me into Liskeard I'll be fine."

Jake laughed. "You will not be fine, Summer Penhalligan. You're drenched and you'll have pneumonia before you even reach the cashpoint. I'm taking you home to dry off and then I'll get Issie or Nick to drive me back with some fuel and we'll rescue the car. And before you argue," he added as, right on cue, she opened her mouth to protest, "I'll lend you some money to tide you over."

The truck was heading back through the sodden lanes to Polwenna Bay now, tyres splashing through puddles and wipers at full speed. They passed the Audi and Summer sighed in annoyance.

"You're just going to ignore anything I say, aren't you?" she said.

"Yep," Jake agreed. "I'll listen again once you're safe and warm. Deal?"

"It's not much of a deal, is it? Not when I don't get any say. You're practically kidnapping me," grumbled Summer. In the warm fug of the cab her hair was starting to curl into ringlets, and he was glad to see that the hot air was beginning to turn her cheeks pink again.

Jake ignored her complaining. If taking Summer back home to warm up while he dealt with her car was kidnapping, then kidnapping was exactly what he was about to do. Alice hadn't raised him to be the sort of man who left someone who was in trouble to fend for themselves: she'd brought her grandsons up to be gentlemen – even if Zak and Nick's behaviour sometimes threw this fact into grave doubt. There was no way Jake could allow Summer to struggle with sopping clothes, petrol cans and greasy wet roads. Ex or not, he felt compelled to take care of her. He told himself he'd do the same for any woman, or indeed any person in need of help.

They drove in silence for a while. Jake sneaked a glance at Summer and saw that her eyes had closed, the thick lashes dark against her skin. She looked exhausted. As he guided the truck through the windy narrow lanes he felt as though he was driving back in time too. They'd travelled like this so many times in the past, him at the wheel and Summer beside him with her hand resting gently on his thigh, sweetly oblivious to the dramatic effect that the slightest brush of her fingertips had on him. Did she remember those days too? Jake wondered. Did bittersweet nostalgia run through her just like the rainwater that was coursing down the sides of the steep lane?

Probably not. She was a big celebrity now and what was he? Just some country boy she'd dated in her less glamorous past. He really needed to get a handle on himself. He was thirty years old, for Christ's sake.

Maybe this was what they called a mid-life crisis?

***

"Where are we?" murmured Summer some twenty minutes later. She'd been fast asleep, lulled into slumber by the warmth and the motion of the car. She was ridiculously tired. Maybe this was the pregnancy taking its toll? For something so small and so new, her baby was certainly determined to take whatever it needed. It had only been because of this bone-grinding exhaustion that she'd given in to Jake.

Well, that and the fact that sitting beside him in the cab felt so normal. Although it was more than a decade since Jake had driven her home from a day out, it could have been only yesterday. That was just the magic of Polwenna Bay, Summer reminded herself; it didn't mean anything more. Cornwall was a timeless county and although the years rolled by with the tides and the scudding clouds, very little really changed. In a world that had recently turned crazy for Summer, this constancy was comforting.

She rubbed her eyes. They were driving through a fairly new estate and were turning onto a rutted track that looked alarmingly as though it was going to plummet over the cliff. "This is the top of the village, isn't it?"

Jake nodded, not taking his eyes from the bumpy terrain. The rain was even heavier here and the clouds were moving in fast. "We can park here now. Nick and Zak have cut a path through the undergrowth to Seaspray."

"I didn't know this was your land," Summer said. She was surprised because she'd thought she'd known everything about the Tremaines. That was twelve years ago, you idiot, she reminded herself sternly. A lot had changed since then.

"It isn't: we just rent half an acre from a farmer, Ben Owens. Do you remember him? He was in your year at school."

Summer did remember Ben. He was tall and ginger and had blushed every time she'd spoken to him. She wondered whether he'd changed.

"Parking here's a bit of a pain because the path's really twisty, but I figured at least this way you don't have to run the gauntlet of the village." Jake pulled up alongside a faded blue shipping container and killed the engine. "We'll get wet walking down but it's only five minutes. Then we'll have some hot drinks and get dried."

It may have been only a short walk, but the downpour had turned the path into deep mud and by the time Jake and Summer had squeezed through the gap in Seaspray's hedge they were both drenched. They threaded their way through the garden, the stunning views smothered by the thick cloud that had rolled in, and Summer's sandals slithered on the sodden grass.

"OK?" Jake reached out and steadied her. His hand on her waist was firm and she found that she was leaning on him as they continued their descent. This was because it was slippery, Summer told herself, and for no other reason. He was just being a gentleman. She remembered now just how much she'd liked this about him. Jake wouldn't have abandoned her at two a.m. in a Marbella club just because he felt she was looking at another man the wrong way, or left her alone in hospital when she *accidentally* broke her wrist and needed it pinned. No, Jake Tremaine looked after his women.

His women? This thought made her throat silt up. Did Jake have a girlfriend? Summer guessed that there must be somebody. He'd been handsome as an eighteen-year-old lad; now that he was thirty he had matured and broadened out into the sort of looks that drew admiring glances everywhere he went.

As they neared Seaspray's back door (still painted the same shade of duck-egg blue that Summer remembered, and fringed with the baskets of tumbling geraniums and nasturtiums that were Alice's passion), both she and Jake became increasingly soaked. His hair plastered to his scalp and his eyelashes starry with rain, Jake pressed his palm against the small of Summer's back and guided her towards the large white house.

Summer stopped abruptly, spinning around to face him. "Hold on a minute. What do you think you're doing?" She'd assumed that they'd been taking a shortcut to Harbour Watch.

"Taking you inside to get dry and warm up. There's no way I'm letting you go back to a damp, cold holiday cottage – not until I know you're not about to contract pneumonia, anyway." Jake's eyes were dark in the gloom, and the set of his mouth had the determination about it that she'd last seen when he'd flatly refused to move to London with her. There was no arguing with him sometimes, but as far as Summer was concerned, now wasn't one of those occasions. She wasn't sixteen anymore.

"That's really kind, Jake, but I wouldn't hear of it. I'm more than happy to go back to the cottage. I've put you out quite enough for one day."

He raised an eyebrow. "Putting me out? Is that really how you see it? This isn't London, Summer. This is Polwenna, remember? People look out for each other here."

It was on the tip of Summer's tongue to point out that Jake and Mo hadn't exactly been there for her when she'd needed them the most, but she stopped herself just in time. This was a can of worms that, once opened, would have to be dealt with; right now, cold and tired, she simply didn't have the strength.

"You've done enough already," was all she said.

"And I wouldn't have completed that if I let you go back without making certain you were warmed up and not about to catch your death of cold," Jake told her resolutely. "I know that cottage. There's only a temperamental storage heater – and the water heater's erratic too. I don't even think there's a tumble dryer. So you're coming back to Seaspray to have some tea and warm up, and that's the end of it. There's no point arguing."

"I don't want to go inside!" Summer recoiled from the very thought of this. It was too painful to return as a stranger to the place that had once been her second home, unwelcome there and unfamiliar now, and knowing that the choices and decisions she'd made as a teenager still had echoes.

"And I don't want to take you back to a cold empty house. There's no way I'd dream of doing that." Jake shook his head and droplets flew from his curls. "While Nick and I go and fetch your car you can have a hot bath and drink gallons of tea. There's no point arguing anyway: I'll pick you up and carry you there if I have to."

Hands on her hips, she glared up at him. "Do you always ignore what people want?"

"Only when what they suggest instead is bloody ridiculous," he countered. "So it would make life a lot easier if you'd just accept my offer of tea, warmth and toast graciously rather than putting up a fight. We'll probably both catch hypothermia otherwise."

They glowered at each other through the driving rain, determined green eyes locking with equally determined blue ones while the drops stung their cheeks and blurred their vision. Summer tried to dredge up some more arguments, but she was getting colder by the second and the world was starting to sway around her. Besides, annoying as it was, Jake was right: the cottage would be chilly and she hadn't any pound coins left to feed the ravenous electric meter. The thought of sipping hot tea by the Aga in Seaspray's cosy kitchen was extremely tempting…

"Come on." Sensing her start to weaken, Jake grasped Summer's hand and towed her the last few yards to the house. He kicked the swollen door open with his rigger boot and they stumbled into the little porch, where a selection of Tremaine wellington boots, damp raincoats and dog baskets jostled for space.

"Jake? Is that you?" called Alice. "That was a quick trip. Did you forget something?"

"I found somebody lost in the rain, so we've come home to dry out. Is the kettle on?" Jake called back, kicking off his boots in two practised movements and tugging Summer into the kitchen.

"You know me, my love; it's always on. Who did you find – oh my goodness!" Alice's hands flew to her mouth and her laughing reply was swiftly halted when she caught sight of Summer.

"I'm so sorry. I won't stay long, I promise," Summer said quickly. A pool of water was gathering on the slate tiles at her feet. "Coming here was a bad idea."

"Of course it wasn't," said Jake firmly. "Was it, Gran?"

Alice never turned anyone away from Seaspray and her kitchen had always been filled with her grandchildren and their friends. Some of Summer's fondest memories were of afternoons spent sitting at the table drinking tea and chatting away to Mo and Alice while the boys ate their way through their own bodyweight in cake. Sometimes even their father would join them, taking time out from the business, and then the whole family would be together. It was almost sad, she reflected, how you never appreciated at the time that this was probably the happiest you'd ever be.

Once Jake's grandmother recovered from her shock at finding Summer back at Seaspray, she smiled.

"Of course it wasn't a bad idea," she said warmly. "Welcome back, my dear."

Stepping forward, Alice Tremaine enveloped Summer in a big hug, not seeming bothered in the least by either the dozen-year gap since Summer's last visit or her soggy clothes. Summer returned the hug, her eyes filling with tears because Alice smelt exactly the same as she'd always done: a mixture of baking and lavender and something that felt dangerously like home. She'd always felt safe here and never before had she appreciated just how precious this safety was. Unlike her beautiful London house, Seaspray thrummed with love and rang with laughter; there were no cold silences followed by hours of nervously trying to second-guess what she'd done wrong and what would happen next because of it.

"You're frozen!" Alice exclaimed, stepping back and looking concerned. Taking Summer's arm, Alice steered her unexpected guest to the armchair by the Aga. "Excuse the hair on it, love. Our cats insist on sleeping anywhere but in their baskets. Now, a cup of tea is what you need – and a change of clothes. Jake, don't just stand there like a goon. Go upstairs and see if you can find some dry things for Summer, and get yourself out if those wet things too while you're about it. You're dripping all over my clean floor."

Jake grinned across the kitchen at her and Summer's own lips couldn't resist curling upwards too. "You can see that I'm still a teenager as far as my grandmother's concerned!"

"Well, if you must act like one," Alice scolded, but she was smiling at him as she spoke. "Now hurry up and get changed. This weather's closed in for a while. We'll have to sit it out."

As if on cue a gust of rain blew against the window and rattled the panes. While his grandmother made tea Jake shrugged off his wet fleece and then pulled his tee-shirt over his head. Even though she was used to Justin's athletic perfection, Jake's torso – strong, broad-shouldered and narrowing down to lean hips – was simply glorious and somehow far more real. Years of physical work had honed and sculpted him, not a flash gym and prancing personal trainer. And she'd bet anything that if Jake were injured he'd simply grit his teeth and get on with it rather than rolling about theatrically on the pitch and gurning. His flat, muscular belly was sprinkled with golden hair that tapered to a delicious V just above the waistband of his jeans, and in a second's weakness Summer devoured him with her eyes. Sensing her gaze on him, Jake grinned at her cheekily. Horribly embarrassed to be caught looking, Summer ripped her attention away.

"Stop showing off, Jake!" Alice swatted her grandson with a tea towel. "What do you think this is? A nineteen-eighties Levi's advert?

Go and make yourself decent, and on the way back down look in the airing cupboard and see what you can find for Summer."

Jake laughed. Water dripped from his hair and trickled over his honed pecs. Something sensual and long forgotten tightened deep in the pit of Summer's belly. To distract herself she caressed the silky head of the tabby cat that had wandered over to investigate the newcomer. Moments later it had leapt onto Summer's lap, where it turned several circles, its needle-sharp claws pie-making, before settling down and starting to purr. When Summer looked up again Jake had gone.

"That's Scruff. I don't think you've met her." Alice lifted the kettle from the hotplate and poured scalding water into a teapot. "Who did we have when you lived here? Bella? Or Paws?"

"Bella. Mo rescued her from Plymouth. She was a stray and some schoolboys were taunting her," Summer recalled. "They were the ones who needed rescuing when Mo was finished with them."

"That's right. Typical Mo, always rescuing things! The amount of injured seagulls and baby rabbits I've had here." Alice folded her arms, leaned against the Aga and smiled, but her gaze was firm when it rested again on her visitor. "Jake's the same, of course: far too kind-hearted for his own good when someone needs help."

Her subtext was obvious, and Summer understood and respected it. She hadn't expected to be welcomed back to Seaspray with open arms, not if Mo's reaction had been anything to go by.

"I'm not here to upset anyone, especially Jake. I never wanted him to pick me up or bring me here. Honestly." Summer needed to make it clear that she hadn't set out to pursue Alice's grandson. "I was perfectly capable of getting to Liskeard on my own but he insisted on helping out."

The older woman nodded. "Yes, that sounds just like my grandson. But Summer, dear, I wasn't referring to you being out in the rain and needing a lift to town. I might be old but my eyes are still working pretty well – and I know a black eye when I see one."

Summer's hand flew to her cheek. That bloody bruise was causing her no end of trouble. Her mother had clocked it for sure and now Alice. She might as well just stand on the village green and announce that Justin Anderson hit her. With the rain and all the stress of running out of fuel, she'd forgotten about trying to hide it.

"It's not what you think, honestly, Alice. I promise. I tripped up in my heels and fell onto the kitchen island."

"Come on, Summer! You can do a bit better than that, surely? You are an actress, aren't you? I didn't come down with that rain shower and neither did Jake. You know as well as I do that he can't bear to see anyone in distress. Especially you."

Especially her? What did that mean? Did Jake still have feelings for her? Summer was alarmed at the warm glow this idea gave her, as though the sun had broken through the louring clouds outside and was shining through the window.

"Won't you tell me what really happened?" Alice asked softly. "Maybe we can help?"

For a second Summer was tempted to tell her everything, fling herself into Alice's arms and sob out the whole sordid tale. Then she laughed at herself. What! Did she really think that Alice could make everything better just as she always had done in the past? This wasn't a case of grazed knees or Ella St Milton being a cow. If only. Justin was far nastier than Ella could ever be.

"I tripped," Summer repeated flatly, and Alice sighed and turned back to the teapot.

"Fine. If you say so." Strong brown tea sloshed into three mugs, followed by milk. Reaching up to the higher shelf on the dresser, Alice retrieved a bottle of Jack Daniel's.

"I don't know why I still keep it here," she remarked, half to herself. "All the children are bigger than me now anyway! Now, a nice drop of this in your tea will warm you up a treat."

"No alcohol for me," Summer said quickly, before the older woman could pour a very generous measure into her mug.

"It's just a tot. It'll do you good."

"No, Alice! I don't want any whiskey. I can't!"

There was a pause during which time seemed to go wrong, each second stretching out for far longer than it should before the next one caught up. Slowly, Alice turned around. The look on her face said it all.

"How many months are you?"

There was no point lying about this. Everyone would know at some point. Summer's hand moved to her flat stomach and rested there momentarily. Then she shrugged.

"I'm not exactly sure. It's only early days. Six weeks? Seven?"

"You haven't seen a doctor?"

"Not yet. I did a home test." Summer knew that the memory of seeing that second blue line appear, and the strange alchemy of mingled dread and wonder, would stay with her forever.

"You really need to see a doctor just to check that everything's all right. Shall I make you an appointment? Richard Penwarren is supposed to be very good."

The thought of going into the Polwenna surgery and having to make small talk with curious locals while she waited to be seen by the GP filled Summer with dread.

"No! I mean, no thank you. I'll sort it out when I'm in London."

Whenever that was going to be, of course. Sometime shortly after hell froze over?

Alice frowned. "Summer, I wish you'd let me help. I know something's really wrong. You ought to tell Jake too. About the baby, I mean. He needs to know."

"Nobody needs to know anything!" Terror clawed Summer's throat and panic fluttered in her chest like a trapped bird. This was how it would get out, a game of Chinese whispers until Justin came after her with his lawyers and his threats and dragged her back. Her heart was racing. "Alice, no one else knows about this. No one! I'd really appreciate it if—"

"Nobody knows what?" Jake strode back into the kitchen, looking from his grandmother to Summer and back again. "Hey, these are serious faces. What have I missed?"

"Nothing, love. Summer was just saying that nobody knows what it's like for her being famous," Alice said without missing a beat.

"Right." Understandably, Jake looked confused. There was an awkward silence, broken only by the purring of the cat.

"I've made your tea," said Alice brightly. "I'll put some whiskey in it, shall I?"

"Not for me, thanks, Gran. I've just called Nick and he's going to redeem himself from my bad books by helping me go and rescue Summer's car. He's going to come over shortly with a can of fuel. I'm worried enough about driving that lovely car and dripping on the leather, never mind negotiating the roads with one of your measures of Jack Daniel's inside me." Turning to Summer, he added, "I've run you a bath and left some towels out and some dry clothes too. I'll be an hour and a half at the most."

Summer felt terrible. "I never meant to cause this much trouble."

He shrugged her protests away. "What else are friends for? Besides, who knows when I'll get to drive a fully loaded Audi TT again? We country bumpkins have to take those kinds of chances whenever we can!"

Nothing Summer said could change Jake's mind, which wasn't really much of a surprise given how stubborn he could be. Eventually she gave up and, taking her mug of tea with her, made her way upstairs to the family bathroom. Seaspray hadn't altered at all, she reflected as she reached the big arched window on the first-floor landing and looked out thoughtfully at the grey sea and even greyer skies. It was reassuring to know that some things had remained unchanged when everything else in the world seemed to have turned upside down. The smell of beeswax polish, the sounds of Alice tidying away in the kitchen and even the drumming of the rain against the windows were all as familiar to her as her own breath.

Once in the warmth of the bath, neck-deep in bubbles and with her head resting on the pile of towels Jake had left for her, Summer's heartbeat started to slow at last. Here, in the peace and quiet of Seaspray, she could press the pause button on the crazy events of her life. Even if this was only for an hour or two, it felt good.

The water lapped over her body, kissing and thawing her chilled skin. Summer exhaled wearily, her eyes growing heavier as she grew warmer.

Moments later they had closed and Summer Penhalligan was sound asleep.

Chapter 18

"Summer! Summer!"

The voice reached Summer through her dreams, far away at first and then drawing closer and closer as though the speaker was calling her name through a long, dark tunnel. For a moment she drifted in the soft never-never land between dreaming and consciousness, before the sensation of fingers touching her shoulder snatched her back to the present.

"Summer? Are you OK?"

She jumped, her eyes snapping open and a fish-hook stab of panic tugging her awake. For a few seconds she struggled to figure out where she was before everything came tumbling back to her. She was now lying in cold bathwater, the luxurious bubbles of earlier on little more than a scummy residue floating on the surface. Every inch of her naked body was visible and, just to make things even worse, Jake Tremaine was kneeling by the side of the bath. The expression of shock on his handsome face as his eyes flickered over her body made Summer want to sink her head under the water. Once, those blue eyes had burned with desire when they'd rested on her. Justin was right: she was far too scrawny these days. One of their last rows had been sparked by him telling her that she needed to get a boob job.

To mask her embarrassment she glowered at Jake and injected anger into her voice.

"What the hell do you think you're doing?"

"Sorry! Sorry!" Thrusting a fluffy towel her way and then averting his gaze, Jake was all apologies. "When Granny Alice said you'd been in here for almost an hour and a half I panicked. Bloody hell, Summer, Nick and I brought your car back in that time! I knocked and I called but when you didn't answer I was worried. I thought—"

"You thought you'd just barge in?"

"Of course not. I was worried about you," Jake said, still with his eyes fixed on the opposite wall. Then he shrugged. "Relax, Sums. It's not like I haven't seen you naked before, is it?"

The only way Summer could ignore the hot wave of shame rushing over her was to channel her annoyance at being disrupted. Clutching the towel to her breasts, she glared at him.

"Well I'm fine, thanks," she said icily.

Jake's blond head turned slowly back. His eyes met hers and in spite of everything Summer's heart fluttered like butterflies on buddleia.

"But you're not though, are you?" he said softly. "Summer, I'm not an idiot. What the hell has that bastard done to you?"

His gaze had dropped to her shoulder and the top of her breast, where her recent encounter with the kitchen island was blooming in purple and brown roses across her flesh. There were silver scars too that Jake had clearly noticed, a faint map of heartbreaks and hot tempers. Summer knew in her logical mind that none of this was her fault; if she'd had a friend in the same position, she'd have been the first to say so. Yet the sad reality was that it didn't feel like this to her. What happened between her and Justin was Summer's secret shame, and a tiny, treacherous part of her couldn't help wondering if in some way she was to blame. Justin had said often enough that she drove him to it, that she was too flirty or that her dresses were too revealing, and that he only got so angry because she made him jealous.

"I'm even more worried now," Jake frowned when she didn't reply. "Come on, Summer, this is me you're talking to. I know you, remember?"

She closed her eyes wearily. Beneath the lids hot tears threatened to spill. Summer fought to contain them because she was afraid that once she started crying she'd never stop. Besides, Jake didn't know her anymore, did he? He'd lost the right to know her when he'd refused to answer her desperate letter all those years ago. She'd wanted to confide in him then and he'd turned her away, so she certainly couldn't trust him now with what had happened between her and Justin.

"I'm fine," she said tightly.

"I know I'm just a bloke but even I know that when a woman says she's fine she's generally not being completely honest." Shifting back onto his haunches Jake crouched beside the bathtub. Slowly, and as carefully as though approaching a wild animal, he reached out his hand and traced the scar on her shoulder with a gentle forefinger. There was something so tender about this simple gesture that she felt herself turn inside out with nostalgic longing. Jake had always been a tactile man, never afraid to show affection. Her memories of their time together were of endless sun-dappled days spent with their arms twined around one another – just the brushing of his fingertips being enough to dust her skin with goosebumps – or walking along the clifftops hand in hand as though unable to be parted even for a second. When Jake had pulled her close Summer had always felt as though she were home: cherished and loved and secure.

What an illusion that had turned out to be! In his own way Jake had been every bit as much of a disappointment as Justin.

"Did Justin Anderson do this?" Jake asked.

Hearing that name was the equivalent of taking the ice-bucket challenge. Image was everything to Justin – image, and his career. Hadn't he told her enough times that he'd ruin her if she ever dared to breathe a word? Summer hadn't doubted him for a second. There was a core of steel that ran through her fiancé; the same steel that had driven him to be top of his game could just as easily be focused on destroying her. It wouldn't be that hard. Who would believe the word of a once well-known party girl and glamour model against that of a national treasure, the brave cancer survivor and the patron of dozens of charities? Nobody. This was why Summer had no choice but to lie low and pray that nobody tipped off the press while she figured out the best way to keep herself and her baby safe.

She jerked her treacherous, melting body away from Jake's touch.

"I told you. I tripped and fell against the kitchen island. It's made of marble, for God's sake!"

Jake's full mouth, the same mouth that had once traced fiery kisses across her neck and her now bruised breasts, was pressed into a tight and sceptical line.

"And did the *kitchen island* give you the scar on your shoulder too?"

Summer glanced down at the thin silver line on her left shoulder. There had been so many rows and so many recriminations followed by tears, promises and passionate make-up sex that she'd lost track of them all. She'd almost forgotten about this old war wound, the now faint evidence of another outburst and a diamond-encrusted signet ring. There were too many secrets; trying to contain them all, like a dam brimful of water, made her head thud.

"That was something else: a cupboard door, I think," she said. "Not that it's any of your business, Jake. Now, is that the end of the interrogation? If it's all right with you, can I get out of this cold water and dry off, or shall I just catch pneumonia while you ask me some more ridiculous questions?"

Summer hated the harsh note in her voice almost as much as she hated seeing the expression of hurt flicker across Jake's open features. He was so honest, she found herself thinking. He'd always worn his heart on his sleeve and had never been able to ignore anyone in distress – which had made it all the more painful when he'd chosen to turn his back on her.

Her and his own child, Summer reminded herself sharply. She mustn't allow herself to be drawn by him. After all, Jake had deliberately and coldly abandoned her just when she'd needed him the most. She must never forget that, or be fooled by him. A man who could ignore the heartfelt letter she'd written – the letter she'd spent hours trying to compose and which had been blotted with her tears and scored with her terror and her heartbreak – was undoubtedly as hard in his own way as Justin Anderson was in his.

"Summer, please talk to me," Jake implored her. He was still crouching beside the bath and he reached for her cold hands, clasping them in his. "Those bruises look nasty. You need to see a doctor."

Summer's ribs did hurt, although she hoped she hadn't actually cracked them in the fall. Her first thought had been for the baby rather than for herself, but so far all seemed well on that score. Soon enough she would find a doctor (maybe Kursa's son, seeing as everyone was raving about him) and get herself checked over, but not until she was sure that she was safe from Justin. The thought of him finding out made her blood freeze.

Jake's strong fingers squeezed hers. "Trust me, Summer, please. I want to help you."

"I'm fine," she repeated, snatching her fingers back. "Or at least I will be once I get out of this bath and am left in peace. Now, do you mind?"

Jake jumped to his feet, holding his hands up in a gesture of surrender.

"OK, Summer, have it your way. Everything's *fine* except for your sense of spatial awareness and maybe your sanity for not telling the truth about the prick."

"I fell," said Summer flatly. "It was an accident."

Jake shook his head in frustrated defeat. "Fine. Whatever you say, Summer, but just bear in mind that I'm not stupid and neither are many other people. With bruises like that it won't take long before somebody puts two and two together as to why you've left him. Cutting your hair doesn't make the slightest bit of difference either." He paused, those bright eyes holding hers. "If anything, you're even more beautiful now."

Summer stared at him. Her heart broke into a gallop and she knew she had to rein it in. Fast.

"Jake, I tripped and—"

"No, Summer, don't say another word about tripping and kitchen islands. We both know that's a load of rubbish."

She swallowed. Part of her wanted nothing more than to tell Jake the truth, to feel his arms close around her, press her face into his strong chest and let him promise her that it would all be fine.

"You can trust me," Jake said softly. "I want to help you. Summer, I still care about you."

For a moment she nearly wavered, almost told him the truth before her sensible self woke up and screamed at her that this was the worst possible thing to do. She couldn't trust Jake Tremaine. He'd already let her down in one of the worst ways a man could let a woman down. Even though she could tell herself that he'd been young or that things were different now, how could she ever trust him again? He might say he still cared about her, but where had he been when she'd needed him? Furious with herself for hesitating, she pushed the moment of weakness aside.

"I've not left him," she said loudly, crossing her fingers beneath the water. "You're letting your imagination run away with you, Jake. I'm engaged to Justin Anderson. We're Summer and Justin, for heaven's sake! We've even had our own reality show."

"But do you love Justin Anderson?" Jake's eyes snagged on hers.

"Of course I do," Summer said, a beat too late to convince anyone. "He's my fiancé."

Jake said nothing. He didn't need to. The delay in her reply had said it all.

"I'm only here to have a bit of a break from the press interest," Summer added. "You have no idea what it's like living with the press. Honestly, it drives me mad. Hiding in plain sight here for a bit seemed like a good idea, that's all." She forced a lightness into her voice that was totally at odds with the millstone heaviness in her heart. This was the performance of a lifetime, Oscar-winning stuff if there ever was. "I love Justin, Jake. I love him and I'm going to marry him. *Hiya* magazine is going to cover the wedding. It's all arranged."

Jake's face was expressionless but a muscle ticked in his cheek. "And there's nothing anyone could say or do to change your mind?"

Summer shook her head.

"Not even if I told you that I still have feelings for you? That maybe those feelings never went away?"

There was a knot in Summer's throat made of tangled hopes and dreams and lost opportunities.

"Jake, I—"

"No, don't say anything, Summer. Please, let me speak. I don't know what's been going on between you and Justin but I sure as hell don't buy into the fairytale that your management likes to spin. I know you, Summer, and I know when you're hiding something from me. I can't undo the past no matter what I do and how much I wish I could, but there's one thing I can do and that's be honest with you now."

The past hung between them. What could have been if she'd never left, Summer wondered? What might life be like now if Jake had been there when she'd needed him?

"I've thought about you every day since you left. I promise not a moment's gone by when I haven't wished that things had worked out differently for us." He smiled ruefully as he raked a hand through his thick blond mane. A lock fell over his eye just the way it always had, and a sudden memory of reaching up from beneath him to push it away from his face made her pulse quicken. "Summer, I know I can't offer you what Justin does. Not in terms of finances anyway. Christ knows, I only have a boatyard that's just about hanging on by the skin of its teeth and a beat-up truck to my name, but I can help you, if you'll let me. Summer, don't you understand? I still—"

"Jake, don't!" cried Summer, although she half longed for and half dreaded hearing what she thought he was going to say next. Did he still love her? Was that it? And did she still love him? That was a question she was too scared to ask herself because it was too painful to contemplate. Too much had happened. There were far too many past hurts and resentments that would have to be explored, and she really didn't think she could face those. Her heart was breaking for the people they'd once been and all that could have been; she knew it was too late for them.

"I know you don't want to hear that I still care about you," Jake said quietly, "but I do. I don't think I ever stopped."

Summer knew that she shouldn't want to hear this, shouldn't even let herself listen, but Jake's words made her feel warm again despite the cold bathwater.

He was watching her, waiting for her to reply. Summer bit her lip because there was only one reply that she could give him. He needed to know the truth about her situation, and that truth was the one thing that would tell Jake that it really was too late for them.

Too late. Were there any sadder words in the English language?

Just as she was screwing up the courage to tell him that she was pregnant, the bathroom door flew open and in charged a small boy brandishing a camera. "There you are, Jake. I've been looking everywhere! Look at the pictures I took with Jules! Dad looks really good in them, doesn't he? He's smiling! Can I use your printer in the office? Can we go now? I need colour and Grand Granny says there's none left in her printer."

"Morgan! You need to knock!" Jake admonished, catching the child by the hood of his sweater and attempting to tether him while an expensive-looking digital camera was waved under Jake's nose.

"I knew you were in here. I heard you to talking to the lady."

Jake raised his eyes at Summer over the child's head.

"The lady is in the bath," Jake pointed out.

"I know *that*," said the boy patiently. "It *is* the bathroom, after all. I heard her talking to you so I knew it was all right to come in if you were in here. Now can we go and print my pictures?"

"My nephew, Morgan," Jake explained. "He has an impeccable sense of timing."

"I like to be on time for things," Morgan replied gravely. "Although time is actually an illusion, you know."

"It feels pretty real when a guy is trying to pour out his heart and soul to someone," said Jake ruefully.

Personally Summer thought that Morgan's sense of timing was spot on. He'd just saved her from blurting out her big secret and she felt very relieved. The fewer people who knew about her baby the better: that way, Justin was even less likely to find out. Making sure that the towel was hiding her body from view, Summer smiled at the boy.

"Hello, Morgan. I'm a friend of your Uncle Jake."

"Is that why you don't have any clothes on?" Morgan asked. "Like when Uncle Nick had a friend come to stay and she had no clothes on and then Grand Gran was cross?"

"Nothing like that at all. Summer got wet in the rain and was warming up," Jake told him, ruffling the boy's hair and grinning at Summer.

He'll make a great father someday, Summer thought with a stab of what felt dangerously like grief; the curly-headed laughing children in Jake's future would be nothing to do with her. Some other woman would feel his baby turn head over heels in her womb and see the wonder on Jake's face when he held his son or daughter for the first time. *It should have been me*, she wanted to yell at him, *why didn't you care enough to help?* All his talk just now was exactly that: talk. When she'd needed him the most Jake had let her down. She'd be doing herself a favour if she kept that in mind.

Instinctively her hand rested against her belly. This little one had Justin Anderson for a father, which for all Justin's wealth and fame was hardly the best start in life for any child. Silently, Summer promised her baby that she would be twice as good a parent to make up for that.

And she wouldn't let Justin near him or her.

"You're Summer?" Morgan's wide eyes swivelled to her, practically out on stalks. "Oh! You're the one Aunty Mo hates. Fact."

It was indeed a fact, thought Summer, recalling how angry Mo had been with her when she'd bumped into her in the village. And it seemed there was nothing she could ever do to change that either.

"Afraid so," she nodded.

"And you need to get out of the bathroom. Fact," Jake told him sternly.

"Aunty Mo won't be very happy to know you're here," Morgan informed Summer. He didn't look at all bothered by this thought, but Summer's stomach lurched. She really didn't think she could face Mo's fury again. Breaking free of his uncle's grasp, Morgan headed for the landing. "Come *on*, Jake. Let's print my pictures."

The moment for confidences had well and truly passed. Jake smiled at Summer and the tenderness in his eyes made her want to cry.

"It seems that I've been summoned. I'll leave you to get dressed in peace. We can catch up a bit later on. Maybe over supper?"

They'd do no such thing, Summer decided as she towelled herself dry. Apart from not wanting to face the wrath of Mo part two, there was also no way she was having any more conversations with Jake; it was far too dangerous. All it had taken was one of his blue-eyed dimpled smiles and she'd been about to sing like a canary.

It was ridiculous.

Cross with herself, Summer pulled on the dry clothes that Jake had managed to liberate from the airing cupboard. He'd certainly found a strange mix: leggings (Mo's), a fisherman's smock (Nick's), thick socks (heaven only knew whose) and a pair of boxer shorts. Maybe those were Jake's? She'd technically got into his pants, Summer supposed, albeit not quite in the way she once had. Her bra was still soggy, so Summer decided to go without it. Losing weight and going down several cup sizes definitely had some advantages, no matter what Justin might think. Besides, she'd only be walking a few hundred yards down to her cottage.

Once dressed in this eccentric attire, Summer crept out of the bathroom and along the landing – but rather than turning right and going down the staircase there, she took a sharp left and then another left. She'd spent enough time here over the years to know the old place pretty well. She knew that in its heyday, Seaspray had required a team of servants to keep it running smoothly, hence the narrow back staircase which led from the servants' quarters towards the boot room and pantry. In the thick socks she padded down it, passing the kitchen silently. The murmur of voices from within told her that the family was otherwise occupied. Within moments she was in the boot room, shoving her feet into a pair of ancient wellies before shooting through the door into the sodden garden.

It was still raining, but the heavy downpour of earlier had eased off to a drizzle now. Summer wound her way down the terraced grounds, showering herself in drops as she brushed past plants that were bowed across the path from the weight of the rain. The air filled with the scent of rosemary as her hand trained through Alice's beloved herbs, which edged the way back towards the village. The mist was starting to lift a little and Polwenna was emerging below, peeking shyly through its white veil like a bride at the altar. Even the seagulls on their chimney-pot perches were looking slightly less miserable than before.

Was running away from Jake the right thing to do? Summer wasn't sure. She longed to tell him the truth and to trust him again, but her fear of Justin and the bad memories of the past held her back. Her heart was telling her to turn around, find Jake and pour out everything, but her head was warning her to step carefully. Only time would tell whether she was making the best choice, she guessed, but unfortunately time was the one thing she didn't have on her side.

Summer was dithering by the white gate at the foot of Seaspray's path, fighting the urge to run back and find Jake, when a slim figure clad in a chic yellow spotty mac, and holding a matching umbrella, joined her.

"Summer?" the woman gasped, leaning closer and narrowing her slate-grey eyes. "My goodness, it is! Fancy seeing you here."

Yellow Mac was none other than her old childhood nemesis, Ella St Milton. Summer's heart plopped into her borrowed wellies. Even in the damp and wearing a plastic raincoat Ella was groomed and elegant, whereas in her peculiar collection of clothes Summer felt as though she'd raided the dressing-up box and ended up looking like a bag lady. All the years of fame and designer clothes vanished like the rapidly clearing mist. She felt about thirteen years old again.

"I can't believe it!" Ella continued, her voice as bright as her raincoat and not giving Summer time to even greet her in return. "Summer

Penhalligan! My God! I don't think I've seen you properly for years – and I barely recognised you looking like that. Whatever brings you back here and up to Seaspray? Fashion tips from Morwenna, maybe, by the look of you?"

Meow. Summer had forgotten just how bitchy Ella could be with her pseudo friendliness and catty comments. More irritating than a G-string under jodhpurs was how Mo had once described her, which Summer thought was pretty much spot on. It seemed that the past decade or so hadn't improved Ella St Milton one bit.

Gritting her teeth, Summer leaned forwards and the two women airkissed beneath the shelter of the umbrella. Ella's tinkling laugh, about as sincere as a politician's promises, sent Summer straight back to school; she was furious with herself for still feeling this intimidated. They were adults now and their childhood animosity was long behind them, surely?

"Yes, I'm just down for a few days visiting family," Summer explained smoothly, once the kisses were over. Her delighted smile was Bafta worthy.

One of Ella's perfect eyebrows arched in surprise. "At Seaspray?"

"I just popped up to say hello to Alice," Summer improvised.

"How nice." Ella smiled at her. At least, Summer thought she was smiling. It was a bit like being grinned at by a shark.

"You can leave the gate," Ella added when Summer moved to fasten the latch. "I'm on my way up to see Jake about this year's charity ball. We've been working on it together – among other things, of course!"

Ella giggled. Her meaning couldn't be clearer. Jake and Ella were a couple. Summer guessed she shouldn't really be surprised. It made sense. Of course it did; they were practically the Kate and William of Polwenna Bay.

As Ella chattered on, doing everything she could short of cocking a leg and peeing over Jake to make it perfectly clear that she was doing a lot more with him than just attending the ball together, Summer silently thanked God she'd not revealed her secret. What a hideous mistake that would have been. She felt sick just thinking what could have happened if Morgan hadn't interrupted her. Ella wasn't exactly discreet. *The Sun*'s news desk would have been running a scoop about Summer's pregnancy within seconds.

"He has invited you, I hope?" Ella continued. She widened her eyes when Summer didn't reply instantly. "Don't say a word; I can see that he hasn't. Naughty Jake. That wasn't very polite of him, but never mind! *I'm* inviting you. It would be brilliant to have you there – and Justin too, of course. It would be wonderful publicity for us." She whipped a mobile from her raincoat pocket. "What agency are you guys with? Shall I get my people to send an invite to your management? Free, of course. I wouldn't dream of charging you."

"No! No, don't do that!" Summer said quickly. "I mean, please don't put yourself out. I'm just having a few quiet days with my family, and I'm sure Justin already has an engagement then."

Something flickered in the dark depths of Ella's eyes. It looked weirdly like triumph. Her finger hovered over the touchpad.

"Really? But I haven't even told you when it is."

Summer could have kicked herself. This was Ella St Milton, who could smell blood from a hundred yards away. Summer plastered on her bland public face but was pretty certain it didn't fool the other girl.

"He's Justin Anderson, Ella. He's always busy. Honestly, I practically have to book an appointment with him myself."

"Maybe I'll just try on the off chance? Then if he could make it at least you guys would get to spend some time together?" Ella glanced at the expensive watch that was hanging on her skinny wrist. "Anyway, I can't stand here chatting all day. I'd better go; we've got a lot to get through."

Strange that Jake hadn't mentioned this, thought Summer. Then again he'd hardly be likely to admit that he was seeing the girl who'd once done her best to make Summer's life a misery, not when he'd been doing his best to… to…

Well, to be honest she wasn't quite sure what Jake had been intending or what he'd wanted to say. Still, one thing was abundantly clear: he'd very nearly been another huge mistake. When it came to men she obviously had zero judgement. So the snippets of the stories that her brothers had told her over the years were true then: Jake wasn't the same guy she'd dated all those years ago. He was as much a player as all the other single guys who lived in this holiday village. Ella was welcome to him.

Not that she wanted him anyway.

Bidding Ella goodbye, Summer turned towards her cottage. Her stomach was in knots. Should she go back and tell Ella that under no circumstances was she to try contacting Justin, or would that just arouse suspicions and complicate the situation even more? Knowing Ella, this would make her all the more inclined to try to reach him, just out of spite.

She glanced over her shoulder but Ella had vanished into the drizzle. It looked as though the matter was out of her hands. All she could do was hope that Ella took her at her word and didn't bother to call Justin's management.

If she did, the consequences didn't bear thinking about.

Chapter 19

While Summer had been fast asleep in the Tremaines' bath, Mo had been sitting in the family kitchen and thinking that she was starting to know how Faust must have felt. Although her particular deal with the Devil meant that she now had sixteen hands of talented horse to enjoy, rather than Faust's unlimited knowledge and worldly pleasures, the nagging sensation that this agreement was going to cost her more than she'd ever imagined was surely one that Goethe would have recognised. Granted, Ella didn't want Mo's immortal soul – but she did want to know Jake's every movement. Mo, who was at heart a very honest person, was growing more and more uncomfortable with that arrangement.

Today was proving far too wet to school the horses, so once all of her stable chores were completed and she'd given herself a headache trying (and failing dismally) to balance the books, Mo had left her four-legged charges rugged up and chomping hay. Then she'd pulled on her waterproofs and stomped over to Seaspray. She'd been rather hoping for a cup of tea, a thick wedge of her grandmother's homemade fruit cake and a big heart-to-heart with Alice about her finances. Mo hadn't dared tell anyone just how bad things were without Ella's contributions, but the constant text messages and interrogations about where Jake might be and what he was doing were starting to make her nerves jangle so badly that the horses could feel her tension down the reins, and now she was longing to tell somebody her woes. Yesterday at a regional qualifier Splash had knocked the show-jumping course flying like heaps of stripy matchsticks, and even the new horse seemed off his game. It was superstitious nonsense, of course, but Mo couldn't help feeling worried that by accepting Ella's strange offer she might have jinxed herself.

It was unusual for Mo to feel in need of reassurance. She was normally secure in her own judgements and never doubted the choices and decisions she made. Sometimes she lost her temper but generally Mo believed she was justified in all that she did, given that she always had the best intentions. The problem was that this agreement with Ella, for all the good it was undoubtedly going to do for the yard, didn't make her feel like this at all. No matter what she told herself, Mo just couldn't shake the fear that she'd made a big mistake. Always frank with herself and others, almost to the point of bluntness, Mo knew that her desperation had enabled Ella to manipulate her and that, in turn, she would be manipulating her brother so that Ella could get her French-manicured claws into him. It made her feel quite sick inside.

The ugly truth was that she'd sold Jake down the river to save her business and boost her career. Not great, Mo, she said to herself. Still, it was too late to back out now; the deal was done. Besides, she'd fallen head over heels in love with The Bandmaster from the second he'd exploded out of the horsebox, all blood-red nostrils, flying mane and ear-piercing snorts. Once she'd sat on his back and felt the power surge through those muscles as he flew over the jumps, each long stride eating out the distances with mind-boggling ease, Mo had known that she was lost. She had to have that horse.

She didn't feel very proud of herself, though. All she could hope for was that Ella and Jake turned out to be a match made in heaven.

So, feeling in need of a change of scene, Mo had headed to Seaspray and arrived to find her grandmother all at sixes and sevens because none other than Summer Selfish Penhalligan was upstairs wallowing in a bubble bath while Jake and Nick were about to race around South East Cornwall trying to sort out her ridiculous sports car. The stupid cow had run out of petrol, apparently.

"Are you mad?" Mo hissed as Jake gathered up his car keys and shrugged on a Helly Hansen jacket. "Let her call the bloody AA; she can afford it. You don't have to run around her. She's not your problem."

Jake frowned. "She's on her own, Mo. She needs a hand."

"Not from us she doesn't! It suited Summer Penhalligan to turn her back on this family once, remember. But now she needs us so we're useful again? Grow a backbone Jake, for Christ sakes! Can't you see she's using you?"

Her brother didn't rise to any of this. If Mo had been given all the fiery genes from the Tremaine pool, then Jake had been awarded her share of the placid ones.

"She didn't ask for help, Mo. I happened to run into her when I was going to Liskeard. Helping out was my idea. So drop it." Jake turned to Nick. "Ready? Got the fuel can?"

Mo decided to appeal to her little brother's innate sense of bone idleness if Jake wouldn't see reason here. "Come on, Nick, don't be such a sap. Why should you run around her on your day off?"

Jake answered for their brother. "Because this isn't his day off. Eddie Penhalligan won't let him come back to work after the other morning's antics and, if Nick wants to keep his job, he needs to get back in Eddie's good books. Isn't that right, Nick?"

Nick, who was looking sheepish at this reminder of his latest escapade, nodded.

"What did you do now?" Mo asked, intrigued in spite of her bad mood. Eddie Penhalligan was regularly threatening to string his crew up by their bollocks for some offence or other. His rants were what often passed for entertainment in The Ship during the long winter nights, with Nick usually bearing the brunt of his ire.

"He turned up for work when he was still drunk," Jake said bluntly, and Alice's hand flew to her mouth in horror.

"Nicky! You didn't?"

Nick's lower lip jutted out just like it used to when he was a baby. Mo knew that lots of women (the stupid ones, in her opinion) found her brother's sulky good looks endearing – sexy, even – but personally she just wanted to slap him. He was a spoilt brat at times.

"You were seriously going to set out to sea when you were pissed?" she asked incredulously. "Bloody hell, Nick. That's really stupid, even for you."

"I wasn't pissed. I was just a bit hung-over," muttered Nick mutinously. "Big Eddie was just making a fuss. It would have been fine."

"It would not," said his grandmother. "You would have put the lives of you and your crew in danger. Nick, how can I get it through to you? Fishing's dangerous. You need your wits about you." Alice looked worried, as well she might. Mo knew that her brother may as well have his fingers in his ears and be singing *la la la*, for all the notice he was taking. He thought he was immortal. It was what made him both a brilliant skipper and also a very hazardous one.

"The Penhalligan boys were hung-over too. When are you all going to stop having a go at me?" he complained.

"When you stop risking your life and being a twat, Nick," Mo told him.

"That's rich coming from you," Nick shot back. "You risk your life every day jumping horses over stupid fixed fences."

"That's totally different! I never ride drunk! I know I need my wits about me to get my job right," countered Mo.

They continued in this tit-for-tat vein for several more minutes until Alice couldn't bear any more.

"That's enough! Both of you! I can't listen to this squabbling for another second. Nick, you know how we all feel about this. If we didn't love you then we wouldn't worry about you."

"I'm twenty-two. I can look after myself," grumbled Nick, sounding about six.

"So prove it," Jake suggested drily. "Stay out of the pub on days when you're working. Now, are you ready? I've got an Audi TT to rescue."

"You're seriously going out in a gale while Lady Muck wallows in the bath?" Mo couldn't believe what she was hearing. "No way. I'm going up there right now to tell her that she can get her skinny butt out of there and sort her own car."

"You'll do no such thing!" Alice's voice might be quiet but there was an edge of steel in it that all her grandchildren recognised. Hands on her hips, she gave Mo a furious look. "Summer is a guest in this house and as such she'll be treated with respect. Do I make myself clear?"

She certainly did. Mo had seen that expression many times over the past twenty-eight years and she'd never yet been brave enough or foolish enough to argue with it.

"Where's all this bitterness come from?" Alice asked, almost to herself. To Mo she added, "People make mistakes, love. It's part of being human. Sometimes decisions that seem good at the time turn out very differently to how we hope they will. Summer was only sixteen. She was still a child; you were all children. How about letting it go and moving on?"

Trying to ignore a nagging little voice that said she now knew *exactly* what it felt like to make a huge mistake, Mo snorted and flung herself onto the battered sofa at the far end of the kitchen. "Well, I think you're all being taken for a ride. Move on and forgive her if you all want to, but I haven't forgotten how she dumped Jake and headed off to the city and her big acting career without so much as a second glance. I haven't forgotten how she chucked away all those years we'd been friends, either – and I never will."

It never ceased to surprise Mo how much it hurt, even after all these years, that her best friend had turned her back on them all so easily. She'd cried her heart out over it and seeing how much pain her big brother had been in had almost destroyed her. Mo thought that if she lived to be a thousand she would still be able to see the greenish-white pallor of his skin and the bruises of sleepless nights beneath his haunted eyes. It was hardly any wonder that when Summer had written to Jake several weeks later and Mo had intercepted the letter, she hadn't felt inclined to pass it on. Instead she'd picked up the pink envelope addressed to her brother in that familiar looped handwriting and taken it down to the beach, where she'd ripped it into a thousand pieces. As the pink confetti had whirled away on the wind, Mo had sworn that she'd never forget the heartache that Summer Penhalligan had caused.

"I haven't forgotten that either," Jake said quietly. His dark blue eyes met hers and Mo saw that there was pain there still. He gave her a tired smile. "But maybe I have forgiven? It was a long time ago. We've all moved on."

Maybe for Jake this was all in the past, but for Mo that windy July morning felt like yesterday. Jake had seemed liked a different person, and eventually he'd packed his bags and gone travelling, on a six-month trip that had stretched into over a decade. They'd not had him back long and Mo was determined not to let Summer drive him away for a second time.

Once the boys had left to collect the Audi, she sipped her tea, ignoring her grandmother's gentle arguments for letting go of the past. Mo was fighting the urge to storm upstairs and have it out with Summer. Her temper simmered. Wasn't blood supposed to be thicker than water? What the hell was wrong with everyone?

The rain was still falling like tears against the windowpanes, and below the house the sea was boiling. It was like her anger with Summer, ceaselessly churning and dashing itself against the rocks. *Or is your anger really aimed at yourself*, wondered that annoying quiet voice of conscience, *and is finding Summer here just an excuse to vent it?*

Her mobile vibrated and Mo's heart sank because this was Ella again, wanting to know where Jake was. God, thought Mo despairingly, the woman kept tabs on him with such diligence that she made an Orwellian totalitarian regime look sloppy. She sighed loudly and slammed the phone down onto the arm of her chair, deciding to ignore the text for a while. Not that this would stop Ella, who was bound to fire several more messages until she got a response. The woman was more persistent than a verruca.

"I take it this bad mood of yours is because of Fernside?" Alice asked. She was sitting at the table now and flicking through the local paper.

"Fernside?" To be honest Mo hadn't given the woods a second's thought for quite a few days. Being in cahoots with your brother's stalker didn't really leave a great deal of headspace free.

"Well, I know it can't be the stables since the St Miltons have decided to place their eventer with you. That must have made life a lot easier. It was a very fortunate decision, wasn't it?" Alice gave Mo a searching look from over her reading glasses, and Mo felt her face start to heat up.

"I'm a good horsewoman," she said, hating the defensive note in her voice.

Her grandmother nodded. "I'm not disputing that, my love. I'm pleased for you if you think it's the right thing. It's just that you seem a bit out of sorts lately and since it can't be to do with the business I thought it must be because the woods have been sold. There's a piece on it in today's paper."

"What?" Mo leapt up from the sofa. "Let me see that!"

Her grandmother pushed the paper towards her. "There's just a paragraph at the bottom on the fourth page but it definitely says Fernside has been sold. Apparently there was a private auction held in Truro. It doesn't mention him by name, but I suppose that Ashley Carstairs has got his way after all. He'll build a drive, of course, and the woods will have to go. What a shame. I played there as a girl, you know. We all did."

While her grandmother reminisced about her childhood Mo scanned the short article. Alice was right: Fernside woods had been sold at auction for an undisclosed sum to a London property company. Mo's fists clenched in rage. It had to be Cashley. Nobody else in London would be interested in a small piece of Cornish woodland. It was worthless to anyone else anyway, since the only place that the woods led to just happened to be his remotely situated house.

"Bloody Ashley Carstairs! I take my eye off the ball for just a few days and look what happens! Well, he isn't getting away with this."

"Sweetheart, I think he already has," Alice pointed out gently. Getting to her feet, she put her arm around her granddaughter's shaking shoulders. "Pick your battles wisely, Morwenna. You can't win this one."

"Want a bet?" Mo wasn't finished yet. She was so angry with herself she feared she'd combust. With her thoughts filled with new horses, the business and Ella's Jake obsession, Mo had make the mistake of thinking that Cashley hadn't been pressing on with his stupid road project. Of course he had. When nobody from PAG had shown up at the auction to raise environmental and ecological objections he must have been rubbing his greasy paws together in glee.

The fact that Ashley's hands weren't greasy in the least, but were actually brown and strong and with nails like seashells, was one that Mo chose to overlook. She didn't want to dwell on that revolting man at all.

How he must be laughing at her now, especially after their argument in the pub. *I never lose* was what he'd told her. Mo's temper, already bubbling, began to boil. He never lost, eh? Well, she'd soon see about that. When she'd told him that she'd chain herself to the trees or lie down under the diggers she hadn't been kidding. Standing at the Tremaine family's kitchen table Mo swore there and then that she'd become the next Swampy to save Fernside, or die in the attempt.

Hmm, knowing Cashley, that was very likely. He'd probably take great pleasure in crushing her with a JCB. Or, truer to form, he'd pay one of his henchmen to do the job and save getting his white Musto sailing jacket dirty.

"Right," said Mo. "This is war."

Grabbing her phone and kissing her worried grandmother goodbye, Mo tore out of the house and stormed through the garden. It was still raining heavily but she hardly noticed the stinging drops that whipped against her cheeks or the mean wind that blew them into her eyes and cruelly spurred white horses across the bay. She was far too busy planning what she was going to say to Cashley.

Mo hurtled through the garden gate and strode down the narrow street, her yard boots stomping through puddles and her waxed riding coat flying behind her like a superhero's cape. Two more texts came through from Ella, each more impatient than the last, but Mo didn't have time to worry about her. She was starting to think that Ella might be slightly unhinged. If she wanted to find Jake then she could brave the weather and walk over to Seaspray, Mo decided. That would soon show how keen she was!

The rain had emptied the village of visitors. Instead of meandering through the streets, gazing into windows or munching pasties on the quayside, they were now squeezed into cafés and pubs, steaming gently in the fug and causing the windows to weep with condensation. A few brave souls tried to carry on, but the driving rain and biting wind soon sent them scurrying into Magic Moon for some shelter amidst the shop's twinkling crystals. Depressed seagulls huddled forlornly on the rooftops, too soggy even to bother squawking. Tripping boats waited at the bottom of the harbour steps, on the off chance that somebody might be crazy enough to want a half-hour tour of Polwenna Bay and the coastline in a heavy rainstorm. May in Cornwall was as changeable as a moody teenager, Mo reflected as she crossed the bridge and took the footpath up to Mariners. Yet like a stroppy adolescent, you still loved it for what it had been before and what you knew it might become in the future.

Mariners was at the top of the village, directly across the bay from Seaspray and, like her family home, only accessible by foot. Today the rain and the boots of Cashley's builders had turned the path into the Somme. Even Mo had to admit that wading through it was a major pain. Nonetheless, she reminded herself that unlike the Tremaines, who'd lived in Seaspray practically since dinosaurs roamed the earth, Cashley had chosen to buy Mariners and had always known that getting there was a menace. So tough tits if it was hard to reach and inconvenient.

Ashley's builders were halfway through building a wall around the two-acre property, a construction that was mockingly known in the village as the Great Wall of Cornwall. All he needed was a moat, some crocodiles and a drawbridge, thought Morwenna wryly, and he'd be there. Should she expect the boiling oil and hail of arrows any time soon?

Probably.

Mariners' wrought-iron gates had a sign cable-tied to them. *Private Property: trespassers will be prosecuted.* That wasn't very friendly.

"So sue me," Mo muttered as she shoved one of the gates open and sloshed through the mud. "Knob."

Inside, the quagmire was so thick from the constant passing of quad bikes and rigger boots that a path of planks had been laid over the ground. As she balanced her way across them like a tightrope walker (if things with Ella went belly up, Mo guessed there was always Cirque du Soleil), several of the builders called out to her and waved. That was another problem that PAG had encountered: at some of the PAG meetings people had voiced the opinion that at least Cashley's renovations were providing employment in the village, whereas the Tremaines had been laying people off for months. It was a bitter pill to swallow because it was true. Mo had let Daisy, her groom, go simply because she had no way of paying her wages – well, not unless the bank suddenly decided to take pony nuts as legal tender, anyway. Jake hadn't hired anyone for the summer season, and Alice had taken to cleaning the holiday cottages herself to help make ends meet. Times were hard – unless you were a city banker who'd done well.

"Afternoon, Mo!" called Roger Pollard, one of the local builders. Even in the rain he and his spotty son, Little Rog, were busy building the latest section of the wall; no doubt it would give the astronauts something to look at from the International Space Station.

Mo waved back. "Wall looks good, Roger." She nodded her head in the direction of the house. "Is Cashley in?"

"Come back for round two?" grinned Roger. "Ding! Ding! Get in your corners! Or maybe it's time for a bit of mud wrestling? Go naked if you like, maid. We won't mind."

She laughed. "You can keep your mud-wrestling fantasy to yourself, Roger Pollard. I've only come to have a chat with him."

"Shame, that, because he's in. Maybe another time? Anyway, better be getting on. This wall won't build itself."

Leaving them to their work, Mo picked her way across the planks to the front door and before she could have second thoughts raised her fist and thumped on it. The sound was so loud in the muffled stillness of cloud and drizzle that it made her jump.

"Christ, what are you trying to do, wake the dead?" remarked Ashley Carstairs when the door swung open. "Jesus, Red, you look like a drowned rat. Did you swim here? Shall I rub you down? Or maybe you'd like a bran mash?"

"Very funny. Anyway, I'm not here to talk about me," Mo snapped. She stepped inside without being asked, ducking under his arm and showering the hallway with muddy water. Good. She hoped it stained the flagstones.

"Come on in. Make yourself at home," said Ashley, his voice laden with sarcasm. "I'll pop the kettle on, shall I?"

Mo didn't answer. She couldn't because she was temporarily shocked into silence by the reality of his renovations. She'd heard all about them, of course. What Cashley might or might not be up to had been the subject of village gossip for months. Sometimes he was knocking it all down to put up something modern, other days he was building flats. She'd even heard that he wanted to open a pole-dancing club; worryingly, Issie had been rather excited about this. Mo usually took village gossip with a shovelful of salt but now she could see that he really did mean business. The house was little more than a shell. The floors and ceilings had all been removed, leaving just one huge echoing void that even on such a gloomy day was flooded with the sharpest, purest light she could have imagined. Mo was bathed in it and she wanted to gasp. To her great surprise she realised that she understood completely what it was that Ashley was trying to achieve here. The space was incredible and the views would be breathtaking. The enormous windows created the sense of being in an art gallery, reminiscent of the Tate over at St Ives, with the seascape framed in them like an ever-changing masterpiece. It was going to be stunning and special and wonderful.

And not at all what she'd expected.

Ashley was watching her reaction, a half-smile playing on his lips. "Do you like it?"

Mo was staggered. She hadn't anticipated any of this. She'd visited Mariners in the past and, in spite of its impressive position, it had been dark and poky inside.

"It's going to be beautiful in here," she gasped.

"The mezzanine isn't up yet, but when it is the place will really come together. I'll be able to watch the sea from my bed." He looked out across the endlessly shifting scenery. "I always wanted a place with a view like this and I've almost done it, got there before—"

There was an expression on his face that Mo couldn't read. It was almost sad, vulnerable even, which was ridiculous. Everyone knew that Cashley didn't have feelings.

"Before what?"

The shutters were down instantly.

"Before anyone else," Ashley said smoothly. "Anyway, I'm glad you like it. See, I'm not all bad, am I? Maybe you've got me all wrong, Red. So how about that dinner? Or if you like we could skip that, of course, and just have sex."

Mo dragged her eyes away from the seascape; the water was emerald green and wildly laced with doily-like foam.

"I don't think so, Mr Carstairs. Anyway, the house was fine as it was."

Ashley stared at her. Amusement was written all over his haughty face. "*Fine?* Who wants to settle for *fine* when you can have awe-inspiring? Why be adequate when you can be the best?"

Usually Mo would agree. Being the best was what drove her, made her confront stomach-lurching fences and risk her neck over the toughest cross-country courses. Still, loath to agree with Cashley on anything, she chose not to answer. Morwenna wasn't here to talk about his bloody house anyway. She was here to discuss the woods.

"I've not come here to chat," she said.

Ashley raised a dark eyebrow. His fathomless eyes bored into hers before sweeping her body insolently and returning to her face. Even though she was wearing a muddy Barbour jacket and her yard boots, Mo felt her insides tie themselves up and her heart did a weird fluttery thing beneath her ribcage. There was something about Ashley Carstairs that made all her certainties vanish like mist in the sunshine.

"You don't want to chat? I must admit I thought you'd be more of a challenge, Mo. I would at least have thought you would hold out for dinner," he drawled.

Sarcasm was better. She could deal with *that* but when he looked at her as though he was the big bad wolf practically licking his lips and ready to gobble her up she felt… she felt… Well, to be honest Mo wasn't quite sure what she felt. All she did know for sure was that he was a horrible person and she despised everything he stood for. He mocked her, he had no principles, he was materialistic – the list of things she hated about him was endless. High cheekbones, glossy dark hair and those intense magnetic eyes didn't negate any of these, and neither did his razor-sharp mind. He ought to put that to better use, anyway.

"I'd rather eat hay with my horses than have dinner with you," she said icily.

"Sweetheart, there's better things you and I could do in the hay than eat it," he pointed out with a grin that made her feel as though she'd just stepped into quicksand. "But I'll leave that to your imagination."

Mo would far rather he didn't, actually. The last thing she needed imprinted on her mind's eye was a vision of what Ashley Carstairs might do to her in the hayloft.

"If you could just be serious for a minute," she said primly, trying to blot out imaginings of his body pinning her down beneath the solid weight of his, as he held her arms above her head and nudged her legs apart with his knee…

Oh God. This was a nightmare. She wasn't thinking that. She really wasn't! This was his stupid fault for making suggestive comments.

"Yes?" said Ashley. The mocking grin on his face and the way he was looking at her made Mo panic for a moment that he might be able to read her mind.

"I need you to take this seriously," she said, yanking her thoughts back from Jilly Cooper land.

"I am very serious, Morwenna. I wasn't joking when I told you in the pub that I always get what I want. I don't like to waste time."

"That's why you've bought the woods, isn't it? So you don't have to waste time walking from the car to the house?"

"The woods?"

"Fernside. You've bought them, haven't you? At a private auction?" To her distress Mo felt tears sting her eyes and she blinked them away furiously; there was no way she was going to give him the satisfaction of seeing her cry. "Don't bother to lie, Ashley. I read it in the papers. There was a private auction in Truro, wasn't there?"

He nodded. "There certainly was. I'm not going to deny it. Why would I? Yes, I put a telephone bid in. I told you, that's where my drive is going to be placed. I need vehicle access to my home. It's a simple financial transaction, Morwenna. I had the money and the price was right. You could have bid too. There was nothing underhand about it. I assure you the whole process was entirely legal."

Mo didn't think she'd ever hated anyone quite so much as she hated Cashley at that moment.

"You know I don't have the money."

He shrugged. "And I do, so I've bought the woods. That's life, I'm afraid. So your point is what exactly?"

Actually, Mo wasn't sure. She'd been so fired up with indignation that she hadn't thought through what she was going to say to him. The reality was that she didn't have a leg to stand on – not legally anyway, although morally it was a very different matter.

"You might have bought Fernside but you're not going to build your stupid road," Mo spat. "Ever. That land has some ancient trees on it, trees that are part of our heritage."

"I'll plant some new ones to make up for it. It's the circle of life and all that jazz. Check my website, Mo. My green credentials are on it somewhere."

"Like planting a few new trees will make everything all right," she said bitterly. "You're destroying a natural habitat and I swear to God I'll do everything I can to stop you. There must be covenants on that land somewhere and I'll find them."

Ashley shrugged. "Well, I won't hold my breath while I wait for that to happen. My lawyers have been over the deeds and it's all totally in order."

"Then I'll arrange a protest. There are loads of villagers who love the woods. We'll make a camp and claim squatters' rights. It'll take you years to evict us," Mo improvised wildly.

He laughed out loud at this and Mo resented him all the more, because even to her own ears these ideas sounded ridiculous.

"Not if I offer them all a pint and a pasty in The Ship. The trees will probably be knocked down in the stampede for free booze; it'll save the diggers a job and me a fortune. Next brilliant plan?"

She glared at him. "This is all just a big joke to you, isn't it?"

"I confess that I can't see what all the fuss is about. It's only a few old trees and as far as I'm concerned making a drive here is progress," Ashley admitted. "But I'm a reasonable guy, so why don't you try and explain it to me? Over dinner?"

He stepped closer and Mo caught a hint of the spicy aftershave he wore. She would have moved away but her back was against the door in a way that she would have found metaphorical if her heart hadn't distracted her by breakdancing in her chest. He lowered his head and when he spoke his warm breath against her ear made Mo's skin ripple with goosebumps.

"And afterwards maybe you can show me your hay barn," he murmured.

Mo shoved her fist down on the door handle as hard as she could and seconds later was stumbling out onto the step. He was taking the piss and she hated him.

"That's right," she spat, "make fun of it all! Well, laugh as hard as you like, Ashley Carstairs, but I promise you that there's nothing funny about what you're about to do. I swear to God there's no way you're chopping down Fernside. No way at all. I'll do anything I can to stop that from happening."

Ashley's expression didn't so much as flicker. "Anything?"

She glowered at him. "You'd better believe it. Anything."

And with this parting comment Mo spun on her heel and strode away, or at least strode as well as she could while balancing on planks. Ashley watched her go and his lips twitched. When she tripped in her haste and slithered through the mud he called after her.

"Anything, hey? I'm going to hold you to that, Morwenna Tremaine! You'll be back here before you know it!"

As Mo, face on fire, slammed the gate she heard Roger senior say to his son, "Things are looking up, boy. Seems like we may see a bit o' that mud wrestling after all!"

Chapter 20

Jake was beginning to regret agreeing to partner Ella for the hotel ball. Apart from knowing in his heart of hearts that he'd said yes to her for all the wrong reasons, he'd never dreamed that the whole deal was going to be so time-consuming. Ella was certainly tenacious and had an attention to detail that was actually rather unnerving; he guessed this was what made her such a formidable businesswoman. Still, he'd had no idea that just being her plus-one would require so much discussion and forward planning. Already he'd had to coordinate outfits and go through a selection of potential corsages, all of which looked identical as far as his bloke's eyes could see. And now here she was again, this time wanting to discuss the menu choices.

He really hoped his irritation wasn't showing. After all, it wasn't Ella's fault that he had zero interest in the entire affair, apart from what she'd promised to do for Zak and Mo.

And neither was it her fault that all he could think about now was Summer…

As Ella chattered away about the latest urgent tasks that required his help, Jake's thoughts drifted up the stairs, along the corridor and into the steamy bathroom. Jake had seen more than his fair share of naked girls but none of them came close to Summer. She was the most beautiful woman he'd ever known. Even now he still felt shaken by the strength of his reaction to her. Everything about Summer, from those striking green eyes to the smoothness of her skin to the fullness of her lips, made him ache with longing. Was it a physical longing? Jake couldn't deny it: he wanted her more than he'd ever wanted anyone, but there was more to his whirling emotions than just wanting to make love to her.

Make love? He meant have sex with her. That was what he meant. Sex, not love. God, the strain of everything must be starting to get to him.

"Don't you think, Jake?" asked Ella.

Jake ripped his thoughts away from the gorgeous naked woman who right now was probably just stepping out of the bath several floors above him. He had no idea what Ella was asking him and he couldn't tell from looking at her. She could be requesting his opinion on anything from the colour of the loo roll at the ball to the state of the global economy.

Luckily for Jake his grandmother, who could see his thoughts were several flights of stairs away, took pity on him.

"Ella, I don't think Jake would mind either way. He likes beef and he likes salmon, so you can decide for him. Isn't that right, Jake?"

"Yes, absolutely." Relieved to be rescued, Jake was more than happy to agree. "Either will be perfect."

Ella dimpled at him. "I'll put you down for salmon then. Omega-three is really good for you and there's less fat in it too. We need to think about your cholesterol."

Christ. She was even scrutinising his diet now! The sooner this ball was over the better.

"I'll have the beef," said Nick, socked feet up at the table and beer in hand. "The more cholesterol the better for me."

"There aren't any places left for you, I'm afraid." Ella didn't look up from tapping notes into her phone. Why she couldn't have just sent him a text was beyond Jake. "The ball wouldn't really be your thing anyway."

"Because I'm a smelly fisherman, you mean?" Nick said. He swigged the last of his beer and waggled his eyebrows sarcastically. "Afraid I'll come in my smock, covered in mackerel scales, and lower the tone?"

This was exactly what Ella thought and they all knew it. Places at the St Milton summer ball were strictly by invitation only and every year a strange kind of social apartheid seemed to be in operation. Celebrities, politicians and millionaire business owners all received a thick cream envelope in the post. Shopkeepers and trawler men weren't quite so lucky. As a humble marine mechanic Jake didn't usually make the grade either. It had never bothered him and now he knew why.

"No disrespect, Nick," Ella said coolly, "but pints of Stella and pork scratchings don't tend to be served at the hotel. You'd be happier with your friends in The Ship."

Nick grabbed a handful of his blond fringe and gave it a tug.

"Yes, my lady. Thank you, my lady. I knows my place," he said in a thick West Country accent. "I'll just toil in the field with the other serfs."

"You're being ridiculous," Ella snapped. She didn't like being teased, Jake noticed, or being disagreed with in any way. She was the sort of woman that a man could only shut up by being in charge in every way and, being an easy-going guy, Jake knew that she wasn't for him. He wanted someone he could just be himself with, someone with whom he never needed to fight. A marriage of true minds, as Shakespeare had put it.

Once this ball was over he was really going to have to spell it out to Ella that nothing further was going to happen between them.

While Ella tapped at her phone, simultaneously firing questions at him about food and managing to glower at Nick, Jake did his very best to make all the right noises and to look pleased to see her. Any other man in his right mind would indeed be thrilled to see Ella St Milton, who today was looking sexy in a tight dress that practically screamed about just how full her boobs were and how taut and toned her stomach was. It wasn't the usual choice of clothing for a resident of Polwenna Bay, that was for certain. Jeans and hoodies tended to be the norm here, plus a pair of stout boots for all the trudging up and down hills. Even Nick's jaw was all but resting on the kitchen table – and Alice's stunned expression would have been comical if Jake hadn't felt at bit like a lion that'd been cornered by a particularly clever big-game hunter.

He sat next to Ella, feeling smothered by the sickly sweet scent she always wore, and doing his best to pay attention to the very detailed seating plan she was now explaining. Yet Jake couldn't help it; his thoughts were drifting upstairs again. This time, though, the bruises blooming on Summer's soft skin were utmost in his mind's eye and he saw again that jagged silver scar snaking across her shoulder. His fists clenched in fury. Someone had hurt her and this filled Jake with a murderous rage. If he saw that person, and he had a good idea who it was, he would kill them. The strength of his emotion took his breath away; it both terrified and thrilled him because it had come from nowhere, as unbidden and as instinctive as his feelings for Summer had always been. Jake wanted to wrap her in his arms and press kisses onto her forehead, her eyelids and her throat. He wanted to promise her that it would never happen again, tell her that if she would just trust him he would keep her safe forever.

Forever? Jake's chest tightened. What the hell was he thinking? Forever?

Did he still love her? Had the past twelve years, a huge part of them spent trying to forget her, been worth nothing? She'd only been back in Polwenna Bay a short while, but already he was finding it hard to think about anything else.

Was this love?

"Jake! You're miles away," Ella was scolding him. "Do try and concentrate! I have to get this finished today. Now, do we sit with Richard and Judy at the celebrity table or do you think it's better if we're with the Earl and Countess? I know you'll love them. He's great fun and she's absolutely beautiful."

Jake couldn't have cared less if she seated him next to Punch and Judy. All he could think about was Summer – and suddenly he realised that he didn't want to waste another second away from her. Before he knew it he was on his feet and heading towards the bathroom.

"Where are you going?" Ella cried. "We've not finished!"

"I'm just checking on Summer. She's upstairs drying out after being caught in the rain," Jake said. Even to him the explanation sounded odd, and Ella's neat brows drew together. Turning to Alice, he added, "She's been up there for ages. Do you think she's OK?"

"You don't need to go anyway, Jake. She's perfectly fine. I met her on the lane when I was on my way up," smiled Ella.

Jake stared at her. "What?"

Ella patted the chair beside her. "We are talking about Summer Penhalligan, aren't we? Glamour model? Reality TV star? Engaged to Justin Anderson, which I guess makes her a WAG? She was just leaving Seaspray as I was arriving. She said that she'd been catching up with you, Alice." She widened her eyes. "Funny, she didn't mention anything about drying off though."

"Summer's gone?" Jake felt as though he'd taken a sucker punch in the guts. She'd left without saying goodbye? Run away from him?

Then again, it wouldn't exactly be the first time she'd done this, would it?

Ella nodded. "She seemed in a real hurry, something about wanting to call Justin? I can hardly believe she's engaged to him, can you?"

Actually, no, Jake couldn't. Not after the bruises and the scars he'd seen.

"We had a lovely chat," Ella carried on, apparently oblivious that with every word she spoke Jake took another blow to his heart. "She even said that she and Justin would do their best to come to the ball! Wouldn't that be amazing! Justin Anderson is a real A-lister. I read somewhere that he's the new David Beckham. Having him attend would really make the headlines. You can't buy publicity like that."

Jake could hardly believe his ears. Summer was going back to Justin? It was true that she hadn't explicitly told him that her injuries were because of Justin; she'd merely given Jake the story about falling against the kitchen island, which he'd swiftly interpreted as she was *shoved* against the kitchen island. But the fact that she'd fled to Cornwall without any money or solid plans spoke volumes. She couldn't possibly want to go back to him. Something was very wrong.

"I need to see her," he said.

"If you're worried about her car keys, I'll give them to Eddie," offered Nick. "I said I'd meet him in the pub later. Just for a half, before you start, OK? I'm not going on the beer again, I promise!"

Jake was torn. He wanted nothing more than to chase after Summer, pull her into his arms and keep her safe – but didn't that make him as controlling as Justin? Summer had walked away from him twice now. She had made her feelings clear. Yet he was sure that there had been something between them earlier. He'd felt it, he knew he had: that unmistakable pull of mutual sympathy and the crackle of sexual attraction. Something was holding her back, he just knew it. She was keeping secrets from him and those secrets were making her run.

"We can finish this later if you like?" Ella offered. "Dinner at mine?"

Alice stepped in. "I think now is a great time, dear. I'll make some more tea in a moment if you'd fill the kettle and wash the mugs?"

Ella looked a bit shocked at the idea of washing up but Alice had a way of voicing her orders as polite requests, so she just nodded her blonde head meekly and rose to collect the dirty cups.

"Nick, you can take those car keys to Eddie now, then there's no need to go to the pub later and you won't be tempted to have a drink," Alice continued. "And Jake, before you get back to the seating plans I need you to help me reach something in the pantry."

This wasn't a request either. Jake followed his grandmother out of the kitchen and along the narrow passageway that led to the northern and cooler side of the house, a place where Alice fought a constant battle against black mould and where the walls crumbled at the slightest touch, as though they were made of chalk. There was a pantry here, a small and chilly room with a window that for some long-forgotten reason was covered in chicken wire as well as a blind. The room wasn't really used very much, since Jake had treated the family to a huge American-style fridge, so he was at a loss as to what his grandmother might need.

"Nothing," was Alice's reply when he asked her. Her lined face was tired and worried and she reached out and touched his cheek tenderly. Her fingertips were as soft as chamois leather. "But I wanted to talk to you alone and this was the only place I could think of. For such a big house it's pretty difficult to try and get a quiet space."

"So we're hiding in the larder?"

Alice smiled. "Can you think of anywhere else, love?"

Actually, Jake couldn't. His gran was right. The larder was dark and still, and far enough from the kitchen for them to talk without any danger of being overheard. A slice of daylight slipped in from beneath the blind and danced through the wire.

Jake had the strangest feeling that Seaspray was holding its breath. He knew he was.

"It probably isn't my place to say this," Alice began. She shook her head and sighed. "Oh, who am I trying to kid? It definitely isn't my place or even my secret to tell, but I love you Jake and I don't want to see you be hurt all over again. I might be old and my eyes aren't what they once were, but there are some things I can still see as clearly as I ever did – and one of them is how you feel about Summer. No, don't interrupt me," she said sharply as Jake began to protest, "and don't treat me like a fool. It's written all over your face. And if I can already tell because I know you, I promise that it won't be very long before everyone else can too."

Jake shook his head in disbelief. He'd only just admitted his feelings to himself yet Alice had already guessed them.

"Are you some kind of witch?" he teased.

Alice smiled. "You don't live this long without learning a few things about human nature along the way. But, Jake love, please be careful with Summer. She's a very troubled young woman and it's complicated for her right now."

"Because Justin hits her?"

His grandmother closed her eyes wearily. "I feared as much when I saw her face. Poor little Summer. What a mess."

"So that's it? That's what's worrying you?" Jake shook his head. "Granny, I'm not scared of Justin Anderson. Any guy who can do that to a woman isn't a man at all."

"No, of course he isn't," Alice agreed. Then she took a deep breath and said the words that turned all Jake's half-formed hopes and dreams to dust.

"But he *is* the father of her baby."

Jake stared at her. The flagstones seemed to shift and heave beneath his feet like the deck of *Penhalligan Girl*. Summer's secret, the way he'd felt that she was holding something from him, the distant look in those hauntingly beautiful green eyes – suddenly all these things made perfect sense.

"What?"

"Summer's pregnant, Jake. She told me earlier on while you were getting changed and running her a bath. I should imagine that's why she's here. She's come to see her family. She hasn't run away, my love. She really is just having a break."

Jake's head spun as the world, a fantasy world that he'd created, spun on its axis. Summer was going back to Justin. Of course she was, because she'd never left him in the first place, had she? That was all in Jake's imagination, all part of his pathetic hope that maybe, just maybe, they could start again. He'd only seen what he'd wanted to see. She'd never told him otherwise, had never given him the slightest indication that she still had feelings for him. In fact, she'd been adamant that her life was fine.

Jake was furious with himself for getting close again. He wouldn't make that mistake twice.

Summer was lost to him. She was engaged to another man and she was going to have his child. It was time that Jake forgot her for good.

Chapter 21

Jules had hoped that the arrival of rain and wind would mean a few days off from the early morning walks, but no such luck. Danny Tremaine hadn't been in the army for nothing and, as he'd pointed out with a laugh when Jules had timidly mentioned the weather, a bit of rain and mud hadn't stopped his men marching twenty miles with fully laden backpacks. Feeling grateful that she was only walking three miles over the cliffs, Jules had stopped moaning and put on her waterproofs.

For somebody with his injuries Danny certainly put her to shame, Jules had soon decided. Even at his most unfit and with a limp he still managed to cover the ground far more easily than she did. She found herself constantly having to sprint to catch him up. Morgan just zoomed ahead with the sickening energy of childhood, snapping away like mad with his beloved camera, and probably running twice the distance as he zigzagged backwards and forwards to show her and Danny the latest shot.

The early starts were hard going for Jules, who was definitely not a morning person, but the grim business of dragging herself out of a warm bed and into the still-dark world was more than compensated for by the stunning sunrises that turned the sea to molten gold and the clouds to cotton candy. Another benefit was that her waistbands soon felt a little looser and she wasn't puffing nearly as much when she climbed up the steep lane to the vicarage. All the fresh air had put colour in her cheeks too; when Jules looked in the mirror (an activity she usually did her best to avoid), she was pleased to see that her city pallor had been replaced by a healthy glow. Maybe there was something in this exercising lark after all? She and Danny had only been walking together for a short time but already Jules thought she could see a difference in them both. Then again, where her new friend was concerned the sparkle in his eyes probably had as much to do with staying away from the booze as it did with the fresh air.

Today Morgan was with his mother and Jules didn't have any morning activities pencilled into her diary, so Danny had chosen a longer route for them. This time they weren't taking the cliff path but instead were leaving Polwenna by means of a very steep back lane and then following a babbling river through an overgrown and heavily wooded valley to the next village. The thought of the extra miles made Jules's legs ache before they'd even started – but Danny had promised that there was a hotel at their destination that served the best bacon rolls ever, and that if she was really tired they could catch the bus back.

Some people would do anything for money or sex, Jules reflected as she followed Danny's broad frame along the footpath, but she was easily won over by a good bacon sandwich!

"How are you doing?" Danny called over his shoulder. "That last bit was pretty steep. Legs OK?"

Actually they were. Jules was surprised. "I didn't really notice how steep it was," she admitted. "I was too busy looking at the view."

Danny smiled. He had a lovely smile; it crinkled the corners of his eyes and made dimples dance across his cheeks. Jules wished she saw more of it because, like the sun that was now peeking out from behind the clouds, it softened everything and made her heart lift.

"That's because you're getting fitter," he told her. "A week ago you'd have been moaning non-stop."

"I would not!" Jules said, outraged. Then she thought about it. "Well, maybe just a bit."

He raised a questioning eyebrow. "At one point I thought I'd need to call the crash team!"

"Cheek! OK, I may have moaned *now and again* but I still did it, didn't I?"

Danny nodded. "You certainly did and now look at you. We've done almost seven miles now, and most of it uphill too, and I don't think you've moaned once. Well done, Private Mathieson!"

Jules saluted. "Sir! Yes, sir!"

"And I think I'm doing pretty well for a cripple," Danny continued. "The damp makes my leg ache like hell but I'm getting there."

"Just as well because I forgot to pack the portable wheelchair," Jules said, patting her rucksack. "Never mind, Danny. If it gets too much I think I could probably carry you over my shoulder. That's how much fitter I feel."

"Oh really?" He raised his eyebrows. "That sounds like a challenge to me. Maybe I should throw you over my shoulder and see how much you like it?"

Jules gulped at the idea of Danny Tremaine throwing her over his shoulder. An image of him carrying her away somewhere quiet where he kicked the door shut, threw her to the floor, and... and...

Yes. Well, anyway. That was quite enough of that. Jules felt quite hot and bothered and was relieved that Danny would think this was from her exertions rather than an imagination that just lately had been going a bit mad. She really shouldn't have read the bodice-ripper that Sheila Keverne had accidentally left behind yesterday when she'd been brass cleaning. It might have been far more exciting reading than the Bible study notes Jules was meant to be ploughing through, but it was wildly inappropriate for a vicar! Now instead of focusing on St Paul's epistles, Jules's brain was full of images of tall alpha males with rippling biceps and bare chests – all of whom seemed to morph into Danny Tremaine.

It was all very unsettling. She must make sure she never, ever read *Fifty Shades*, not even just to see what her outraged flock were making all the fuss about!

"You'd give yourself a hernia if you tried to lift a lump like me," Jules quipped hastily. "I'm sure you're lighter than I am anyway, so I'll go first."

Danny frowned. "Why do you always do that?"

"Do what?"

"Put yourself down."

"Do I?" Jules had never really thought about it before. It was a bit of a habit with her; make the quip about being fat herself before anyone else could. She'd been doing it for years, ever since primary school when Sarah Sutton had pointed out with an evil seven-year-old's glee that Jules Mathieson was too big to fit through the Wendy-house door. Funny, wasn't it, how even all these years on that particular memory still had the power to send a hot wave of shame washing over her.

Danny nodded. "Yes. You do it non-stop and it does you no favours. Why don't you give yourself a break? It must he bloody hard work living with all that negative self-talk."

Jules shrugged. "Habit, I guess. Anyway, you're a fine one to go on about negative talk, aren't you?"

"Touché! Although, to be fair, I am working on it. I don't think I've called Tara a bitch for at least two hours. That deserves a celebration."

Danny leaned against a tree, pulled a cigarette from his pocket and, placing it in his mouth, lit it. Catching Jules's disapproving expression he rolled his good eye. "Oh, don't look at me like that, Rev. It's one cigarette."

"Seems a shame to survive Afghanistan and then give yourself cancer," Jules said. "Still, up to you I guess."

The tip of the cigarette glowed crimson as Danny inhaled. "Come on, Jules. A guy's got to have one vice."

"So why not just stick to being a miserable git who wakes people up too early?" Jules suggested.

"Very funny. Look, I've given up the booze, the women and the self-pity. At least let me have a smoke," Danny said. "I daren't light up at home. Morgan will give me the lowdown on the hideous way I'll die and Gran will look so disappointed in me that I'll need even more counselling than they say I already do. Everyone has one secret vice and this is going to be mine." He blew a couple of perfect smoke rings and then pinned her with a challenging stare. "So, go on then. What's yours?"

"What's my what?"

"Your secret vice? Or don't vicars have them? Are you all perfect?"

She laughed at this. "Far from it. Gosh, I don't know. Eating cake?"

"That's pathetic and hardly a secret. Come on, spill. Do you long to throttle Sheila Keverne? Have a penchant for expensive wine? Secretly fancy the Archbishop of Canterbury?"

No, but I think I might secretly fancy you, thought Jules despairingly.

Jules wasn't sure when this crush had started. It had crept up on her with a stealth that had taken her by surprise. It certainly wasn't something that she'd looked for or expected. It wasn't even something that she wanted. It had been Jake who'd first caught her eye, which seemed crazy now that she knew him, and Danny was the closest thing that Jules had to a friend here in Cornwall.

Being a vicar was a lonely job sometimes. There was God to talk to, of course, and He was a brilliant listener – but He wasn't quite so easy to have lunch with or to buy a coffee for. Jules knew that she couldn't grow too close to anyone in the congregation for fear of being accused of favouring one person over another. Her job held women friends at bay too; they didn't feel that they could talk about their boyfriends or their sex lives in front of a vicar, which meant that they met without Jules and sooner or later she was excluded from their gatherings. It hurt but Jules understood, and she had prayed very hard to try to let go of her resentment and bitterness over it.

Then along came Danny. Difficult, damaged, angry Danny, who was the antithesis of everything Jules had ever wanted in a companion. He dragged her out in the worst weather, was responsible for her blistered feet that now looked like something out of *Alien*, and challenged her on everything from her faith to what she wanted to eat. He was so spiky that he made a cactus seem cuddly, had a chip on his shoulder the size of Cornwall and was probably the most infuriating person she'd ever met in her life.

But Danny was a contradiction too. He was a wonderful father – beyond patient with Morgan, who could be bloody hard work at times. He bore his physical pain stoically, had a determination that almost bordered on the obsessive, and possessed not only a sharp mind that loved to debate politics but also a surprisingly wicked sense of humour. As they'd walked together over recent mornings, his anecdotes about his childhood and impressions of various residents of Polwenna Bay had made Jules laugh so hard that she hadn't known what had hurt more – her sore feet or the stitches in her sides. Danny didn't care that she was a vicar (he said he'd seen enough on the battlefield that he couldn't give a hoot what God thought of anyone), and with him Jules knew that she could be totally and utterly herself.

"God, I'm dying to know what it is now!" Danny exclaimed. He stepped forwards and mimed warming the palm of his hand against her flushed cheeks. "You should see the expression on your face! You've gone scarlet!"

"Ha very ha," said Jules. "FYI, I was thinking about carrot cake."

"Really? And what exactly were you doing with that carrot cake? Or maybe I shouldn't ask?"

Now she was having inappropriate thoughts about doing things to Danny Tremaine with cream cheese frosting, which would have made her blush even more if that had been possible. To hide her embarrassment Jules made a big thing about looking at her watch and needing to be back at the rectory by lunchtime. By the time she was composed enough to be able to look at him again, Danny was finishing his cigarette and stubbing it out on the gatepost.

"Last one to the hotel buys the breakfast," he grinned. "Which is probably going to be you."

"My legs are shorter," Jules complained, but Danny wasn't sticking around to hear her excuses and was already striding ahead. Hitching her rucksack higher onto her shoulders, Jules followed him over a stile and into another wooded area.

She was being ridiculous, Jules scolded herself as they continued on their way, laughing and chatting easily. Maybe the Lord had set this as a test? A way of teaching her about the pangs of unrequited love – or perhaps to see if, like Job, she could suffer anything and still praise Him? Or maybe it was nothing to do with God at all but just her being an idiot. It made no sense that her heart lifted when she saw Danny's smile, or that just sitting in silence with him was more meaningful to her than hours of chatter with anyone else. When she opened the door in the mornings to see him waiting on the doorstep she felt as though she'd scooped the lottery. Just spending time with him gave her the kind of contentment that she'd never imagined was possible.

It was hopeless, of course. First of all Danny was a married man, albeit a separated one, and as a vicar – and as a person – Jules had the utmost respect for that sacrament. Secondly, even if they were separated now, she knew that Danny was still head over heels in love with his wife. He talked about her endlessly, even if it was in a negative way, and all of Jules's pastoral training told her that Danny's level of anger towards Tara was actually a reflection of how much his true feelings for her were tearing him apart. Just to add to her own private agony, Jules had cracked late one night and typed *Tara Tremaine* into Facebook, then proceeded to torture herself over pictures of a willowy brunette with the kind of figure that made Rosie Huntington-Whiteley look like a heifer. Tara looked even more attractive than Jules had recalled from that eventful night in the pub. She definitely wasn't as round as she was short, with disastrous purple hair and a cake habit. No wonder Dan was heartbroken at losing her.

So. A crush it was and a crush it would remain. Like a schoolgirl infatuation with a boy band, Jules knew that it would pass and that one day she'd look back on it and laugh at herself. She hoped so, anyway – but until that day she'd keep her feelings to herself. She'd just have to settle for being lucky enough to spend time with him.

This was the final stretch of their walk, the woods linking Polwenna Bay with the smaller village of Waterbridge. Ancient trees were tangled above her head and to the left where the land dropped away Jules glimpsed the River Wenn sparkling between the branches. The woods were magical, full of dappled light and deep pools of green solitude. Unseen eyes watched them as small creatures paused in the undergrowth before scampering away, while on the far side of the estuary a lone horse and rider cantered along a track. Jules wondered whether she might spot a heron today, or maybe even a kingfisher; at the very least, there were usually oystercatchers paddling in the shallows.

She sent up a quick prayer of gratitude for the beauty of the world around her. Moving to Cornwall had been a shock after the pace and drama of the city, but with every day that passed Jules was falling a little more in love with her new home and, of course, the people in it.

The bacon roll at The Coach and Horses in Waterbridge was every bit as good as Danny had promised. By the time their breakfast arrived (thick slices of local bacon crammed into floury baps almost the size of Jules's head), the summer had decided to turn up as well and the world was bathed in warm sunshine. Taking their food outside, Danny and Jules sat down at a picnic table to eat.

"Food of the gods," Danny said happily, squirting ketchup into his roll and taking a huge bite. Red sauce dripped from the corner of his mouth and Jules was suddenly filled with a dreadful compulsion to reach across and lick it off. She looked away hastily and dragged her thoughts back to other matters.

"God is singular," she said piously, and Danny laughed.

"It's too nice a morning to argue over theological issues with you. 'God' it is!" He raised his face to the sun; both eyes were now closed. "This is what it's all about. Good exercise, good food and good company. Beats being hung-over and miserable."

Jules bathed in the glow of his words and then, emboldened by them, she reached into her bag and drew out the thick cream envelope that had been hand delivered to the rectory two days earlier. Inside was an invitation to the St Miltons' summer ball, a masked affair with a Versailles theme – whatever that meant. To her astonishment it was addressed to Jules and a plus-one. Jules had heard of the ball, of course; it was the talk of the village. But she'd never expected to be one of the privileged few who were actually invited. It seemed that being the vicar of Polwenna Bay came with more than just a dwindling congregation and a draughty rectory. It also came with social status – a bit like something out of a Jane Austen novel.

Hmm. Jules really hoped this didn't make her the twenty-first-century equivalent of Mr Collins.

She tightened her grip on the envelope, which she'd been carrying around with her since she'd received it. Surely if Danny thought she was good company and was having fun hanging out with her then he wouldn't mind accompanying her to the ball? It might even do him good to socialise somewhere other than the pub.

"Bloody hell, those are rarer than hen's teeth," whistled Danny when Jules passed the invitation across the table. "Only Jake, Zak and Mo have been invited from our lot. Nick's furious. Says he and Issie are going to gate-crash."

Wiping his mouth with a napkin, he took the thick cream card between his fingers and started to read.

Reverend Jules Mathieson (plus one)
You are cordially invited to attend a
Versailles themed Masquerade Ball
at the Polwenna Bay Hotel
to benefit the
Devon and Cornwall Air Ambulance.
Saturday, the first of June,
Six-thirty in the evening.
The Starlight Ballroom,
Polwenna Bay Hotel,
Cornwall.
Formal attire.

"What on earth does it mean by 'Versailles themed'?" Jules wondered.

"You've got to dress like Marie Antoinette, I guess. Big hair, boobs out, beauty spots and all that, but hopefully without the guillotine! Sounds like a laugh."

It did? Fancy dress was Jules's idea of hell. It was all very well if you were skinny and gorgeous but not much fun otherwise. Her last attempt at fancy dress had been as a telly tubby. She'd rocked Tinky Winky, but somehow Jules didn't think that a purple onesie would cut it at the Polwenna Bay Hotel.

"Where on earth can I get an outfit like that?"

"If you're not Ella St Milton with a huge budget? Or Mo, who'll probably just go in jods?"

Jules nodded. She dreaded to imagine what she'd look like in jodhpurs. There would need to be an awful lot more hill walking first.

Danny passed the invitation back. "Shame it has your name on it. You could have made a killing touting this. Still, since there's no way out we need to make a plan. There's a really cool fancy-dress shop in Plymouth that I've used before for New Year's stuff. We could check it out if you like? You'll have to drive though – unless you want to go round in circles, that is!"

He was actually laughing at himself. This was a major step forward. Encouraged, Jules said quickly, and before she could chicken out, "I don't want to go to the ball on my own, Dan. Do you fancy coming too?"

"As your plus-one?"

"No, as my hat. Of course as my plus-one. Besides, if I have to look like an idiot then I don't see why I should do it alone. Are you up for it?"

Jules held her breath. Suddenly, dressing up as Moll Flanders didn't seem nearly as bad if she had Danny there too to make her laugh.

For a moment he hesitated. "I've been to it before. With Tara."

Jules could only imagine what he was thinking. He'd have been glorious in his dress uniform and Tara would have been stunning in her ballgown. What a beautiful couple they would have made, dancing beneath the stars and smiling into one another's eyes. Poor Danny. The contrast of going now, injured, wifeless and with a fat vicar, must be painful in the extreme.

"I didn't mean to bring back any difficult memories," she said quickly. "Forget it, Dan. It was a daft idea."

But Danny was shaking his head. "Tara was a right pain in the arse. Moaned all night that her shoes hurt. No, it might be fun to actually go and enjoy myself for once. I can keep Zak in line too, seeing as he's headlining. Yeah, why not?"

She stared at him. "You want to go with me? Seriously?"

"Seriously. It'll be a right laugh. Nothing like a spot of dressing up," Danny said cheerfully. There was a twinkle in his eye and he gave her a smile of such genuine sweetness that Jules's heart floated up and away like a balloon. Then Danny pointed at her half-eaten bacon bap. "If you don't want that, can I have it?"

Jules pushed the plate across the table. It was the weirdest thing but her appetite had suddenly vanished. Normally she could have eaten all of it and had room for seconds. Now, though, her stomach was filled with thousands of fluttering butterflies. There was no way she could eat.

Cinder-Jules was going to the ball!

Chapter 22

It was late afternoon on the first Saturday in June and anyone who was anyone, or at least considered to be so by the St Milton family, was busy getting themselves ready for the Polwenna Bay Hotel summer ball. All across the village costumes were being hastily pulled together. Kursa was flat out styling hair and Patsy's Pasties had suffered a big hit in takings as people had tried to diet away their spare pounds at the eleventh hour. Up at the hotel the staff scuttled around like busy ants, stringing fairy lights through all the bushes, looping shabby-chic bunting from the trees and setting out the gleaming cutlery in the dining room. The helipad was raked and prepared, the smooth green lawn was good enough for a game of bowls and inside the hotel every wooden surface was beeswaxed and buffed to shining perfection. In the kitchen saucepans bubbled and hissed while chefs yelled and pots were clattered in the race to be ready in time. Polwenna's teenagers, always keen to earn some extra money, had been recruited as waiters, and were now busy ransacking bedrooms to unearth smart black skirts or trousers before begging their mothers to iron their shirts.

It was the same every year and, if she was honest, it was an event that usually passed Mo by. There wasn't much time for ballgowns and bling when you spent most of your days mucking out and riding. Ella had bragged about the ball all the way through school, and lots of Mo's friends had been pea green with envy at the thought of being bought a new prom-style dress by their parents and getting to meet celebrities. Mo and Summer had found it all very amusing and hadn't been jealous in the least: after all, Summer had an innate belief that one day she would be one of those famous people, whereas Mo was happier in jodhpurs and only cared about the kind of celebrities that had four legs.

Well, Summer's vision of the future had certainly come true, but it hadn't seemed to bring her much joy. Mo had only glimpsed her briefly since the day she now referred to as *bath day* and had been shocked by how thin and pale her former best friend had looked. Summer had been leaving the Penhalligans' cottage with Susie and hadn't noticed Mo sitting on the quay – but Mo had seen her, all right. She'd been taken aback at the dark circles under Summer's eyes and the jutting collarbones. Her heart had lurched as a dreadful thought had occurred to her: was Summer seriously ill? Was that why she'd come home and not brought Justin with her?

Mo had tried to ask Alice but her grandmother had remained tight-lipped, so she'd soon given up. It was easier to prise limpets from the rocks than it was to get information out of her grandmother if she'd decided to stay quiet.

As Mo sat at the big mirror in what had once been her mother's dressing room at Seaspray, attempting to drag a brush through her wild red curls, she reflected that Jake had been in a very odd mood lately too. For the last week or so he'd been foul, snapping at them all – and staying out late drinking in The Ship, according to Nick, who spent most of his time there. Issie said it was like Jake and Danny had swapped personalities, because Dan was far more cheerful nowadays, whereas every time she spoke to Jake he practically bit her head off. Even Morgan, who wasn't usually very good at picking up on people's moods, was giving his uncle a wide berth.

Mo narrowed her blue eyes thoughtfully as she looked at herself in the mirror. She was willing to bet her entire overdraft that Summer was at the bottom of Jake's terrible mood. That girl, no matter what her problems, was nothing but bad news for him – and the sooner she pushed off back to London, the happier Mo would feel. The image of those shredded flakes of pink envelope drifting away on the breeze kept returning, though; last night she had even dreamed of them. Mo sighed, impatient with herself for dwelling on such things for so much as a nanosecond. Alice would have said her dreams were the sign of a guilty conscience but Mo shoved such daft thoughts firmly aside. She hadn't done anything wrong by not passing Summer's letter on to Jake. Quite the opposite in fact: she'd been trying to spare him any more pain. There was nothing for her to feel guilty about.

The woodland, on the other hand, was a whole different issue. Mo felt dreadful that she'd not acted more quickly where Fernside was concerned. Not that she would have had the money to buy the woods herself, but at least she could have drummed up some press interest or picketed the auction.

It had been a while since her row with Cashley but every moment was as fresh as though it had only happened minutes earlier. When she relived his mocking comments and the way his dark eyes had raked over her body as if she was just another object that he could buy for his collection, Mo felt close to combusting with rage. The worst thing of all was that there didn't seem to be much she could do, because Ashley was right: the woods were now his, fair and square.

It looked like she really was going to have to chain herself to the trees – and alone too, given that none of the other members of PAG seemed that keen to join in. Even Issie, who was usually up for a good bit of anarchy, had been doubtful.

"At the end of the day we might not like what he's going to do, but he's totally within his rights to do it because he owns Fernside now," Issie had pointed out sadly. "There's no covenant and no preservation orders on the trees. He's even bought outside the conservation zone. He's clever – I'll give him that much, sis – or else he's got a good solicitor. There's nothing technically wrong. PAG hasn't got a hope."

"But the trees are ancient!" Mo had flared. "He can't cut them down. He's a bloody philistine!"

Issie had given her a hug. "He's an arse, Mo. Fact. But, unfortunately for us, he's an arse with the law on his side."

Well, Mo didn't give a hoot for the law. Fact. She loved those woods. When her mum had died she'd spent hours alone there with no one but the wildlife and the silent trees to see her cry. It was a special place, a beautiful place, and she'd do everything in her power to save it.

Losing patience with her hair, Mo shoved in onto the top of her head and anchored it with a clip. There, that would do. The girl in the mirror glowered back at her. The last thing Mo felt like doing was plastering her face with make-up, putting on the ridiculous dress that Danny, of all people, had fetched from Plymouth, and spending the evening making small talk with folk who wouldn't usually give her the time of day. But the St Miltons had invited her to the ball and, since they had her by the short and curlies right now, Mo hadn't dared say no.

As she attacked her surprised eyelashes with the dregs of some dried-up mascara, Mo supposed that since she was officially the St Miltons' three-day event rider it made sense that she would be expected to attend. They'd want to be able to show off about their horse and impress their guests. Not that any of the St Miltons had shown the slightest bit of interest in their horse since the day The Bandmaster had been delivered. Nobody had turned up to watch her put the horse through his paces or, as owners tended to do, give her a million and one useless tips on how to ride him. They hadn't even offered the poor boy so much as a carrot.

Which just proved Mo's worst suspicions: Ella had thrown the horse at her purely because she wanted to get close to Jake. Did that mean that when things didn't work out she'd take The Bandmaster back again?

This thought made Mo feel panicky and close to tears. Bandy hadn't been with her long but already he'd managed to make his way into her heart in that sneaky way that animals did. Unlike some horses, who looked down their thoroughbred noses at Mo most of the time and only just about managed to acknowledge her when she was weighed down with a hay net, Bandy already whinnied to her when she crossed the yard. He also had a habit of shooting across the paddock like a rocket if he so much as caught sight of Mo. He was a dream to ride too, with a mouth as soft as a ripe peach and only needing the slightest of aids to move across the school in his floating trot. He was careful over coloured poles, and when she'd taken him into Devon for some cross-country schooling he'd done so well that a certain high-profile rider had tried to buy him. Bandy was a once-in-a-lifetime horse and Mo knew with every fibre of her being that he was the one who could take her all the way to the next Olympics.

She couldn't lose that horse. She simply couldn't. There had to be a way to persuade Jake that Ella would be a good choice for him. The only problem was that Mo couldn't even convince herself of this, never mind her brother. Ella's constant texts and demands were extremely wearing, and although Mo had done her best to further the other girl's cause with Jake, nothing seemed to be working. Whenever Mo had broached the subject he'd almost bitten her head off. This was so unlike her usually sunny-natured big brother that Mo was becoming quite worried about him. He wasn't eating properly – already his cheekbones seemed even more pronounced than usual – and the only person with worse shadows under their eyes was Summer.

The whole thing was a mess. Mo could only hope that Ella would look so good tonight, and that Jake would have enough to drink, that the magic would finally happen between them. During her schooldays Mo had witnessed the consequences when Ella didn't get her own way, and nothing Mo had seen of her lately suggested that her old rival had improved with age. Mo groaned and buried her face in her hands. If she could only turn back the clock and tell Ella to stick her horses and her bribes where the sun didn't shine. She might well have lost her business and her chance of winning Olympic gold, but at least she'd still have liked herself. Right now Morwenna Tremaine was finding it very hard to look in the mirror.

Which was making getting ready for a fancy-dress ball somewhat difficult.

"Knock! Knock! Get your kit on! I'm coming in!"

The door flew open and in walked Nick. Or at least, she assumed it was Nick; it was pretty hard to tell underneath the powdered hair and glittering carnival mask. He was dressed like something out of the three musketeers, in tight breeches and a flowing green velvet cloak. The look quite suited him, in fact. There was one problem, however: Nick hadn't been invited. Neither had Issie, who'd followed him in, dressed in an identical outfit and brandishing her plastic rapier like a demented Zorro.

"Aren't you ready yet?" Issie looked alarmed. "Hurry up, Mo. Zak will be here any minute if you want a lift. He's setting up at six."

Mo frowned. "I'm sharing a taxi with Jake and Danny and we're picking Jules up on the way. What on earth is Zak up to now? I thought tonight was supposed to be his big chance to meet a record producer? He'd better not mess that up."

Lord. She hated the tone of her voice; she sounded such a nag. A wave of grief for her mother, who would have done a much better job of keeping the twins in line, hit Mo afresh. The loss still felt as raw as it had done when she'd sobbed her heart out in the woods all those years ago.

"He's sneaking us in. It's going to be sick," Nick explained, while Mo tried to recover from the unexpected tide of emotion that had almost floored her. "We'll be in the back of The Tinners' van with all the kit and a blanket over us. When Zak sets up we'll just look like we're with the band. Isn't it genius?"

"No, not really," said Mo bleakly. Sometimes the twins made her feel like an old woman. "It's a high-security event. What if you get caught?"

"Don't stress, Mo. Of course we won't," said Issie blithely. "And if we did, so what? They can't shoot us, can they?"

"I thought you'd be pleased to have some decent company," added Nick. "Jake's had a face like a slapped backside all week and I can't imagine you want to hang out with Danny and his vicar. Amen!"

Issie walloped him with her plastic sword. "Leave it out. Jules is all right when you get to know her."

Nick looked doubtful. "Yeah, whatever. At least she can sit on Tara and squash her flat if she turns up and tries to give Danny a hard time. It'll save me a job."

"Aren't you supposed to be going to sea tomorrow?" Mo pointed out.

After his last performance, Nick had been lucky to escape without Eddie throttling him, never mind be given a second chance to skipper *Penhalligan Girl*. It had taken a lot of tactful persuasion by Jake, grovelling from Nick and calling in of favours by Alice to have him reinstated. Mo wasn't sure quite how seriously Nick had taken the whole escapade. He still seemed to think it had been a huge overreaction on Eddie's part, and unfortunately most of the younger folk in the village agreed with him. Still, in fairness to her little brother, he seemed to have cut down his drinking and his last fishing trip had yielded one of Polwenna Bay's best hauls in months. Seeing over ten grand's worth of bass being landed had gone a long way towards softening Eddie's heart when it came to his maverick skipper.

"Chillax, sis. I'll only have the one; two max," said Nick. He held up his fingers and winked. "Scout's honour."

"You were never even in the Scouts," grumbled Mo, hating the fact that her lips were twitching even though she was trying hard to be stern. Nick's charm was like a superhero power – it overcame any obstacles. "Now push off and let me get dressed in peace. Issie, could you help me zip up my dress?"

Danny had come up trumps with Mo's outfit, although she strongly suspected that the peacock green-and-blue silk dress and the ornate feathery mask had been selected by Jules rather than her brother. His friendship with the vicar was a curious one, Mo thought, but it seemed to be doing him the world of good. Dan was out walking every day and she'd not seen him with a drink for a while. Best of all, though, Jules made him laugh, which was saying something. Poor old Dan hadn't had a great deal to joke about lately.

"You look great," Issie told Mo once the dress was zipped up. She stepped back and admired her sister. "That colour is amazing with your hair and eyes. You'll pull for sure!"

Mo, who had no desire whatsoever to pull, grinned. "It feels dead weird to have a skirt on, though. Thank God it's only for one night."

"I'm not sure about the yard boots, mind," Issie remarked, looking down at her sister's feet. The boots were peeking out from under the hem of Mo's long dress.

"Well," reasoned Mo, "since I'd probably break my neck trying to walk in heels, I reckon this is the more elegant option. Compared to going arse over tit, anyway."

"Who knows, maybe you'll set a trend," said Issie with a wink.

The two sisters made their way downstairs to the kitchen, where Morgan was busy cataloguing his latest pictures with painstaking detail. When he saw his aunts, Morgan insisted on snapping photos of them too. For a few blissful moments Mo was able to forget all about Ella and the woods. When a text from Zak sent the twins hurtling down to the village Mo heaved a sigh of relief that they hadn't bumped into Jake first. He'd been so grumpy lately that there was no way he'd find their plans to gate-crash the party amusing. Danny wouldn't have been pleased either. She was equally glad that Alice had been out at a WI meeting and missed them. The less her grandmother knew about the twins' antics the better.

Mo whiled away the next hour or so Googling environmental protests with Morgan, who was more than happy to tell her lots of facts about carbon dioxide and global warming. Apparently the new teacher at Polwenna Primary was into green issues and had been doing a project with her class, and Morgan was full of it. Mo filed this titbit of information under L for later on; maybe the teacher would be able to help her. Mo wasn't intending to use the children as a human shield to stop Cashley's diggers, which was Morgan's preferred action plan, but maybe his teacher would have some ideas or know people who could help.

If Ashley Carstairs thought Morwenna Tremaine was beaten, he was in for a shock!

"What are you up to?" asked Jake when he and Danny finally joined them. He raised his eyebrows when he saw what was on the laptop.

"'Top ten successful ways to stage a peaceful protest'," he read. "What's going on here, Mo?"

"Nothing," Mo said quickly, slamming the lid down and giving Morgan a *don't say a word* look.

"Now why don't I believe that for one second? Are you planning to chain yourself to a tree and sing *we shall not be moved* to Ashley?"

It was a plan of sorts, Mo supposed – and, annoyingly, about all she'd managed to come up with so far. PAG hadn't been very inspired though, and the new vicar had quickly vetoed the whole idea. Maybe Jules was going to suggest that they prayed their way through it in a peaceful protest? Somehow Mo couldn't imagine Cashley taking that very seriously.

"Try not to wind him up too much. He's our best customer and if he takes his boat to Fowey we're in big trouble," Jake warned her. His stern look suggested that he meant business but Mo wasn't impressed. This was nothing she hadn't heard before. Everyone else in Polwenna Bay might be terrified of Cashley and be grovelling and all but tugging their forelocks to have his business, but Mo wasn't going to give him the satisfaction. Besides, you couldn't put a price on the woodlands. If she upset Ashley and he pushed off from Polwenna Bay forever then losing his business was a small price to pay.

"Mo?" Jake repeated. "Do you hear me? Please don't wind him up."

"Yes, yes." She flapped her hand at him impatiently. "Don't panic, Jake. I'm not going to do anything to upset Cashley." *Yet*, she added silently.

"Now we've got that settled, can we get ready to leave?" Danny wanted to know. He was looking dashing in a scarlet frock coat and ornate silver mask, which hid his injuries. Momentarily, Mo was thrown. He looked almost like his old self, the confident and happy brother she loved so much.

"The taxi driver's just called," Danny added. "He's waiting for us by the bridge."

Jake sighed. "We may as well get it over with."

He hadn't bothered to dress up Versailles style or even found a mask. Instead he was wearing a tux and bow tie. His hair was in loose ringlets to his shoulders and he'd not even shaved, but somehow the golden stubble made him look even sexier, in a dishevelled and dangerous way. Although he was her annoying big brother, Mo thought that it would be hard to find a better-looking guy at the ball than Jake. He could have walked straight out of an Armani advert.

No wonder Ella was crazy about him.

"This is supposed to be fun," Danny reminded his brother as Jake rummaged in the fridge for a beer and, opening it with a hiss, proceeded to down the can.

"Fun for whom?" Jake asked wearily. "I tell you, life wasn't this complicated in Antigua."

Mo didn't think she'd ever seen him look so miserable, not even when Summer had dumped him all those years ago. There was such despondency in his eyes that she wondered what on earth had happened. Was it the business? Or was Ella starting to drive poor Jake around the twist?

"Look on the bright side, fam. It's a free party and you're the plus-one for the hostess. It's a dead cert you'll get lucky," Dan told him cheerfully. "I'm the one who looks like the thing from the swamp and who's supposed to be the miserable bastard in the family. Step away from my role! What the hell's got into you this week, anyway?"

Jake shrugged. "Everything, I guess. The business isn't doing so well and Dad's interfering again with it. He's down at the office now and I dread to think what he's up to. He's probably remortgaging the whole lot behind our backs or buying a ticket to Vegas so he can put it all on red."

This was nothing new. Jimmy Tremaine had always been hopeless with money but he had buckets of charm and generally got away with murder. It was no secret whom Nick took after.

"Dad's just being Dad," said Mo. "He won't change now, Jake."

"Absolutely. All the more reason to come out and party if Dad's being a menace," agreed Danny. "Come on, the taxi's waiting and so is Ella St Milton."

"Great," said Jake bleakly. "Just great."

Mo's heart was sinking. From the expression on his face and the way he reached for another beer, Jake was far from being in the party mood. Even worse, he wasn't inclined to spend much time with Ella. He could make all the excuses he liked about the business and their father but Mo knew the truth: something had happened between him and Summer, and it was eating him up.

Mo's fists clenched in the folds of her dress. Why on earth did Summer Penhalligan have to come back to Polwenna Bay? Nobody wanted her here. She was spoiling everything and breaking Jake's heart all over again.

While the boys fetched their coats Mo flipped open the laptop once more and headed back to Google. Several clicks of the mouse gave her exactly what she needed and with tingling fingertips she reached into her bag for her mobile. This was a long shot; Mo didn't even know if anyone answered calls to celebrities' agents on a Saturday evening, but there was only one way to find out...

Maybe somebody should tell Justin Anderson to come and fetch his errant fiancée home?

Chapter 23

Summer had forgotten just how physically exhausting life could be in Polwenna Bay. As beautiful as the village was, and as romantic as narrow streets and steep cliffs were in theory, in reality going about daily life somewhere designed for horses and handcarts was tough. London, with branches of Waitrose on every corner and parking right outside the house, had spoilt her, Summer had realised. Here every task involved the strategic foresight of a grand chess master because otherwise you soon found yourself walking miles up and down the steep lanes carrying bags of shopping and then being forced to retrace your steps because you needed the bank or more coins for the electricity meter. Nobody needed to go to the gym here; that was for certain. Trekking half a mile to fetch the car or lugging the groceries home from the parking spot was a workout in itself.

She'd kept herself busy over the past few days and, although she was no stranger to hard work, Summer couldn't remember when she'd last felt this shattered. Jake had been as good as his word and filled the Audi up as well as returning it to her parking space, so she'd been making the most of it: in between driving back to the bank and picking up groceries, Summer had also visited Patsy, made an appointment to see Dr Penwarren and bought herself a pay-as-you-go mobile. These were all small things but to Summer each was a baby step on the road to claiming her life back.

While in town she'd sneaked into the newsagents to glance at the tabloids and the celebrity magazines, feeling weak with relief when there was nothing at all about either her or Justin. His silence made her uneasy; it normally meant he was building up to something. Summer didn't kid herself into believing that he might have washed his hands of her or accepted that their relationship was over. Justin didn't think like that. As far as he'd be concerned, she was his possession and he'd make certain she came back home one way or another. He knew how to manipulate her. Sometimes it was tears; sometimes it was a grand gesture. (The Audi had originally been filled with red roses and delivered after a heated disagreement. Even now Summer couldn't think of red roses without remembering the equally red bruises on her wrists.) Worst of all, though, was the guilt when Justin reminded her of just how dreadful his childhood had been.

"It's bollocks, Summer," had been Hattie's reaction when Summer had told her about Justin's mother walking out on him. "I don't care if his therapist says that's given him trust issues. Plenty of men have had shit mothers. They don't all take it out on their girlfriends. Stop trying to make excuses. Justin's not a victim; he's just a bastard."

Summer knew all this and she also knew her friend was right. She'd just been waiting for the right time to leave. The day had arrived when the second blue line had appeared. As much as Summer might have felt that deep down she deserved whatever Justin literally threw at her, there was more at stake now.

When she felt even braver she would ask Hattie to make an appointment for her to see a solicitor too. Justin would play nasty, so she would need to be prepared.

Just as Summer had anticipated, Justin had stopped all her bank cards – a move that would have left her stranded had it not been for Hattie, who'd kept her promise and wired money over to Summer's secret account. According to her agent, Justin was fuming and demanding to know where Summer was. Fortunately, with a big game coming up, his manager had him on a tight leash. Summer had been with her fiancé long enough to know that he would only simmer for a while before he exploded. Then, manager's veto or not, he'd come looking for her. Hattie had said that he'd accused her of hiding Summer and had then been through a list of her friends. It was only a matter of time until he realised that she'd done something extremely out of character – returned to her estranged family.

After bumping into Ella St Milton, Summer had been almost sick with fear that Ella would contact Justin's management to invite him to the ball. Summer knew that if Ella had the slightest inkling that there was an issue, she'd love nothing more than a chance to exploit it; the hair-cutting episode would never be forgotten and it certainly wasn't forgiven. Summer could only hope she'd managed to pull off the performance of a lifetime and had convinced Ella that everything was fine. Still, it had been a while. Surely if Ella had done something Summer would have known about it by now?

For the past few days these thoughts had been whirling around her head like malicious little wasps, every now and then stinging her with a terror that made her pulse race and caused her to jump at the slightest noise. Only the exhaustion from walking up and down the village, her nerves jangling in case somebody spotted her, had stopped Summer from lying awake at night with her heart thumping with dread.

It was a Saturday evening now, at the start of June. As she curled up on the window seat, sipping tea and watching the waves roll onto the beach, Summer knew that she couldn't continue hiding away indefinitely. Her absence was bound to be noticed. Sooner or later somebody would mention that they'd seen her in the village, and before she knew it the press would descend. No, at some point she would have to screw her courage to the sticking place, face Justin and sort everything out. Right now just the thought of this made her mouth parch as though somebody had tipped half of the beach into it. She needed to be strong enough to make sure she was able to stand her ground and didn't crumble. There was a better chance of gaining that strength in Polwenna Bay, where she could listen to the gulls and spend time with her mother in the family home. Here, where she was breathing in the thick salty air and had the whispering waves to soothe her, Summer felt that slowly but surely she was starting to heal. Just as her bruises and the soreness in her ribs were fading with every day that passed, so too were the scars inside that nobody else got to see.

Nobody else, that was, apart from Jake.

Summer sighed and leaned her head against the windowpane. She'd been trying very hard not to think about Jake since their half-conversation up at Seaspray. Her life was far too complicated to involve him any further, Summer told herself sternly, and he'd let her down so badly in the past that in his own way he was just as much of a disappointment as Justin. At least, this was what she was trying to believe – but her heart didn't seem to want to listen to reason, and she'd replayed his words over and over again until she was almost driven insane.

It must be her hormones making her feel this emotional, Summer decided; this longing for him didn't make any sense. They'd been apart for a lifetime, were little more than strangers now. He'd never brush his lips against hers again, his golden stubble grazing her skin as his mouth caressed her throat and trailed kisses across her collar bones, and those arms would never pull her close again to hold her against his heart. The too-short nights spent talking until the moon had sailed high and dawn had scratched the sky were just memories now. She'd never again curl into him in the darkness, wrapping her arms around his strong torso and burying her face into the nape of his neck. These were just shadows of another life that had ended a long time ago, memories that somehow kept slipping through her mind with a bittersweet insistence. She and Jake were strangers now and that was all they would ever be. Once she left here she'd not see him again for a very long time. For all she knew, when she next returned to see her family he might even be married to Ella...

At this thought a sharp pain stabbed her right below her breastbone, exactly in the centre of her heart, and she gasped out loud. Imagining Jake married to another woman hurt more than anything Justin had ever done. Maybe coming back to Polwenna Bay hadn't been such a smart move after all? Although in her mind time had stood still – the village with its crumpled cottages and golden horseshoe beach looking exactly as it had the day she'd left – the reality was that everyone had moved on. Even her gruff father seemed less worried about his embarrassing daughter than he'd been before; he hadn't bothered to give Summer the customary lecture. In fact, the couple of times she'd seen him, Big Eddie had been far more concerned about the antics of her brothers. He hadn't even remarked on her bruises or made so much as one snide comment. Susie was glad to see her daughter back at home, though, and it had been good to catch up with Patsy too. Nevertheless, Summer knew she didn't really fit in anymore; she didn't belong anywhere.

The celebrity world no longer held any appeal and Summer was effectively homeless, since there was no way she could return to the

London house. Polwenna held her heart in a way that nowhere else ever would – but there were too many memories here for comfort, and being close to Jake was proving surprisingly painful. The bruises from her final row with Justin were healing far more quickly that the betrayals and disappointments of twelve years ago. She'd never really loved Justin, Summer realised with a jolt, but she had loved Jake Tremaine with every beat of her tender sixteen-year-old heart.

As though her thoughts had conjured him up, Jake was suddenly outside the window and only inches away, walking past her cottage and looking breathtakingly handsome in a tuxedo. The evening sun turned his hair to flame and gilded his tanned skin. Mo, dressed in shimmering greens and turquoises, was beside him, laughing at something he'd said, and on his far side was a tall limping figure in a long curly wig that shielded his face. This had to be Danny, Summer realised, and her heart went out to him. It was hard to equate the sunny-natured boy she remembered with the stories her brothers had told her about a drunken and violent man whose injuries were truly shocking. Poor, poor Danny. All he'd ever wanted was to be a soldier. Summer, who'd been equally driven by her own childhood dream, could understand only too well how the bottom fell out of your world when the dream crumbled away from underneath you.

She shrank back against the curtains, not wanting the trio outside to think that she was spying on them. Try as she might, though, she simply couldn't look away. The Tremaine siblings still had that magic which drew the eye and made you long to be with them. It was an innate confidence, an ease at being within their own skin, that was so attractive. All the family had that magic, Summer recalled. Patsy said they got it from their father, and Summer could well imagine that.

Jimmy Tremaine was charming and handsome and great fun, even if he wasn't the most effective parent. The Tremaine children had inherited all of his charisma, although it was tempered by Alice's influence – except perhaps in the case of Nick, whom her father was ready to strangle.

Summer needn't have worried about being spotted: the trio were so caught up in their conversation that not one of them glanced her way. Jake was saying something that made Mo throw back her head and laugh, and her giggles were so familiar that Summer felt the loss of her friend all over again. There had once been a time when she would have been with them too, off on some adventure and joining in the laughter, the d'Artagnan to their Three Musketeers. Now she was as much of an outsider as any holidaymaker just visiting for a few weeks. This wasn't her place anymore. It was time to move on.

Long after they'd vanished from sight Summer sat on the window seat staring after them, lost in thought until the sun had slipped behind the headland and shadows pooled across the path. Down in the village lights began to shine in cottage windows, and across the harbour the fairy lights of The Ship threw trembling rubies and emeralds into the water. This was a safe time of day to wander through the emptying streets, Summer had learned. The locals were at home or sinking a few pints in the pub and the holidaymakers had drifted back up the village to their coaches and cars. If she wanted to stretch her legs and clear her head for a moment, then now was the time.

Minutes later her baseball cap was rammed on her head and she was locking the cottage door behind her before walking down the hill and into the village. Now that the evening had fallen the shops were all closed and the seagulls had headed out to the cliffs. Symon Tremaine's restaurant was open for business; as Summer passed by, the aroma of garlic drifted on the breeze, making her mouth water and filling her mind with images of Paris and romance. She quickened her pace just in case Symon was about, then headed left towards the harbour where two trawlers were moored against the quay, their engines running. Fork-lift trucks buzzed up and down as the fishermen landed the day's catch. *Penhalligan Girl* hadn't moved all day, though – which was a bit puzzling, since the weather had been fair and, judging by the stacks of yellow fish boxes, it looked as though the catch was good. Maybe they'd saved tide and were going to go in the small hours instead?

Or had something awful happened to her father? Had Eddie had another heart attack?

Feeling sick at the very thought of this, Summer turned towards the row of ripple-patterned stone cottages and soon found herself at the bottom of the damp and narrow steps that led to the lower door of her parents' cottage. The door was never locked; fisherman had a habit of either returning unexpectedly from sea or staggering home drunk and without keys, so this had always been the family's preferred entrance. As usual an assortment of oilskins and rigger boots were piled up on the weathered bench beneath the plastic overhang, and somebody had heaped logs in a leaning tower, like Pisa's, against the wall. Summer was just about to step inside when the door flew open and she was almost flattened by her brothers charging out of the cottage. At any rate, Summer guessed they were her brothers. It was difficult to be sure because they were both dressed up in masks, plumed hats and frock coats. It made a change from smocks and wellies, she supposed.

"Bloody hell, Summer! You're right in the way!" cried the first, narrowly missing a collision with his sister by walloping into the log pile and causing a wooden avalanche. "Bollocks!"

"Be quiet, you harris! Do you want the old man to hear?" hissed the other brother. It was hard to tell them apart: they were both over six feet tall and fairly broad, and both had the dancing green Penhalligan eyes, so in fancy dress they were more or less interchangeable. It was only when they slid their masks up to see where they were going that she was able to determine which was Bobby and which was Joe.

Both of the boys scrabbled about grabbing logs and piling them back up in a haphazard fashion, trying to make as little noise as possible. It would have been comical if not for Summer's growing suspicions that they were up to no good.

"What's going on?" she demanded.

"Nothing," said Bobby quickly – too quickly for Summer's liking. The boys might be in their twenties now but the guilty looks on their faces were exactly the same as when they'd been kids and caught truanting or selling Eddie's copies of *Playboy* at school in order to buy fuel for their jet skis.

"Nothing? Really? So you often go out dressed like Louis the Fourteenth then?"

"Eh? Who's he?" Joe said.

"A French king, you twat," Bobby told him scathingly. To his sister he explained, "We're going to the St Miltons' ball and it's going to be wicked. There's loads of free booze and Nick says all the birds will have their tits out in low-cut frocks."

"Tits everywhere," said Joe happily. Not for the first time, Summer reflected that the lads'-mag culture might have made her fortune but it hadn't done much for the intellectual development of the likes of her brothers.

"How come you two were invited?" she asked, surprised that the boys had been included. Fishermen weren't usually at the top of the St Milton family's list of desirable guests.

Joe and Bobby laughed and then shushed each other loudly.

"Don't be daft, Summer. Of course we weren't invited," grinned Bobby. "Zak's playing and Nick's persuaded him to smuggle a load of us in. Issie and some of the others have already gone up. Apparently it's a piece of piss to get through security."

"You're gate-crashing the ball?" Summer was impressed at their nerve, although this sort of thing was typical of Nick Tremaine, from what she could gather of him. She supposed that as their big sister she ought to disapprove, but part of her liked the idea of Ella's snobby gathering being infiltrated by the boys and their friends glugging all the free Moët and working their way through the canapés. Then a thought occurred to her. "So why are you sneaking out? What's the problem with Dad? He's no fan of the St Miltons."

Her brothers exchanged a look.

"You look just like you did when your football smashed Sheila Keverne's greenhouse," Summer told them. "Guilty, in other words. Come on, out with it. Why can't Dad find out?"

"Because we're supposed to be going to sea at four and he'll probably have another heart attack if he knows we're up at the party," Bobby confessed. He couldn't quite look his big sister in the eye. "He's got a real bee in his bonnet about everything these days. Like he never had a few beers before he went out."

"Don't look like that; we're not getting totally pissed," added Joe, seeing her concerned expression. "It's only a couple of drinks and a few laughs. We're not going to get bolloxed."

"Yeah," nodded Bobby. "We're not total twats, you know."

"Are you sure about that?" Summer was beyond exasperated with her brothers. She shook her head in despair. "What is it with you two? Don't you realise just how serious this is? Haven't you listened to anything the older fishermen have said?"

"Don't start nagging," said Joe.

"Nagging?" Summer could have grabbed her little brother and shaken him until his eyeballs rattled in his thick and empty skull. "You think pointing out that you're taking risks with your lives is nagging?"

Her brothers looked mutinous but Summer didn't care. They needed to listen.

"I think I got here just in time," she said wearily. "Come on, you two; get back inside."

Joe crossed his arms and glared at her. "No way. It's going to be sick at that party. No way am I missing it."

"Me neither," said Bobby.

"Fine. Then I'll tell Dad, shall I? He can decide whether the boat goes or not." Summer knew that there'd already been the mother of all rows recently over the boys turning up for work hung-over. Maybe a blast of Eddie Penhalligan's wrath was what they needed to see sense.

Joe shrugged. "Fine, tell the old man if you must. Go on, wind him up – but if it gives him a heart attack then it'll be *your* fault. Just remember that the doctor said another one could be fatal. In the meantime, sis, we've got to meet Zak. Come on, Bobby. Let's go."

Summer stared after her brothers, furious with both of them because they'd well and truly outmanoeuvred her. Whatever decision she made now, Summer knew she couldn't win.

She sighed and pushed open the door, calling hello to her parents and trying to ignore the uneasy churning in the pit of her stomach. All she could hope was that her brothers were true to their word and really did have only a couple of drinks. There was no way she could speak to her father about all this, because he'd fly into a white-hot rage and go charging after the boys, causing another almighty scene – hardly what the doctors would recommend for a man with sky-high blood pressure. Joe was right: it could be fatal.

But then again, so could three hung-over boys on a trawler…

Chapter 24

When the daylight started to bleed away from the sky and twilight draped its turquoise veil across the countryside, the narrow lanes leading to the Polwenna Bay Hotel began to fill with more supercars and Bentleys than all of Park Lane's showrooms put together as the great and good of Cornwall made their way to the St Miltons' ball. By the time darkness was falling in earnest, the hotel windows blazed with light and loops of white fairy lights danced in the trees like fireflies. Excited guests chinked glasses and chattered, their words popping in the breeze like the bubbles in their champagne.

In a past life, before death duties and the cost of upkeep had become issues, the Polwenna Bay Hotel had been the country residence of a wealthy family. As such, it occupied a breathtaking headland position, from which its floor-to-ceiling windows gazed across the formal gardens and out to sea. A sweeping gravel drive wound its way to the hotel, taking a leisurely route through several acres of grounds and up a gradual incline before circling the building like a scarf and ending at the foot of a flight of elegant steps leading to the vast front door. As each vehicle crunched over the immaculate gravel, valets in white gloves stepped forward to open doors, assist the passengers as they alighted and magic the cars away to the parking area. All that remained for the guests to do was air-kiss the hosts, take their flutes of Moët and drift away to the terrace where Zak Tremaine was channelling his inner Frank Sinatra by crooning about flying to the moon and playing among the stars.

Jules certainly felt as though she was no longer on planet Earth. With a glass clenched tightly in her fist, she leaned against the balustrade and watched the other guests drift about like gorgeous butterflies. It was like being on a film set, she thought dreamily; none of this felt anything like her real life. The sensation that this was all make-believe was heightened by everyone being dressed in eighteenth-century clothing, unrecognisable behind an array of Venetian carnival masks. The music floating on the breeze, the fairy lights swaying gently, the champagne now fizzing through her bloodstream – all of these things gave the evening even more of a magical quality. Jules knew she wasn't looking like her usual self either: her sweeping claret velvet gown pulled her stomach in and gave her a cleavage that Katie Price would envy, and her long silvery wig and glittery butterfly mask complemented the dress perfectly.

Catching a glimpse of her reflection in one of the shiny windows Jules felt a little thrill of pride, which she made a mental note to ask forgiveness for at some point. The costume suited her well; it was far more feminine and flattering than her usual attire of clerical shirt and black trousers.

It was just her luck not to have been born in the eighteenth century when boobs and killer curves were in. Still, vanity was a sin; she really must be careful.

"Having fun, mate?" Danny asked, chinking his glass of orange juice against her champagne flute.

Jules nodded, the feathers on her mask bobbing enthusiastically. The past three hours had been perhaps the most glamorous of her life. This certainly beat dressing up in a cassock. "It's great. I can't tell who anyone is though, can you? Apart from Jake, of course."

Danny's mouth, or rather the uninjured corner of it, turned upwards. "Yeah, but even if he *had* dressed up the fact that Ella St Milton is practically hanging off his neck is a bit of a giveaway."

"She's certainly keen," Jules agreed. Dan wasn't exaggerating. From the moment they'd arrived at the hotel, Ella had glued herself to Jake's side. Not that Jules blamed her. Jake really was a gorgeous-looking man – although now that she knew him better, Jules wasn't nearly as intimidated by his beauty as she'd once been.

Besides, he didn't make her sides ache with laughter or drive her mad with infuriation like Danny did…

"Keen!" Danny was snorting into his orange juice. "That's diplomatic, Rev. You must be good at your job. *Stalker nut job* is how I'd describe her, even if she is hot."

"Don't be mean," Jules scolded. She glanced across the terrace to where Ella, dressed in white and with her blonde hair tumbling down her back in snaky medusa waves all threaded with roses and ribbons, was holding court while Jake stared out over the inky sea, looking deep in thought. "She's beautiful."

Danny's good eye, a blue circle behind his mask, narrowed. "You mean she *looks* beautiful. Personally, I wouldn't trust her a single inch. She's up to something. Mark my words, there's something she wants."

Goodness, but men could be thick sometimes, Jules thought in amusement. It was as obvious as the pretty nose on Ella's face that it was Jake she wanted. Her body language was all but screaming it. Jake didn't seem particularly interested in all the arm touching and hair tossing but, because he was a gentleman, he was trying to do a good job of being her partner – even if he looked as though the experience was on a par with having a root canal.

"That's his fourth drink just since we've been watching," Danny observed as they saw Jake take a glass of Moët from a passing waiter and knock it back. "God knows how many he had before that. Still, if in doubt get pissed."

"That's the worst advice I think I've ever heard," said Jules disapprovingly. "Just remember, I can't walk you home if I'm in heels – and besides, it'll cost us a fortune if you start smashing glasses here."

"Your feet are safe, Rev: I'm doing my best to stay on the wagon. Besides, a masked ball is perfect for someone like me. Second only to Halloween," Dan quipped.

His tone was light but Jules felt the pain underneath the words and her heart ached for him. His injuries were certainly life changing but Jules no longer noticed the scarred face or missing arm. To her these things were just part of him being Danny, as much as his piercing blue eye colour, the fiery temper and the tinder-dry wit.

She couldn't say this though – not without sounding as though she was dolloping out platitudes or, even worse, being patronising. Fortunately at this point one of the Polwenna teenagers who'd been hired to hand out canapés came waltzing past with a plate of miniature bruschetta, and she was able to shut herself up by cramming several into her mouth.

Unlike Jules, Danny waved the food away. Ever since they'd arrived he'd been searching the crowds of people and she guessed he was looking for Tara. In a strange masochistic way she was eager to catch a glimpse of his wife again too. Although she knew that she and Dan were only friends and would never be anything more, Jules was curious to take another look at the woman who'd walked away from him just when he'd needed her most. It was just part of her pastoral duty, she told herself. She wasn't at all bothered by how thin or how pretty Tara might look in a ballgown.

"There you are! I've been looking for you all evening!" Here was Mo, striding across the terrace looking flushed and rather fed up. Jules had to smile because under her gorgeous dress Mo was still wearing her yard boots and thick socks.

"Having fun?" Jules asked.

"I'm bored stiff. How long before we can get out of here?" Mo grumbled, swiping a drink from a passing waiter and glugging it thirstily.

"Hours and hours for you yet, missus," Dan told her. "Anyway, aren't you supposed to be talking about nags with all the important people? You're here to schmooze your way to the Olympics as I recall."

Mo rolled her eyes and tossed her mane of red curls, which had come unpinned about five minutes after leaving the house. She looked as highly strung and as ready to bolt as any of her horses.

"That was what Salmonella *said* I was here for, but I can't find anyone who's remotely interested. Richard and Judy were very sweet about it but they're not horsey, and some of the other celebrities I spoke to were encouraging but not up for sponsoring an eventer. I tried talking to Ella's father but he didn't have a clue what I was on about. I don't think he even knows about Bandy – and if he does then he was far too busy trying to put his hand on my bum to listen to a word I said," she sighed, pushing her mask up onto the crown of her head and rubbing her eyes wearily. "At least Zak's having a good time. I really hope there is a record producer here tonight. If Ella's fibbed about that as well I'll murder her."

Across the terrace, and on a small stage set up at the edge of the lawn especially for him and his band, Zak Tremaine was crooning into a microphone while surrounded by a rapt audience. He had a beautiful voice, Jules thought wistfully, rich and dark like Bourneville chocolate and so soulful that it made the hairs on the nape of her neck stand to attention. Add to this the sexy dishevelled looks of a fallen angel and those compelling Tremaine eyes and there you had it – the kind of artist that Simon Cowell would trample over One Direction in order to be the first to sign. The Tremaine family had some impressive genes, that was for sure.

"The place is full of VIPs," Jules assured Mo. "I'm sure one of them would be interested."

Mo crossed her arms and looked fed up. "I'll give it a couple more hours and then I'm out of here. The horses still need feeding and exercising tomorrow morning. Shall we grab some more drinks and listen to the band for a bit?"

They made their way across the terrace and down to the lawns where, with fresh drinks in hand and plates piled high with canapés, they found a space at one of the white wrought-iron tables. Each table was topped with a huge glass bowl filled with water in which bobbed floating candles and white roses. Jules supposed she could try something similar with the font if she ever felt the urge.

With her foot tapping beneath her long skirts, Jules soon lost herself in the music. The night grew thicker, a slice of moon smiled down at them and stars sprinkled the sky as though the St Miltons had put in an order with the Milky Way. Even the weather was mild enough to sit outside and enjoy the evening, although the army of patio heaters that had been lined up with regimental precision probably helped. Jules sighed contentedly. This was all a materialistic show, and she was fully aware that she should be in the world but not of it; nevertheless, there was something truly wonderful about being here tonight, all dressed up and watching the beautiful people at play. Tomorrow she would be back to the reality of an empty church and Sheila Keverne's complaining, but just for tonight Jules really did feel like Cinderella.

And Danny, even though he didn't know it, was her Prince Charming.

Thankfully, Dan was oblivious to her train of thought as he watched the brightly dressed guests flitting across the lawn. Although he was wearing a mask Jules could tell he was frowning.

"Please tell me I'm hallucinating," he said slowly, pointing at a group of wigged and masked guests who were dancing with flutes of champagne in each hand and laughing loudly. "Tell me that isn't Nick, pissed out of his head and making a tit of himself?"

Even as Danny was speaking a tall man staggered into one of the tables, knocking it sideways and sending water and candles slopping everywhere before ending up lying on the grass and laughing hysterically in the way that only the totally drunk can. A smaller figure, dressed identically in tight white breeches and a powdered wig, pulled him to his feet, giggling and swaying under his weight. Seconds later they were both back in the huddle of equally merry young people and out of sight.

"Mo?" Danny turned to his sister, who was affecting sudden interest in the floating candles. "Is that Nick over there?"

Mo was still peering into the rose bowl, so Danny gave her a prod. When she looked up, her face was a study in guilt.

"Mo?" said Dan again. "Is that Nick?"

His sister sighed. "Who else? He's gate-crashed with a load of his mates."

"And now he's on the piss as usual. Of all the bloody idiots!" Danny's fist thumped down onto the table. "Zak sneaked him in, I suppose? And Issie?"

His sister nodded miserably. "I think half the youngsters from the village were stowed away in the band's van."

"Including the Penhalligan brothers, no doubt." Danny shook his head despairingly. "Jesus Christ. Were we ever that stupid?"

"Probably," admitted Mo, "but at least we didn't work on a trawler."

"And they're supposed to be going to sea at four," Jules said, horrified. She was recalling an earlier conversation with Alice after they'd initially been discussing the flower arrangements at St Wenn's. Alice, clearly worried, had spoken to Jules at length about Nick's latest antics and Big Eddie's rage. As a general rule, Birmingham didn't have many fishing boats so this was all Dutch to Jules – but even as a newbie she could appreciate the dangers involved. The sea was an unforgiving environment, as the Bible often highlighted. That aside, Jules had worked with enough young people to know that so often the only way they would ever learn for themselves was the hard one, with each painful lesson taught through bitter experience. Polwenna Bay might not have the gang crime or drug problems of the inner city but Jules was learning fast that life in a fishing village had its own unique brand of danger.

"Why didn't you stop him?" Danny demanded. His hand was shaking and orange juice slopped onto the table.

"He's twenty-two, Dan! What was I supposed to do, send him to his room without any supper?" Mo jumped to her feet, her red curls flying. "He promised me that he was only going to have a couple of drinks."

"And then a pig flew by," Danny replied sarcastically. As though driven by some destructive instinct, his hand reached for Mo's champagne glass; it hovered over it for a few seconds, before returning to the table with a thud of clenched fist. Jules felt relieved. A drunk and angry Danny was not a good prospect either.

"I'll kill Zak when I see him next," Danny promised. "As if Nick and Issie need any encouragement to be stupid. And the Penhalligan boys as well? Bloody idiots."

"Getting angry isn't going to help, Dan." Jules put her own drink down. "Let's just find Nick and take it from there."

"Yes, we'd better grab him and get him home – and the Penhalligan boys as well – before it's too late and they head off to sea," agreed Mo.

Danny squinted into the dancing crowd but there was no sign of Nick anywhere now. He'd completely melted into the whirling colours.

"Where the hell is he now?"

"Probably at the bar," said Mo.

"Let's split up and see if we can find him," Jules suggested. It was scary how easily she slipped into vicar mode when there was a crisis. "How about I sweep the dining room and the bar? Danny, you can do the terrace and the ballroom, and that leaves Mo to search the grounds."

Her eyes met Mo's and saw in them unspoken agreement that Dan shouldn't be left to wander the uneven gardens and cliffs.

"Fine," said Danny flatly, and Jules knew from his tone that he'd seen her and Mo exchange that glance. He'd hate feeling that they were making allowances for his physical problems and would hate even more knowing that neither woman wanted him near the cliff edge when he was in a volatile mood. She felt some of the trust they'd built up lately slip away, and this was followed by a sensation like barbed wire tightening around her stomach.

Danny checked his watch. "If there's no sign of the moron then we'll meet back here in half an hour."

"If either of you finds him, text me," Mo said, checking inside her clutch bag that her mobile was on. "And if I find him first then he'll need Jules to do the last rites!"

There was a look of such grim determination on Mo's face that Jules almost felt sorry for Nick Tremaine. Almost but not quite. This was supposed to be a fun night out, not a rescue mission.

Walking towards the hotel, it occurred to Jules that she seemed to be making a bit of a habit of sorting out drunken Tremaine men since she'd arrived in the village. Was God trying to tell her something about the evils of drinking too much, Jules wondered as she headed inside, murmuring apologies as she wove her way through the guests and cannoned into waiters, or was this part of His plan? If so, Jules wished she knew what the plan was. Mysterious ways could be marvellous, of course, but sometimes they were slightly frustrating to a weak and frail mortal. A *For Dummies* guide might have helped.

As she crossed the lobby Jules recalled Alice's anxious expression and Danny's stricken face. The deep dark sea stretching away below the hotel was full of dangers and no place for anyone who didn't have their wits about them. Danny would never forgive himself if anything happened to his brother, and Jules knew that in turn she would never forgive herself if anything happened to set Danny back. She had to find Nick.

Jules bit her lip. Her feelings for Danny were more complex than any theology lectures or confusing doctrine, and she knew she must put them aside. They were inappropriate and unfair. She had to focus on being his pastor and his friend; anything else would just cloud the issue. She felt a sudden stab of longing for her old, safe life in Birmingham. So much for having a quiet few years in a sleepy rural parish.

Being the vicar of Polwenna Bay was proving to be much more complicated than she had ever imagined.

Chapter 25

The hotel's grounds were deceptively large, stretching from the headland almost to the sea in a series of beautifully landscaped terraces, and the further Mo walked from the house the darker the night became. Now it was the stars that lit her path rather than pools of lamplight from the hotel, and instead of music the pounding of the waves beat time and filled her ears with an endless melody of their own. An owl hooted from the big cedar tree that guarded the top terrace, and Mo shivered at the lonely sound and the sensation of being watched by the curious eyes of unseen night-time creatures.

Thank God she was wearing her yard boots, Mo thought as she crunched along the path. It led to a sharp flight of steps, plunging her into the blackness of the next terrace. She couldn't imagine trying to make her way down here in a pair of heels; she'd probably have broken her neck in the attempt. With her skirts bunched in her fists and feeling like something from Poldark, Mo cautiously made her descent. She was relieved when the land became level again. Now she remembered why she lived in her jeans or jodhpurs.

There were no fairy lights or lanterns on this lower terrace. Mo supposed the guests were meant to remain on the smooth lawns of the upper formal gardens, away from the dangers of steps and uneven ground. Heaven forbid that an A-lister might trip and seek to sue the St Miltons. Still, knowing her brother as she did, Mo was certain that if Nick was in the garden and up to something she would find him in the very place where he wasn't supposed to be. If he wanted to smoke a quiet joint somewhere then he was bound to be down here. She just hoped that he hadn't had so much to drink that he'd passed out somewhere or, even worse, tripped and knocked himself out. Mo supposed this would save Big Eddie a job, but if Nick was injured the logistics of getting him back to the house would be complicated to say the least.

Her eyes had adjusted to the dark now, and as the slither of moon peeped out from behind a ridge of building there was just enough silvery light for her to see that there was no sign of anyone. There was a sundial in the middle of the lawn and there were some low-lying ornamental hedges, but nowhere that Nick could be hidden from view. If her brother was outside then he must have climbed down to one of the terraces below this one. From the few occasions that Mo had been to the hotel as a child she remembered how narrow and tricky the climb down was; she didn't really relish trying it in the dark and wearing a long skirt.

She paused for a moment, half inclined to turn back and fetch a torch from someone, when there was a noise from the next terrace. Was it the footfall of another person, or just a rabbit scampering over the path?

"Nick!" Mo called. Her voice seemed too loud against the stillness. "Nick!"

There was no reply but Mo was certain that she wasn't alone. There was definitely somebody else out here; she could sense it in an almost primitive way. Her pulse began to skitter. Her fear was atavistic and illogical, and Mo was furious with herself for it. She'd ridden round Badminton, for heaven's sake. Searching a deserted Cornish garden was quite literally a walk in the park.

The step to the next level had somehow managed to escape the St Miltons' latest round of redesigning and manicuring of the grounds. This flight of granite steps was worn and furred with moss, the stone balustrades cracked and crumbling beneath her fingertips – a far cry from the almost mathematical perfection of the higher levels. The storms of the last winter had caused parts of the cliff to plummet into the sea and Mo supposed that in the name of safety the lower gardens had been closed. What better place for Nick and his friends to slink away to if they wanted to have a sneaky smoke?

This level was home to the long-neglected fountain, once a favourite spot for the wealthy owners of the old manor house, but now just a bowl filled with sludge and guarded by stone cherubs with sightless blank gazes. Two stone benches, covered with lichen and weathered by decades of storms, were placed either side. Mo remembered Alice telling her how, when she'd been courted by Ella's grandfather many years ago, they'd spent hours sitting on one of the benches, holding hands and watching the water play in the sunlight. Nick was bound to have heard these stories too, and he'd probably decided to slip away to this spot to be sure of avoiding his older siblings. Mo felt a little glow of triumph that her brother couldn't outsmart her.

Just as she'd suspected, there was someone there: once she was at the bottom of the treads, Mo made out the silhouette of a tall figure perched on the edge of the fountain and staring out over the inky sea. She was just about to call out when the vibration of her mobile announced the arrival of a text. Mo reached into her clutch purse and slipped her mobile out, fully expecting a panicked message from Danny asking if she'd had any luck with her search.

found N in bar - totally wasted. J and I will get him home. Gd luck with networking!

Mo stared at the screen, stunned because she'd been so certain that the figure by the fountain was her brother. Now she looked more closely, though, she could see quite plainly that this man was taller than Nick by at least a head and not nearly as burly across the chest. He also held himself with a coiled tension that was at odds with her brother's Labrador-like enthusiasm.

The light thrown by her mobile had illuminated her and the hidden man turned to look at her. The top half of his face was masked, so Mo couldn't see his expression fully, but she had the feeling that he was surprised to see her and more than a little irritated at having his solitude interrupted.

Who was it? And why on earth would he have wound his way down to such an isolated spot? There was no tell-tale glow of a cigarette. He was alone, so she wasn't interrupting a romantic tryst. Neither was he checking a BlackBerry or taking a private call. The eyes behind the mask were pools of blackness and his mouth was set in a sardonic smile. Mo's heart twisted into a tight knot; even though he was in the shadows and wearing a disguise, she knew exactly who this was, and as they stared at one another goosebumps rose on her arms.

Not good, Mo, not good. She should turn around and run now if she knew what was best for her.

"You just can't stay away from me, can you?" drawled Ashley Carstairs.

There weren't many occasions when Morwenna Tremaine was lost for words, but this was one of them. Of all the sodding bad luck. If there was anyone on the entire surface of the planet Mo would have wanted to see less than Cashley, she couldn't for the life of her think who it would be. God, fate really seemed to have it in for her lately. She must ask Alice which fairy her parents had forgotten to invite to her christening and try to put things right.

"What are you doing, skulking about down here?" she demanded, crossing her arms and glaring at him.

"Skulking?" The dark eyes glittered, although whether with annoyance or amusement it was hard to tell. "You really do have the most interesting perception of situations, Morwenna Tremaine. I could ask you exactly the same question, couldn't I? Why are *you* skulking about in the gardens and all alone in the dark?"

He stood up and advanced towards her, closing the distance between them with just a few strides of his long legs. His white breeches clung to and sculpted the muscular lines of his thighs and showcased a neat and tight backside. Mo glanced away quickly, shocked at herself for even looking in the first place. It was the champagne that was making her head spin and her eyes wander. It must have been much stronger than she'd realised.

Even though she'd only had a few glasses…

"I'm looking for my brother actually," said Mo quickly. Her voice sounded high and squeaky.

"Well, as you can see, he's not here, whichever one you want. Not unless he's hiding under a daisy or something," Ashley replied. He took another step forwards and Mo could smell his spicy aftershave. It made her feel nervous and she only just stopped herself from stepping back.

Cashley made her feel nervous? What the hell was that all about? This wasn't a sensation Mo was used to – or one that she liked.

"I can see that for myself, thanks," she said through gritted teeth.

Ashley nodded slowly. He was wearing a Venetian-style mask of gold, from the top of which sprung funeral-black plumes. He was so close to her now that Mo could feel the draught from the feathers as his head moved. The dark eyes held hers.

"Well, well, Red, looks like it's me and you all alone in the dark. What do you think of that?"

What did she think of being alone with him, in the dark and on the edge of the cliffs? The quick answer to this was that she was suddenly more unnerved than she wanted to admit. Oh Lord, she'd annoyed Ashley for weeks, months even. PAG had thrown obstacles in his way, blocking his plans for Mariners at every turn and probably costing him more money in one year than she would ever earn, and then she'd told him exactly what she thought of him in front of everyone in The Ship. Men like Ashley were used to everyone kissing ass. They didn't take kindly to being defied and challenged.

"What I think is that I'm going back to the hotel," she told him haughtily.

"In such a hurry? I'm hurt." He placed his hand over his heart, but below his mask his lips twitched upwards. Piss-taking bastard.

"You'll get over it." Mo turned on her heel to leave but Ashley reached out and caught her wrist, spinning her back around to face him, and she gasped.

"Take your hands off me!"

"What are you scared of?" Ashley asked. Something crackled between them and Mo attempted to snatch her hands away, trying to ignore the weird jig that her heart was doing.

"Nothing! And certainly not you! Let me go!"

But Ashley didn't let go. Instead his grip tightened and he pulled her towards him. His other arm snaked around her waist and somehow Mo found that she was held tightly against his chest. He was even taller than she'd realised and she had to tilt her chin right up to look at him.

"I don't believe you; it sounds insane but I know you, Mo, and I know that you're absolutely terrified, even though it's just me and you here. Or is that the very reason why you're so scared?"

His words were heavy with a suggestion that Mo didn't want to contemplate for so much as a millisecond. In the cold moonlight his mask shone, bright and eerie, and those dark eyes seemed to see right through her.

"I'm not afraid of you!" Mo glared at him. He was still holding her close and she could feel his heart racing against her breasts. Who was afraid of whom here?

"Even though we're all alone, Morwenna? Totally alone? How about that? If I don't want to let you go, what can you do?"

"I'll scream," Mo threatened.

Ashley laughed. "Go right ahead. There's nobody else about for miles." He paused. "In an empty garden nobody can hear you scream."

The implied menace in his words made Mo shiver. As always her first defence was attack and she was pretty sure she could fight him off. She had five brothers, after all, and had learned early on in her childhood that some of life's battles were physical. Symon still had a Harry Potter style scar on his forehead from the time he'd tried to wrestle the TV remote from her and change the channel over from coverage of Hickstead – and she'd once knocked Zak out by accident.

"And what's that supposed to mean?" she demanded, her blue eyes narrowed and her curls bobbing with rage. "Are you going to bump me off? Drown me in the fountain maybe? You'd like that, wouldn't you? There'd be nobody then to stand in your way when you try to destroy the environment and ruin the village."

Ashley laughed. It was a deep mocking sound and it did strange things to the hairs on her forearms.

"Drown you in the fountain? That's certainly tempting, but no, I don't think so. Not this evening anyway."

"Throw me off the cliff then?" Mo suggested. "Smother me with a wad of your money?"

He pulled her closer and lowered his head so that this time the feathers brushed her cheek and she felt his warm breath against her ear.

"How unimaginative you are, Red. I can think of much better things to do to you than any of that," he murmured. "And I know you're thinking about them too. I can see it in those gorgeous angry eyes of yours."

His hands were on the bare skin of her shoulders now, the fingertips skimming over her flesh before falling to trace her collarbones and just stopping above the swell of her breasts. All this time his intense gaze never left her face.

"It's a crime that all this is usually hidden under a fleece," he remarked huskily. "Christ, you're a beautiful crosspatch, Morwenna Tremaine, absolutely beautiful. What am I going to do with you?"

Mo's heartbeat thudded in her ears like Mr Dandy's hooves across the paddock. Something very peculiar was going on. She really ought to slap him hard and walk away but she was frozen, her stomach cartwheeling as though she was about to leap the biggest ever fence, because Ashley was right. She *was* thinking about what he could do to her – and none of her wild imaginings involved murder. Instead, and to her absolute bewilderment, she was thinking about how much she wanted him to make love to her.

"You could kiss me," she whispered, shocked at herself but unable to hold the thought back. It was like having an out-of-body experience and Mo didn't think she could have avoided it if she'd tried.

Ashley's inky pupils dilated but before he could say another word, or she was able to stop and think straight, Mo reached up and wound her fingers into his dark hair, pressing her mouth against his and gasping as his lips met hers with equal urgency. Their tongues duelled in passion just as effectively as they did when they argued, and when Ashley pulled his body against hers there was no finesse or tenderness, just an all-consuming hunger that matched her own. One of his legs moved between hers and Mo couldn't help herself drawing him even closer, and gasping in pure pleasure because those tight breeches left nothing to the imagination.

"Is that a hedge fund in your pocket or are you just pleased to see me?" Mo murmured, tilting her head back as his lips trailed molten lava kisses over the tender skin of her throat while his thumbs traced the swell of her nipples through the thin fabric of her gown.

"Stop taking the mickey," Ashley told her. His teeth nipped at her earlobe before his mouth moved back to claim hers again, causing Mo to forget everything except arching closer to feel every delicious sensation. She was melting, her whole body like Cornish ice cream left out in the sunshine, throbbing and aching for more. She didn't think she'd ever felt so turned on in her entire life, and when he drew his mouth away from hers and moved his hands back up to her shoulders it was nothing short of torture.

"For your information, for once I am most definitely pleased to see you," Ashley said softly, his eyes still holding hers and his fingertips tracing shivers all over her body. "I always knew it was going to be good with you, but I had no idea just how good."

Something about the way he said this, maybe it was his utter certainty that this moment had been a foregone conclusion, was enough to make Mo's desire-dazed brain whir back into life.

"What do you mean, you *always knew*?"

Ashley's lips quirked upwards. "This. You and me. I could feel there was something from the moment we first met and I knew you could feel it too. You've always wanted this. Why else would you have gone out of your way to be so difficult? It's wasted far too much time."

Mo stared at him. The passion of seconds earlier that had heated her blood to volcanic temperatures was starting to cool rapidly, bubbles of boiling desire popping away just like the bubbles in the champagne she'd clearly had far too much of earlier on.

"Difficult?" She could hardly believe her ears. "You think I was just being difficult? You arrogant bastard! I believe in all those principles!"

Ashley sighed. "So touchy, Mo. Maybe 'difficult' is the wrong word. Feisty? Angry? Trying too hard to go against everything I did? I knew when you came around to my way of thinking that there'd be fireworks between us. Playing hard to get is always as sexy as hell."

Mo's libido did a massive U-turn. This was the sexual equivalent of a bucket full of iced water.

"You think I was playing hard to get?"

Ashley shrugged. "Call it what you like. I'm useless with words. Trying too hard to fight your feelings? Not wanting to give in? Using the woods as a cover when really you were terrified of how you felt?

Come on, Red; don't look at me like that. There's no shame in it. You want me just as much as I want you."

Mo's head was spinning. *I always get what I want* was what Ashley had said in the pub that night – and it was true, wasn't it? Money, houses, planning permission, beautiful woodlands; the list was endless. What he wanted he would always get. This was just another move in his twisted game of social chess.

Well, he wasn't having *her*!

"I do *not* want you," Mo hissed. "Don't kid yourself. I've had too much to drink and you've taken advantage of that."

Ashley ripped his mask off. His face was almost as unreadable without it but a raised eyebrow implied that he didn't believe a word she was saying. Why should he, Mo realised with despair, when only moments ago every part of her had longed for him, her body reacting to his with ferocity and an urgency that appalled her now? She was hardly able to believe it herself.

"We both know that's rubbish," Ashley said with a calm confidence that made Mo want to scream. "You want me and I certainly want you." His gaze roved over her body and suddenly Mo felt far too aware of the thin and clinging silk of her dress that showed every swell and curve. His eyes flickered back to hers. "We're the same, you and I, Mo. Don't fight it. Just enjoy it."

She shook her head. Mo was damned if she'd be Ashley's latest conquest. This was just a game to him, and no doubt there was a queue of identikit skinny blondes, dressed in Musto and thrilled to be whizzed around the bay on his penis boat and then whisked up to the hotel for a five-star meal and presumably a five-star shag. He was messing about with her, that was all, and she'd almost been caught up in it. Of course she knew that she wasn't Ashley's type. He hated her. This was just another of his devious mind games.

Yet there was a tight knot in her throat because – for a strange few moments, anyway – she'd felt a genuine connection with him and part of her had cried out to that with a passion that had completely taken her aback. Amazed and horrified to find she was so hurt, Mo glowered up at him.

"We are *not* the same," she said so icily that it was a wonder the garden didn't frost over. "I actually care about things, whereas you're just playing games."

"That's not fair," said Ashley. He glanced down at the impressive bulge in his breeches and then looked back at her. "From where I'm standing it feels like you've been playing with me. Anyway, this was your idea as I recall?"

There was a glint in his eye as he said this and Mo was livid with herself.

"I meant about the woods!"

"The bloody woods again?" For a second he looked defeated. "Look, can we talk about all that later? Start again? Everything I say has all come out wrong. I can't think straight when I'm around you. Come here, Mo. Let's not waste time."

"I don't think so," said Mo, ignoring the pounding of her blood as his dark eyes raked her body hungrily. "This was all a big mistake. I don't even like you, Ashley."

Again, his lips curled into that sardonic smile. "Who said anything about liking me? You don't have to *like* me, Mo. Anyway, somebody once told me that love and hate taste pretty much the same on a woman's lips. Shall we see if that's true?"

"It's all just a joke to you, isn't it?" Mo was consumed with a white-hot rage, although whether this was with Ashley or herself it was impossible to tell. "The village, Fernside, Mariners, me…" She shook her head. "I suppose you just kissed me because you thought it might shut me up about everything that you've been up to. It'll suit you if I let you just get on with all your crooked deals."

Ashley looked amused. "The kissing was your suggestion, actually, but admittedly a bloody good one. And for your information none of my deals are crooked. You said so yourself; everything with the woods was above board."

"There'll be something dodgy somewhere."

"Always wanting to believe the worst," sighed Ashley. "Enough talking, anyway. Had we but world enough, and time, this chatting, lady, were no crime."

He was quoting Marvell? Ashley was certainly full of surprises. For a second Mo was impressed before she remembered that the poem was all about telling a woman to get her kit off and to stop wasting time.

Typical.

"The grave's a fine and private place, but none, I think, do there embrace," he added softly. "Mo, I need to tell you something—"

But Mo didn't want to hear whatever it was that Ashley wanted to tell her. She was through with his games.

"Look, I've had too much to drink and I know you just wanted to make some pathetic point," she said angrily. This was familiar ground and she started to feel a little more like her usual self. The person who'd been kissing him and tingling from head to toe at the slightest touch was a total stranger. Mo never wanted to see her again. "Well, congratulations, Ashley. I hope you feel really proud of yourself. You're not a man. You're pathetic."

"Is that what you really think? Strangely it didn't feel like that a few minutes ago." Ashley's face didn't so much as flicker with emotion. God, thought Mo, he really was a heartless bastard.

"Yes," she told him. "It's exactly what I think."

Ashley shrugged. "Well, you protest all you like, Red, but we both know the truth. You want me more than you've ever wanted anyone and you can't bear to admit it. Why not just give in and enjoy it? We're both adults. Why not live a little? Have some fun?"

He was so infuriating! Mo could have smacked his smug face.

"What kind of inadequate person are you that you get your fun playing with people's lives?" she hissed, spinning around on her heel and marching across the uneven grass, her skirts flying out behind her and her whole body shaking with a heady cocktail of fury and frustration. She was angry with Ashley but most of all Mo was furious with herself because he was right: for a moment there she'd wanted nothing more than to *just give in and enjoy it*. Part of her still did.

What the hell was wrong with her?

"Come back, Mo," he said. "Let me show you just how serious I am."

But Mo wasn't turning back. She didn't think she could trust herself if she did.

"Anyway," she thought she heard him call, although it was hard to hear his words over the drumming of her heart, "there's no time left anymore for *playing*."

Chapter 26

It wasn't the sunlight slicing through the curtains, the loud calling of the gulls or raging thirst courtesy of far too much free-flowing Moët that woke Jake the following morning. Instead it was the growing awareness seeping into his consciousness that he wasn't alone. With his eyes closed, he gingerly stretched out his foot and was jolted well and truly awake when his toes encountered a silky smooth and unmistakably feminine calf. It took a few moments for his champagne-saturated brain to adjust before, peeling open his eyes, Jake saw a sight that would have gladdened the hearts of most red-blooded males: a stunning and totally naked woman was curled up against him.

Oh God. He'd broken the dry spell then…

"Morning, handsome," murmured Ella, nestling against him sleepily. "That was some night."

Christ, thought Jake in alarm, it must have been. If only he could remember it.

"Morning," he replied, sliding his arm from beneath her and grimacing at the sudden rush of pins and needles. Something similar was going on in his brain. Glancing around the room he saw various items of clothing strewn about like a formal-dress snowstorm. Over there by the door was his tux flung onto a chaise longue, while hanging out together rather jauntily on the curtain rail were a lacy bra and a bow tie. His boxers were hooked on the bedpost. Gradually, like some sort of Sudoku puzzle, scenes of the previous night started to fall into sequence.

Ella sat up, pushing her blonde mane back from her face and yawning widely. The glimpse of her sharp white teeth and vividly red tongue gave Jake a sudden sensation of déjà vu and in spite of himself he felt a twinge of lust. Danny was right that Ella was hot, and last night she'd gone all out to prove just how high that temperature could go.

"God, I'm exhausted," she said, leaning across and removing her panties from the bedside clock so that she could read the time. "Jesus! It's only nine a.m., Jake. No wonder I'm tired. We've only had a few hours' sleep."

Ella's eyes might be heavy with yesterday's mascara but they glittered triumphantly as she said this. Jake had another groin-tightening flashback of what those pink lips had been up to not so long before. *Sleeping* hadn't exactly been high on their agenda, as he recalled...

He hadn't been in the mood to party and once at the hotel Jake had swiftly got stuck into the champagne, ignoring the disapproving looks lobbed in his direction by Mo and Danny and focusing all his attention on being Ella's date for the evening. This had proved to be far less onerous than he'd been expecting. Not only did Ella look incredibly sexy in her outfit, her gym-honed body and silky blonde hair drawing the eyes of all the men present like iron filings to a magnet, but she'd also turned out to be surprisingly good company too. Granted, she had an acerbic tongue and was as spoilt as hell, but she'd made him laugh too and that rapier-sharp wit had kept him on his toes. Any guy would be proud to partner her. The problem wasn't Ella, Jake had realised as she'd smiled up at him, angling her body in order to give him the best possible view of her cleavage.

The problem was *him*.

While Ella had worked the room, showing an impressive knowledge of the various businesses of her father's guests and being more than able to hold her own as she discussed politics or industry, Jake couldn't help but admire her astute mind. Yes, she was Polwenna Bay's equivalent of Machiavelli, and he didn't like knowing that he'd been played, but she was certainly highly intelligent. As the evening had worn on, he'd begun to enjoy sparring with her.

Do I find her attractive? he'd asked himself. The answer, of course, was that he did. Could they have some fun together? That was a certainty, given that the air between them crackled with sexual possibilities. Were they well matched? Since they were both from the oldest and most established families in the area, this went without saying. If they'd been characters in a Jane Austen novel their mamas would have been practically booking the church. On paper it all looked great, but did Jake actually want it to go any further than an evening of no-strings fun?

The answer was no. Fun and sexy as Ella was, Jake knew in his heart of hearts that she wasn't the one for him.

So no, the problem wasn't Ella. It was him, Jake had concluded – or perhaps more accurately, it was the woman who was alone in Harbour Watch Cottage, a woman whose bruised face and fierce pride made him want to fold her into his arms, hold her close and protect her from anyone who dared try to harm her.

He still loved Summer.

While Ella had flirted and chatted and played the part of hostess to perfection, Jake had worked his way through the champagne and tried his best not to think about those dark curls, sea-green eyes and curves softer than a ripe peach. He'd forced himself to listen to Ella and laugh at her anecdotes. Now and again he'd even found that he was enjoying himself. But there was no escaping the truth: Ella was not the woman who still held his heart even after all this time, the woman who was every bit as out of his reach as the moon rising above the sea. None of Ella's high-maintenance beauty, intelligence or acid-tongued humour came close to Summer's natural grace and wit. He'd have done anything to hear her laugh and see that sweet smile light up her eyes like sunlight shining on the Cornish waves. To know that he wasn't going to be the man to do so was ripping him into pieces.

He'd reached for another flute of champagne, hoping that the alcohol would soon kick in. There was no hope of him ever being with Summer. She was having another man's baby, for God's sake. It was time he moved on, and some fun with Ella – who couldn't have been giving him clearer signals if she'd dressed up as a traffic light and turned red, amber and green – was exactly what was needed, or so he'd thought.

Now, as he was starting to sober up, Jake was wondering just how wise this decision had been. What had looked like some no-strings fun at three a.m. suddenly felt very different in the bright morning light. Judging by the way that Ella was running the tips of her nails along his forearm and snuggling into him, she was up for a repeat of the night before. Appealing as this idea was on one level, and as much as Jake knew that any red-blooded male would think him crazy to turn her down, there was something deep inside telling him that it was a bad idea. He didn't want to be with Ella. Superficially a relationship with her might seem great, but where it mattered Jake knew that it was never going to work.

"Ella, don't." Gently he caught her hand in his and removed it from his arm. "This shouldn't have happened. I wasn't supposed to come back with you last night."

Hurt flickered in her eyes. God, Jake really didn't like himself some days. "Shouldn't? Weren't supposed to? Says who?"

My conscience, thought Jake. He must have got Zak's share but in any case it was a major killjoy.

"This isn't a good idea," he said.

Ella's free hand wandered beneath the duvet, where it took a leisurely stroll up his thigh and brushed against the part of him that most definitely wasn't listening to his brain. "Funny, it feels like a great idea to me. Come on, Jake, there's no point fighting it. You wanted to come back to my room, so let's not pretend otherwise. I always knew you'd spend the night here. We both did."

Jake closed his eyes. "Ella, when a beautiful, sexy woman invites a single guy back to her hotel room after he's had a few drinks on board then it's a pretty inevitable conclusion he's going to say yes."

The hand strayed higher. "And we had a good time, didn't we?"

"I'm sure it was great," he told her. "Of course it was. You're a gorgeous woman."

Ella shot him a triumphant smile. "See, I knew that once you gave me a chance and got to know me, you'd like me."

"I said you were gorgeous and sexy and beautiful," said Jake, catching her other hand and dragging it out from beneath the covers, where it had been determined to do all it could to distract him. "I never said I liked you!"

"You didn't say much at all," Ella reminded him. "As I remember, talking wasn't really on the agenda. Shame you passed out when you did. It was all looking so promising." The hand slipped from his grasp again, strayed lower and found exactly what it was looking for. In spite of the immense relief of discovering that he'd passed out before anything else could have taken place, Jake felt himself harden. Sometimes he was ashamed to be a guy.

"Ella, spending time with you last night was a lot of fun and, yes, I was pleasantly surprised just how much of a good time we did have." It was time to level with her. "Look, we both know I only came to the party for Mo and Zak's benefit. I didn't have any desire to be here – but you took me by surprise, because when you're not being pushy, you're actually a nice girl."

"How about that for a backhanded compliment?" said Ella drily. "Who says romance is dead?"

"But what's happened between us isn't romance, is it? You manipulated a situation and I let you because I was enjoying it. Nothing's changed, Ella. You knew that I came here as a single guy – and I'm leaving as one too."

"But not so soon, surely?" Ella slid on top of him, her blonde hair falling over her perky breasts, and ran her hand across his chest. "I think the least I deserve is a chance to make you dislike me even less."

Jake's hands slid around her slim waist. "You're really determined, aren't you?"

Her lips were against his neck now. "I think we'd be good together. What's wrong with that?"

His body didn't protest but Jake's brain was yelling at him to push her aside. She'd stop at nothing to get what she wanted and the bottom line was that nothing she did could change the way he felt. He had to stop this now, even if she didn't seem to think they needed to. It wasn't fair otherwise.

"Come on, Jake," Ella murmured, her teeth nipping the flesh of his throat and her soft hot tongue making his senses reel. "Just enjoy it. There's no point fighting; I always get what I want."

This determined whisper was the trigger he needed to drag himself out of this logic-melting sensation of desire and back to reality. Tightening his arms around Ella, Jake pinned her beneath him in one swift twist of his strong body. Those dangerous hands were both held in one of his, and finally he could think clearly enough to tell her exactly how things were going to be.

"Last night we both got what we wanted, Ella," he said firmly, "but this is where it ends. It was a good night and we can still make it a great morning, but let's see it for what it is. I've never led you to believe that anything serious was going to happen between us, even if I did have a much better time with you than I'd expected."

She stared up at him. "So that's a good thing, isn't it? Can't we see what happens next?" The pink triangle of tongue licked her lips. "You never know, Jake, it could be a lot of fun finding out."

Jake didn't doubt this for a second. "Ella, I'm tempted as hell but can't you see? It would be totally wrong of me to do that. Having a fun night together is one thing, but my leading you down the garden path pretending this could go somewhere when I know that it won't isn't fair."

"You don't know that it won't go anywhere," Ella insisted. "You said yourself that you like me far more than you ever thought you could. We're good together. You fancy me and I fancy you. The sex is amazing. You don't know that it couldn't work out."

Releasing her hands, Jake rolled onto his side and smiled sadly.

"Of course I fancy you and yes, last night was great – but, Ella, I *do know* that this isn't going further. Last night I saw you as a person I find sexy and intelligent, and after a few drinks my inhibitions were gone. It was fun but something deep inside tells me that it isn't right. I'd be lying to us both if I pretended we could try to make this into something it isn't."

Ella pushed her hair back from her face and gave him a sharp look. "Is there somebody else?"

Was there? Jake couldn't answer that truthfully. He knew that the woman he wanted heart, body and soul belonged to another man; Jake could love her with every fibre of his being but she could never be his. Anything he had left and gave to Ella would just be a poor shadow of what he felt for Summer, and that wasn't fair. Ella deserved better than second best.

"Hopefully there is for both of us." He'd sidestepped the question neatly but Jake could tell that Ella wasn't fooled. Of course she wasn't. She was a smart woman. He exhaled slowly. "Let's not waste any more of each other's time and risk missing out on finding those people one day."

Ella shook her head. "Don't give me all that bullshit, Jake. It's got nothing to do with missing out on potential soulmates." She paused and made sarcastic speech-mark gestures with her fingers around that word. "It's Summer Penhalligan, isn't it?"

Jake stayed silent, which only served to incense Ella. Her hand lashed out and caught him with a stinging slap on the side of his face.

"You spent the night with me but it's her you want! It's always been her!" Ella kicked off the covers and leapt out of the bed in a whirlwind of rage, her hair flying as she snatched up her robe. Jake touched his cheek gingerly. Gym-fit Ella could pack a punch, that was for sure. He guessed that somewhere along the line he deserved this.

"There's nothing happening between Summer and me," he assured her, but Ella just laughed.

"But you wish there was, don't you? God, you're utterly pathetic. Summer's never going to be interested in you, a Cornish spanner turner! She's engaged to Justin Anderson, for God's sake. She's probably with him right now and having a right laugh that you're still her puppet after all this time!"

Jake didn't reply as she hissed abuse at him, her words as deadly as any viper's sting. He wasn't going to react, partly because he knew that he'd hurt Ella badly, however unintentionally, and partly because she was right: he did love Summer and it was pathetic. Nevertheless, every ugly word that Ella threw at him confirmed that his instincts about her had been spot on. Attractive and sexy and entertaining as Ella was, she was not a person he wanted to spend the rest of his life with.

Right now the rest of the next five minutes felt far too long.

Jake was hastily gathering his clothes and simultaneously hopping into his boxers when there was a furious knocking on the door of the suite.

"If that's room service then you can fuck off," shrieked Ella. She glared at Jake and crossed her arms over her chest. "I've lost my appetite for smoked salmon and scrambled eggs all of a sudden."

There was another knock, followed by a round of nervous throat-clearing.

"I'm sorry to disturb you, Miss St Milton, but there's an urgent message for Mr Tremaine at reception. His grandmother has asked that he calls home at once."

There was no point in Ella trying to deny that Jake was in her suite; most of the guests at the party had seen them leave together.

"He's coming," Ella called back coldly. Jake heard sounds of acknowledgement from the other side of the door, followed by the messenger's shoes shuffling away down the hotel's carpeted corridor.

Throwing Jake a look that should have shrivelled him at her feet, Ella stalked into the bathroom. Moments later the sound of running water could be heard. Even the gushing faucets sounded angry, Jake thought. What a mess.

Clad in only his boxers and feeling about sixteen, he dithered for a moment at the bathroom door, torn between trying to apologise again and just wanting to get the hell out.

Getting the hell out won.

He was about to step into his trousers when there was another sharp knock on the door.

"Mr Tremaine, please open up."

"One minute," Jake called, pulling on the trousers and raking a hand through his hair. Then he opened the door, expecting to see the concierge with an elaborate breakfast that Ella had ordered – more evidence of her planning ahead and moulding him to her own agenda. Instead, he was taken aback to see his father standing beside the hotel manager.

Jake's heart went into free fall. It was unlikely that Jimmy Tremaine had decided that now was the perfect time to have a father-and-son chat. Even if Jimmy's face hadn't been porridge grey, just his being at the hotel told Jake that something was very wrong.

"What's happened?" he demanded. Fear made his voice harsh.

Jimmy Tremaine gripped the door handle for support. He suddenly looked every one of his sixty-three years. Even his moustache and ponytail seemed to be drooping.

"Dad? Tell me what's happened!" Jake felt like shaking his father. A hundred horrible possibilities were racing through his mind. "What's wrong? Is it Gran?" Oh God, while he'd been wasting time messing around with Ella had something awful happened to Alice?

His father took a deep breath. He was shaking. As an icy finger of foreboding traced a path down Jake's spine, he realised that he'd never seen his father so upset.

"You need to come home," Jimmy said quietly. "There's been a dreadful accident." He paused and passed a hand across his face. When he looked up his eyes were bright with tears. "Oh Christ, there's no easy way to tell you this, Jake, but there's just been a call from the coastguard. *Penhalligan Girl*'s gone down."

Chapter 27

Summer stood at the furthest end of the quay, her hands curled around the metal handrail as she scanned the horizon, desperately willing *Penhalligan Girl*'s small life raft to appear. She wiped her face with the sleeve of her jumper, unable to distinguish now between her tears and the sea spray. She wasn't alone; many villagers had joined the Penhalligans on the quay in a silent vigil and were now staring with her out across the endless waters. Like a pet cat that suddenly lashes out and scratches, the sparkling sea now felt both familiar and alien to Summer, and she could scarcely grasp what was happening. The whole scene had a nightmarish sense of unreality, only there was no hope of waking up from this horror.

The phone call from one of the Polwenna skippers had come only twenty minutes earlier, but already Summer felt as though that had been another life altogether, a more innocent one in which she'd chatted easily with her mother over breakfast while Eddie had sat grumbling about the low-cholesterol offerings and plotting his later escape to score a sausage roll from Patsy. During the ordinariness of that day's breakfast time, they'd been so blissfully unaware of the unimaginable horror that lay in wait. Summer might have been worried sick about what was going to happen with Justin and her heart might have ached with the loss of any future with Jake, but now these things seemed unimportant compared with the news that the trawler and all hands had been lost.

"Tell me his isn't happening," Susie said quietly. She glanced down at her mobile phone just in case some good news had miraculously appeared, but the screen was stubbornly blank in her trembling hand. "This has got to be a mistake."

Summer put her arm around her mother, pulling her tightly against her side. She knew there was nothing she could say that would offer the slightest comfort, because this wasn't a mistake. The coastguard didn't make errors about fishing boats sinking and emergency distress beacons being activated. This was as serious as these things could ever be, and now they were waiting for a rescue helicopter to be scrambled as soon as one was available. Every fishing boat from the Polwenna Bay fleet had abandoned its towing in order to steam to the last known co-ordinates of *Penhalligan Girl*. No mistake had been made, or at least not by anyone who wasn't on board *Penhalligan Girl*.

Of course, Susie knew this just as well as Summer did – and so did every other resident of the village. All fishing families dreaded a call like this and prayed that they would never receive one, even though the churchyard at St Wenn's was filled with evidence that such things did happen.

Summer had woken early that morning with the rays of the sun dancing across the floorboards of her bedroom, and filled with a resolve to tell her family the truth. Seeing Jake the day before, so near and yet a million miles away, had been something of a wake-up call and a vivid reminder that her life was hurtling in a very different direction. Knowing that the Penhalligans were always up at the crack of dawn, she'd walked through the newly born morning before letting herself into the family's cottage and drinking strong tea with her parents. Nobody had mentioned anything about the boys being out the previous night and, since the boat had gone, Summer had heaved a sigh of relief that she hadn't stressed her father unnecessarily. Her relief was short-lived; moments later Eddie's mobile had rung and the whole nightmare had begun in earnest.

It had taken both Susie and Summer several minutes to get any sense out of Eddie. He'd slumped at the kitchen table, the phone clutched against his chest and with his mouth gaping like something from his nets. White faced, and after downing a shot of emergency whiskey from the bottle Susie kept hidden in her knitting basket, Eddie was eventually able to stutter out the dreadful news. Once he'd done so, Susie had also needed a drink.

The call had been from one of the other skippers, who'd heard over the VHF radio that *Penhalligan Girl* had sent out an emergency Mayday signal. All vessels in the vicinity had been requested to change course immediately and head to the area in which the boys had been going to fish that day. The hope was that they might find survivors, although the reality was that this was unlikely. For the boat to have vanished without any of the crew having made a call over the radio meant that disaster must have struck *Penhalligan Girl* incredibly fast. The emergency signal itself didn't need to be activated manually, so there was no crumb of comfort in that either. Summer knew that big waves from a coaster could submerge a boat; she knew too that when frigates headed straight into the course of trawlers, the smaller boats were unable to change direction fast enough because their towing gear was spread miles out behind. These things had happened in Polwenna Bay before. Then there were the heartbreaking tales of young men who'd gone to sea alone and never returned, having been caught in their winding gear or washed overboard by a freak wave. Everyone had a story to tell and it was generally taken for granted that fishing was a perilous way to earn a living. You dealt with this by not thinking too hard about it and telling yourself that it was just as hazardous to cross the road. You had to think that way, Summer knew, because otherwise the worry and the statistics were enough to drive you insane. It was all about putting safety first every time and never taking risks. The sea was an unforgiving entity and there was no margin for error. Enough of the fishermen in the village had missing fingers or tales to tell, to make everyone aware of the dangers. Everyone, it seemed, except for her stupid, reckless brothers and bloody Nick Tremaine – who'd all been determined to party hard no matter what the risks.

Now, standing on the quay while her mother choked out gasping sobs, Summer felt close to hysteria herself. She might not have been in the wheelhouse but she was every bit as responsible for this disaster as her brothers. If only she'd said something to her father rather than hoping that Bobby and Joe would be sensible and only have a few beers. Eddie would have been furious, erupting so violently that he'd certainly have risked his heart, but that now looked like the lesser evil compared with this far greater one. If only she'd spoken out then, he would have stopped the boys from going to sea.

It was her fault. Yet again she'd brought nothing but misery to the people she loved.

"Summer Penhalligan? Susie?" A small plump woman with the kindest eyes Summer had ever seen and a crazy mop of purple hair joined them. Although she was wearing jeans and a Quiksilver hoody, the dog collar peeking out gave away her identity and a cold claw scraped Summer's heart. If the vicar was here then it could only mean that bad news was expected – or maybe had already reached the village.

The woman held out her hand. "I'm Jules Mathieson."

"The vicar," Susie whispered. She grasped the outstretched hand, clutching it as though it was a life raft, and her eyes filled with tears that spilled onto her cheeks. "Are you praying for us, Vicar?"

Jules took Susie's hands in her own. "Mrs Penhalligan, I've been praying for your boys from the second I heard the news and I'll carry on praying until they come home, but I'm not strictly here on church business. I'm a friend of Danny Tremaine and last night we had to carry his brother Nick home from the party up at the hotel."

Susie stared at her. "Nick? Our skipper, Nick?"

"I'm afraid so. He went to the St Miltons' ball last night and had far too much to drink. From what I can gather quite a few of the youngsters gate-crashed the party."

"And my boys were there too, weren't they?"

The vicar sighed and was about to speak when Susie interrupted.

"It's all right, Vicar; you don't need to tell me that. I know they were. If there's a party then Bobby and Joe will be the first ones there. But to take the boat out when they've been up all night drinking?" Susie looked utterly defeated. "They know that's asking for trouble."

Summer couldn't keep the truth in for a second longer. "This is all my fault! Mum, I knew they were going up to the hotel – I caught them sneaking out – but I didn't say anything because I was scared that Dad would upset himself. Nothing I said was going to change their minds." Her vision blurred, the sea shimmering dangerously. "If I'd said something then they'd be safe."

"You need to know something," said Jules. She was still holding Susie's hands and amid the swelling despair she was a calming presence. "Nick didn't go to sea this morning – as far as I know he's still unconscious up at Seaspray – but Danny and I did see your boys last night, because they helped us carry Nick to a cab, and I can promise you that neither of them was drunk. In fact they shared the taxi back down to the village with us. Bobby was furious with Nick because it would leave them short-handed, but your son certainly wasn't drunk. He said that he'd only had a couple of beers."

"And do you believe that?" Summer desperately wanted this to be true; two beers was nothing out of the ordinary for a fisherman the night before a fishing trip, and she knew that if that had been all both her brothers would have been fine after a sleep and some breakfast. If they'd really been careful then whatever had happened at sea might not have been down to an error of their judgement – although not having their more experienced skipper and being short-handed could certainly have made a difference. They'd be guilty of being a little rash, but hardly the first fishermen who'd gone to sea light on crew.

Jules looked thoughtful. "I don't know either of them, of course, but Danny does and he didn't seem to think they were in a bad way. They were in high spirits but that was all. Actually they seemed keen to get back so that they'd have some sleep. It was Nick who'd taken it too far."

"Sounds about right." Susie's face darkened with anger. "Nick's done that several times before." She looked at Summer. "Jake promised us that it wouldn't happen again. He promised."

"With all the good intentions in the world, I don't think this was something Jake could really promise," said Jules gently, "and I should imagine that when he gets home and speaks to Nick there'll be hell to pay."

"So because Nick got drunk the boat had to go out short-handed, with two boys who'd been out partying and were probably still half asleep," Susie said wearily. "Why did they have to be so stupid?"

"They would have thought they were doing the right thing, Mum. They wanted to keep the boat earning," Summer began, but Susie rounded on her, eyes flashing with fury.

"And as for you, how could you not tell us what was going on? Didn't you care that your brothers were putting their lives at risk? Or don't they feature any more either? If anything happens to them, Summer Penhalligan, it will be your fault!"

"I didn't want to upset Dad," Summer cried, stung by the unfairness of this. "I was worried about his heart. I didn't know what to do for the best."

"So you decided it was easier to let them go to sea? Risk their lives? Cross your fingers none of us would be any the wiser?" Susie's contempt was so sharp that Summer recoiled. "Who are you, Summer? I don't feel I even know you anymore."

"I thought I was doing the right thing!" Summer couldn't hold back the tears any longer. "I was so frightened that Dad would have another heart attack."

"This is a really difficult time for all of you," Jules said softly to Susie, "but I'm sure Summer was trying hard to think of everyone, and we all know just how ill Eddie's been. Danny's certain that the boys weren't drunk at all; he was actually impressed that they had the sense to know when to stop."

But Susie wasn't prepared to let her daughter off the hook this easily.

"But Summer didn't know that the boys hadn't been drinking." Susie shook her head slowly and the look of disappointment in her eyes made

Summer feel sick. "If anything's happened to them then I'll know who's to blame. If we'd known then we could have stopped them! They wouldn't be... be... out there!"

Summer couldn't bear to listen to another word. Nobody could blame her more than she blamed herself. With a sob she spun around, elbowing her way through the crowds until she was running along the quay and away from her mother, but no matter how fast she ran Susie's accusing words followed her. Blinded by tears and with her emotions as tangled as the nets strewn in bins alongside the fish market, Summer fled through the winding streets.

Her brothers were missing at sea and it was all her fault. Susie would never forgive her and Summer knew that she would never forgive herself. She was like a curse to everyone and everything she had ever loved. Her shoulders shook. She should never have come back to Polwenna Bay. Returning had been a big mistake.

By the time she was almost back at her cottage, Summer's breath was coming in aching gasps and it felt as though an industrial sewing machine was needling stitches across her stomach. With one hand clutching her abdomen and the other frantically trying to jab the key into the lock, she sobbed in frustration. All she wanted to do was hide away from everyone, curl up in the window to watch the horizon for a returning boat, and pray harder than she'd ever prayed for anything in her life that Bobby and Joe would come back to them.

"Summer! Summer! Are you all right?" Suddenly, miraculously, Jake was at her side, gently taking the key from her hand and slotting it into the lock. "Jesus, bloody stupid question. Of course you're not."

Summer couldn't help herself; the sound of that familiar voice and the kindness in his words were all it took to breach the dam of her despair. The grief was a tsunami sweeping her away and with it all the barriers that she'd tried so very hard to maintain. Nothing mattered anymore apart from having her brothers safely home again.

Somehow Jake managed to steer her inside, kicking the door shut behind them, before sinking with her into the window seat and pulling her close against his chest. There he held Summer against his heart and let her cry and choke out her sorrow and her awful guilt, stroking her hair away from her hot face until eventually there were no tears left and her breathing began to calm. Then, after pressing a kiss onto the crown of her head, Jake crossed the kitchen and filled the kettle. Tea had always been the Tremaine family's answer.

"This isn't your fault, Sums," he said, leaning against the counter and crossing his arms. "If it's anyone's fault then it's mine for not taking a harder line with Nick. He's let your brothers down in a big way and, believe me, right now he feels bloody awful. We both do."

Summer shook her head. There was no way the blame lay with Jake. She knew only too well who was really responsible.

"I should have told Dad what they were up to. I knew it was stupid."

"And risk Eddie keeling over for nothing? I saw him that day when he lost his temper with the boys and I was terrified he was going to have another heart attack. Christ, I was on my way to see him and I dread to think what sort of state he'll be in. Your Dad's not a well man. You were only trying to protect him. Summer, trust me on this one, there was no way you could have known what would happen."

Summer wiped her eyes on her sleeve. "I thought I was doing the right thing, but it's meant the boys have been at risk."

"Your brothers are both adults, Sums. They know the job and they know the dangers. There's nothing they've done this morning that they haven't done a thousand times before. Your mum knows that really."

"But the boat's gone down!" Summer sobbed. "The boys are lost at sea."

Jake couldn't deny it. Everyone who lived in a fishing community knew what it meant when the coastguard was alerted.

"They have a life raft," he said gently. "That's where they'll be. The coastguard will be able to track them. Their EPIRB gave a signal."

He meant that a distress beacon had indicated their position. But Jake and Summer knew of enough instances of fishing boats sinking so fast that their life rafts didn't have time to detach and inflate. Neither of them needed to voice their fears. Even if the location beacon had given out a signal, it didn't always mean that a rescue attempt was successful.

Summer glanced out over the ever-shifting waves. Somewhere out there were her brothers. Her eyes filled again. *Please, God*, she prayed, *bring them home safely. I'll do whatever it is you want. I'll leave the village, stop thinking about Jake – I'll even go back to Justin if that's what it takes. Just bring my brothers home.*

Jake, oblivious to Summer's frantic pleas with the Almighty, made tea and together they sat sipping their hot drinks and watching the horizon. His quiet presence steadied her but still, even half an hour on, none of the Polwenna fleet had returned. Was this a good thing or not? Summer wondered miserably. She glanced down at her pay-as-you-go phone but there was no message from Susie or Eddie. The villagers were still gathered on the quay and now a TV crew had joined the throng. No matter how many times she told herself to stay positive, Summer knew that this didn't look good.

"I can't stay here any longer," she said. "I know it's pointless but I'd feel more use down on the quay."

Jake nodded. "I totally understand but, sweetheart, the news teams are there. This is a big story. Are you sure you want to risk being spotted?"

Justin, the media and her anonymity all seemed irrelevant now. Summer wondered why it had ever seemed to matter so much.

"I just want to be with my family," she said sadly. Even if Susie and Eddie hated her right now, she knew that her place was with them. "I always have done."

"Then that's where we'll go," Jake said firmly, and Summer found that she liked the way that they were a "we" again, a unit against the world. "Come on. Let's go and find your parents."

So together they made their way back into the village and through the crowds, until they arrived at the quay. Summer heard ripples of interest as she passed and felt their stares follow her, but this no longer made her pulse race; with Jake beside her she knew that she could face whatever was coming – however bleak.

Chapter 28

Mo's horror at the events of the night before had paled into insignificance now. After taking a call from her distraught grandmother, she had broken the habit of a lifetime by not mucking out and exercising the horses but instead turning them straight out into the paddocks. While they rolled in the mud like trophy wives enjoying a spa treatment, she sped into the village, little caring that her hair was still wild from the night before and her face was full of smudged make-up.

Like anyone who'd grown up in a Cornish fishing village, Mo was only too aware of the dangers of the sea; hearing that *Penhalligan Girl* had gone down turned her blood to ice. Was it wrong to be so thankful that Nick had been too drunk to go to sea? He might well be consumed with guilt and regrets but for once in her life Mo was glad of her brother's heavy drinking habits; ironically they'd kept him safe.

The news had not long broken but already a crowd was gathering on the quayside and shocked villagers were huddled together, staring out to sea as though sheer willpower would be enough to bring back the trawler. Patsy Penhalligan was crying and Jules was already with the family. Shit, thought Mo. This looked bad.

What could she do? Usually filled with energy, Mo hated feeling so helpless. Standing here on the quayside while everyone milled around talking in hushed whispers as they speculated about what might have happened was enough to drive her crazy. Surely there was something she could do to help? She glanced around just in case Jake was about with a plan but there was no sign of her brother. Given that the last time she'd seen him Ella had been draped all over him like a python clad in designer labels, it didn't require a huge leap of Mo's imagination to figure out where Jake might be. Ella was probably re-enacting scenes from *Misery* right now so that he wouldn't be able to leave her bedroom for a very long time.

Mo felt a pang of guilt. If Ella got her manicured claws into Jake it would be partly her fault. Wonderful as The Bandmaster was, she was starting to feel that he didn't quite make up for Evil Ella being a permanent fixture in the Tremaine family. She was going to have to make some tough decisions. On the other hand, nobody had forced Jake to spend the night with Ella. It was a strange way to behave with somebody whom he claimed not to like.

God. Was there a man alive who wasn't a total disappointment?

"I can't bear it!" A dreadlocked whirlwind hurled itself into Mo's arms and almost knocked her flying. It was Issie, green with a hangover and haggard with grief, and now howling into Mo's shoulder in between hiccoughing "Bobby!" and "Joe!" at regular intervals. Mo wasn't feeling sympathetic though. If anyone had been looking for a sign that her little sister and her crowd's partying had got completely out of control, then there couldn't have been a more obvious indicator than this. Still, now wasn't the time to give her sister a lecture; instead, Mo just hugged Issie until the storm of weeping subsided.

Catching sight of Danny above her sister's golden head, Mo waved him over, her surprise at seeing her usually reclusive brother out in the crowds was less important than the need to know what was happening.

"Any news?" she asked.

"Nothing yet." The good side of Danny's face was set in a grim line. "Andy Penrice said he had a Mayday call come through to *Wave Dancer* and he alerted the coastguard straight away, but that's all we know.

They're going to scramble the chopper from Culdrose to search for them once it's back from a shout on the other coast. The call's gone out for a lifeboat though."

Mo felt sick. This was about as serious as it got.

"What about Eddie?" she asked. This dreadful situation wouldn't do his heart any good at all, and for all his bluster everyone knew that he was a very ill man; his last heart attack had shocked the village. Mo hoped that Dr Penwarren wasn't too far away.

"In a terrible state, as you can imagine," Danny said tersely. "I'm on my way down to see him now to apologise on Nick's behalf. Jules is with Susie."

"And Summer," Issie reminded him. She dabbed her eyes on her sleeve. "They're her brothers, after all. They weren't even drunk either. Bobby said they only had two because Summer read them the riot act before they left. They wanted to try a new tow as well. Bobby said something about Nick finding some really good grounds and that they wanted to go back and make a killing."

"Did they say where?" Danny asked. His hand gripped Issie's shoulder and she yelped. "Sorry, Issie, but I think it could be really important. If we can tell the fleet where that was it could help. The lifeboat has the EPIRB co-ordinates but I don't know how close they are to launching it."

"I think they were towing near the Shindeeps," Issie whimpered. Tears rolled down her cheeks and splashed onto the cobbles. "They were looking for bass. Nick caught a load there the other day."

Danny and Mo's eyes met. Mo's stomach flipped with terror. The Shindeeps were a treacherous cluster of submerged rocks some fifteen miles west of Polwenna Bay where a sharp reef rose up from almost two hundred feet, causing big surges and eddies that bass loved. The area was notorious for shipwrecks and there were endless local legends about the men who'd perished there over the centuries. If Nick and the boys had been fishing these grounds, then it had only been a matter of time before disaster struck.

"Think or know?" Danny demanded. "Tell me the truth, Issie! This really could be the difference between life and death!"

"They were fishing there. They've been there a couple of times and caught loads. They said it was OK with their equipment," Issie wept.

Danny's hand fell away. He looked grey. "Bloody idiots. I'd better let the coastguard know. If they've hit the Shindeeps…"

His voice tailed away. There was a knot in Mo's throat. Joe and Bobby were brash and a bit dim at times but they were nice boys and she couldn't imagine them not being here. It was impossible. Those two boys were as much a part of Polwenna Bay as the seagulls and pasties. Images of playing with them when they were tiny flickered through her mind's eye. Mummifying them in loo roll had been a favourite game of hers and Summer's, Mo recalled, and her eyes filled with tears.

All of a sudden Mo wished with all her heart that she was still friends with Summer. What did any of the hurts and grudges matter in the face of this morning's awful developments? Everything was in very sharp focus now.

"And the boys really weren't drinking?" Mo asked Dan.

"Apparently not; just bloody Nick. I've just left him with his head over the toilet and Zak's going to keep an eye on him. I've had words with him as well for being so irresponsible. They're both feeling pretty awful, as you can imagine." He grimaced. "The bloody Shindeeps. No wonder Nick had such a good haul the other day and managed to shut

Eddie up. Of all the stupid idiots. If I get hold of Nick he'll wish he'd never gone there."

Mo could imagine that Nick was already wishing he'd never fished those grounds. What must it be like to know that your thoughtless, reckless behaviour could be responsible for something so dreadful happening to your friends?

Danny sighed wearily. "Was I that stupid at their age? No, don't answer that, Mo. I've been pretty bloody stupid at twenty-nine."

Mo raised her hands. "Hey, if anyone's had a reason, then it's you. Besides, I didn't say a word."

"Yeah, you don't have to. The damage bill from the pub said it all. Anyway, I'm going to update the other boats and then find Jules. She's going to want to do her bit to help Susie and Eddie, and it might make things a little easier if I'm with her."

Jules again? It was the most unlikely friendship she could think of, but at least it was one that was doing Dan good. Maybe he'd found God? Whatever the reason, Mo had seen snatches of the old Danny back recently, like glimpsing sunshine through clouds, and it was wonderful; if this was what religion was doing for him then she was all for it. She might even check it out herself.

"Have you heard from Jake?" asked Issie quietly. She depended on Jake a lot, Mo had noticed, and he was a soft touch when it came to his baby sister. Quite how forgiving he'd be this time, however, remained to be seen.

"Last I heard Dad was going up to the hotel to find him. Jake wasn't answering his mobile," Danny told her.

Mo wasn't surprised to hear that Jake was incommunicado – Ella had probably smashed his phone and broken his legs by now, if Stephen

King was to be believed – but she was taken aback to learn that Jimmy had ventured out before eleven. Much as she adored her father, Mo knew that he wasn't an early riser. Things were really serious.

While Danny and Issie made their way to the Penhalligans, Mo wove through the crowds towards the marina and tried to lasso her galloping thoughts. It was unbearable to think that the helicopter was elsewhere and that the lifeboat was still on land, even though its crew were no doubt trying to respond to their alerts as quickly as possible. The Polwenna Bay fleet was heading to the last known co-ordinates of *Penhalligan Girl*, but the fishing boats were built for strength rather than speed and would take ages. If Bobby and Joe were in the water they wouldn't have long before they succumbed to the cold. Every moment that passed by was critical. There had to be something she could do…

"What's all the fuss about, Red? One of you lot caught a fish at long last? Or is it that you really can't bear to stay away from me?"

Mo had reached the first of the floating pontoons and Ashley Carstairs, aboard his ridiculously expensive powerboat and dressed head to deck-shoed foot in Musto gear, was smirking up at her. His ropes were cast off and the rod holders of his boat were rammed with expensive fishing gear for a day on the water. His mirrored Maui Jim shades glittered in the sunshine and Mo caught sight of herself in the lenses, pale faced and hollow eyed.

"I knew you'd come looking for me," he added, his lips curling upwards. "I could tell last night how you felt."

If that had been the case then Mo was pretty certain he'd have put the boat flat out for the horizon and never shown his face in the village again. Before she could yank her thoughts back under control and think of a sufficiently barbed reply, Ashley gestured to a sticker on the side of the controls. It depicted what looked like a skirt and sweater, with a huge cross through both items in the style of a no-entry sign.

"I'd say hop on," he said, with that mocking grin of his that made Mo itch to punch him, "but you're a little overdressed."

"God, you're disgusting. All you can think about is sex!" she snapped. Yuck, she'd kissed this idiot. She was never drinking again.

"Who mentioned sex?" Ashley pushed the glasses onto the top of his head. His dark eyes regarded her thoughtfully. "Freud would have a field day with you, Morwenna Tremaine, although he'd have to fight me first. Anyway, why's sex disgusting? Filthy maybe, dirty definitely, but disgusting? Not the adjective I'd have chosen."

"Not sex! You!" Mo shrieked. "A boat's gone down and all you can think about is sex!"

"A boat's gone down? As in sunk?" Ashley said. The mocking note had vanished and a concerned frown now dug itself in between his eyes. "Not a Whaler then – these beauties are bloody impossible to sink – but one of the trawlers, I take it?"

"Yes, *Penhalligan Girl*." Mo was beside herself now. "The coastguard's been alerted but it's taking too long to get there and the helicopter is on another shout. I know you think we're all just a bunch of inbred pasty eaters but those boys could die of hypothermia if they're not rescued in time."

"Christ. You really do think the worst of me, don't you?" Ashley held out his hand. "Come on. Jump on board. Yes, you're overdressed and you'd look better in a string bikini, but what the hell are you waiting for?"

He was still trying to embarrass her even at a time like this? Mo was just about to spit a sarcastic retort right back at him when she caught his eye and suddenly understood exactly what he was suggesting. It was as though their thoughts had collided somewhere above the white deck, with a fizz of electricity and a flash of genius that would have impressed even Stephen Hawking.

Mo wasn't the daughter of a marina-owning family for nothing; although horses were in her heart, boats were in her blood. Cashley was on the flashiest boat for miles around, wasn't he? A brand new unsinkable Boston Whaler with all the gizmos, including state-of-the-art GPS and, even more importantly, a pair of three-hundred-horsepower engines. It was faster than any trawler and probably even faster than the lifeboat. Before she could even question the wisdom of what she was about to do, Mo jumped.

"Good girl," Ashley said softly. His hands caught her waist, resting there briefly before setting her down on the deck. Mo was pretty sure it was the movement of the deck that made her knees quiver, but there was no chance to think about this: already Ashley was at the console, the engines were roaring into life, and the boat was making its way out of the berth and through the harbour gates before heading out onto open water.

"Put this on." Ashley shrugged off his life jacket and thrust it at Mo. OK, so he wasn't about to drown her then. Not yet, anyway.

"That's yours," Mo replied.

"I'm not risking your life. Besides, no matter what you may think of me, I like to think I'm a gentleman."

His tone of voice said that he wasn't going to be argued with, so Mo obeyed.

"Thank you," said Ashley. He glanced at her and winked. "I see you're ignoring the bikini rule, but since these are extenuating circumstances I'll overlook it this once."

He was so annoying that he made Mo's teeth itch but right now he might be all the hope the boys had, so she kept quiet and pretended to be busy tying the cords.

The chart plotter beeped into life and his finger hovered over the touchscreen.

"I fish all around here," said Ashley, seeing Mo stare at the on-screen charts peppered with tracks and plot points. "I have to have some fun when I'm not running the evil Empire or plotting how to cut down ancient woodlands. Besides, fishing is cheaper than building a Death Star."

Mo was taken aback. Did Cashley have a sense of humour or was he really Darth Vadar? Sometimes it was hard to tell.

"So," he said as they passed the quay. "Any ideas where they were when their EPIRB gave its signal?"

"The Shindeeps."

Ashley stared at her. "You aren't serious? They were trawling at the Shindeeps? Bloody hell. Even a worthless incomer like me knows enough of this area not to go anywhere near those rocks."

"They wanted to catch some bass." Mo bit her lip. "They've been taking huge risks lately and catching loads of fish. I think they've snagged the trawl in one of the wrecks off the rocks and the boat's gone down. Maybe a wave caught it? I don't know, but the Shindeeps is the place. Issie just told me."

"Red, angel, this boat's unsinkable, not indestructible. You'd better make this worth my while."

He'd pushed his glasses back down, so Mo couldn't tell whether he was joking or not. Quite how he'd like her to repay him she wasn't sure, but her imagination was coming up with some suggestions that made her face feel hot. Luckily Ashley was far too busy pulling in fenders and throwing ropes into the hold to notice.

"Ready?" he said as the boat passed the final buoy that marked the channel out of the harbour, and Mo nodded. She wasn't sure she'd ever be ready for what they might discover but at least this way she felt as though she was doing something.

Ashley pushed the throttle forward and the boat surged into top speed and up onto the plane with all the grace and power of a racehorse bolting out of the starting gates. Lace-doily wake spread out behind them and within minutes the village was just a collection of specks amid a smudge of green.

The run across the sea to the Shindeeps was a relatively smooth one and under any other circumstances Mo probably would have enjoyed it. The sea was glittering and although there was a slight breeze and the water was lumpy, Ashley's boat skipped across the waves as easily as a pebble skimming over a flat pond. The speed snatched Mo's breath away and she clung to the handrail with all her might; she felt as though she was riding every one of the six hundred horses under the engines bareback and without a bridle. Mo loved speed and adored galloping her horses flat out across countryside, but this was something else again. The speed whipped tears from her eyes and made her cheeks wobble. She wedged her backside against the bolster seat and stole a glance at Ashley. The wind blew the dark hair back from his face and she could see how hard he was concentrating.

"How much longer?" she shouted to him.

"We're doing almost sixty miles an hour. About five more minutes," Ashley called back. "She's at full speed now."

Polwenna Bay had vanished and there was nothing around them but miles of water and the blue sweep of sky. Mo shivered. She loved the sea but there was something about being this far out and no longer able to see the land that she found unnerving. Surprisingly though, far from being the clueless show-off that she'd expected, Ashley actually knew how to handle the boat, coaxing maximum performance from her and trimming the engines perfectly so that she flew over the waves and surfed across the big troughs. If her sister was right, Mo knew that Ashley's boat would easily reach any survivors a good ten minutes faster than the nearest lifeboat.

Abruptly, Ashley pulled back the throttle, sinking the boat back into the water and jolting Mo backwards.

"What are you stopping for?" she cried, frustrated beyond all belief that he could waste time like this. "We can't be far away."

"I just saw a plastic milk container float by." Ashley knocked the boat out of gear and peered over the side. "There! Do you see?"

Mo did. Only metres away the remainder of two pints of Trewithen Dairy's semi-skimmed milk bobbed merrily past. A can of Foster's followed, evidence if she ever needed it that Bobby and Joe had been close to this spot.

"Unless the fish are brewing tea or going on the piss, then that's debris from their boat," Ashley observed drily. "I daren't go flat out in case I get something trapped in the props or, God forbid, run a survivor down. It might have escaped your notice but it's hazy now and visibility is down to about half a mile. Is that all right with you?"

Mo felt thoroughly chastened. "Yes, sorry."

Ashley raised an eyebrow. "An apology from Morwenna Tremaine? If only I had a witness."

Mo chose to ignore this dig. She was too busy squinting at the horizon.

"Get up onto the bow." Ashley put the engine back into gear and the boat began to creep forward. "If you see anything, shout and point at it and don't take your eyes off it, whatever you do."

Mo didn't argue. Ashley knew what he was doing here and she appreciated his expertise. Just as she was in charge at the yard, with safety as her top priority, he was in charge here. It was just as well; she wouldn't have had a clue.

"There's the Shindeeps," Ashley called, pulling the boat around in a broad sweep and pointing to where white water was boiling across the sharp teeth of the rocks. "We can't go much further or we'll risk running aground ourselves. I'll hold her here. Shout if you can spot anything."

At first Mo thought it was just the glinting sunlight on the water playing tricks on her eyes, a mirage caused by longing, because she was sure that she could see a bright orange blob at least a quarter of a mile away to the east. Eyes narrowed, and with her hand blocking the glare, Mo peered closer and her heart leapt. It was the life raft!

"Over there! Portside!" she cried. "It's them!"

"Got it!" Ashley turned the wheel and pushed the throttle forward, and within moments they were pulling alongside the small orange craft where a white-faced Joe and Bobby were waving frantically and shouting.

Everything seemed to happen very fast after this. Ashley knocked the engine into neutral and leaned across with the boat hook, which Joe grabbed with an expression of great relief, and flipping down the boat ladder the Whaler's owner helped the shaken boys on board.

"There's chocolate and a flask of coffee in the locker under the console," he said to Mo, wincing as the life raft scraped the side of his pristine engine. "They're shocked and they'll need some sugar."

Mo did as she was told. Ashley's confidence and authority were very reassuring and, besides, he was right: the boys looked terrible. While she rummaged through Ashley's dry bag for a couple of Snickers bars and the flask, she heard his conversation with the coastguard as he marked the waypoint on his plotter and told them that they could stand down the rescue mission.

"Both survivors of fishing vessel *Penhalligan Girl* are on board 280 Outrage *Big Rod*, and you have our co-ordinates," he was saying over the VHF. "Returning to Polwenna Bay now and requesting an ambulance on standby." He put the radio back in its holder and caught Mo's eye. "Maybe you should have some coffee too? You look dreadful."

Actually, Mo *felt* dreadful. Her hands were trembling and she was lightheaded. In her haste to reach the village she'd skipped breakfast, and she'd hardly eaten anything the night before either. This, added to the huge adrenalin rush of earlier, made her feel quite peculiar and shaky.

"Here, have this." Ashley shrugged off his Musto coat and draped it over her shoulders. It was warm with his body heat and to her surprise this wasn't the unpleasant sensation she'd anticipated.

"Thanks," Mo said.

Ashley shrugged. "Can't have three of you hypothermic. There isn't enough coffee or room in the ambulance."

"You're all heart," Mo told him, and Ashley laughed wryly.

"You'd better believe it, Red."

The journey back to the village was slower. Bobby and Joe, wet and dazed, sipped the coffee and gradually stuttered out their version of what had happened. Just as Mo had suspected, they'd been fishing off the rocks when they'd snagged the trawl on the seabed and run into difficulties.

"Nick made the turn no problem the last time," Bobby said quietly. "We didn't have his tracks in the plotter, though. I thought I could do it from memory but…"

"But we're not as good as Nick," Joe finished. Wet and tearstained he looked about twelve, and Mo could have swung for her careless, reckless sibling. Nick Tremaine had that instinctive edge of brilliance laced with the luck of the Devil, which made him both a fantastic and a very dangerous skipper. Of course the less experienced Penhalligan brothers would struggle to pull off his stunts. Still, this wasn't the time for lectures. They'd already learned a very hard lesson.

"We couldn't pull free," Bobby continued. He could hardly speak; his voice was so hoarse from yelling for help. "I didn't want to cut the gear – Dad would go mental if we lost the trawl – so we thought we'd steam back to the harbour and maybe pull it free that way."

Mo groaned. It was an amateur mistake and one guaranteed to end in tragedy.

"But you were snagged on a wreck and couldn't break away? And the boat was under too much loading, wasn't it?" Ashley guessed. "What happened next? Was it the wind direction? Did a wave hit her side on and that was it?"

Joe nodded. "It was so quick. One moment I was in the wheelhouse and Bobby was working the winch, the next she was under." He paused and passed a shaking hand over his face. "We thought we'd die."

"Lucky for you then that Mo guessed what was going on and had the guts to do something about it, " Ashley said icily. "Otherwise the rescue mission would have been still on the way while you clowns drifted to France. You owe her your lives."

"I take it Issie grassed us up?" said Bobby bitterly.

"And lucky for you she did," snapped Ashley. His face was black with anger. "You're a pair of stupid, reckless idiots and you've got away with it today by the skin of your teeth. Value your lives. You don't know how lucky you are, so learn from it. The sea won't forgive you twice and I certainly won't be burning good fuel to save your necks again. Don't be surprised when you get a bill from me."

There wasn't much more that anyone could say to this and the rest of the journey home passed in silence. Mo stole a couple of glances at Ashley but he was focused on the helm and didn't look her way once. She wasn't sure whether to be relieved or disappointed. How she could thank him for listening to her, and quite why he'd done so, she couldn't figure out. Mo had the uneasy feeling that she really owed him now.

By the time they returned, the good news had reached the village and the quay was packed with people waving and cheering as Ashley steered through the harbour gates. As he drew alongside the quay Susie came running, followed by a puffing and dangerously red-faced Eddie. Of Summer there was no sign, and in spite of everything that had passed between them, Mo found herself worrying about her old friend.

Ashley, ignoring the excitement and the calls of congratulations almost to the point of rudeness, busied himself examining the damage to his engines. Mo leapt off the boat intending to help moor up but found herself surrounded by friends and villagers who were all desperate to hear the story, while Bobby and Joe were safely delivered into the care of the waiting paramedics. By the time the crowds had thinned Ashley had moved the boat back to his mooring and was walking along the pontoon. His face was set in a scowl and he'd clearly abandoned the day's fishing trip.

"Ashley!" Mo called to him, her voice echoing across the water. "I've still got your coat and your life jacket!"

He paused and looked her up and down. Mo felt hot – and not because of the heavy coat. "So you have. Just as I said earlier: overdressed for a boat trip."

"Shall I bring them over to you?"

"Good idea," Ashley agreed. "Bring them up to Mariners this evening, about seven, and for God's sake don't wear those bloody jodhpurs."

She stared at him. "You want me to come to Mariners?"

"I think it's time we had a talk, don't you? There's something you need to know."

"And what's that?"

His expression was inscrutable. "Come over later on and you can find out. I'm not discussing it here."

And with that he leapt up the steps from the pontoon, slamming the marina gate behind him. He vanished from sight, leaving Mo staring after him with her stomach churning and the ground shifting beneath her feet as though she was still at sea.

Chapter 29

By the time Jake and Summer reached the quayside an ambulance had arrived and snippets of speculation were rippling through the crowd. The sight of paramedics parked up on the slipway sent Summer's heart plummeting. Was this good news or bad? And as for the rumours that air and sea searches had been called off; did this mean that the boys had been found or that there was no further point in searching for them? What was happening?

Following her anxious gaze, Jake squeezed her hand. "Don't panic. I'm sure that's just here as a precaution. We'll grab Danny. He'll know what all the latest developments are."

Summer nodded. She felt giddy. Shock and an empty stomach topped up with a large measure of guilt were certainly taking a toll on her blood pressure. Bless Jake for trying to ease her nerves though, even if it wasn't working. As they'd walked back into the village she could feel his worries just as keenly as her own and she knew that he was as torn and as shredded inside as she was. He always had done his very best to protect her and take care of her, she remembered, which was why his silence when she'd needed him the most had been so inexplicable and so very hurtful.

The crowds were deep now, a churning spin-cycle mix of holidaymakers and locals, and she couldn't see past them. She supposed she could push and barge her way through but there was an odd buzzing in her ears and the scene was starting to swim. Only the firm grasp of Jake's hand was keeping her anchored; otherwise Summer feared that she would pass out. The edges of her vision were fuzzy and speckled with weird black dots, and every few moments sharp pains spiked her right in the abdomen. Something was very wrong but until she knew what was happening to her brothers she couldn't afford to think about herself.

"There's Issie!" Jake waved his hand. Being over six feet tall, he could see exactly what was happening and had no trouble attracting his sister's attention. "Issie! What's going on?"

"They've called the search off!" Issie shouted, waving back excitedly. Her blue eyes were shining with relief. "Ashley Carstairs found the boys over by the Shindeeps – the boat's lost but they're safe!"

Relief was too bland a word for the all-consuming, overwhelming, swamping sensation that Summer felt as she heard those words. Joe and Bobby were safe and her silence hadn't killed them. For once it seemed that fate was inclined to be kind.

Still holding Summer's trembling hand tightly, Jake threaded a path to his sister.

"You're sure?" he demanded once Issie was beside him. "You've seen them? They're home?"

His sister nodded. "They're home, safe and sound. Actually, they've only just come in; you've missed it by seconds! Honestly, Jake, it's a miracle. Mo and Ashley took his boat out and found them out by the Shindeeps. The boat had gone down and everything."

Jake made a noise in the back of his throat that was halfway between a growl and a moan. "I'm not even going to ask what they were doing fishing out there. The main thing is that they're safe. Or they will be until Eddie gets hold of them."

"They're not hurt are they?" Summer asked. Her heart was racing and she could hear the blood pounding in her ears.

"They seemed all right to me," Issie assured her. "A bit wet and scared looking, but otherwise they were OK. I think they're only going to hospital for a check-up. Your folks are going with them."

The strange roaring sound in Summer's ears was growing louder. Although she tried her hardest to make out Issie's tale of trawls catching in wrecks and Mo's commandeering of a second-homer's powerboat in order to launch her own rescue operation, nothing was really sinking in apart from the massive relief that Joe and Bobby were safe. The pain in her stomach was growing sharper with every second that passed and Summer knew she couldn't ignore it much longer.

There was something really wrong...

"Summer?" Jake's voice sounded very far away. "Summer?"

The roaring was motorway loud now and the quayside scene was fading fast. It was as if a curtain was coming down in front of her; the last thing she saw before her legs buckled was Jake reaching out to catch her, and she found herself thinking abstractedly, and she guessed wholly inappropriately, that both inside and out, he really was the most beautiful man she had ever known...

***

Summer knew straight away that her baby had left her far behind. Before she even opened her eyes to make out the green walls of the village surgery and the edges of the narrow examination couch, she understood exactly what had happened. She didn't need the gentle words of Dr Penwarren or the quiet presence of Jake, holding her hand at her bedside, to tell her what her heart instinctively knew. There was a deep and echoing emptiness within her, a ringing silence when before she'd heard the companionable whisper of another soul curled up next to hers and sharing her every thought and heartbeat. The warm, fuzzy sensation of no longer being alone had vanished. Her little *almost* person was gone and already Summer missed that tiny being more than she would ever be able to say. Although her eyes were closed, a tear rolled down her cheek.

"It's all right," she said quietly, "you don't need to tell me. I know."

All she longed to do was turn her head to the wall and weep. The baby might have been Justin's, and only just there, but it had been *hers* and somebody she would have loved and lived for. After what had happened before, this little one had felt like a second chance, and regardless of who its father was Summer would have given her life for it.

The loss was indescribable.

She took a deep breath. Was this the price she'd had to pay for having her brothers returned? A cosmic balance sheet with the ins and outs on the ledger weighed in lives? If so, her sin of keeping quiet about the boys' antics had been paid for very dearly. She wondered what Jules Mathieson would have to say on the matter.

Opening her eyes, Summer saw that she was indeed inside the Polwenna surgery, in a small consulting room that had hardly changed since she used to visit with her mother. The same kinds of dog-eared posters proclaiming the benefits of immunisation were tacked onto the wall, and the small window still revealed a slice of sky above a wedge of acid-green hillside. The only real difference was that the doctor taking her pulse today was a young man with kindly grey eyes and thinning sandy hair, rather than Dr Kussell, the scary elderly gentleman with horn-rimmed glasses who'd terrified them all as children.

"Take it easy," the doctor said as she tried to sit up. "You've been in and out of consciousness for about five minutes and your blood sugar's very low. You've not eaten today?"

Summer pushed herself into an upright position. The room dipped alarmingly.

"Was it something I did wrong? Did I eat something bad for the baby? Or was it the stress of today? Could that have done it? Or what about a fall? I fell over not that long ago." She realised that this volley of questions sounded like an interrogation, but she had to know the truth. If this miscarriage were her fault then she would rather be told so. "Was it something I did?"

But Richard Penwarren was shaking his head. "Absolutely not. These things sometimes happen, I'm afraid, especially in the very early stages. Often women don't even realise they're pregnant. It's pretty common. You mustn't blame yourself at all. There was nothing you could have done that would have made the outcome any different."

Jake squeezed her hand. "Don't blame yourself, Summer, please."

But Summer did blame herself. This was her punishment for being careless before. While the doctor wrote her a prescription for painkillers and advised her to rest for twenty-four hours, she drifted twelve years away and back to a grotty shared house in a sooty London terrace, where she'd sobbed into her pillow and hated herself more than she'd ever thought possible.

To be sixteen, pregnant and all alone in a strange city was probably top of the list of the most terrifying things that could happen to a young girl. Summer still tasted the fear now and her heart ached for the frightened teen she'd been. She'd tried to reach Jake, pouring everything out to him in a heartfelt letter, but there'd been no reply. After several weeks had limped past, Summer had come to the painful realisation that he wasn't interested and certainly wasn't about to help.

Rudely awakened from all the half-formed, hazy little daydreams that she'd started to weave, involving flowers and white dresses and a cute toddler bridesmaid with Jake's blonde curls and her own green eyes, Summer had made a panicked appointment with the nearest family-planning clinic. She'd made it as far as the waiting room, where she'd sat studiously avoiding the gaze of the other women there. As the clock had ticked the minutes away, her resolve had started to evaporate; before her name had even been called, Summer was heading back towards the bus stop, cold with horror at how close she'd come to making a decision she would have regretted. She might have been young and on her own but Summer's mind had been made up: no matter what happened, she was keeping her baby.

Later that night, when she'd woken wracked with cramps and an overwhelming sense of bereavement, Summer had cried bitterly. The mixture of sadness and relief had haunted her ever since and she still wondered whether what had happened was her punishment for even thinking about a termination.

Of course, the adult Summer knew that this was utter nonsense. The logical part of her would have argued with anyone that sixteen was far too young for her to have been a parent and that everything had worked out for the best. Yet sometimes when she caught a curly blonde head out of the corner of her eye or saw eleven-year-old girls ransacking Claire's Accessories, her heart twisted painfully with grief.

So right now, in the doctor's surgery, she couldn't help but wonder whether this was yet another punishment. Richard Penwarren could go on as much as he liked about statistics and how one in five pregnancies ended in a miscarriage, but none of that eased her guilty conscience. Maybe it was the superstitious Cornish blood in her?

Once she'd sipped some water and reassured both the doctor and Jake that she was feeling well enough to stand, Summer was left alone with Jo, the practice nurse, who was in charge of the practicalities. Summer had been at school with Jo, a kind but bossy girl who'd been in the year above and gloried in her role of head prefect; she didn't seem to have changed much. As Jo weighed her and took her blood, Summer thought that there was something comforting about being fussed over by her now. She half expected to be told to tuck her shirt in and not to fidget in assembly, the crime that had always driven Jo half demented.

Would her babies have been little wrigglers, unable to sit still just like her? The lump was back in her throat because she'd never know now.

"Here, have these," Jo said, catching the misery on Summer's face and thrusting a box of Kleenex in her direction. "I know you're feeling dreadful right now. It's OK to cry, love. It's a horrible thing to happen and your hormones will be all over the place."

"Thanks." Summer dabbed her eyes and blew her nose. God, all she seemed to do was cry these days. When had life become so complicated?

"Jo, was it anything I did wrong? I was really anxious today. Could that have done it?"

"I doubt that very much. I'm afraid it was probably just one of those things. It happens more than you'd think. Still, you are very thin and quite underweight," Jo observed, peering at the charts. A short woman, as round as she was tall and with rosy apple cheeks, she obviously saw this as a bad thing. "You need to build yourself up a bit. I really don't think you could have done anything to prevent what happened; I'm just concerned that you should look after yourself going forwards."

"I've been stressed," Summer said. Her hand rose to her fading bruise. Stressed? What an understatement that was. Bloody terrified came closer.

"That must have been quite a shiner," Jo remarked casually. "How did that happen?"

The scene in the kitchen flashed before Summer's vision: Justin's face red with rage, the bulging vein crawling across his temple like an obscene worm, the spittle gathering in the corners of his mouth, and then the kitchen island flying up towards her.

"I fell over a while back. I tripped. Could that have been it?"

Jo's candid hazel gaze met hers and Summer knew instantly that the other woman understood exactly what kind of fall it had been.

"It's unlikely but it could be something to do with it, although a foetus is generally pretty tough. Still, take my advice, Summer, and make sure that you don't have that kind of *fall* again?"

"I'm fully intending *never* to fall like that again," Summer promised her. She meant it too. Let Justin do his worst now; she really didn't care. He could badmouth her to the press as much as he liked. She couldn't give a hoot. In fact, let him try. Maybe she'd hire a top lawyer of her own and see how much he liked it? The tabloids and celebrity magazines would love to know the truth about football's golden boy.

"I'm glad to hear it," said Jo as she scribbled detailed notes onto labels and stuck them onto the test tubes of dark red blood she'd just drawn. "We'll send these off to the lab but I bet you're anaemic too. I'll ask Richard to write you a prescription for iron tablets. Put some weight on, relax a bit and it'll all work out. You'll see."

"Thanks." Summer didn't have the heart to point out that in her world you could never be too thin and that feeling permanently hungry was just a fact of life to her. Jo looked as though she inhaled clotted cream and pasties. As for iron, Summer guessed that avoiding red meat for almost a decade hadn't helped.

"And how long are you staying here for?" Jo was asking. "I'm not being nosey, by the way. I'm just wondering what's best to do with your notes and where to send the results of these bloods."

This was a very good question. How long was she staying at Polwenna Bay? Until her mother spoke to her again? That could be a very long time. She only had another few days in the cottage before the next booking meant she had to move out. She'd have to return to London at some point.

It was time to face the music.

"It's lovely to see that you and Jake have got back together," Jo continued cheerfully, not waiting for a reply. She rammed the test tubes into a plastic bag. "You always were such a lovely couple at school, and it was so romantic the way he had to travel the world before coming back and finding you again. He never stopped loving you, did he? And hasn't he improved with age? He's gorgeous! We all adore Jake here. He's a guilty pleasure for lots of us! Not like my Steven. Bald as a coot he is now, bless him! You must remember what a lovely head of hair he had?"

Summer didn't remember Steven at all, but then she'd never had eyes for anyone apart from Jake.

"Jake and I aren't together," she said quickly. "I'm engaged to Justin Anderson. The footballer?"

Jo pulled a face. "Can't say I know much about him but I'm sure he's not a patch on Jake. That man adores you, Summer. It's obvious. Don't walk away from him again, that's my advice. There's plenty here who'd snap him up in a heartbeat. Annie Fanny from the hotel, for one. Me for another, if I can get someone to take on my Steve! You two are meant to be together. Like Romeo and Juliet."

"It didn't end too well for them as I recall," Summer pointed out.

Jo flapped her comment away with her hand. "Minor details! Lizzie and Darcy then! Or even Kate and Wills. Take your pick."

Summer smiled. "You're a hopeless romantic, Jo. Jake's just a good friend, that's all, and he's got a kind heart. There's nothing else between us."

"And if you really think that then we'd better do another test. This one, I think!" declared Jo, pointing to the vision chart and grinning. Then the smile slipped away and her expression settled into serious lines. "Teasing aside, Summer, please be kind to yourself. You've been through a horrible thing today and you need to rest up. Take the painkillers and let those who care about you, hot male *friends* or otherwise, in. OK?"

"You don't get that kind of advice in Harley Street," said Summer. It was a weak attempt at a joke but at least she was trying. Right now she wasn't sure she'd ever be able to laugh again.

Jo's nose wrinkled in disdain. "Harley Street? What do you need to go up country for when you've got everything you could ever need in Polwenna Bay? That's what I say."

As Summer left the consulting room she was inclined to agree with her old school friend. London wasn't holding much appeal right now and she could hardly wait to return to her cottage and burrow under the duvet, listening to the gulls arguing on the rooftop and being lulled to sleep by the waves. She'd get some rest as Jo had suggested, cry a bit more maybe, and then she'd screw up her courage and visit her parents. What would come next she had no idea. Afraid of the black void before her, Summer pushed all thoughts of the future away.

That was a problem for another day.

Chapter 30

Jake wasn't the kind of man who would dream of imposing his will on a woman – being brought up by Alice and alongside two strong-willed sisters had taught him a thing or two about how the female mind worked – but neither was he the kind of person to abandon someone in need of some care. Today he knew that Summer was shaken and needed looking after. Two horrible shocks in such close proximity were too much for anyone to cope with.

"I'll be fine back at the holiday cottage," Summer insisted once they were walking away from the surgery and back through the village. Her chin was set at the familiar stubborn angle he remembered so well and her green eyes were filled with a determined expression. "I can look after myself."

"I don't doubt that for a second," Jake told her calmly. "But the point is that you don't *have* to look after yourself, because you're coming up to Seaspray where we'll take care of you. You've been through far too much for one morning. Anyway, those look like bloody strong painkillers to me and I'm not going to leave you on your own to take them. Once your folks are back home then by all means go back to the cottage, but until then we're looking after you up at the house. No arguments. It's not up for debate."

Summer opened her mouth to object but swayed unsteadily on her feet. Jake could tell by the waxy pallor of her cheeks that she was feeling dreadful.

"I'm not meaning to order you about. Please just humour me on this one?" he said gently, cupping her face in his hands and gazing down at her. God, but he just wanted to take care of her, keep her safe from harm. He was just a breath away from telling her how she still made him feel, because Ella had been right: he was still in love with Summer. Jake didn't think he'd ever stopped loving her and seeing her so broken now was tearing his own heart into ribbons. He would have done anything to wipe the tears away from her eyes and make her smile again. Tenderly, his fingertips traced the curve of her cheek before resting against her soft lips, stopping any protests before she could voice them.

"You've been so brave, Summer. Not just about what's happened today but also about what's brought you here too. You don't have to tell me about any of it, not if you don't want to, but I've seen enough of the world to be able to draw my own conclusions." He smiled at her sadly. "I guess what I'm trying to say is that you don't have to be brave when you're with me. I want to take those burdens away, even for an hour or two. I want to take care of you."

His hands slipped to her shoulders and Summer exhaled, a deep shuddering breath, which felt to Jake as though she'd been holding it for far too long.

"I'd like that," she told him quietly.

So together Jake and Summer walked through the village, skirting the harbour – where crowds still lingered and a BBC local news team was busy putting together a report – before making the slow climb up to Seaspray. By the time they reached the house Summer was looking exhausted. She didn't even protest when Jake helped her up the steps to the door and into the kitchen. This alarmed him because Summer was always so independent, so single-minded, traits that he loved and was driven crazy by in equal measure.

For once the house was empty; Jake supposed that everyone was still in the village or dealing with the aftermath of the almost-tragedy. While the kettle hissed away on the hob and Summer settled onto the tatty sofa, the cat instantly claiming her lap, he checked Nick's room in case his brother had passed out again, but it was deserted. Only the stale smell of beer and the still-closed curtains gave evidence that Nick had been there at all. Zak's room was also empty; his holdall was gone and the bed covers had been stripped away. Jake gritted his teeth in annoyance because it was typical of Zak to run at the first hint of trouble and leave Nick to carry the can. The patterns and habits of childhood died hard, it seemed.

It was just him and Summer here then, and this knowledge made Jake's resolve harden. It was time they had an upfront conversation. He'd seen enough of Summer now to guess what her life had been like recently. Behind the glitter of her fame and the glossy celebrity-magazine photo shoots lay something ugly and destructive.

And he loved her far too much to say nothing and risk her going back to it.

The kitchen was quiet in the bright light that swept in from the sea and bounced off the white walls. The clock ticked gently, the cat purred and the mugs chinked as Jake carried them over to the sofa.

She smiled up at him. "Tea. How very British."

Jake laughed. "Yeah, they gave me hell for it in Australia. They were always bemused by my filthy PG habit. They thought I should be drinking Foster's like all the other Bruces."

"So did you?"

"Ever tried dipping Rich Tea biscuits in lager?" Jake shuddered. "No thanks."

Summer smiled, her eyes lighting up just like deep rock pools when the sun shone into them, and he found himself thinking that he would do anything to make sure that she smiled every day for the rest of her life.

It was time to be honest.

Jake placed his mug on the floor and sat down beside her, reaching out and taking her hands in his. Just this simple gesture knocked him sideways at the kick it gave his emotions. Those small hands fitted into his as though they'd been designed that way. Maybe they had.

"Sums, what's been going on?" he asked, tracing her bitten fingertips with his own. "I don't want to seem like I'm prying and you don't have to answer if you'd rather not, but I'm worried about you."

She sighed. "I will tell you the truth about what's been happening with me, I promise, but first I need you to tell me something and I need you to be honest, no matter how painful you think it might be."

His eyes held hers. "Summer, I've loved you since the moment I first saw you and every moment since. There's nothing that you can't ask me."

She hesitated for a while, her teeth worrying her bottom lip, before sliding her hands away from him and clasping them tightly in her lap.

"If you loved me so much then why didn't you come when I wrote to you?" she said quietly. "I was so scared, Jake, and I didn't know what to do for the best, but I thought you would be there for me. It broke me when you ignored the letter."

Jake frowned. "What letter? Did you send it before you arrived? I wonder if Gran's tidied it up? It's probably on the dresser with a pile of Dad's credit-card bills."

"Not a recent letter. I mean the one I sent you from London when I first moved there for drama school. The one where I told you that I was pregnant and that I needed you." Tears fell now and she brushed them away angrily. "I poured my heart out in that letter. I couldn't understand how you could have ignored me."

Jake stared at Summer, his mind whirling as he sought to process what she'd just told him.

"Are you saying that when you left here you were pregnant? That you were having our baby?"

"Yes!" Summer cried. Her eyes shone with more tears. "I didn't know until I'd been there a week or so, but as soon as I did I wrote to you and I told you everything. How sorry I was that I'd left the way I did, how I wanted to come home, how much I loved you, how much I wanted to have the baby even though we were so young…" She paused, pinching the bridge of her nose and trying to slow her breathing. Once her emotions were sufficiently under control to continue, she added, "When I didn't hear from you I knew that it was over and that I was on my own. I understood that your being a part of my life was over."

"That's why you hardly ever come back?" Like sea mist clearing and revealing the village, everything was suddenly starting to make sense.

"How could I after that? It was far too painful."

She was weeping bitterly and Jake couldn't bear this. Pulling her into his arms he held her close and pressed his face into her hair until the torrent of emotion began to ebb. As she wiped her eyes, Jake struggled to grasp what he had just learned. The mental landscape of the past decade or so had shifted and the seismic impact was so enormous that he felt disorientated. Summer had tried to tell him that she'd still loved him. She'd wanted to come back to the village and hadn't just turned her back on him without a second thought, as he'd believed for so long. She hadn't stopped loving him. She'd wanted to come home to him. She'd thought that he had turned his back on *her*.

This changed everything and his heart broke at the thought of all the time they'd wasted because of these misunderstandings.

Jake dropped a kiss onto Summer's damp forehead then released her gently, wiping her tears away with his thumbs.

"I had no idea," he said quietly. "Summer, I swear I never knew anything about any of this. I certainly never saw any letter, let alone got to read it. Christ, if I had I would have been on the first train to Paddington. There's no way that I would have let you go. When I didn't hear from you again I assumed it was because you'd moved on and didn't want to know me."

Summer's gaze flew to Jake's. Her face was a study in horror. "You never read my letter?"

"I didn't even know it existed until a few moments ago. Why didn't you just phone the house?"

Back then, in the days when both their families had relied much more on landlines, Summer and Jake had spent hours hogging the phone and driving the others mad. For months Eddie Penhalligan had resisted all suggestions of Summer having her own mobile, for fear of her wasting money on her endless calls. He'd yielded on the matter only because Summer was about to move away from home, and he'd been furious when she'd lost the new handset within weeks of owning it.

"I did! I tried ringing you several times," Summer cried. She could still remember standing in the red call box that was papered pitifully with cards advertising the charms of desperate women, clutching her twenty-pence piece and plucking up the courage to dial. "The first time I rang, Mo told me that you didn't want to speak to me, and another time when I managed to get through she just slammed the phone down. That was why I wrote." Her hand flew to her mouth. "Oh my God! Mo! She was so angry with me. I think she felt I'd betrayed her just as much by leaving as I did you. Do you think she would have taken my letter?"

Jake loved his fiery, stubborn sister but he knew that this was exactly the sort of thing Mo would have done. Up at dawn every day to deal with her beloved horses, she wouldn't have found it hard to intercept the post, which in those days had always arrived through the letterbox first thing in the morning.

"I think it's exactly what she'd do," he sighed. "She would have thought she was helping but instead she's let me waste years of my life thinking that the person I loved didn't feel the same way about me."

"And I thought that you hated me. I've thought it for years," Summer whispered. They stared at one another, aghast. "Oh God, Jake. What a mess."

Jake swallowed back his anger. "It's all the years spent thinking… Well, I guess there's no point going over that now. But, Sums, what did you do? What happened to the baby? Am I a father?"

She slipped her hand into his. "I was only sixteen and I was so scared, Jake. I didn't know how I was going to cope on my own. I thought about a termination and I even made an appointment with the clinic, but I couldn't go through with it. My baby was all I had left of you; there was no way I could part with it. I guess fate had different ideas, though. I started to lose the baby that same night." Her voice clotted with tears. "It broke my heart and ever since I've always wondered whether that was my punishment for even considering a termination. It was just like what happened today. Maybe that was another reminder of what I almost did?"

The image of Summer alone and scared made Jake savage. He couldn't bear to think of her frightened in the city and believing that he'd deliberately turned his back on her.

"None of this was your fault," he said firmly. "What happened then wasn't a punishment and what happened today wasn't either, was it?"

Her head drooped. "No. It wasn't. Today was probably down to Justin."

Ah yes, Justin Anderson. Jake had been coming to that part of the story. His fists clenched but he was determined not to shy away from the truth, no matter how painful.

"Are you ready to tell me about him?"

She grimaced. "Maybe if you can put a slosh of Alice's secret whiskey in the tea?"

"Just a small one," said Jake firmly. "You've had a couple of strong painkillers."

Retrieving the bottle from the top shelf, Jake poured some of the whiskey into two tumblers before joining her back on the sofa. Then he listened quietly and without interruption – even though each word roused in him a fury deeper and darker than anything he'd ever known – as Summer told him the truth about her relationship with the famous sportsman.

It was a familiar tale, of a younger and vulnerable woman who had met an older glamorous man and been amazed to be the dazzled focus of his full-beam attention. He was damaged and had warned her to keep away from him, yet had bombarded her with gifts and flowers and the kind of adoration that she'd thought only existed in movies. He'd woven their own little world where no one else was welcome, and that had been seductive. She'd felt loved, cherished, adored – and later trapped. Friends and family had slipped away until there was nobody for Summer except Justin. Slowly, and imperceptibly at first, his closeness had turned into control. As Summer described how just tiny, seemingly insignificant things such as talking to the wrong person or smiling at a stranger could send Justin crazy, Jake clenched his jaw. It was classic emotional abuse. Justin would fly into a rage, take it out on Summer and then be filled with remorse. Slowly he'd distanced her from her family, undermining the already strained relationships like an artisan manipulator, until there had been nobody close to her but him. It was because he loved her so much, had never loved anyone as he loved her, had been hurt in the past; there were a million excuses for his behaviour. But to Jake's mind there was only one reason: Justin Anderson was a cowardly, controlling piece of shit. Every time he thought about how Summer had gained her bruises and why she'd lost her baby, Jake was consumed with rage. When she told him about the ugly night when she'd become pregnant, it took all his self-control not to leap into his truck, drive to London and kill the bastard. Only knowing that this would be for his own benefit, rather than for hers, kept Jake from grabbing the keys and storming to the city.

"Why did you stay for so long?" he asked.

"It sounds pathetic, I know, and I tried to leave so many times," Summer said quietly. She'd hardly touched her drink as she'd told the story, and couldn't look at him. His heart broke to see that she was blaming herself. "I wanted to get away but I must be so weak, Jake."

"Summer, you're probably the strongest person I know," Jake told her. "You've survived. That's brave."

"Is it?" She looked doubtful. "I never felt brave. Every time, he talked me around again and I gave in. He loved me, couldn't bear to be without me and, later on, he swore he'd ruin me if I left."

"Ruin you?" Jake didn't understand.

"He meant that he'd destroy my reputation and my career. Honestly, Jake, you don't know what he's like. He's got lawyers on tap and the press loves him, especially after the cancer thing."

"Does your career really mean that much to you that you'd put up with him?" Jake couldn't fathom this. The fear and the emotional blackmail made sense but the career part baffled him. Maybe this was because he'd never had a burning desire to be a marine engineer? In contrast, Summer had always wanted to act and Susie had never tired of pushing her.

Summer shrugged. "Not really, but I've been sending money home for years – quite a lot of money actually. Dad remortgaged the house; he ran up debts on the business and there have been all sorts of problems with the boat, so I tried to help out. I bought *Penhalligan Girl* for them, although I guess they'll need another trawler now, and money's going to be really tight if nobody's working. Just the kind of leverage Justin loves. He'd know I couldn't risk upsetting him." She gave Jake a sad smile. "I guess in some ways I felt like I deserved him. Justin was my punishment for screwing up when I was younger, but as soon as I found out I was pregnant again then everything changed. When he shoved me into the kitchen island I knew I had to get out, because it wasn't just about me anymore, was it? So I ran out of the house, jumped in the car and hit the M4 and just drove until my head began to clear. The rest you know."

"You've been really brave," Jake told her. Slowly, not wanting to panic her, he added, "but you do know that you can't keep this to yourself anymore, don't you? You have to go to the police. He can't be allowed to get away with it."

"I know I do, but not right now, Jake. I don't feel strong enough. Give me a few days just to get my head together and I'll do something. There's nothing he can do to me now."

Jake nodded. Gently, he helped her to her feet.

"I think you need to rest," he told her. "You've had a hell of a day, and I'm more sorry than I can ever say that you've had to go through all this. Forget everything else; it can all wait until later. There's no rush, Sums. You're safe now."

She exhaled slowly and, as he put his arms around her and helped her up to the guest bedroom, Jake felt the tension start to slide from her slim frame. By the time she was beneath the thick white duvet her eyelids were drooping.

"I'm so tired," she said sleepily. "Sorry, Jake."

Jake leaned forward and kissed her forehead tenderly.

"Just rest," he said. "You're safe here."

Summer had been through so much and he instinctively knew that there was still more that she hadn't shared with him yet. She didn't need someone telling her what she should do – God knew, she'd already had more than enough of that – but what she did need was someone to love and support her while she figured out what the next steps were.

Jake wanted those next steps to be with him. He wanted to take her hand and tell her that he would be beside her, every day for the rest of their lives if she would let him. He loved her with a passion that shocked him but he knew that now was not the time to talk about feelings or plans. The events of the day so far were too raw. The past, too, was still painful, with its effects echoing even into the present day, but Jake hoped that if he was patient Summer would realise that she still loved him.

Whether she'd want to be with him though, or with anyone after what she'd been through, was a different matter.

Chapter 31

Mo was buzzing. The excitement of the dash out to the Shindeeps and the adrenalin of finding the boys and bringing them home to safety, combined with the weird pulses of electricity that always seemed to zip between her and Ashley, had left her nerves jangling. Knowing that if she sat on a horse she'd send it crazy, Mo decided to abandon riding for the day and pop up to Seaspray to catch up with her family.

Her head was still spinning from Ashley's earlier command that she should deliver his coat and life jacket in person. He really was the most infuriating man! Who did he think he was, ordering her about like she was one of his underlings? Mo thought indignantly. She had a good mind to ignore him and let him collect his own stuff. That would show him that she wasn't the kind of person he could boss around.

Mo shoved the garden gate open and paused to catch her breath after the steep climb. The village dropped away below her; the boats in the marina were all lined up neatly, and beyond the harbour wall the tide was on the turn and hopeful seagulls strutted at the water's edge. There were still a lot of people left on the quay. The local news crew had arrived and managed to grab Mo for a few sound bites and she'd been hailed as the hero of the day. Mo felt quite a fraud because Ashley was the real hero. If it hadn't been for him then who knew whether Bobby and Joe would have been found so quickly, or even at all? Fishing off the Shindeeps, and with the rescue vessel still miles away, they could have drifted for hours and quickly become hypothermic. She'd tried her best to explain how the rescue was really down to Ashley and how his confident and expert handling of his boat had made all the difference, but he'd vanished and instead the glory of the day had rested with her. By lunchtime Mo knew that her frizzy red hair and mad eyes (she was under no illusions as to what she looked like on camera) would be beamed into houses across the West Country. I didn't do anything, she thought guiltily, apart from tell Ashley that he had to find the boys. Thank goodness he'd listened though. They'd spent so much time arguing in the past that she was amazed he hadn't told her to get lost.

Why had he been so quick to help, rather than being his usual belligerent self? Unless she was a better kisser than she thought, of course. And what was all that stuff about valuing your life and living every moment? He was the most intriguing man she'd ever met, and no matter what she did to distract herself Mo just couldn't stop thinking about him. She'd contemplated those moonlight kisses so many times that it was making her feel exhausted.

Mo was stumped. This made no sense. She was everything that Cashley hated: a Cornish bramble thorn in his gym-honed London flesh. And as an arrogant, capitalist second-homer he was certainly everything that she despised too. Why she kept reliving those kisses and replaying the image of his haughty profile, hair blown back from his face and jaw set in grim determination as he danced his boat over the waves, was a mystery.

Mariners was directly opposite Seaspray, and as usual the builders were toiling up and down the garden like ants as they built the Great Wall of Cornwall. The place was a testament to Ashley's sheer determination. He was going to defy gravity, global recessions and PAG to have his house built the way that he wanted it, and in record time too. He was certainly used to getting his own way, so to have taken orders from her earlier was unheard of. What was it with him?

And what was he so keen to tell her?

Trying to figure it all out was giving Mo a headache, so she turned her back on the view and climbed the final few steps up to her family's house. A cup of coffee, some toast and a slice of Alice's fruitcake were what she needed. She couldn't possibly figure Ashley out on an empty stomach.

Mo was spooning coffee granules into a mug and waiting for the toast to spring out of the toaster when Jake entered the kitchen. He looked terrible; his eyes were shadowed and his usually smiling mouth was set in a grim line. Even his golden curls seemed to have lost their bounce. Lord, Mo hadn't realised just how upset he'd been by this morning's events. Knowing Jake, Mo guessed that he was blaming himself for failing to get through to Nick. He'd always taken it upon himself to look after them all.

"Hey, cheer up. It's all OK: Bobby and Joe are fine. They were lucky." Mo poured the boiling water into her mug and lobbed in a spoonful of sugar for good measure. After the morning she'd had, she figured it was the least she deserved. "Do you want a coffee? Or some toast? I've put a couple of slices in."

Jake didn't reply but just stood in the doorway. His arms were folded across his chest and there was an expression on his face that made Mo uneasy all of a sudden. If she didn't know better, Mo would have said it was fury and directed at her, which was ridiculous because she hadn't done anything wrong. Quite the opposite, in fact. She was the hero of the hour. Everyone in the village was talking about how she and Ashley had rescued the boys. Jake didn't have any reason to be mad at her, unless it was because she'd not managed to stop Nick drinking last night. Personally Mo thought that it would have been easier to stop the tide. Nick on a mission to drink was a force of nature.

"Don't look at me like that," she grumbled. The toast popped up and she whipped it onto a plate, wincing at the heat and blowing on her hot fingertips. "It's not my fault if Nick chooses to get off his face. He's a big boy now." She opened the fridge and rummaged around until she located a jar of Alice's home-made strawberry jam. "I'm having this on mine. Do you want the same?"

"Did you destroy the letter Summer wrote me?"

The question was so unexpected and so shocking that Mo was totally thrown. She stared at Jake, hardly able to believe her ears.

"What?"

"I asked you whether you've ever destroyed any letter that Summer sent to me." Her brother stepped forward. "It's a simple enough question, Mo, so why don't you put the bloody toast down and just answer it?"

Mo glanced at the toast, almost surprised to see it; her appetite had vanished the moment that Jake had mentioned the letter. How on earth did Jake know about that? It had been Mo's guilty secret for years.

No, not a guilty secret, she thought furiously; that wasn't the right way to describe what had actually been an act of love. Mo had only been thinking of protecting her brother from any more heartbreak. Having seen him fall apart when Summer had chosen to walk away, Mo had been filled with a bitter determination not to allow her to do any further damage. As far as Morwenna Tremaine was concerned, Summer had had her chance and she'd blown it long ago. Nobody treated her brother like that and was ever forgiven.

Mo adored Jake. Like her, he was old enough to remember their mother. When Penny Tremaine had died, Jake, Danny and Mo had clung to one another for comfort. Jake and Mo had been especially close. It had pretty much stayed like that throughout their childhood. Jimmy had never been much of a hands-on father – he was far too busy chasing the latest money-making scheme or impressing holidaymakers in The Ship – so the eldest Tremaine siblings had been left to their own devices. It was Jake who'd taught Mo to ride a bike and throw a mean right hook, and who'd patiently let her learn to drive in his beloved Fiesta. Mo loved him fiercely and wanted to kill anyone who might hurt him.

Even if they happened to be her best and oldest friend.

Summer had called the house on a couple of occasions and Mo had happened to pick up both times. This had given her the perfect opportunity to tell her ex best friend exactly what she thought of her. Summer hadn't said much in response but had simply and quietly taken Mo's ranting and raging, probably knowing she deserved it, Mo had thought savagely. If she'd seen how pale and defeated Jake had been, then Summer would have realised that actually Mo had let her off lightly. A few days later Mo had been up early to ride and by chance had bumped into the postman, a portly character who was often complaining about the hilliness of his delivery round. Seeing Mo, the postman had recognised an excuse to avoid climbing the steep path to Seaspray. He'd thrust a pink envelope into her hand and called over his shoulder to make sure to give it to her brother. Mo had taken one look at that familiar loopy handwriting, and the letter's fate had been decided. The second the postman was out of sight, Summer's words to Jake had been pocketed in Mo's jacket. Not long afterwards, they'd been pink confetti drifting on the sea breeze. No good would come of anything Summer had to say, Mo had told herself. As she'd watched the pieces of the letter land on the waves, the words bleeding away into the water, Mo had been convinced that this was all for the best.

Now, years on and with Jake glaring at her across the kitchen, she wasn't quite so sure.

"What on earth are you going on about that for? It's ancient history," she said, defensively.

Jake's eyes narrowed. "Nice try, Mo, but don't avoid the question. Did you or didn't you?"

"All right, yes I did!" Mo flung down her toast and put her hands on her hips. "I ripped it up and do you know what? I'm glad I did!"

Jake's expression didn't flicker. "What on earth did you do that for?"

"Jesus, Jake! I don't know. It was years ago."

Jake gave a harsh laugh. "Come on. You're better than that. You know exactly why you did it."

Mo was stung by her brother's accusing tone. "All right, then, I'll tell you why I did it. I was sick and tired of seeing you being manipulated. Summer made it pretty damn clear that she didn't give a toss about you or any of us when she pushed off to London. She showed her true colours then, didn't she? She's nothing but a hard-hearted bitch."

"She was sixteen, Mo," Jake said wearily. "Sixteen. A kid. Can't you see that she was confused? She'd had Susie pushing her for years. Looking back now, I can see that I wasn't being fair either by putting pressure on her to stay. I should have supported her, not issued an ultimatum."

Mo, who until the arrival of Ashley Carstairs had never been confused in her life about what she wanted, snorted rudely.

"She's been telling you some sob story, hasn't she? God, Jake, don't be such a sucker. You might not remember how in bits you were about it all but I do. She was utterly selfish and I hated seeing what it was doing to you. She's certainly never looked back, has she?"

"You don't know anything about Summer. What on earth made you think you had the right to interfere? Have you any idea what you've done?" Jake said. Although he didn't raise his voice the steeliness in his tone was at odds with the laid-back brother she knew and loved – the brother whom she'd been protecting.

"I know she broke your heart, walked out on you and never looked back," Mo shot back.

"And did you know she was having our baby?"

"What?" Mo felt her blood turn to ice in her veins.

"You heard. Summer was pregnant."

"Pregnant?"

Jake nodded. "She found out a week or so after arriving in London and she was desperate to get in touch with me. She called a couple of times but you put the phone down on her." Striding across the kitchen, he glowered down at Mo. "So she wrote instead, but of course I never answered. You can imagine what she thought."

Somebody had stolen Mo's voice and all she could do was whisper. "So what happened?"

"She was sixteen, alone and frightened," Jake said shortly. He couldn't even look her in the eye, Mo realised. "What do you *think* happened? What choices did she have?"

Normally Mo's life was full of certainties. This horse spooked at those kinds of fillers. That cross-country course was lethal if wet.

Summer had betrayed Jake and, by association, Mo too. She liked life being black and white. Grey was far too complicated.

"She didn't get rid of it, did she?" Her voice was hardly audible. If Summer had been forced to terminate the pregnancy because of her, then Mo didn't think she could live with herself.

"She thought about it but she lost the baby – not before she'd been to hell and back first, though. Can you even begin to imagine how that must have been? She went through all that by herself, and while thinking that I'd read her letter and chosen to turn my back on her." He passed a hand over his eyes in despair. "I can't bear to even think about it."

Neither could Mo. She felt sick.

"I didn't know," she said. "I swear to God, Jake! I had no idea. I would never have done it otherwise. You know I wouldn't!"

"You shouldn't have done it anyway!" Jake's voice was shaking with anger. "Christ, Mo, don't you see what your interfering has done? I've spent twelve years of my life thinking that Summer didn't want to be with me, twelve bloody years, and the same goes for her too. Twelve wasted years, Mo! We can never get that time or that child back now. Have you any idea how that feels?"

Mo's throat tightened. "I didn't know, Jake. I thought I was helping you."

"*Helping* me?" He sounded incredulous. "Jesus Christ, Mo. That's the kind of help I can do without. Do me a favour, will you? Don't ever try to help me again."

"I'm so sorry, Jake." Mo could see her brother was devastated and to know this was her fault, however well intentioned, was more than she could stand.

"I think it's a bit too late to be sorry, don't you?" Jake held up his hand when she started to apologise again. "No, don't. There's nothing you can say that could possibly make things feel any better right now. What you forget, Mo, is that you've known about this for a long time. I've only just found this out and it's changed absolutely everything."

"But not us!" Mo cried now. "Nothing's changed between us! I only did it because I cared – and I was just a kid, Jake! I was sixteen! I had no idea what was going on! I was angry and scared. I wasn't deliberately trying to hurt anyone. Don't look at me like that. I'm still the same person."

But Jake held up his hands again. "I need some time to get my head around all this, because it doesn't feel like you're the same person. Do you understand? I have to figure this out and I need some space. Quite frankly, Mo, I can't stand the sight of you right now."

Mo didn't want to hear any more. She was out of the kitchen, through the back door and tearing across the garden almost before she was aware of it. All she wanted to do was put as much distance between herself and Jake as she could before she fell into a thousand pieces. It was unbearable. One swift, hot-headed teenage decision, made in the heat of the moment all those years ago, had come back to haunt her. Even worse, that impulsive teenage gesture had hurt her beloved brother in the worst way possible.

Mo didn't think she would ever be able to forgive herself.

Chapter 32

Jules couldn't remember a time when she'd ever felt quite as drained as she did right now. Her daily walks with Danny definitely left her breathless and with her legs aching as though she was coming down with flu. Since she'd been living by the sea and taking in all the fresh salty air, she'd often found that her eyelids had felt weighed down, but this profound exhaustion was something else entirely. By the time she'd made the climb back up to the rectory Jules was struggling even to summon enough energy to unlock the front door. She'd known she was unfit but this was ridiculous! Why, even filling the kettle was a task of Herculean proportions.

While she waited for the kettle to boil, Jules slumped at the kitchen table and contemplated opening the biscuit tin to rummage for a chocolate digestive or two, but the effort of crossing the room to fetch it was too much like hard work. It was also a strange development that she was feeling a lot less inclined to snack on Hobnobs and shortbread these days. Was it just her imagination, Jules wondered as she tested the waistband of her jeans, or were her clothes starting to feel just a little bit looser lately too? If so, maybe Danny Tremaine could have a whole new career as a personal trainer to look forward to; in next to no time he had achieved what endless slimming clubs and miracle supplements had failed to do.

Now that the kettle had boiled, Jules dragged herself to the worktop and sloshed the hot water onto a tea bag. With the tea brewing, she leaned against the counter and gazed thoughtfully out of the window. How many rectories came with a view like this? Jules asked herself. If she stared at it all day she didn't think she would ever get bored. The sea was never the same from one minute to the next and the village below her was a moving picture as people and vehicles wiggled their way through the narrow streets. She'd only been here a short while but already Polwenna Bay felt like home. From the beady-eyed seagulls always on the scrounge for leftovers or dive-bombing for ice creams, to the people she was coming to know and care about, Jules knew she'd been right to listen to that small firm voice that had insisted that coming here was the right thing to do. Whether it had been intuition, fate or God really hadn't mattered to Jules initially – and nor had the shocked expressions of her fellow young vicars, all of whom had been surprised at Jules jumping at the idea of a rural parish, even if she had become increasingly convinced that she was being called by God to go there. One of the other vicars had even suggested that she might be bored…

Now, standing by the window and watching BBC Cornwall packing away their broadcast equipment, while down on the quayside people still huddled in groups and discussed the events of the morning, Jules laughed out loud. Bored? Hardly. Nothing in all her years of training had prepared her for life in a small seaside parish. Particularly with the speed and the drama of *Penhalligan Girl*'s disappearance, the responsibility of having the entire community looking to her for comfort and support had been heavier than Jules could have ever imagined. Her role as the vicar of Polwenna Bay had been thrown into sharp relief. There was much more to it than fighting Sheila Keverne over the brass-cleaning rota or striving to make her sermons more exciting, and Jules had found herself thrust right into the centre of the action. People had wanted prayers and reassurance and answers – and who else did they turn to for these things, even in the multimedia age, but their vicar? Today Jules had really felt a part of their community: their pain had been her pain and their joy her joy. The relief of seeing the two boys brought home safe and sound had been overwhelming. Talk about an answer to prayer, Jules thought as she splashed milk into the mug. Still, she was willing to bet that it was the first time anyone from Polwenna Bay had seen Ashley Carstairs in quite that light!

The local property developer was quite a mystery. Generally he seemed about as popular in the village as the Ebola virus, and from what Jules could see Ashley tended to spend most of his time searching for ways to upset as many people as possible and flashing his money about. He wanted everything done yesterday and seemed in a constant race against time. Jules frowned; she couldn't help thinking that Ashley worked a little too hard to cultivate his cavalier image. It certainly didn't tally with the quiet man she often saw sitting in St Wenn's – and neither did today's heroic rescue of the Penhalligan brothers. There was far more to Ashley Carstairs than met the eye; of that Jules was certain.

Mug in hand, Jules was just about to wander into the churchyard to soak up the sunshine and doze for a minute in the warmth, when there was a knock on the front door. Sending up a quick plea to her boss upstairs that this wasn't Sheila Keverne demanding an apology for the short-notice cancellation of today's service in favour of prayers at the quayside, Jules abandoned her drink and went to answer it.

Opening the door, Jules thought that on reflection she would have preferred Sheila Keverne. Although they had never been introduced formally, she instantly recognised Tara Tremaine.

"I need to speak to you, Vicar," Tara said. "Is it a good time?"

Jules's first thought was for Danny. Why was Tara looking for a priest? Had there been a problem? Had he done something awful? Please Lord, no, anything but that.

"Is Danny OK?" Jules demanded as her heart screwed itself up into a tight ball. All sorts of horrible scenarios danced across her vision. "Has something happened?"

"Danny's fine," Tara replied calmly. She held out a slender hand which Jules shook politely, wincing at the contrast of Tara's slim manicured fingers with her own stubby digits with their short and practical nails. "Actually I ought to say that he's as fine as he'll ever be."

Jules stared at her. The relief was overwhelming.

"I hope this isn't inconvenient? I can imagine you've been flat out this morning." Tara dropped Jules's hand and stepped back, her hazel eyes narrowing. "You look very pale. Maybe I should go?"

"It's certainly been hectic, but no, it's not a bad time at all," Jules assured her visitor, doing her best to click into vicar mode rather than gawp at this woman who'd been the cause of so much of her friend's heartache. "How can I help?"

Tara shrugged. "I don't know if you can. It's just that I know you and Dan are... close?"

Jules felt a flush creep up her neck. There was something about the way Tara said this that made her, however innocent, feel horribly guilty.

"We walk on the cliffs together," she said carefully. "He's been very kind to me by showing me all the best routes."

Tara gave her a sideways look. "I'm not sure *kind* is a word I'd apply to Danny these days."

Jules chose to ignore the dig. "He's been through a lot. You both have."

Tara laughed bitterly. "That's an understatement, but I won't bore you with the ins and outs. Besides, Dan's probably told you all about it anyway, hasn't he? He won't talk to me but it seems he's more than happy to speak to you."

Actually Danny hadn't said much about his ex at all lately, but Issie certainly didn't hold her contempt back. Even some of Morgan's innocent comments had helped Jules build a rather unflattering mental picture of Tara, which didn't really tie in with this unhappy woman standing before her. Jules was cross with herself for judging.

"Look, I'm sorry if I sound jealous," Tara added while Jules struggled to find the right words, "but if I do sound that way, then I suppose it's because I am. My husband, the man I've been with since I was fifteen, couldn't talk to me. He totally shut me out, in every way. In the end it was impossible to live with him. He drove me away, Vicar. Can you imagine how that felt? Yes, I've left him – but he gave me a bloody big shove."

"I'm sorry. That must have been very painful," Jules said, and Tara inclined her head in agreement.

"It broke my heart. He wouldn't reach out to me at all. Did you know that when he was in rehabilitation he refused to see me?"

Jules didn't know this but she wasn't surprised to hear it. Danny was hugely proud and independent; he would hate anyone to see him vulnerable, or feel obliged to help him, especially his wife.

"I went there every day for a month and every day I had to go away," Tara continued. "The staff must have thought I was such a loser." She shrugged. "Not that they said so, of course, but that was definitely how it felt to me. I wasn't needed. They offered me counselling but what was the point? I wasn't the one who'd given up, was I? I knew the truth. Dan didn't want me anywhere near him and he still doesn't. I belong to the old life and every time he looks at me I remind him of how things used to be."

"I don't think that's true—"

"You don't know enough to comment," Tara cut through Jules's protest. "I promise you that's exactly how it is. So forgive me if I say that when I heard he was spending time with you and telling you everything, I was jealous and hurt too. Nothing I've been able to say or do has helped him or stopped him drinking. In fact I've probably made it worse by threatening to take Morgan away unless he quits. But you've made a huge difference in just the short time you've known him." She paused, her eyes flickering over Jules's body, probably comparing it to her own slim frame and feeling even more confused. "What's your secret? Why you and not me?"

Jules suddenly had a sense that she was being weighed, measured and found rather lacking. There was no sexual threat here, was what Jules guessed her visitor was thinking; Danny really had just been going for a walk. So what on earth did this plump vicar have that she didn't? Jules didn't blame her visitor for making such a sweeping assumption. Tara was one of those delicate, doll-like women whom nature blesses with perfect features, a taut flat tummy and hair that never seems to frizz or straggle. She was the antithesis of Jules, who daily waged – and lost – the Battles of both the Frizz and the Bulge. In contrast to the baggy jeans and hoody that Jules had opted for today, Tara was dressed in a Breton tee-shirt and skinny jeans that exaggerated her long slim legs. Jules knew she'd have looked like Billy Smart's Big Top in that stripy shirt, and she'd have struggled to get jeans like that over one ankle.

There was no doubt about it; Tara Tremaine was a very attractive woman.

No wonder Danny had been heartbroken to think she would leave him, but to learn now that Tara was hurting too put a very different complexion on things. This was a married couple and marriage was a sacrament. Danny shouldn't be spending his free time with another woman when his wife needed him, still loved him even. From what Tara was telling her, this marriage was very far from over. With sadness tightening her throat Jules knew that as a vicar, and as a decent person, it was her responsibility and her duty to help make things right between them – even if doing so squashed flat the tiny shoots of happiness that, like hyacinth bulbs planted and placed in the dark, had been growing in her heart. Their walks had quickly become one of the highlights of her life in Polwenna Bay, but if these were at the expense of Danny's marriage then they came at a price too high to pay. As a vicar Jules knew that the needs of her flock must always come above her own. That was the example set to her by Jesus and she strove every day to follow it.

This wasn't always easy though…

"Danny doesn't talk about himself very much," Jules said gently. "But whenever he has done I guess it's because I'm a vicar." She touched her dog collar and smiled. "This makes me easy to approach and it comes with a whole plethora of assumptions and understandings. Call it confession, if you like – even if that's the other team!"

Tara nodded slowly. "That makes sense, I guess."

"Listening to people is a huge part of my job," Jules said. "I'm impartial too," she added, knowing that this was at least her intention, "and that helps a lot. Sometimes people find it too hard to speak to those they love the most. Somebody from the church, somebody who doesn't have the same emotional investment, can just listen. It's the same reason why people might be able to talk to a counsellor or the Samaritans."

The other woman exhaled. "You're right; of course you are. That's exactly why Dan can't talk to me. I'll get too upset and he'll always be holding back. I didn't think of that when I came up here. I just thought that..." She pulled a wry face. "Vicar, I feel really stupid now. I actually thought Danny and you might be having an affair! Isn't that ridiculous?"

Jules smiled back but inside it felt as though somebody was wrapping barbed wire around her heart. Of course it was ridiculous. *She* had been ridiculous at best, unprofessional at worst, and she'd allowed herself to grow far too close to Danny. Well, that would have to stop, Jules decided sadly.

Tara didn't stay much longer – she'd clearly felt far too awkward to come in for a cup of tea – and once she'd departed Jules abandoned her now cold mug of PG tips and headed for her church. She had a sudden longing to be somewhere quiet where she could just be still and close to God. Although she knew that He was always with her, there was a particular kind of serenity in St Wenn's, with its cool pools of silence and rainbows of light. Tara's visit and her revelations had been hugely unsettling; Jules needed time to come to terms with what she'd learned and to pray for answers and guidance, both for herself and for the Tremaines. With any luck Sheila Keverne wouldn't be there. Jules was crossing everything that there would be far too much excitement and gossip going on in the village for her verger to come up to do a spot of brass cleaning today.

As always the church door was unlocked, and as Jules stepped into the nave the stillness immediately soothed her. The smells of polish and old hymn books were comforting and familiar and the atmosphere was blissfully calm, as though the centuries of prayers and deep reflection had seeped into the walls and pews. Jewelled sunshine poured through the stained-glass windows and onto the worn flagstones, revealing dust motes dancing and spinning in the light. The deep recessed windowsills were filled with the flower displays made by Alice, forming bright splashes of colour against the grey stones, which bore plaques honouring the young men of the village whose blood had soaked the faraway fields of the Somme.

Sheila wasn't there, thank the Lord – but Jules wasn't alone, which took her by surprise. St Wenn's was often visited by tourists (those fit and interested enough to wander off the beaten track to find the church, anyway), but this usually happened on wet and miserable days when there wasn't much else to do. It was unusual to find holidaymakers in here between services on sunny Sundays when there were ice creams and boat trips on offer elsewhere. Jules grabbed one of the guides to the church, a slim leaflet pointing out all the things worth looking at, but as she neared the chancel she realised that this wasn't a holidaymaker at all: it was Ashley Carstairs.

He was sitting in the second pew from the front and his dark head was bowed as he either prayed or was lost in deep thought. There was less of a difference between these two states than people realised, Jules often thought, and as a vicar it was interesting to learn that people you seldom saw at a service often came into the church at other times. She'd seen Ashley here three times already this week. Jules was thoughtful; he looked troubled.

Hearing her footsteps, Ashley glanced up. Something flickered in his dark eyes when he caught sight of her. Annoyance? Irritation? Jules wasn't certain but she could tell that he wasn't pleased to lose his solitude. Instantly he rose to his feet.

"Please, don't mind me," she said quickly. "I didn't mean to disturb you. I'm just here to pray."

But Ashley was already sliding out of the pew. "I was on my way anyhow."

This was blatantly untrue but Jules decided to ignore it. Just as the dog collar made some people feel reassured, she knew full well that it often had the opposite effect on others; Ashley was clearly one of these folk. Before she could think of the right words to put him at his ease, or point out that he'd left a sheaf of papers behind on the pew, he was striding up the aisle. Seconds later she heard the church door click shut behind him.

Jules sighed then slipped into his vacated pew to scoop up the papers. She'd take them back to the rectory for safekeeping and maybe drop them up to Mariners later. The walk would do her good.

The papers looked important. Legal documents? Jules couldn't help but glance down at them out of curiosity and was surprised to discover that she was holding a letter from a solicitor, along with the historical deeds to Fernside. This was the piece of land that PAG had been fighting Ashley over, wasn't it? The remainder of the ancient woodlands that linked Mariners with the lane out of the village, and which kept Ashley's property inaccessible by road. The last time Jules had attended a PAG meeting (generally she tried to avoid them, as things tended to become very heated) there had been great agitation because apparently Ashley had purchased the woods. Morwenna had been all for a

Swampy-style protest with villagers chained to trees and all but singing *we shall not be moved* while the diggers and bulldozers crept nearer.

Jules frowned. She was totally confused. None of the upset of that meeting made any sense at all now. According to the solicitor's letter she was holding in her hands, Ashley Carstairs didn't own the woods at all.

Morwenna Tremaine did.

Chapter 33

Summer let herself into the holiday cottage, closing the door behind her with a soft click. The cottage was open, which surprised her. She guessed she'd left in such a tearing hurry to get to the harbour that she must have forgotten to lock up. She leaned against the back of the door and closed her eyes, savouring the peace and quiet of just being alone in her own space, even if it was borrowed. Being at Seaspray had been wonderful; Jake and later on Alice had been so kind, but after resting for several hours she really felt the need just to be alone. Jake hadn't wanted her to go but Summer had insisted, and in the end he'd reluctantly walked with her to the bottom of the garden.

"I'll come and find you later," he'd said, pressing a kiss onto the top of her head. "No protests, Sums. It's not up for discussion. I want to check that you're all right. I'll send Morgan down in a bit to see if you need anything, and then you really need to get some more rest. It's been quite a day."

He wasn't wrong there, Summer now thought wearily. Her body ached, her head throbbed and she felt as though she could sleep for about a month. It seemed a lifetime ago that she'd heard the dreadful news about her brothers. Her hand rested for a moment on her stomach and her eyes stung with tears. She blinked them away and bit down on her lip until she could taste the metallic taint of blood. Slowly, piece by minute piece, her control returned. There would be plenty of time to grieve later.

It hadn't even been a day since she'd left this house to wander down to see her parents at Cobble Cottage, but she felt years older. The house too felt different. Its energy had shifted so that, rather than being the quiet haven she'd been enjoying, it made her feel oddly on edge, as though she was being watched from the shadowy corners or spied on from the dark stairwell.

Hormones, she told herself. That was what this was. Her body was in shock, her emotions were reeling and she was all over the place. The cottage was the same as it had always been. This was just her imagination playing tricks on her; the goosebumps dusting her skin and the acceleration of her heart rate were all caused by the trauma she'd been through, nothing more.

If she could fall asleep right now and not wake up for several years, Summer didn't think she would mind too much. Coffee: that was what she needed. A strong cup of coffee that would jolt her senses awake and hopefully drive away this creeping sense of unease.

Grinding her knuckles into her eyes until she saw stars, Summer went to fill the kettle and fetch a mug. It was as she was stretching to pick one from the highest shelf, balancing on her tiptoes to reach it with her fingertips, that she heard a tread on the stair.

The mug flew from the shelf and shattered with a sickening crash. Shards of china peppered the floor – but Summer barely had a moment to register this, because an arm had snaked around her waist, pulling her backwards with such force that she lost her footing.

"Having fun without me, Summer?"

It was Justin.

"Nothing to say?" he hissed, yanking her backwards so roughly that she stumbled and would have fallen were it not for his vice-like grip. "That's unusual. Or have you been saving all your conversation for your lover up at the big house?" His breath was hot on her neck and, catching the taint of whisky on it, Summer's insides turned watery with terror. Justin angry because he thought she'd been cheating was one thing. Justin angry and drunk was another entirely.

"He's not my lover," she choked, but it was hard to speak when his other arm was pressing against her windpipe. It was hard to breathe, even.

"Liar!" Justin spat. Although she couldn't see his face Summer knew exactly how it would look. His lips would be drawn back from his teeth in a snarl and his eyes would be blank with rage, all signs of the handsome Dr Jekyll who graced magazine covers and ads for trainers totally eradicated by this violent and jealous Mr Hyde. "I've been told exactly what you've been up to. You've made a fool out of me, you bitch, and nobody does that. Nobody!"

He was dragging her across the kitchen now and towards the stairs. Every jolt of his arm left Summer gasping for air. If he carried on like this he would choke her. How on earth had he got into the cottage? How did he know which one she was in? How had he managed to make his way through the village without being recognised?

These questions raced through her mind but there was no point trying to search for answers. Justin had found her. That was the only fact she needed to worry about.

In the past Summer had been rendered limp with terror when Justin was in this frame of mind, but today she was filled with fury rather than with fear. Maybe it was because she felt that she had nothing left to lose, or maybe it was because she'd finally had enough of being bullied. Who the hell was Justin Anderson to treat her this way? She'd spent most of her adult life on the run from the guilt that had shadowed her for so long and believing that Jake hadn't loved her enough. Today had turned all of that upside down.

She wasn't the same person who had fled from their London house. Justin Anderson wasn't going to push her around anymore.

Summer ducked her head to avoid his hand clamping over her mouth.

"How the hell did you get in?"

Justin laughed. "The key was under the potted bay tree where your friend told me I'd find it. Shit security you country bumpkins have. It wasn't hard, Summer."

Who was the friend? Summer's brain was tying itself into knots as she tried to figure this out. Ella? It had to be.

"Don't I even get a hello?" he continued. His voice was deceptively friendly, at odds with the strength of his grip. "I've driven all this way for you, Summer. You could at least look pleased to see me."

Summer had been with Justin for long enough to know his moods. This one was particularly dangerous, a faux bonhomie that could flip at any time into white-hot rage. Usually she went rag-doll limp and did as little as possible to aggravate him. Sometimes it worked but mostly it didn't. Hitting the kitchen island had been one such example. He'd be waiting for her to do exactly that now.

Well he'd been lucky before. This time Summer had nothing to lose.

"I'm *not* pleased to see you," she told him, as best she could once his arm was away from her windpipe. "I don't love you and I don't want to be with you. It's over."

The back of Justin's hand cracked against the side of Summer's head with such force that fireworks blazed in front of her eyes.

"You don't get to decide that," he snarled. "We're Justin and Summer, you stupid bitch. We're a product worth millions. The next Posh and Becks. You don't get to choose to walk away from that. You don't get to choose."

But this was where he was wrong. Things had changed since she'd arrived at Polwenna Bay; they'd changed in ways that Justin couldn't possibly contemplate. She was no longer the same person who'd walked away from him.

"You need me," he was saying. "You need the money. How else will you bail your pathetic family out every time? How will they ever afford another boat now unless you cough up? I made you and I can ruin you too."

It was all rubbish of course. Justin hadn't made her: Summer had enjoyed success long before she'd met him, but he'd been telling her this for so long now that she'd started to believe it. His constant put-downs and reminders that she was just clinging to the coat-tails of his fame and talent had been mental water torture – a steady drip, drip, drip of negativity into her subconscious. Eventually she'd bought into it. Not now though. Being away from him and back in the place where she'd once belonged and been so happy – and spending time with a man who respected and supported her – had thrown Justin's lies into sharp relief.

"And when I speak to the papers I can ruin you too!" she gasped.

Justin laughed. "As if they'll believe you – a slut who's cheated on a national hero. A man in remission from cancer, too. Your word's worth nothing compared to mine. You're just some cheap lads'-mag tart. You'll never work again by the time I've finished."

Out of the corner of her eye Summer saw the coffee container still on the counter. It was a heavy and very large glass jar which Patsy, being a staunch tea drinker, had donated to her niece. If she could somehow reach it, Summer thought, then she'd stand a chance of surprising him. All she had to do was get close enough to grab it. If there was ever a time when she needed to call upon her acting skills, however rusty, it was now.

"Baby, you're hurting me," she said softly. "You don't need to hold me so tightly. I'm not going anywhere."

"You're coming back with me." His grip tightened and Summer cried out as Justin tugged her back towards the stairs. "You can get up there and pack your damn case, and show me some appreciation while you're at it."

No! Not that again. Anything but that! Her heart drumming as he yanked her towards the staircase, Summer forced herself to stop struggling and become soft and pliant in his arms. Nothing turned Justin on more than a struggle, she knew that much, and the more she protested the more he'd enjoy it.

Summer wasn't going to give him the satisfaction.

"OK, baby. Maybe you're right; it is time I came home." She took a deep breath and tried to sound as though she was agreeing with a well-meaning suggestion, rather than fighting a man who was half drunk and who loved force. "I'll come upstairs and pack my bags. Just let me go first, hey?"

Justin's fingers loosened their grip a little, just enough for Summer to stamp on his foot, twist and try bolting for the door. His howl of pain was followed by a short tussle as he grabbed her hair and snatched her head back so hard that she heard her neck click. The agony almost made her vomit.

"You bitch!"

The smack of his hand against her face made Summer's vision fade and the force sent her stumbling forwards. She slammed into a cupboard gasping as her hip collided with the corner, and then Justin was behind her and tugging her jeans down.

"Stand still," Justin rasped. Summer heard the zip of his flies as he pushed against her, and panic clawed her chest. This was not going to happen again. It wasn't!

Stars were still twinkling before Summer's eyes and she was struggling to breathe, but as Justin was occupied with freeing one hand she saw the moment and somehow managed to stretch forward and grab the coffee jar. Twisting around desperately, she brought it down onto his head with all her might.

Justin didn't even cry out but dropped like a stone to the floor, where he lay crumpled at her feet. Summer stood over him, jar in hand and panting as though she'd just had a workout. She was profoundly shocked at what had almost taken place – but not nearly as shocked as Justin, who gazed up at her blearily, blood trickling from his head and onto the flagstones. His eyes didn't seem to be able to focus at all; he just blinked while his mouth opened and shut like something from her brothers' trawl.

Oh my God, thought Summer, stunned. She'd done it. She'd really done it: stood up to Justin and defended herself.

There was no way she was ever going to let him hurt her again.

It was at this point that the cottage door flew open and Jake hurtled in, fists held as though ready for a fight. When he saw Summer standing over Justin, he pulled her straight into his arms and held her tightly against his chest.

"Sweetheart, are you all right? Had he hurt you?" Jake tilted up her head and gazed down at her. His blue eyes were bright with anger. "If he's dared to lay a finger on you then I swear to God I'll kill him. Your face is bleeding. Christ, I'm going kill him."

Summer knew that although Justin was an athlete, Jake, with his body hard and muscular from the hours of physical work in the boatyard and being out on the water, was more than a match for him. She could feel the fury pulsing through him and she knew that he meant every word. It both thrilled her and made her feel so safe to know that Jake was ready to fly to her defence. Still, she was pleased that he didn't need to. Summer had seen enough aggression for one day.

She reached up and placed her finger on his lips.

"I don't think you need to. He's not going to do anything to me now," Summer said. "I must have hit him really hard."

They both looked down at Justin, whose eyes seemed to be looking in different directions. Summer could practically see the birds tweeting above his head. Then, tenderly, Jake uncurled her fingers from the jar and placed it onto the counter.

"Not hard enough," Jake said grimly. He crouched down next to Justin. "If you *ever* come near her again, that bash on the head will seem like nothing. Do you understand that, you piece of shit?"

Summer's ex was far from his groomed celebrity self now. Dribbling snot and blood onto the flagstones and moaning pitifully, he looked pathetic.

"She hit me," he whimpered, one hand clutching his head. "The bitch hit me."

"Don't you dare speak about Summer like that, you scum." Jake put his face so close to Justin's that their eyeballs were almost touching. "You broke into her house and assaulted her."

Justin made a spluttering sound. It might have been a protest or a laugh; it was hard to tell because his voice was clotted with mucus and blood from his nose, which had evidently hit the stone floor.

"Call an ambulance," he gurgled. "Christ. That bitch has really hurt me."

"Sod the ambulance. I'm calling the police," Jake told Justin, whipping his mobile out of his pocket. "They can decide what to do next."

"Call them then. I'll sue for assault."

Summer's mouth parched. "It was self-defence!"

"Prove it," Justin wheezed. A hint of the old vindictiveness had crept back into his tone, but for once she actually felt relieved to hear it. If Justin was still capable of being a bastard then she couldn't have done too much harm.

Jake gave him a scornful look. He was itching to thump Justin himself, Summer realised, and it was an act of real restraint that he'd managed to resist.

"She doesn't have to prove anything." He stood up, squeezed Summer's shoulder reassuringly and strode to the open door. "Morgan!"

Morgan's curly head appeared at the door. His eyes widened when he saw Justin lying on the kitchen floor.

"That's him, Jake! That's the bad man who was hurting Summer. I saw him through the window."

"A kid?" Justin pushed himself onto one elbow. His eyes were crossing. "Big deal."

"A kid with a camera and an obsessive passion for taking photos." Jake turned to Summer, who was staring at him in confusion. "I sent Morgan down to see if you needed anything," he explained. "He saw what was happening and called me straight away. While I ran down he took lots of pictures for me."

Morgan held up his camera with its big telephoto lens.

"Thirty-five actually. I might be a paparazzi man when I grow up," he remarked thoughtfully. "Look, Jake: I took lots of them."

Jake took the camera and scrolled through the images. His eyebrows shot into his thick blond fringe and a muscle began to tick in his strong, clenched jaw. Summer knew only too well what he was looking at. She had the bruises and the cuts to match the photographs.

"I ought to finish you right now for this," Jake grated, and Justin shrank away.

"He's not worth it." Summer laid her hand on Jake's arm. "Leave him. He won't be coming anywhere near me again. Not once we go to the press." She turned to Justin. He looked so ridiculous sprawled on the floor it now seemed impossible that she'd been terrified of him. Justin was just a bully, and like all bullies once you stood up to him he was actually pretty pathetic.

"My face is cut," he whined. "If I lose modelling work I'll sue your arse off."

"Sue away," said Jake to Justin. "There's enough evidence here to prove every word you say is a lie. I shouldn't think there's a company on the planet that'd want you to endorse their products after this. Men who beat women aren't very popular."

"Fact," said Morgan, nodding.

Jake handed his mobile to Summer. His face was serious.

"Sums, call the police. That was a serious assault and I know it wasn't the first, no matter what you've said before. You owe it to yourself and to whatever poor girl falls for him next to make sure he never has the chance to do it again. Don't be afraid, sweetheart; he can't harm you anymore. He'll never lay a finger on you again, I promise."

She glanced down at her ex-fiancé. Justin's eyes had closed and he looked utterly defeated. He wasn't going to hurt her now and neither was he about to go anywhere – not unless it was in the back of a police van, anyway. Jake's words about needing to make a stand for the next girl Justin met struck a chord with Summer. It was too late for her and her baby but nobody else was going to suffer because of him. That was the one thing she could do in honour of that little soul who'd never really had a chance.

Her eyes met Jake's and the love she saw in them made her stomach turn somersaults. He touched her cheek tenderly, his fingertips skimming the shadows of her old bruises before gently brushing over the new swellings.

Jake was there for her in every way, she realised. He always had been and her heart was telling her that he always would be. All she had to do was trust it.

But was she strong enough to do the right thing? Brave enough to stand up to Justin once and for all, and publicly too? For a second she quailed, but then Jake smiled at her and instantly Summer knew the answer. She might be aching, trembling and physically weak, but with Jake Tremaine there beside her Summer felt stronger than she ever had before. She loved him and, in loving him, she knew that at long last she had come home. And she never wanted to leave.

If she really wanted to be free, stop running and make her peace with everything, then it was time to take the final step. With a shaking finger, Summer began to dial...

Chapter 34

Mo was distraught. She couldn't remember ever feeling quite so sick. Every time she recalled her earlier conversation with Jake her blood ran cold. She thought that the expression of disappointment and disgust on his face would probably stay with her forever.

Mo had torn out of the house and raced through the village back to the stables. She'd known that there was no point staying at Seaspray and trying to plead with her brother; the withering look he'd given her before he'd gone back upstairs, presumably to comfort Summer, had said it all. He despised her and it didn't matter how sorry Mo was or that she would have given anything at all to turn back time and change things. She knew she could tell Jake over and over again and until there was no breath left in her lungs that she loved him, that he meant the world to her and that she wished with all her heart that she'd never thrown the letter away, but it wouldn't make the slightest bit of difference. Mo knew Jake inside out and he had a stronger sense of right and wrong than anyone else she could think of.

She had also never seen him so angry…

For the rest of the afternoon Mo felt as though she was trapped in a nightmare, with her day seeming hell-bent on going from bad to worse. If she was searching for a sign that the universe wanted to punish her for the stupid, childish mistakes she'd made all those years ago, then she didn't have to look much further than the big horse lorry that, when she arrived back at the stables, was parked up in the yard. Mo instantly recognised the smart blue and gold crest of The Bandmaster's previous owner, Alex Ennery, on the side of the vehicle – and her heart sank.

Before she'd even made it through the yard gate a smart female groom in cream breeches and spotless Dubarry boots was leading The Bandmaster out of his stall and up the ramp of the lorry.

"What do you think you're doing?"

Charging across the yard, Mo tried to snatch the lead rope but she was too late; Bandy was already loaded and the ramp had been slammed firmly shut behind his muscular rump.

"Hey! What do you think you're doing? That's my horse!" Mo cried. She marched around to the jockey door, ready to have it out with the groom. "You can't just take him. There's been a mistake."

The groom, a tall willowy blonde girl Mo recognised from the local eventing circuit, sighed. "Look, Mo, this is bloody embarrassing enough. Please don't make it worse."

But Mo didn't care about being embarrassing. She just wanted Bandy out of the lorry and back in his stable.

"That's my horse! Unload him right now!" she demanded. Her heart was hammering in her chest and she felt dangerously close to tears. "You can't just turn up and take him."

"He's not your horse though, is he? Technically this is Ella St Milton's horse – and she's asked me to collect him."

"But I'm training him! Ella left him here because she wants me to ride him." Mo glanced around frantically in the hope that there might be somebody about to back her up, but she was out of luck and the groom just shrugged.

"Well, it looks as though she's changed her mind then, doesn't it? She's asked me to deliver him to Alex Ennery."

"There's got to be a mistake." Mo was beside herself. She couldn't lose The Bandmaster, the horse that was going to take her to the

Olympics. She dug her phone out of her pocket and furiously scrolled through her contacts list. "Please, give me a minute to just call her. I'm sure she'll be able to explain."

It took several rings before Ella picked up.

"What?" she snapped.

"Ella, somebody's here to fetch The Bandmaster." Mo's voice sounded panicked even to her own ears. "Can you please tell them it's a mistake?"

"I most certainly won't," said Ella. "There's no mistake. I have asked for the horse to be moved. Alex Ennery will do a much better job than you."

Mo felt as though she'd been punched. "But I've not even had him a month yet! That's not long enough to be able to tell. Ella, come on, be fair. I need more time. Let me take him over to Bicton next week. I know he'll do really well."

"Come on, Morwenna, don't be deliberately obtuse. This isn't about the horse. This is about our little business transaction. You haven't delivered so I'm taking back my part of the deal."

"But I did everything you asked! I spoke to Jake. I sang your praises. I even got in touch with Justin Anderson for you and told his people exactly where Summer was." Mo felt sick. She'd sold her soul to do all this, broken her brother's heart and interfered in Summer's volatile relationship, and for what? Ella was still taking the horse away. Mo supposed it was no more than she deserved.

"Well it wasn't enough," Ella retorted. Her irritation crackled through the mobile network. "You haven't kept your end of the bargain, I'm afraid. Where's your brother now? He's not with me, is he?"

"I can't help that!" Mo cried out in frustration. "I can't make Jake want to be with you, Ella, can I? If he still loves Summer and isn't interested in you then there's nothing I can do about it! It's not my fault he prefers her!"

She heard a sharp intake of breath from Ella's end of the line and could have kicked herself for being so blunt. This wasn't the way to talk Ella round. On the other hand, Mo couldn't lie either. It simply wasn't in her nature.

"And if I decide that I want my horse to be trained at another yard then there's nothing you can do about that either," Ella shot back, lightning quick. "It's not my fault I prefer another trainer."

"I tried, Ella!" Mo felt as though the very cobbles of her yard were shifting beneath her. "I did my best."

"Then it wasn't good enough, was it?" replied Ella. "Don't bother me again, Morwenna."

The call was ended abruptly. There would be no continuing the discussion; that much was clear. Mo sagged against a stable door and listened to the flapping of all her chickens coming home to roost.

"Sorry," said the girl groom, who could see from Mo's face exactly what the answer had been. As one horsey woman to another she was gruffly sympathetic. "That's a shitty thing to happen. You're bloody good, Mo, and he'd have done really well with you."

Mo nodded. "Look after him for me? And he likes to be scratched just above his withers."

The girl hopped up into the cab and started the engine. "He'll be looked after, I promise."

The lorry backed slowly out of the yard. Mo shut the gates and watched miserably as it drove away down the lane, taking the horse and all her Olympic hopes away. Her brother hated her, she'd betrayed her old friend in the worst way possible and now her career was probably over too. Add to this the loss of the woods and Mo felt like hurling herself off the cliff top.

As she worked her way through her chores, all afternoon Mo wept quietly. She supposed she'd had these things coming to her; she certainly wasn't very proud of her behaviour. She filled hay nets, scrubbed buckets and mucked out stables as though on autopilot but couldn't face riding any of her horses. Mo simply didn't have the heart, and she knew that she couldn't do them justice in this frame of mind. She didn't think she'd ever felt so miserable in her life.

By the time the evening sun's fingers were creeping across the paddock and the light was fading from the sky, Mo had come to a decision: she was going to apologise to Summer and tell her everything. There would be no more guilty secrets and festering grudges. Summer needed to hear about what Mo had done from her own lips, and she also needed to be aware that Mo had contacted Justin Anderson.

Getting hold of Justin hadn't been as hard as Mo had first imagined; as soon as she'd mentioned Summer, his agency had been more than happy to take a message. At the time, Mo had pushed away any doubts.

Now, though, as Mo brought the last of the liveries in for the night and secured the stable doors, she couldn't stop thinking about the way her erstwhile friend had kept such a low profile in the village and she felt awful. It was so obvious now. Summer was hiding from Justin, and revealing her whereabouts was an unforgivable thing to have done – but Mo had deliberately chosen to ignore this just because she was desperate to have The Bandmaster.

What sort of person had she become?

The answer was one that she didn't like very much.

Having completed her chores and decided on a course of action, Mo headed back into the village. She didn't even pause to change her jeans or to have something to eat. All she wanted to do was get back to her family and to Summer so that she could put things right. Nothing else mattered.

Although it was twilight and the night was falling fast, Mo decided to take the path through Fernside. The shadows and the pitch-blackness didn't bother her in the least because she knew every twist and turn of the track by heart; nor did the calling of the rooks or the flutter of bats trouble her. Mo was more unnerved by the darkness in her own heart than that of the woodland. Instead, the solitude of her surroundings soothed her. Here nobody would see her tearstained face or stop her for a chat about the morning's heroics. The last thing she deserved was anyone's congratulations. There was nothing about her that was admirable or courageous, Mo thought unhappily. If anything she was a total hypocrite.

Eventually the trees thinned out and the path turned a sharp left, revealing the lights of the village twinkling below. Beyond them, the glittering waves silvered by the full moon looked almost magical. Mo paused for a minute to gather her racing thoughts and to make the most of this scenery. After all, she realised sadly, there probably wouldn't be many more times she could stand here and enjoy the gull's-eye view of Polwenna Bay. Ashley was sure to have the place flattened and covered in tarmac any day now. Mo sighed. He was infuriating and yet a complete mystery. On the one hand he was everything she loathed – arrogant, materialistic and domineering – but on the other there was something about him that was dangerously appealing, no matter how hard she tried to deny it. The way he'd kissed her last night still made the blood gallop to her cheeks, and today he'd handled the boat with surprising skill and a mastery that was extremely attractive. Mo would have found her feelings towards him disturbing if she'd only had the heart to contemplate them.

Oh Lord. Ashley. She was supposed to have returned his coat and life jacket this evening, wasn't she? Both of these items were still in the porch at Seaspray, abandoned there what felt a lifetime ago when, so full of exhilaration and certainties, she'd charged home after the morning's adventures. That was when Summer was still the bad guy and Mo had been the brave and justified defender of her brother's broken heart.

How was it possible that everything could change so much in just a few hours? How could the firm ground become quicksand in little more than the beat of a heart?

She was just heading around the final bend in the path when the flashing of blue lights from the village caught her eye. An ambulance? Or maybe a police car? It was hard to tell from here. All she knew was that the vehicle was parked by the boatyard, which was as far as a vehicle could go if it needed to reach either Seaspray or Cobble Cottage, as the ancient streets were made for horses and far too narrow for cars. What on earth had happened now? Was it Eddie Penhalligan? Or even Summer? Oh God, she prayed, please don't let anything else have happened!

She picked up her pace, tripping over tree roots and stumbling down the steps in her haste to reach the top of the steep lane behind the church which would lead her into the village. She was in such a hurry that in the darkness she failed to see another figure rushing towards her from the opposite direction. Seconds later Mo collided with a tall and decidedly strong male form, whose arms instantly closed around her.

Mo couldn't help it; she cried out in terror.

"That's not the effect I usually have on women, Red," Ashley Carstairs remarked. "They have been known to scream, of course, but not with fear."

The shadows made his sculpted features seem even more pronounced and his teeth gleamed white in the moonlight. Mo shivered.

"What are you doing here?" She injected a note of hostility into her voice, although oddly she didn't think she actually felt that way about him anymore. Still, it made her feel more like her usual self. If she was losing her antipathy to Cashley then Mo really did fear that her world was turning upside down.

"Looking for you, actually. I've just been over at Seaspray. You were supposed to come over to Mariners, remember?" He released her and stepped back, frowning. "No offence, Miss Tremaine, but you might have made a little more effort with your outfit, and the *eau du cheval* is a little overpowering too."

Mo ignored this jibe. "I've been flat out. Not everything revolves around you."

Ashley raised his eyebrows at this. "Did I ever say that it did?"

He hadn't and Mo knew she was being sharp. She took a deep breath. "Sorry, that was out of order, but I'm not going to make dinner tonight."

He nodded. "I'd already figured as much. Still, dinner or not, I wanted to give you something." Ashley released her and, stepping back, reached into his jacket pocket to pull out a folded envelope. "I'd stupidly mislaid it, which is why I was sprinting back home in case I'd missed you." He held it out. "Go on. Take it."

Mo did as he asked. The envelope was thick and heavy between her fingers.

"What is it? A writ?"

He threw back his head and laughed. "So suspicious, Red. No, it's not a writ, although maybe it should be, seeing as you're trespassing on my property."

She glared at him.

"Joke!" Ashley said swiftly. "It's just something I thought you might find interesting and that I wanted you to have. I have to go away for a while and I thought you ought to have it before I leave. Call it a little goodbye present. Don't read it now though. Open it later on."

What on earth was all this about? Mo guessed it was the latest move in his game of chess with PAG. Ashley was certainly weird.

"Why would *you* want to give me a present?"

"Jesus, Mo, you're hard work. I don't know. Take a wild guess. Maybe because I like you? Because it feels like the right thing to do? Because for once I don't mind losing? Take your pick."

She scowled at him. "Stop taking the piss. Everyone knows we hate each other."

Ashley's face was deadpan. "Do they?"

"Yes, they do. And it's true. I told you before, I can't stand you."

His lips twitched. "And I told you that on the lips of a woman love and hate taste pretty much the same."

Before she could avoid him, Ashley stepped forward and brushed his mouth against hers. The heat of his lips and the rasp of his stubble against her skin turned Mo's blood to fire and, horrified with herself, she shoved him away.

"See what I mean?" grinned Ashley. "Stop fighting it, Red."

"I'm not fighting anything," Mo lied. A pulse was beating in her most secret place and her knees felt decidedly watery. To distract herself she said, "Where did you say you were going?"

"I didn't, but I'm flattered you want to know."

Mo could have kicked herself. "I just want to make sure I can avoid it."

"Just away." Ashley ran a hand through his hair and then shrugged. "It's personal business."

Mo thought he looked sad, but then again that was ridiculous. Nothing ever bothered Cashley; he was as hard as nails.

"What did you want to tell me earlier?" she demanded.

He looked away. "Nothing that won't wait for another time, the right time. This isn't it."

God, he was being strange. Mo decided that she preferred it when Ashley was horrible to her. The air of sadness around him this evening was unnerving.

Mo stuffed the envelope into the back pocket of her jeans. "Look, fun as this is, I can't hang around here chatting. I need to find my friend Summer."

"So you've already heard the news then? I was on my way to find you first. I didn't think it was something you should hear over the phone," Ashley said. His dark hair was ruffled and now she was looking more closely Mo noticed that his cheeks were flushed. He must really have been in a hurry to reach her. This, too, was oddly out of character.

Usually a sardonic quip was never far away and he behaved as though he had all the time in the world.

It drove Mo mad.

Usually.

"News?" She thought of the blue lights down in the village and her hand flew to her mouth. All thoughts of the envelope were instantly forgotten. "What news? What's happened? No one's hurt, are they?"

"Hey, calm down, Red. There's nothing to panic about, OK? Everyone is fine. Everyone is safe." He placed his hands on her shoulders and the strong grip of his fingers felt like the only thing stopping Mo from spinning into orbit with agitation. She found herself hoping that he wouldn't let go. "I do have to say that for a small fishing village an awful lot seems to go on here, though. Mo, look at me and try not to panic, but there was an assault on your friend Summer earlier this evening. A violent assault by all accounts and perpetrated by her partner."

Mo stared at him. The words seemed to echo in her ears. Violent assault on Summer… Violent assault on Summer… Round and around they went, and she felt dizzy with dread and guilt. What had she done?

"There's been an arrest already," Ashley was saying. His hands felt like all that were holding her up. "The village rumour mill has it that the police have just carted away none other than Justin Anderson himself. Hey, don't look like that, angel. It's not your fault."

Mo couldn't look him in the eye. It was her fault. All of it.

"Is she all right?"

"As far as I know she's fine," Ashley reassured her. "I promise you. From what Sheila Keverne told the Rev, who then told me, Justin Anderson's come off worst. Close encounter with a coffee jar, apparently – and your little nephew seems to have captured most of it on film. He was busy showing everyone until the police took his camera. Apparently he went crazy at that."

Mo laughed in spite of herself. "Yes, he would."

"So panic not; she's safe. Your brother's a hero and the local press have got two good stories from Polwenna Bay in one day," he finished. "Honestly, it's the village that keeps on giving." His eyes narrowed. "Hey, you're really pale."

Mo felt pale. "I need to find Summer."

"I'll walk you into the village," Ashley said. He let her go and she swayed for a minute. She'd not eaten all day and this, added to the shock of hearing about Summer, made her feel weak.

"I'm fine."

"No arguments, Mo. I know you think I'm a bastard but there's no way I'd leave you alone when you've had such a shock. I'm walking you down." He paused and then a ghost of a grin flickered over his mouth. "Fact."

They walked down into the village, side by side but without speaking. It was dark now and the restaurants and pubs spilled warm light and delicious smells into the cool air. Holidaymakers strolled through the streets, lingering to read menus or to peer into shop windows, and music from one of the pubs trembled on the air. As they passed the village green a police car drove by with a slumped figure in the back, unmistakably Justin Anderson. He must have driven like fury to get down here and reach Summer, Mo thought. She'd given him exactly what he wanted.

The lights were blazing from Harbour Watch Cottage and there was a crowd of people gathered outside. Mo spotted Sheila Keverne and some of the old biddies from the church as well as Kursa Penwarren and the vicar. When they caught sight of Mo and Ashley, there was a fresh ripple of excitement.

"I'll leave you to it. I'm not exactly flavour of the month with that bunch," Ashley said, grinning at Mo. "If they come for you with faggots and a stake, give me a bell and I'll see what I can do." He bent down to kiss her cheek and she shuddered at the charge of electricity that jolted her to the core. What on earth was this about? She hated him. He stood for everything she despised.

It must just be a strange reaction to the strain she was under. That was it.

He touched her face almost tenderly and then, stooping down again, he brushed her lips with his own in another kiss as soft as butterfly wings.

"Take care, Red," he said gently. "I'll see you around."

Ashley melted away into the crowd, dismissing the congratulations for his earlier rescue and being his usual disagreeable self. Mo stared after him, her fingertips touching her mouth wonderingly, but the darkness had consumed him. Suddenly Mo realised that she would miss him being there to spar with and to challenge her. Unnerved by this, she swallowed back the uncomfortable feeling and made her way inside.

Inside the cottage Summer was sitting at the small kitchen table next to Jake, who had his arm around her shoulders and was holding her close. Meanwhile Alice was brewing tea and Danny was trying to convince Morgan that having the police take his camera was actually a very exciting thing indeed. Issie and Nick were texting on their phones, their father was deep in conversation with Bobby Penhalligan and even Symon had abandoned his restaurant. Eddie Penhalligan leaned against the cooker, his meaty arms folded over his ample belly, and spouted forth about what he'd like to do to Justin, while Susie sat on the other side of Summer, holding her daughter's hand.

"Mo!" Alice's face lit up when she caught sight of her granddaughter. "There you are, my love. We were going to call but Jake didn't want to alarm you."

Mo met her brother's eyes across the room. They both knew the truth. Jake's gaze still simmered and Mo didn't blame him one bit for feeling this way.

She had nothing to lose now by telling the truth. If Summer and Jake and everyone here despised her forever because of what she'd done, then so be it. She deserved it. Looking at Jake now, his mouth set in a grim line and with anger in his eyes, Mo felt a stab of grief. After what Mo had done to Summer, the girl Jake had loved for so long, she would understand if he never found it in his heart to forgive her. She had to face that. She dredged up all her courage and the words came tumbling out.

"I'm so sorry for everything," she said to Summer. "This is all my fault. If I'd given Jake your letter none of this would have happened."

But Summer shook her head at this. "Of course it isn't your fault, Mo. You were just a kid. You weren't to know what I'd said. Besides, you thought you were doing the right thing. You wanted to protect Jake."

"She's right, love," agreed Alice. "It was a long time ago and you were very young."

Mo wasn't going to let herself off the hook that easily, though.

"But it's not just the letter, although that was bad enough." Her eyes filled with tears. "Summer, it was me who called Justin's people and told him where you were."

There was a ripple of astonishment. Jake inhaled sharply.

"You did what?"

Summer looked stunned. "Mo, why on earth would you do that?"

Mo hung her head. She didn't think anyone could despise her right now as much as she despised herself.

"I've been riding one of Ella's horses and she only put him with me on the condition that I helped her get close to Jake. She said she'd take him away if Jake didn't take her to the ball." The tears spilled over Mo's cheeks, splashing onto the floor. "I love that horse but I know that's no excuse. I shouldn't have listened. I didn't have to do what Ella told me but I was still so angry with you, Summer. I thought you'd come back to hurt Jake all over again and I couldn't bear it. I just wanted you to go away for good and for everything to go back to normal. I thought if Justin came and you made up then it would be fine."

Alice had put her hand to her mouth in shock. "Oh, Morwenna, you didn't? Summer's ex is violent. That was why she was here. Wasn't it obvious?"

"I didn't think about why she was here," Mo choked. She dashed her tears away with the back of her hand and fought to gather sufficient control to carry on speaking. "I didn't know any of the other stuff Summer had gone through and I had no idea that Justin Anderson was violent." Her voice shattered and she was sobbing in earnest now. "I'm so, so sorry, Summer, and I wish to God I'd never done any of it. Everything that's happened to you, it's my entire fault! All of it!"

The room was quiet and her sobs sounded harsh against the stillness. Then Summer pushed her chair back with a loud clatter, and moments later she was hugging Mo and sobbing too.

"Of course it isn't your fault," she said, wiping Mo's tears away with her thumbs. "Mo, it's nobody's fault! It's just life. You made mistakes but so did I and so did Jake. We've all messed up."

But Mo shook her head. "Summer, didn't you hear what I just said? I called Justin's people and I let them know you were here. It's totally my fault he came to find you."

"Mo, stop. Listen to me! Justin didn't find out from his agency. My agent, Hattie, had already told them not to breathe a word about where I was. She knew what he's like and so do they. Believe me, the last thing his team want is another scandal." Summer stroked Mo's tangles back from her damp face, just as she'd done when they were children and Mo had broken her heart over losing her mother. It was such a tender and familiar gesture that Mo wept even harder. "Nothing you did made any difference. He'd already figured out for himself where I was. I expect he saw me on the news when the trawler story broke."

"She's right," Jake said quietly. "This isn't your fault, Mo."

"But Ella is," Mo choked.

"I'm far more to blame for that than you are." Jake looked troubled. "I've not been fair to her in some ways and I will make that right, if I can. And Mo? I know I was really angry with you earlier but I was being unreasonable. Summer's right: we were just kids. You ripped up a letter. Big deal. I should have fought harder for Summer and been mature enough to see that she needed to have a chance at a career in the theatre."

"But I still did it all," said Mo bleakly. There was no getting away from the fact that she'd allowed her temper and latterly her ambition to get the better of her. She glanced at everyone and then hung her head again. "I'm so ashamed."

There was quiet. The clock ticked and outside somebody laughed. Down in the harbour a boat engine spluttered into life. Summer didn't speak; instead, she hugged Mo even tighter.

"We've all done things we regret," she said softly. "I put my career above Jake and then I made choices with it that could have been better. I embarrassed my family and I stayed away from them rather than coming back home and admitting that I'd made some huge mistakes. I should have stood up to Justin a lot earlier too."

"Summer's right. We've all done things we're ashamed of. Me more than most." This comment was from Danny, who smiled at her encouragingly. "It takes balls to admit it though."

Eddie Penhalligan pulled a face. "Christ! What's this? Confession? You'll have the bloody vicar in here next."

"No we won't," Danny muttered. There was a bleak look on his face. "She's not so keen on hanging out with me anymore. Says I need to sort things out with Tara." He snorted. "As if that will happen. Tara's playing her usual games again and Jules is far too soft to see it. Tara's latest boyfriend's probably dumped her so she's decided she needs me again."

Alice glanced at Morgan and then frowned at Danny.

"It's all right, Grand Gran. Don't look so worried," said Morgan kindly. "I know that my mum and dad are going to get divorced. It will be all right. Issie says I'll get twice as many presents. And if I have stepparents, probably even more because everyone will want me to like them. Fact."

"Oh, Issie! That's dreadful! You shouldn't tell him such things," scolded her grandmother, looking appalled. Everyone else was laughing though and, shaking her head in resignation, Alice smiled too. The tension was well and truly broken.

"You saved my brothers' lives today as well," Summer pointed out to Mo. "Don't you dare deny it either. Dad's already told me that if you hadn't thought as fast as you did and reached them they could have died. I think that more than makes up for anything else that might have happened. There's nothing to forgive, Mo."

"She's right," Jake agreed. "It's time to put all this behind us." His eyes slid to Summer's and he smiled at her, a slow and secretive smile that spoke of the tender words they'd already shared, the promises made and the future yet to come. Then he winked at Mo and added, "Just do us both a favour, Mo? Don't tear up any more letters."

Mo wiped her eyes on her sleeve. She felt wrung out. "I don't deserve any of this after everything I've done. Why should you forgive me?"

Summer smiled at her. "Because you're my best friend, Mo. You always were and I know that you always will be. I've missed you so much."

Susie Penhalligan rose from the table to join her daughter. "I think there've been enough grudges and misunderstandings to last a lifetime, don't you?"

"So you forgive me too?" chipped in Nick, hopefully. He was always one to chance his luck.

"Don't push it," growled Eddie. He stepped forward and Nick paled, shrinking back to cower behind Symon. Then the big fisherman shrugged his burly shoulders. "Man up, you great girl's blouse. I'm not going to deck you now, am I? There's been enough hitting for one day. Just be grateful I've got a heart condition and more important things on my mind." His brows drew together in a dark scowl. "And somebody way up higher on my hit list than you. Or you," he added, glowering at Mo.

"Oh stop it, Eddie." Susie's voice was firm. "There's been quite enough of that sort of behaviour for one day." To Mo she said, "We can never thank you or Ashley enough for what you did for our boys today. It won't be forgotten by any of us, Morwenna. You can count on that."

"So the subject's closed," Summer said, smiling at Mo. "It's all behind us now."

"I'll make some more tea and we can drink to new beginnings," suggested Alice. Tea was her solution to most things. Mo sometimes thought that her gran, armed with a teapot and a bumper box of PG tips, could probably do a fantastic job of running the UN. Militant groups and sworn enemies would be chatting away over a brew within minutes.

Nick opened his mouth, probably to say that a toast like this deserved something stronger, but he caught Jake's eye and shut up hastily.

"Great idea," Symon, always the peacemaker, agreed. "I'll have a quick cup before I go back to the restaurant."

Mo had been so upset that she'd almost forgotten about Ashley Carstairs and the envelope. While Alice made a fresh pot of tea, Issie bickered with Nick and Summer returned to Jake, who held her close and as though he'd never let her go again, Mo tugged the crumpled paper out of her back pocket. What it could possibly be she had absolutely no idea. Knowing Ashley, it was probably a fuel bill for running his boat all the way to the Shindeeps and back. She wouldn't put anything past him.

Mo pulled up a chair next to Summer and, as Eddie flung the door back on its hinges and invited any villagers who *just happened* to be passing by to join them, she tore the envelope open. Inside was a letter from a solicitor.

It must be a threat of legal action. The absolute bastard, Mo thought furiously. That would teach her not to ever trust him again. He'd probably only kissed her as a twisted way to lull her into a false sense of security.

She scanned the words, mentally preparing herself for a call to the family's own lawyer and hearing the bang of the final nails being hammered into the coffin of the stables, when through the legalese Mo began to make sense of what she was actually reading. With a strange rushing of blood to her brain and the room starting to spin, Mo finally understood exactly what it was that she was looking at, although quite *why* Ashley had done this was beyond her. There was no rational explanation.

The letter stated that Fernside now belonged to Mo.

Before he'd left, Ashley Carstairs had given her the woods.

Chapter 35

Summer watched as Nick and Symon lugged the last of her boxes up the path to Seaspray. The Tremaine boys and her brothers had been climbing up and down from the car for the best part of the day and now, just as the sun had decided to slide down the rooftops and the seagulls were starting to doze, they were almost finished. Whoever knew that she'd had so much stuff stored in the London house? She hoped that it was all going to fit into Seaspray.

She could still hardly believe that this was happening, that she really was moving in with Jake. Every now and again she had to give herself a sly pinch just to make sure that she wasn't dreaming. Catching sight of Jake – her beautiful, golden, glorious Jake – as he shouldered the final trunk as easily as though it was made of cardboard, Summer had to pinch herself yet again. Sometimes her life seemed too good to be true.

"Ouch!"

Yes, she was definitely awake! Impossible as it seemed, this really was her life. She was indeed the luckiest girl on the planet.

Since that terrifying day in the cottage when she'd feared for her survival at Justin's hands, Summer's life had changed in just about every way. Of course there had been the inevitable media circus as well as statements to make to the police. Nevertheless, her medical records, the bruises from his last assault and Morgan's photographs were evidence enough that she, and not Justin, had been telling the truth. Summer had decided to press charges. She anticipated that there would be more bumpy times ahead, but with Jake beside her she knew that there wasn't anything she couldn't do. She wasn't a victim. She was a strong woman

– and with Jake's love she was even stronger now than she could have ever imagined.

Predictably, the press had gone crazy and ridiculous money had been offered for her side of the story, but Summer hadn't been tempted in the slightest. From this moment on she was determined that no area of her life would ever be up for sale again.

Packing up the house in Kensington had taken only a few weeks, and today everyone had made time to come and help her move in to Seaspray. Her parents were thrilled to have her back in the village and all the Tremaines (apart from Zak, who was recording somewhere for the record-label boss he'd met at the ball) had downed tools to help. Mo was in the bedroom unpacking the boxes and trunks and, if Summer knew her best friend, was still trying to figure out why on earth Ashley Carstairs had made the woods over to her. Summer had her own theories on that one but thought it best to leave it to Mo to figure things out for herself. Besides, there was something about Ashley that made Summer hesitate. He was keeping secrets, of this she was certain.

She ought to know. She'd kept enough of her own over the years…

Summer raised her face to catch the late rays of the sinking sun. Her bruises had long since faded and her skin was turning the colour of honey, the bridge of her nose scattered with a cinnamon dusting of freckles. Her hair was starting to curl over her ears, growing out a little now, and the dark glasses and baseball cap were things of the past. Her arrival in Polwenna Bay had been a short-lived wonder and the locals' excitement at having a celebrity living in their midst was soon eclipsed by other news – not least that Morwenna Tremaine had mysteriously acquired the woods, and that the new vicar was losing weight faster than a reality-TV star with a fitness DVD deal. People here weren't impressed by fame, although they were impressed that the sale of Summer's London home would go a long way towards sorting her family out with a new trawler. There would be some serious ground rules this time though, Summer thought. And if Nick Tremaine thought that he was going to be the skipper, then he was in for a huge shock. Summer already had plans for who could fill that role.

She gazed at the sky. It was a perfect blue, the kind of July blue that she associated with childhood. It made her think back to summer holidays where the weather had always been good and the days had been spent on the beach eating curling ham sandwiches and drinking lemonade. In the distance, the sea was that stunning oily-petrol blue unique to days without so much as a breath of wind. The tide was way out now, the sand a golden horseshoe that grew dark at the edges where the water lapped it and the waves sighed and hissed. These were the sights and smells of home, and Summer couldn't put into words just how happy she was to be back. It seemed that nowadays she always woke up with a smile on her face and fell asleep exactly the same way.

Happiness was wonderful. Being with Jake was wonderful. Life was wonderful, and Summer smiled to herself as she turned back to the terrace to help Jake with the last cases. Once those had been carried into the house, everything she owned would be here in Polwenna Bay for good. Her new life with Jake was ready to start.

"What are you smiling about?" grumbled Nick, staggering past with two suitcases.

"Being back here," Summer said simply.

Nick grimaced. "You're mad. You escaped the place – and once I do that, I swear to God I'm never coming back."

"Ignore him," said Jake, joining them and wiping his brow. "Wow. That was a steep climb up. Spending all that time in London has made me soft."

"Hardly," said Summer. She looked into his beautiful blue eyes, the same colour as the perfect sky above, and marvelled again at the love she saw there. It was exactly the same love that she'd seen all those years ago when they'd snatched stolen kisses in the coves and made love in the long grass that fringed the cliff tops. She'd been foolish enough to put fame and fortune above that love once, but Summer knew that she'd never make the same mistake again. This time she had a fortune that couldn't be valued in money.

Jake grinned wickedly. "Maybe soft is the wrong word?"

Nick pulled a face. "You two are gross. Worse than teenagers. I'm leaving you before I hurl."

Once they were alone, Jake abandoned the case and pulled Summer into his arms. His lips brushed the tender spot at the base of her neck and she shivered while butterflies fluttered in her stomach. The nights, filled with his touch, his lips, his strong body against hers, had seemed to pass in a billow of the drifting muslin curtains; there was never time to get enough of him, and somehow she felt certain that there never would be. They had so much time to catch up on that neither Jake nor Summer ever wanted to be far apart again.

Lord, maybe Nick had a point? She felt just like a teenager. At last she was acknowledging her teenaged self, who'd known beyond all doubt exactly how love should feel.

Together they stood without speaking and yet closer than words, watching the seascape below, a silken sheet of blue that stretched to the horizon and beyond. Jake rested his chin on her head and Summer could feel the steady beating of his heart against her back. His arms wrapped around her and held her against him.

Summer felt herself melting like ice cream in the sunshine. The fears of the last few years, the sadness of losing her unborn children, the ugly truths that would soon surface in one of the UK's highest-profile celebrity court cases; all these things were easier to bear now that Jake was there too. Together they were a team. Together they could do anything.

A seagull wheeled in the sky above them, calling over and over again with the same harsh cries that, no matter where she had heard them, had always sent Summer's soul racing back to Polwenna Bay. How many times had her heart constricted with that sound as jigsaw memories of Jake and Mo and Cornwall had tumbled through her memory? Hearing those calls now though, Summer felt only happiness. With Jake's arms around her and the next chapter ready to be written, Summer knew that she was staying here forever. She was in love with Jake and she always had been. They were entwined in each other's history and hearts, always and forever.

Runaway Summer was finally home.

THE END

Epilogue

Ashley Carstairs checked his watch for the umpteenth time and watched the nurse with the long sexy legs sashay past the door of his private room and back around the ward for what had to be at least the fifth circuit. Was she doing this for his benefit? he wondered. She certainly seemed to clatter the trolley into his door exceedingly often and, unless this was just typical woman-driver behaviour, he was rapidly coming to the conclusion that she was trying to get his attention.

It was odd being back here again. He'd hoped that his last visit had been the final one but no, it seemed that his body was determined to have the last say. How many times had he lain in bed at night, terrified that this was going to happen again? He'd wake up with a pounding head and the sheets rank with sweat, his hand fumbling for the lamp so that the pitch-blackness where the nightmares bred was quickly obliterated by soothing light. There he would lie, staring up at the ceiling and counting down from one hundred, trying to calm himself while his heart hammered against his ribcage. Sometimes it worked and sometimes it didn't, but he was always rendered weak with relief that it had just been a dream and that his old enemy, small and creeping and deadly, hadn't managed to catch him unawares this time.

Today, Ashley had a gut feeling that he wasn't going to be so fortunate. He'd managed to dodge this opponent not once but twice. To hold out for another victory was probably pushing his luck. Besides, he'd read all the literature and spent hours of what life he did have left browsing web pages and terrifying scientific journals in order to know exactly what he was up against. In business it was always prudent to know your enemy; Ashley didn't see why his health should be treated any differently. Face it, he often said to himself wryly, your health is the biggest asset you have. Without it what's the point of the properties, the fast cars and the expensive toys?

Headaches. Insomnia. Feeling breathless and dizzy. Inability to concentrate. Out of character behaviour. Ashley could tick off his symptoms one by one, although for a while he'd convinced himself that Morwenna Tremaine was the cause. Waking up in a sweat after a particularly erotic dream about Mo wasn't anything to be concerned about and all the other symptoms on the list could be put down to the frustration she caused him. The rows over the woods and his development project, her cutting comments, the way she refused to be impressed by anything he said or did. God, she drove him mad! He was used to women dropping at his well-shod feet and practically causing a gale with their fluttering eyelashes when he tossed a little attention their way, so Ashley was perplexed to find that Mo actually seemed scornful of all the usual things that women liked. She'd laughed at his car ("phallic symbol", was what she'd called it), rolled her eyes at his boat ("Do you really need that to catch one little fish?") and even stood him up for dinner.

It didn't make sense. Women usually loved him – but not Morwenna Tremaine, it seemed. What on earth was her problem?

The nurse came by again with the drugs trolley. This time Ashley knew it wasn't his imagination; she really did slow down when she passed, and he was sure that the poppers on the top of her uniform really ought to have been done up. Not that he was complaining about seeing the creamy swell of her breasts. Lying in a hospital bed with nothing more to do than stress about his results wasn't much fun and any distraction was welcome. If she came past again he'd ask her to examine him properly, Ashley decided. After all, he was paying a fortune to go private and speed things up. The least he deserved was a very thorough bed bath.

The nurse was tall and slim, with dark hair slicked back in a sexy bob. She'd look a bit like a boy from behind, Ashley thought distractedly, which really wasn't his thing. Jutting bones and sharp angles might look good on the catwalk but he'd dated enough models to know that these attributes didn't translate so well in the real world. Besides, Ashley liked his women curvy. He loved full breasts and soft thighs and long curly red hair…

Damn it. Morwenna was still right there in his head and, no matter what he did, Ashley couldn't get her out. She was spiky and rude and bloody-minded – but with her amazing blue eyes, the irises circled with a deeper almost navy blue, her determined heart-shaped face framed with tumbling auburn ringlets, and her small, sexy body that always teasingly threatened to fall out of her clothes, Mo was also one of the sexiest women he'd ever seen.

He had to have her. If he didn't get her out of his system he'd go mad. From the way she'd kissed him at the masked ball, Ashley knew that she wanted him every bit as much as he wanted her; she was just too proud to admit it. Just the recollection of how she'd felt in his arms, her gorgeous body pressed against him and her curvaceous backside cupped in his hands, was enough to make him grow hard.

Ashley brightened. This was a good sign, surely? He couldn't be too sick if *that* part of him was still functioning. Maybe the whole health scare was just the product of his overactive imagination, and when the doctors finally got around to seeing him Ashley would be packed off with nothing more than a patronising lecture about continuing to monitor his health and eating tinned tomatoes.

He'd also have transferred ownership of those bloody woods to Mo (and be getting his shoes muddy reaching his house every day) for absolutely nothing...

"I must be going soft, "Ashley muttered to himself. "That land's worth a bloody fortune to me, but all she'll do is hug the trees and sing to the birds."

Ashley didn't have much time for eco-warriors; in his opinion they just held up his inevitable developments and cost him far too much money. Mo, though, was different. He could see how much Fernside meant to her and, in spite of himself, on the last few occasions when he'd walked through the woods to fetch his car, Ashley had even found himself looking at it all through her eyes. The trees were ancient, their gnarled and knotted limbs furred with moss and intertwined like the aged hands of a long-married couple, and in the springtime the blues and yellows of the harebells and primroses had been just as striking as the bright hues of the Klimt in his office. He'd even found himself thinking that perhaps Mo and her crackpot cronies had a point after all. The woods certainly teemed with life, and to turn them into a road did seem somewhat philistine.

When the knife-sharp headaches had returned, the first thing Ashley had done was atavistic but he hadn't been able to help himself: he had headed straight for the church. There he'd pleaded with God, making bargain after bargain, or rather trying to; that chubby vicar had an extremely annoying habit of continually interrupting him. On his last but one visit to St Wenn's it had seemed to Ashley that he'd had a zap of divine inspiration. Maybe if he left the woods alone then he in turn would be left in peace? The more he'd pondered this thought the more solid it had become in his mind, until he'd actually instructed his attorneys to make the woods over to Mo.

Was it superstitious? Yes.

Did he give a toss about that if it worked? No.

Would it make Mo happy? Yes.

God. He hadn't even slept with the girl – or had a civil conversation with her, come to that – and yet he cared about whether or not she was happy? Ashley was alarmed. He didn't need the results of the scan or the biopsy to know that if this was the case he really must be sick.

Squeak. Squeak. Here came the sexy nurse again with her trolley. He'd distract himself for a bit, Ashley thought. It was the least he deserved.

He rolled onto his side, hoping to beckon at her through the door of his private room, but as he turned the sudden pain in his head was so sharp that his vision turned black and Ashley had to grip the side of the bed hard to focus his mind and stop himself from falling out.

Jesus Christ. Did it all really have to hurt that much? What the hell was he paying for? Surely if you went private it was supposed to negate the discomfort as well as the waiting lists? Then Ashley recalled that he'd turned down the earlier offer of pain relief, having considered himself too manly to need it. Never again. Next time he'd have all the drugs they suggested.

Not that there was going to be a next time…

He panted and gasped. Slowly his vision cleared, but unfortunately the nurse, her breasts and her long, stockinged legs were gone. Instead, the grim forms of his consultant and the registrar had taken her place.

It was not a swap for the better. The serious set of his consultant's mouth and the nervous way the registrar was clicking his pen filled Ashley with icy dread. He wished that he were anywhere but here.

"Don't just stand there. Tell me," Ashley barked. He didn't mean to sound rude or blunt but he couldn't bear the not knowing for a second more. The hideous suspense alone would kill him. He fixed the medics with a determined stare.

"Don't pretend things are fine when we both know it's a lie; just tell me the truth."

The consultant inclined his bald head. The registrar coughed awkwardly. His fingertips were yellow, Ashley noticed.

It was time for some gallows humour…

"You really shouldn't smoke," Ashley remarked. "It kills you, apparently. I've never even had a puff. How's that for irony?"

The registrar couldn't meet his eye. It seemed that there was suddenly something very interesting on the floor.

Ashley's consultant cleared his throat. His expression said that the time for joking was over, and for once Ashley couldn't have agreed more.

This was a *deadly* serious business, after all.

"I'm very sorry, Mr Carstairs," the consultant began, flipping open his notes and fixing Ashley with serious grey eyes. "We need to face some tough facts because I'm afraid it's not great news…"

To be continued in the next Polwenna Bay novel
A Time for Living

Ruth Saberton is the bestselling author of *Katy Carter Wants a Hero* and *Escape for the Summer*. She also writes upmarket commercial fiction under the pen names Jessica Fox, Georgie Carter and Holly Cavendish.

Born and raised in the UK, Ruth has just returned from living on Grand Cayman for two years. What an adventure!

And since she loves to chat with readers, please do add her as a Facebook friend and follow her on Twitter.

www.ruthsaberton.co.uk
Twitter: @ruthsaberton
Facebook: Ruth Saberton

Printed in Great Britain
by Amazon